Goodloe Harper Bell

Natural Method in English

Consisting of a Series of graded lessons for the use of schools. Arranged for the

convenience of teachers, and especially adapted to private study

Goodloe Harper Bell

Natural Method in English
Consisting of a Series of graded lessons for the use of schools. Arranged for the convenience of teachers, and especially adapted to private study

ISBN/EAN: 9783337780463

Printed in Europe, USA, Canada, Australia, Japan

Cover: Foto ©Andreas Hilbeck / pixelio.de

More available books at **www.hansebooks.com**

Natural Method

IN

ENGLISH

CONSISTING OF

A SERIES OF GRADED LESSONS

FOR THE USE OF SCHOOLS.

———•———

ARRANGED FOR THE CONVENIENCE OF TEACHERS,

AND

ESPECIALLY ADAPTED TO PRIVATE STUDY.

BY G. H BELL,

Professor of the English Language and Literature in Battle
Creek College.

BATTLE CREEK, MICH.:
STUDENTS' PUBLISHING COMMITTEE.
1881.

PUBLISHERS' NOTE.

The remarkable success which has attended Prof. Bell's method of teaching English in Battle Creek College, has created a rapidly increasing demand for copies of his lessons. Some of the students have been so desirous of using these lessons in teaching elsewhere, that they have, at great expense, procured copies by the use of the pen. This increasing demand, coupled with the belief that the method should have a wider sphere of usefulness, has led the students to undertake the publication of this work, having first corresponded with a large number of the graduates of the College, many of whom are engaged in teaching, and are using this system in their schools. The responses were hearty and unanimous, and the author has reluctantly yielded to the solicitations of his pupils to give the work to the public, and supervise its publication.

We confidently hope the reception given to the work will justify the heavy expenditure incurred in thus bringing it before the educational world, and that the call for future editions will be such as not only to re-imburse the author for his painstaking toil in gratifying the wishes of his numerous pupils, but also to induce him to give them the benefit of his experience in teaching the higher branches of this important study, by the publication of his lessons in Rhetoric and Literature.

Students' Publishing Committee.

Battle Creek College.

PREFACE.

This book, as its title indicates, is an attempt to present a *natural method* of teaching the English language. The author does not claim to have fully reached the end in view; but from the success which has attended the use of these lessons in manuscript form, it has been thought that their publication might aid in the promotion of rational teaching, and thereby lead to a truer appreciation and better use of our language.

The peculiarities of the method may be briefly stated as follows:—

1. The language is developed, not with special reference to the parts of speech, but so as to meet the demands of thought,—first showing a need, and then how that need is supplied. For example, we think of *objects*, and in speaking of them must *name* them; we think of the *qualities* and *actions* of objects, and in expressing such thoughts must have words to denote qualities and actions; we think *when, where, how,* and *why* certain actions took place, or certain conditions existed, and must have *words* for the *expression* of such thoughts. This plan is adhered to, not only in the introductory lessons, but throughout the entire work.

2. The examples are so selected and arranged that the pupil, from the first, is able to understand and explain the use of every word in them; for, with slight exceptions, the examples of each lesson contain nothing new but the special truth to be taught in that lesson. This work of selecting and arranging, as experienced teachers will realize, has been no light task.

3. Instead of stating principles first, and giving examples afterward, the new truth to be taught is drawn from the examples themselves.

4. The analysis of sentences is logical rather than grammatical, dealing *primarily* with the *thought;* and with constructions, as *mere conveniences* for *expressing* the thought. Technical terms are, in the main, avoided ; and the analysis is soon made general by dropping its minuter parts. Thus the energetic teacher will be enabled to prevent his pupils from losing the *thought* in the intricacies of grammatical analysis, and to make the thought better understood and appreciated than it could be by the most careful reading without analysis. This is of the utmost importance ; for how often the pupil becomes wholly oblivious to the meaning of a sentence while giving its grammatical analysis!

5. An interest is awakened, not only by noticing how admirably the different constructions are adapted to the various modifications of thought, but also by observing the peculiar fitness, force, and beauty, of rhetorical figures. The name of the figure, being in itself of little consequence, is made wholly incidental; but the figure is so explained as to show why it is appropriate, and what gives it its chief charm. Thus the learner is given an early introduction to the beauties, as well as to the strength and adaptability, of our language.

6. The essential rules of syntax have been so combined with the parsing as to lose their formality, without any diminution of their force. But few examples of false syntax have been given, for the reason that, in general, more benefit is derived from admiring the good than from criticising the bad.

7. The ultimate aim of the author has been to cultivate such a love for the study of language as will finally lead to the formation of a correct taste. This accomplished, the best practical results are sure to follow; but without this, rules and definitions will prove of little value. Even the slightest grammatical inaccuracies should, of course, be avoided; yet language may be free from all these, and still fail of its end,—the clear and forcible expression of thought. In language, as in other things, effectiveness should be regarded as the highest proof of excellence.

The writer would take this opportunity to express his appreciation of the many excellent books on English grammar; and as he has rejoiced in the success of other authors, and enjoyed the fruit of their labors, he confidently expects that they will be the first to discover and commend any excellences which this book may contain. Whatever errors or imperfections may have escaped notice will be corrected as soon as discovered, and any aid to this end, by way of friendly criticism, will be most gratefully received. It is to be regretted that active employment in the school-room, together with a multitude of other cares and labors, has made it impossible to give the book that completeness and finish which such a work deserves. Imperfect as it may be, however, it is, at the solicitation of many teachers and students, submitted to the public, with the hope that upon thorough trial it will be found to meet at least some wants that have long been felt.

G. H. BELL.

BATTLE CREEK, MICH., May 29, 1881.

HINTS TO TEACHERS.

1. Let your chief aim be to call out thought. Talk in such a way as to show at once what a necessity, as well as convenience, our language is. Without urging them to talk, lead your pupils to ask questions and express their views.

2. Do not let your pupils forget, from first to last, that *language is the expression of thought*, and therefore subservient to it. First promote the clearest possible appreciation of the *thought*, and afterward notice how the clauses, phrases, and words, of the sentence, are adapted to the expression of the thought.

3. In order to keep the *meaning* of the sentence continually in mind, require the class to *remember* the shorter sentences, after having them once read, and to analyze and parse them with their books shut.

4. Whenever the analysis or the parsing grows monotonous, bring out the same thoughts by questions, returning, after a few minutes' exercise, to the ordinary method of recitation.

5. Do not neglect the written exercises required as seat work. If the task assigned in the book is too heavy, lighten it; but do not omit it, unless occasionally, and from special causes. Have the work *thoroughly* and *neatly* done; and be sure to read and criticise the papers *yourself*. It is a good plan to mention some of their excellences and defects at the recitation, without betraying the name of the writer.

6. If the examples given for analysis, parsing, etc., are too few in any lesson, add others of your own selecting; if they are too many, use only what you need, but be sure to be thorough. It is thought that in some lessons there are so many examples that a part of them may be reserved for reviews and examinations.

7. If in any school there is serious opposition to the form of analysis given in the models, you can bring out the same thing by questions until the prejudice is removed.

8. Do not be too strenuous or exacting in those mere technical forms of parsing that have no practical bearing upon the use of the language. Remember that parsing is only a means to an end, and is valuable only so far as it promotes a correct use and ready interpretation of the language.

CONTENTS.

(ix)

ACTIONS PREDICATED.—(VERBS.)

ALLUDING TO OBJECTS.—(PRONOUNS.)

DISTINGUISHING OBJECTS OF THE SAME KIND.—(LIMITING ADJECTIVES.)

ACTIONS AND QUALITIES MODIFIED.—(ADVERBS AND AD-VERBIAL PHRASES.)

OWNERSHIP, AUTHORSHIP, ORIGIN, FITNESS. ETC.—(POSSESS-IVE CASE AND ADJECTIVE PHRASE.)

VERBS.—THEIR CLASS, FORM, VOICE, TENSE, MODE, PERSON
AND NUMBER.

DESCRIBING OBJECTS BY REFERRING THEM TO A CLASS.—
(APPOSITION AND NOUN IN PREDICATE.)

ASSUMING ACTION.—(PARTICIPLES.)

NAMING ACTIONS AND QUALITIES.—(VERBAL AND ABSTRACT NOUNS.)

RELATIONS.—(CONJUNCTIONS.)

ELLIPSIS, ADDRESS, EMOTION, COMPARISON.

COÖRDINATE CLAUSES.

ADVERBIAL CLAUSES.

ADJECTIVE CLAUSES.

INTERROGATIVES.

SUBSTANTIVE CLAUSES.

POTENTIAL MODE.

IMPERATIVE MODE.

INFINITIVE MODE.

PHRASES IN PREDICATE.

PHRASES ABSOLUTE.

SUBJUNCTIVE MODE.

COMPLETE CONJUGATION, ETC.

CORRELATIVE CLAUSES.

ENGLISH LANGUAGE.

LESSON 1.

Introduction.

To the Teacher. — If we would arouse the minds of children, and awaken in them a permanent interest in any subject, we must lose no time in giving them *something to do*. To that end, the first exercises in this book are made so simple that every child can take part in them.

As soon as the pupil finds that he can do what the teacher requires of him, he becomes courageous and hopeful. He has been victorious in the first encounter, and expects to conquer in those that are to follow. This courageous, hopeful spirit is indispensable to success, and the first aim of the teacher should be to inspire such a feeling.

If these exercises seem inappropriate to the age and intelligence of your class, pass on the more rapidly, taking two or three lessons at a recitation; but be sure that the work is *done*, and *well done*.

1. The Study of Language.

We are now to begin the study of language. Language is what we use in telling our thoughts. We speak to those who are present, and write to those who are absent. When we *think*, we think about some **thing**, and when we talk about that thing, we have to *name* it; so we must have a *name* for every thing we talk about.

We talk about the trees, the grass, the flowers, the sky, the sun,—about rivers and lakes, mountains and forests, hills and valleys, fields and brooks,—about our hopes and fears, our joys and sorrows, our successes and disappointments; our friends, our relatives, our playmates, and thousands of other things.

2. Exercise in Naming Objects.

For all these things we must have *names;* and in order that you may see how necessary these names are, we will notice how many of them we use in talking of the commonest things.

You may give the names of,—

1. The objects in this room.   3. Articles of furniture.
2. The rooms of a house.   4. Things that people wear.
                5. Things seen in the street.

Suggestions. — Whenever the members of the class hesitate in giving the names of objects, and the delay is sufficient to cause dullness, drop in names yourself until they get started again. Do not dwell too long on any one thing, but get all you can from the class without too much delay. We do not care so much to exhaust the subject, as to give an idea of the multitude and variety of names in our language, thereby making the study of those names seem important.

As fast as the names are given, write them on the blackboard, as illustrated below. Do not be too formal: the chief object in this exercise is to awaken an interest in the study of language. Make the exercise *lively* at any cost. While writing the names upon the blackboard, it would be a good plan to have each member of the class write them on his slate, or upon paper.

ILLUSTRATIONS.

(a) **Objects in the Room.**—Desk, boys, box, pointer, chair, girls, paper, clock, picture, flowers, pencils, rostrum, blackboard, vase, pens, iron, crayons, pipes, ink, boards, books, windows, ink-bottles, paint, bell, doors, rules, scholars, charts, maps.

(b) **Rooms of a House.**—Sitting-room, parlor, kitchen, bed-room, closet, pantry, library, dining-room, drawing-room, hall, cellar, garret, chambers.

(c) **Articles of Furniture.**—Chairs, tables, bedsteads, stoves, bookcase, bureau, stand, sofa, ottoman.

(d) **Things that People Wear.**—Hats, coats, vests, boots, rubbers, furs, shoes, dress, apron, bonnet, slippers, muff, collars, cuffs, neck-ties, sacks, shawl, overalls, hood, overcoat, wrapper, mittens, gloves, vail, muffler, cape, cap, scarf, cloak, hose.

(e) **Things Seen in the Street.**—Horses, wagons, carriages, men, women, houses, carts, flowers, trees, walks, dust, mud, water, grass, birds, churches, cars, dogs, fence, stores.

3. Questions.

1. Why must we have names for all these objects ?— *Because we cannot talk about them without naming them.*

2. What are we studying ?—*Language.*

3. How do we use language ?—*In telling our thoughts.*

4. How do we tell our thoughts to those who are present ?

5. How to those who are absent ?

6. When we wish to talk or write about *anything,* what is it necessary to do ?—*Name the thing.*

7. For what, then, must we have names ?

4. Written Exercise; for Seat Work.

Write the names of things that are raised in the garden; things that are raised in the field; different kinds of fruit; wild animals; domestic animals. Put these names upon paper, just as we have put names upon the blackboard to-day, and bring the papers to the next recitation.

LESSON 2.

Naming and Classifying Objects.

1. Questions.

1. What use do we have for language ?

2. When do we tell our thoughts by writing ?

3. What do you expect to learn from these lessons ?

4. Can you not talk and write already ?

5. Why do you come here to learn what you already know ?—*We must learn to speak and write* **better** *than we now can.*

6. What kind of words have we found to be very necessary ?

7. Why are names so necessary ?

8. What classes of things did we name yesterday ?

9. What classes of things were you to name on the papers that you have brought in to-day?

10. Without looking on your paper, name as many as you can of the first class.

11. Name as many as you can of the second class; of the third class; the fourth; the fifth.

12. Why do we need so many names in language?— *When we talk, we must first name the thing that we wish to talk about.*

2. Naming Objects.

Give the names of different kinds of,—

1. Wild birds.   3. Trees.
2. Domestic fowls.   4. Flowers.

3. Nouns.

All names are called *nouns.*

Which words are nouns in the sentences that I will now speak?

EXAMPLES.

1. The clock ticks on the wall.
2. Two boys are skating on the ice.
3. The meadows by the road-side were sweet with new-mown hay.
4. Time is money.
5. Fishes draw water through their gills as men draw air through their nostrils.
6. The lost child had yellow hair, blue eyes, and a freckled face.

4. Written Exercise; for Seat Work.

Select fifty names from your reading-book, and pass them in, neatly written on paper, at the next recitation.

LESSON 3.

Naming the Parts of Things.

1. Questions and Exercises.

Sometimes we wish to speak of the *parts* of objects, and then we need names for those *parts* just as much as we need names for the *objects themselves*.

1. What two parts has a broom?

2. What three parts has a pin?

3. What two principal parts has a knife? 4. What do you call that part of the blade that is farthest from the handle? 5. What do you call that part of the blade that is nearest to the handle? 6. What other parts of the blade can you name? 7. Which part is called the hilt? 8. What do we call the thin plates of iron or brass that line the handle on each side? 9. What other parts of the handle can you name?

10. What do we call the thin coat that covers an apple? 11. What do we call the central part? 12. What do we call the part that is between those just named? 13. What do we call the part that fastens the apple to the tree? 14. What do we call the part just opposite the one last named? 15. What part of an apple is called the pulp? 16. What does the core contain?

17. Name the parts of a wooden pail.

18. Name the parts of a plow.

19. What parts of a wagon can you name?

20. Name the parts of a clock.

Suggestions.—While talking about an object, such as a knife, a pin, or an apple, have the object in your hand, and point to the parts as they are named. In this way you will be more likely to secure the attention of all the members of your class, and a more lasting impression will be made. Whenever practicable, take pains to point out the parts of such objects as the plow or the wagon to all who are not familiar with them. The writing of the words will be a good exercise in spelling.

2. Written Exercise; for Seat Work.

Write about wagons, naming and describing their parts, and telling what purposes they serve. Draw a line under every noun.

LESSON 4.

Parts of the Human Body.—First Steps in Composition.

Questions and Exercises.

You may now give the names of the parts of the human body, while I write the names on the blackboard.

1. Questions.

1. What are the principal parts of the human body? —*Head, trunk, and limbs.*

2. What are the principal parts of the head? 3. What name is given to the bony wall that protects the brain? 4. What is that part called which covers the skull? 5. What is borne upon the scalp? 6. Name the parts of the face. 7. Name the parts of the mouth.

8. What are the principal parts of the trunk?— *Chest, abdomen, hips, breast, sides, back.*

9. What does the chest contain?

10. Name the different parts of the arm.

11. Name the parts of the leg.

12. What names are given to the different parts of the hand?

13. What names are given to the different parts of the foot?

14. What parts of the body are most used?

15. Which are most useful—the hands or the feet?

16. Which could you best bear—to be blind, or to be deaf? Why?

17. Tell some things that can be done with the hands.

18. For what purposes are the eyes chiefly used?

Suggestions.—These questions should be varied, increased, or diminished, according to the intelligence of the class and the kind of answers given. These lessons are meant to meet the wants of children, and are none too simple to serve that purpose. It will also be found, upon trial, that they are well adapted to such older persons as are called *hard to learn*. If they are too easy for your class, ask fewer and harder questions, and, if need be, combine two lessons in one.

2. Written Exercise; for Seat Work.

Write something about the most important parts of the body and their uses. Begin the first word of each sentence with a capital letter, and put a period at the close of each sentence, unless it is a question or an exclamation. Do not forget to cross the t's and dot the i's.

LESSON 5.

Geographical' Names.

Suggestions.—It is a good plan to gather the papers at the beginning of each recitation, and, glancing over them, praise the excellences, point out the most glaring defects, especially in form and arrangement, and give instruction for future work. Do not be severe. Let your remarks be brief, and of an encouraging nature. You can accomplish more by approving the good than by censuring the wrong.

1. Questions and Exercises.

As I write these names on the blackboard, you may write them on your slate or paper.

1. What do we call a body of water that is surrounded by land? 2. What do we call a point of land extending into the sea? 3. What name do we give to a large stream of water? 4. What do we call very small streams? 5. What do we call a body of land with water all around it? 6. What do we call a very high ridge of land?

7. In what State do you live? 8. What other States can you name? 9. Which is the largest river in the world? 10. Which is the longest? 11. What other rivers

can you name? 12. What countries? 13. What city is the capital of this State? 14. What is the capital of the United States? 15. Name other cities.

Each of these names of cities, rivers, States, etc., must begin with a capital letter, as you see on the blackboard.

2.   Seat Work.

Write names of—

Lakes, oceans, seas, gulfs, bays, counties, townships, villages.

LESSON 6.

Class Names and Individual Names.

1.   Questions and Instruction.

Get ready to copy names as fast as I write them on the board.

1. Give me names of boys.

2. Give names of girls.

3. If several boys were playing on the ice, and I should say, "*A boy fell*", could you tell which boy I meant? If I should say, "**John** *fell*", could you tell which one I meant?

4. If I should say, "*A girl is singing*", could you tell which particular girl I meant? Could you, if I should say, "**Ellen** *is singing*"?

5. If I should say, "*My uncle lives in a* **city**", could you tell what city I meant? Could you tell, if I should say, "*He lives in* **Boston**"?

6. Can **boy** mean *any* boy? Can **city** mean *any* city? Can **Andrew** mean *any* boy? Can **Detroit** mean *any* city?

7. If I should say, "*A* **pupil** is careless", could you tell which one of this class I meant? Could you if I should say, "**Jane** *is careless*"?

8. We may use the noun *merchant* in speaking of any one of the class of men called merchants; *friend*, in speaking of any one of my friends; *doctor*, in speaking of any one of that class; and *teacher*, in speaking of any one of the class of persons called teachers.

But if we wish to speak of some **particular** *merchant, friend, doctor*, or *teacher*, we have to use a different kind of noun; such as, *Mr. Ford; Joseph; Alonzo Palmer; Miss Boardman.*

9. So we may use the noun *island* in talking of any one of that class of things; *village*, in speaking of any village.

But if we wish to talk about a **particular** island or village, we must use a different name; such as, *Borneo; Bloomfield.*

10. A noun like *friend* or *village* that may be applied to any one of a class is called a **common noun;** but a noun that means some particular one of a class, like *Joseph* or *Borneo*, is called a **proper noun.**

2. Exercises.

(*a.*) Each give a proper noun that names a person. Each give a proper noun that names a place. Give a common noun that names a place; a person.

(*b.*) Tell which of the following nouns are common, and which are proper :—

EXAMPLES.—Niagara, lake, corn, John, paper, map, Boston, hill, Ellen, wheat, gold, Detroit, Italy, knife, mountain, Alabama, book, Mexico, vase, field, Johnson, Lowell. car, corn, bread, ice, snow, sugar, Iceland, apple, glass, Mary, Maine, lily, house, Montreal, Hudson River, Casco Bay, Bay of Fundy, Elk Rapids, song, poetry, flowers, Harper's Ferry, Glenn's Falls, Lake of the Woods, Mountains of the Moon.

Note.—Names of substances, such as gold, chalk, snow, etc., are classed among the common nouns.

3. Seat Work.

Write fifty common nouns in one group, and forty proper nouns in another group.

LESSON 7.

Initial Letters.

1. Instruction and Exercises.

1. We will now give attention to the list of nouns in the last lesson. The first letter of a word is called the **initial** letter of that word.

2. What kind of initial letter have the common nouns ? With what kind of letter does each proper noun begin ?

3. Write the following nouns correctly :—

EXAMPLES.—andrew, Baltimore, Nation, country, london, plain, Desk, moses, Ida, Map, book, Boston, detroit, emma, a Lord and Lady, england, europe, ocean, peninsula, Cataract, forest, Richmond, levi, Riches, buffalo, a Buffalo, cleveland, Moscow, paris, peru, poverty, Silver, sorrow, Gratitude, virtue, goodness.

4. Some common nouns begin with a capital letter, such as the names of the *months*, the names of the *days of the week*, and the names of *tribes*, *races*, *political parties*, *etc.*

EXAMPLES.—January, May, Monday, Wednesday, Choctaws, Circassians, Whigs.

But the names of the seasons take a small initial.

EXAMPLES.—The four seasons of our year are spring, summer, autumn, winter.

2. Seat Work.

Write the following sentences correctly :—

1. My Friend Arthur is in brazil.

2. He expects to start for Home on the first tuesday in july.

3. One day in early Spring, philip, jane, and lucy went into the woods to gather wild Flowers.

4. naples is a beautiful City in Italy.

5. The shortest Days of the year are in december.

6. september, October, and november are called the Autumn Months.

7. The grand divisions of the eastern continent are europe, asia, and Africa.

8. The warmest season of the year is called summer.

9. The first day of the week is called sunday.

10. in the valley of Elah, david, the young Shepherd, fought with goliath, the Giant of gath.

11. The democrats and the republicans are the leading parties in our country.

12. The sioux are a warlike tribe.

LESSON 8.

Proper Names Consisting of Two or More Words.

1. Instruction and Exercises.

(*a.*) When a common noun is used with a proper noun, or when two common nouns are used together, to name a person or place, each noun usually has a capital initial.

EXAMPLES.—Gulf of Mexico, Hudson's Bay, Cape Ann, Captain Brown, Colonel Shaw, Otter Creek, Isle of Man.

(*b.*) Write the following names correctly :—

EXAMPLES.—Cape cod, Staten island, elijah, river, columbia river, bay, casco bay, Lake, house, Horse, lake Geneva, michigan city, mount Washington, bay of panama, gulf of Darien, Mount Holyoke, boston harbor, Hampton roads, shenandoah valley, Washington Prairie, Straits of magellan, florida Peninsula, isthmus of suez, Cape of Good Hope, Victoria land, london Bridge, moosehead lake.

(*c.*) Write the following sentences correctly :—

1. The odd fellows have built a hall at silver creek.

2. Malays and indians, as well as negroes,* have a dark complexion.

3. The picts and scots were tribes of ancient britain.

4. The waldenses reside in the valleys of piedmont.

2. Seat Work.

Write a composition on what you have learned about common and proper nouns.

*NOTE.—It is customary to begin *negroes* and *heathen* with a small letter.

LESSON 9.

Number.

1. Instruction and Exercises.

(*a.*) Tell which words are nouns in the following sentences:—

1. A river is a large stream of water.
2. The tall pine waves in the wind.
3. The mountain and the squirrel had a quarrel.
4. The robin and the wren are flown, and from the shrubs
   the jay;
   And from the wood-top calls the crow through all the
   gloomy day.

How would you change the noun *river* to make it mean more than one river? What change would you make in the noun *stream* if you wanted to speak of more than one stream?

In sentences 2 and 3 how would you change each noun to make it mean more than one?

What noun in sentence 4 means more than one? How would you change it to make it mean only one? How would you change each of the other nouns to make it mean more than one?

(*b.*) Which of the following nouns name only one thing? Which of them name more than one thing?

Ex.—Tree, men, field, children, lake, brooks, pebbles, flute, harps, chains, bonnet, willow, kitchen, tongue, face, village, leaf, crosses, castle, violets, garden, park, sword.

(*c.*) Give other nouns that name just one thing. Others that name more than one.

When a noun names just one thing, *a single object,* it is said to be in the **singular number;** but when it means more than one thing, it is said to be in the **plural number.**

(*d.*) Which of the following nouns are in the singular number, and which in the plural ?

Ex.—Valley, picture, stones, doors, vase, lamp, tents, boat, rocks, vines, curtain, pinks, paths, man, sky, sphere, homes, life, scenes, world, seasons, herd, flock, stoves, schools, mob, clouds, family, woodlands, swarm, armies, shores.

(*e.*) Change the number of each of these nouns.

MODEL.

Valley, is a noun, common, singular number ; its plural is *valleys.*

2. Seat Work.

Copy the following sentences; put *c* over every common noun and *r* over every proper noun; draw one line under every noun in the singular number, and two under every noun in the plural number.

EXAMPLES.

1. The vessel brought tea from China, tigers and elephants from India, parrots, bananas, and coffee from Brazil, and sugar from Cuba.

2. At the door on summer evenings sat the little Hiawatha.

3. With the ebb of the tide, the ships sailed out of the harbor.

4. Day after day, in the gray of the dawn, plodded the German farmer, with flowers and fruits for the market.

LESSON 10.

Collective Nouns.

1. Instruction and Exercises.

1. Examine the list of nouns under (*d.*) last lesson, and tell which of them name collections of objects.

2. Names of *collections* are called **collective nouns.**

3. Which of the following nouns are collective ?

Ex.—Houses, assembly, plains, council, rivers, soldiers, army, torrents, band, voices, forests, company, senate, sailors, regiments.

4. Is soldiers a collective noun? Why not?—*Because the word soldiers does not necessarily name a collection of objects; the soldiers may be in different places far apart.*

5. Would the soldiers make an army unless collected together in one place?

6. What other collective nouns can you give?

7. Turn to the ——— page of this book, and see how many you can find.

8. Now listen while I read from another book, and tell me when I come to a collective noun.

2. Seat Work.

(*a.*) Make lists of common nouns in both numbers, putting the singular nouns in one column, and the plural in another.

(*b.*) Make a list of collective nouns in both numbers.

(*c.*) Make a list of proper nouns in the singular number.

Can you make out a list of proper nouns in the plural number?

LESSON 11.
Formation of the Plural.
1. Instruction.

1. Examine the nouns below, and notice how the plural is formed. The dark, broad-faced letters show what has to be added to the singular noun to make it plural.

EXAMPLES.

Singular,	Plural.	Singular,	Plural.
1. Time,	time**s**.	1. Gas,	gas-**es**.
2. Hill,	hill**s**.	2. Hiss,	hiss-**es**.
3. Loom,	loom**s**.	3. Box,	box-**es**.
4. Window,	window**s**.	4. Piece,	piec-**es**.
5. Roof,	roof**s**.	5. Maze,	maz-**es**.
6. Hand,	hand**s**.	6. Wish,	wish-**es**.
7. Tree,	tree**s**.	7. Arch,	arch-**es**.
8. Lake,	lake**s**.	8. Barge,	barg-**es**.

2. How are the plurals formed in the first column? Does the addition of the **s** increase the number of syllables?

3. How are the plurals formed in the second column? Does the addition of **es** increase the number of syllables?

4. Can you tell any reason why **es** should be added to these words instead of adding **s** as in the first column?

Add **s** instead of **es** to each of the words in the second column, and then try to speak the words thus formed, without increasing the number of syllables.

5. Try to speak the word *foxs.* Speak *gas* and *gass*, and see what difference you can make in the two words. Try to speak the words *lashs, fishs, waltzs, taxs, glasss,* each in one syllable.

By these experiments we see that when a noun ends in the sound of **s, j,** or **z, sh** or **ch**, we cannot easily add **s** without forming a new syllable, and that is the reason why we add the syllable **es** to such nouns.

6. The letter *x* sounds like *ks*, so any noun that ends in *x* really ends in the sound of *s.* Nouns ending in *ge* end in the sound of *j*, for the *g* is soft, and the *e* is silent, as it is also in *piece, maze,* and many other words.

Silent *e* at the end of a word is dropped before adding *es*, as it always is before a syllable beginning with a vowel.

2. Exercises.

(*a.*) Which of the following nouns form the plural by adding **s**. Which by adding **es**, and why?

EXAMPLES.—Council, ocean, march, flood, bush, mountain, topaz, cage, lens, ax, hedge, lace, case, field, atlas, town, race, ridge, conscience, forest, porch, adz, plain, prairie, lynx.

(*b.*) Why are the following plurals improper?—

EXAMPLES.—Watchs, cloudes, taxs, bookes, dishs, inchs.

Correct them.

3. Seat Work.

Change the number of the nouns in the following sentences, making such other changes as are rendered necessary by the change in the number of the nouns.

EXAMPLES.

1. Every porch and arch of the church was highly ornamented.

2. Sword and shield, mace and battle-ax, lay together in a confused heap.

3. Chart and compass, book and atlas, were alike unknown.

4. A dried fish hung from the ridge of the wigwam.

5. Every ray of the setting sun gilded the bush with burnished gold.

6. As the gondola passed under the bridge, my attention was attracted by a sudden splash, and when I turned my face, the gondolier had disappeared.

7. A fox leaped over the fence, and hid beneath a branch of hemlock.

LESSON 12.

Nouns Ending in o and y.

1. Instruction.

1. Notice how the plural of the following nouns is formed.

EXAMPLES.

Singular,	Plural.	Singular,	Plural.
Valley,	valleys.	Cargo,	cargoes.
Money,	moneys.	Potato,	potatoes.
Lady,	ladies.	Cameo,	cameos.
Balcony,	balconies.	Seraglio,	seraglios.

2. In the first column the nouns all end in **y**. *Valley* and *money* form the plural by adding **s**, but *lady* and *balcony* change the **y** to **ie** (the old-fashioned spelling) and then add **s**.

3. These different ways of forming the plural of words ending in *y* are caused by the different kinds of letter

that come before the *y*. In *valley* and *money* the letter just before the *y* is a *vowel*, so the *y* is left unchanged; but in *lady* and *balcony* the letter just before the *y* is a *consonant*, so the *y* is changed to *ie* before adding **s**.

4. In the second column the words all end in **o**. In the first two words, **o** comes after a *consonant*, and for this reason, **es** is added to form the plural; but in the other two, **o** comes after a *vowel*, and so **s** alone is added.

How many syllables in cargo? How many in cargoes? Then does the **es** added to nouns ending in **o** increase the number of their syllables? Nouns ending in **u** or **i** commonly form the plural like those ending in **o**.

5. The letters *a, e, i, o, u* are vowels. All the other letters are consonants, except *w* and *y*, which are sometimes vowels and sometimes consonants. **W** is a vowel when it has the sound of **u**, and **y** is a vowel when it has the sound of **i**.

6. Some of our nouns ending in *o* are taken directly from other languages. Such nouns form their plural by adding **s** instead of **es**. But when they have been long and familiarly used in our language, they generally form their plural like ordinary English nouns. With regard to some of these nouns, however, custom is not uniform, even among good scholars, some preferring the plural formed by adding **s**, and others the plural formed by adding **es**. For example, the plural of *domino* may be *dominos* or *dominoes*; of *portico, porticos* or *porticoes*; of *piano, pianos* or *pianoes*; etc.

2. Exercises.

(*a.*) Which of the following nouns form the plural by adding **s**? Tell how the plural of each of the other nouns is made.

EXAMPLES.—Echo, forest, volley, sky, flood, chimney, pony, volcano, sash, tax, adz, torch, larch, watch, folio, grace, bay, country, pulley, cage, hippopotamus.

2

(*b.*) Correct the following plurals:—

EXAMPLES.—Flys, bushs, tornados, monkies, berrys, folioes, countys, monies, chimnies, cherrys, boy's.

3. Seat Work.

Rewrite the following sentences, changing the number of the nouns in italics, and making such other changes as are rendered necessary by the change of the noun.

EXAMPLES.

1. *Bridges* with several *arches* spanned the limpid *streams* at the bottom of the narrow *valleys.*
2. A *fairy* dances about the *marsh.*
3. A *tomato* is under the *dish.*
4. With *torch* in hand, we traveled on through *porch* and *arch.*
5. A *face* peeped over the *wall.*
6. An *emu* is taller than a *crane.*
7. A *volcano* belches forth a *mass* of liquid rock.
8. He writes a *folio* in an *hour.*
9. The *hero* boldly dispatched the *mosquito* that had annoyed the *lady.*
10. The rocks on the opposite shore gave a distinct *echo* of the *waltz* played by the *mulatto.*
11. The *rhinoceros* is not a *native* of this *country.*
12. A *gnu* is sometimes called a horned *horse.*

LESSON 13.

Nouns Ending in f and fe.

1. Questions in Review.

1. How do nouns ordinarily form their plural ?
2. What nouns add the syllable **es** to form their plural ? Give examples from the sentences on the paper just written out.
3. How do nouns ending in *y* make their plural ?
4. How do we make the plural of nouns ending in *o* ?

5. When we add *es* to a noun ending in *o,* do we increase the number of its syllables ?

6. What may be said of the plural of foreign nouns ?

2. Instruction.

1. The following nouns ending in *f* form the plural by changing *f* to *ve* before adding *s* :—

Loaf,	thief,	shelf,	half,	leaf,	wolf,
self,	sheaf,	beef,	elf,	calf,	wharf.*

2. Some nouns ending in *fe* change the *f* to *v* before adding *s;* as, *knife, knives; wife, wives; life, lives.*

3. Exercise.

Change the number of the following nouns, and use their plurals in sentences of your own :—

EXAMPLES.—Roof, thief, chief, fife, life, strife, leaf, grief, sheaf, gulf, wolf, shelf, waif.

4. Instruction Resumed.

. The plural of letters, signs, figures, and words mentioned merely as words, is formed by adding the apostrophe and *s* ('s).

EXAMPLES.

1. You are careless about dotting your i's and crossing your t's.

2. There are too many **and's**† and me's in your composition.

3. Your 9's and +'s are neatly made.

5. Exercise.

Write the following sentences correctly :—

1. Two Chieves lay upon the fallen leafs.

2. Ahs and Ohs are found in almost every line.

---

*NOTE.—*Wharf* has two ways of making its plural,—wharfs and wharves. When *staff* means a stick, its plural is *staves;* but when it means a band of officers, its plural is *staffs.*

†NOTE.—This method of forming the plural of other parts of speech used as nouns is taught by some of our most recent authors. See *Whitney's Essentials of English Grammar*, p. 54. Some, however, prefer simply to add *s* without an apostrophe.

3. There are some bookes on my shelfs that have been much read ; such as the lifes of Great men, the voyages of Columbus, captain cook, and commodore Kane, and the conquest of mexico by cortez.

4. As soon as the wolfs had devoured the sheep, they attacked the calfs.

5. Printed 9es look some like 6es inverted.

6. His ors and buts came so often that all began to laugh.

6. Seat Work.

1. Write sentences containing the plurals of the following words, letters, and signs :—

EXAMPLES.—Knife, sheaf, hoof, half, thief, grief, 7, *, p, q.

LESSON 14.

Peculiarities in Number.

To the Teacher.—It is not expected that the lists of words given in this lesson will be committed to memory : indeed it would be a waste of time for the pupil to do so. Frequent reference to the lists will after a time make them sufficiently familiar.

The *Exercise* and the *Seat Work* should be required ; and in connection with these, some general questions should be asked.

1. Lists for Reference.

(*a.*) Some nouns have very **irregular** ways of forming their plural.

EXAMPLES.

Singular,	Plural.	Singular,	Plural.
Man,	men.	Foot,	feet.
Woman,	women.	Tooth,	teeth.
Child,	children.	Goose,	geese.
Ox,	oxen.	Mouse,	mice.

(*b.*) Some nouns **have no plural.**

EXAMPLES.

Gold,	wheat,	chalk,	tar,
silver,	rye,	ice,	hemp,
copper,	corn,	clay,	vinegar,

tin,	millet,	flesh,	gratitude,
lead,	barley,	mortar,	darkness.

REMARK.—Some nouns of this class may take the plural form to denote different kinds of the same substance.

EXAMPLES.—1. Most of the *wines* now in market contain very little of the juice of the grape. 2. Vegetable *oils* are the most wholesome.

Others take the plural form when the name of the material is used to name the things made of it. So the glazier has *tins* for fastening panes of glass, the housewife has *tins* for baking purposes, the printer has his *leads*, and cents are sometimes called *coppers;* but in their ordinary use the words given above, and many others, have no plural form.

(*c.*) Some nouns **have no singular.**

EXAMPLES.

Annals,	clothes,	oats,	scissors,
ashes,	dregs,	pinchers,	shears,
bitters,	eaves,	nippers,	snuffers,
breeches,	embers,	riches,	stairs,
cattle,	wages,	remains,	stilts,
suds,	thanks,	tongs,	victuals.

REMARK.—Some of these words, such as *dregs, embers, oats, nippers, stairs, stilts,* are in a few instances and with some meanings, used in the singular number, but such uses are very rare. *Molasses*, although plural in form, is regarded as singular.

(*d.*) Some nouns have the **same form in both numbers**; that is, whether singular or plural in meaning.

EXAMPLES.

Sheep,	species,	couple,	salmon,
deer,	series,	bellows,	odds,
swine,	means,	wages,	gallows,
news,	apparatus,	shad,	mathematics.

(*e.*) Nouns are sometimes **plural in meaning**, although **singular in form.**

EXAMPLES.

Fish,	yoke,	ton,	brace,
pike,	dozen,	head,	cannon,
pair,	score,	sail,	shot.

(*f.*) Some nouns have **two plurals with different meanings.**

EXAMPLES.

Singular,	*Plural.*
Penny,	pence or pennies.
Brother,	brothers or brethren.
Fish,	fish or fishes.
Die,	dies or dice.
Index,	indexes or in'dices.

REMARKS.—We use *pence* to denote a sum, or so much in value ; and *pennies* to denote separate pieces of money.

Brothers denotes those of the same family ; *brethren,* those of the same society.

We use *fishes* to denote separate individuals ; but *fish* to denote quantity or the species.

Dies are stamps for coining ; *dice* are small cubes for gaming.

In'dexes are tables of contents or reference ; but *in'-dices* are algebraic signs.

(*g.*) Most **compound words** form their plural by changing only that part which is described by the rest.

EXAMPLES.

Singular,	*Plural.*	*Singular*,	*Plural.*
Cherry-tree,	cherry-trees.	Brother-in-law,	brothers-in-law.
Gentleman,	gentlemen.	Hanger-on,	hangers-on.
Step-father,	step-fathers.	Pailful,	pailfuls.
Tooth-brush,	tooth-brushes.	Armful,	armfuls.
Saw-tooth,	saw-teeth.	Court-martial,	courts-martial.

(*h.*) In **some** compound words the two nouns are so

nearly **equal in importance** that both are changed in forming the plural.

EXAMPLES.—Man-servant, men-servants ; woman-servant, women-servants ; knight-templar, knights-templars.

(*i.*) **A name and a title** are often united to form a proper noun. With respect to the plural of such compounds, authorities are not agreed. It is generally conceded, however, that the word, which, in any given instance, conveys the leading thought, and is therefore to be made most prominent, is the one to be changed in forming the plural. The following may be of some service.

EXAMPLES.

Singular. Dr. Hoyt.
Plural. The two Dr. Hoyts, or the Doctors J. and L. P. Hoyt.
Sing. Miss Latham.
Plu. The two Miss Lathams, or the Misses Ellen and Jane Latham.
Sing. Mrs. Chatterton.
Plu. The Mrs. Chattertons.
Sing. Miss Brown.
Plu. The Misses Brown, and sometimes the Miss Browns.

REMARK.—In speaking of the difference of opinion as to whether the title or the name should be changed in forming the plural of these words, Goold Brown says, " Both opinions are right if neither be carried too far"; and further, " It appears that each of these forms of expression may be right in some cases ; and each of them may be wrong, if improperly substituted for either of the others".— *Grammar of Eng. Gram.*, p. 245.

(*j.*) The following nouns ending in **o** after a consonant, on account of their **foreign origin,** commonly have their plural made by the addition of **s** only.

Albino,	fresco,	memento,	proviso,
canto,	halo,	octavo,	quarto,
duodecimo,	lasso,	piano,	sirocco,
solo,	stiletto,	tyro,	zero.

(*k.*) **Foreign nouns** sometimes retain their foreign plurals.

EXAMPLES.

Singular,	Plural.	Singular,	Plural.
Antithesis,	antitheses.	Bandit,	Band'tti.
Analysis,	analyses.	Beau,	Beaux.
Axis,	axes.	Genus,	genera.
Basis,	bases.	Cherub,	cherubim.
Ellipsis,	ellipses.	Larva,	larvæ.
Emphasis,	emphases.	Minutia,	minutiæ.
Oasis,	oases.	Nebula.	nebulæ.
Parenthesis,	parentheses.	Vertebra,	vertebræ.
Focus,	foci.	Miasma,	miasmata.
Fungus,	fungi.	Magus,	magi.
Calculus,	calculi.	Stimulus,	stimuli.
Synopsis,	synopses.	Terminus,	termini.
Synthesis,	syntheses.	Proboscis,	proboscides.

Some of these nouns have also a regular English plural, for example, *beau, bandit, focus, fungus, cherub.*

2. Exercise.

Correct the following sentences :—

1. We saw five deers quietly feeding in the Park.
2. Gallies were once used in the navys of some countrys
3. The book cost two pounds seven shillings and six pennics.
4. My uncle has several bellowses in his shop.
5. The fishing Companys caught fifteen barrels of shads.
6. I like algebra better than any other mathematic I ever saw ?
7. To what specie does that Plant belong.
8. The prophet elisha was plowing with twelve yokes of oxes.
9. My two brethren, Joseph and Marius, were both under five years of Age
10. The ice was so heavy that it broke the eave on the West side of the house.

3. Seat Work

Suggestion.—If this is too much for *seat work*,—as it may be for some classes,—require as much of it as will best meet the wants of your class.

(*a.*) Correct the following words, and then use each

word properly in a sentence, preserving the meaning that seems to be intended here:—

EXAMPLES.—Serieses, tong, scissor, apparatuses, swines, snuffer, victual, folioes, lilys, skies.

(*b.*) Write the following sentences correctly :—

1. Don't scatter an ash on the floor?
2. The bow of one snuffer is broken.
3. We bought five dozens of Peaches.
4. He sold two barrel of fishes?
5. We pasture forty heads of cattle
6. The man is four scores and ten years old.
7. People knew nothing of such apparatuses in those days
8. Molasses are brought from the west india islands.
9. The news are that there is ice in the gulf of mexico.

————•————

LESSON 15.

Gender.

1. Instruction.

Man,	woman,	box.
Boy,	girl,	tree.
Uncle,	aunt,	house.
Lion,	lioness,	brook.
Ox,	cow,	field.
Tiger,	tigress,	mountain.

1. Which of these words are names of *males?* Which are names of *females?* Which are names of objects that have no *sex?*

2. What other names of males can you give? What other names of females? Of objects that have no sex?

3. Names of males are said to be in the **masculine gender;** names of females, in the **feminine gender;** and names of objects that have no sex, in the **neuter gender**, since they are neither masculine nor feminine, and *neuter* means *neither.*

2. Exercises.

(*a.*) Give proper nouns in the masculine gender; in the feminine gender; neuter gender. Give common nouns in the masculine gender; in the feminine gender; neuter gender. Change the number of each.

(*b.*) Give the gender of the following nouns :—

EXAMPLES.—Matron, master, mother, James, book, uncle, map, niece, youth, brother, landlady, nun, Nancy, priest, monk, girl, London, rose, bird, son, hero, negro, goose, man, duke, queen, wagon, spinster.

(*c.*) Go through this list of words, and change the gender of all the nouns that can be so changed.

(*d.*) Tell which of the nouns in the above list are common, and which are proper; which are in the singular number, and which in the plural.

(*e.*) Change the number of each.

3. Seat Work.

(*a.*) Take up each of the following words separately, and tell (1) whether it is a common or a proper noun, (2) its number, (3) its gender.—*See model below.*

EXAMPLES.—Hero, countess, maid, wife, nephew, daughter, bride, governor, witch, lord, bachelor, Josephine, lad, husband, Philip, widow.

(*b.*) Do the same with the nouns in the following sentences.

EXAMPLES.

1. Nauhaught the Indian was a deacon.
2. My brother Nathan was a soldier in the war.
3. The Empress Eugenia is said to be a kind woman.
4. Lucy Marvin, the only sister of Peter Cook, is a seamstress.
5. Nathaniel, her son, chops her wood, and goes on errands for the neighbors.

MODEL.

Hero.—Noun, com., sing. n., mas. g.

LESSON 16.

Peculiarities in Gender.

1. Instruction.

If I should say, "*My cousins came to see me yester-day*," could you tell whether they were men or women, boys or girls? If I should say, "*My pupils are kind*," could you tell their sex?

So we see that there are nouns, which, although they are applied to persons, do not distinguish their sex; that is, they do not show whether the persons are males or females. For *cousins* or *pupils* may be either males or females, or they may be of both sexes; that is, some of them may be males and some females.

Just so it is with *friends, associates, parents, children, people, scholars, etc.*

2. Exercises.

(*a.*) Change the number of the nouns given above. Does their singular form distinguish sex any better than their plural does?

(*b.*) Give other names that are applied to persons without distinguishing their sex.

3. Instruction Resumed.

(*a.*) Nouns that distinguish sex are called *gender-nouns*. When a noun does not distinguish sex, it is as well to say nothing about its gender; but if we do refer to the gender, it is probably better simply to state that the noun under consideration does not distinguish sex.

(*b.*) The word *poet* applies to males and females alike; but when it becomes necessary to distinguish a female poet, we may use the term *poetess*. So we use *lion, horse, dog*, without regard to sex, unless it is particularly necessary to make a distinction. For the purpose of making this distinction in special cases, we have the feminine forms, *lioness, mare, bitch.*

(*c.*) Sometimes the *feminine* form is used to denote both sexes. For instance, we speak of *ducks* or *geese* without regard to sex; but if we wish to make a distinction, we use a different word for the male. What is the masculine gender of *goose?* Of *duck?*

(*d.*) The sex of young children, and of lower animals, is often disregarded. Ex.—*The child cries because* **it** *is hungry. The mole makes* **its** *path under ground.*

(*e.*) Nouns distinguish gender in three different ways:—

1. By different words. Ex.—*Boy, girl; uncle, aunt; king, queen.*

2. By different endings. Ex.—*Tiger, tigress; hero, heroine; governor, governess.*

3. By prefixing or affixing other words. Ex.—*Man-servant, maid-servant; male friends, female friends.*

4. Lists for Reference.

Masculine,	Feminine.	Masculine,	Feminine.
Bachelor,	maid.	Beau,	belle.
Buck,	doe.	Cock,	hen.
Drake,	duck.	Earl,	countess.
Husband,	wife.	King,	queen.
Lord,	lady.	Nephew,	niece.
Ram,	ewe.	Stag,	hind.
Wizard,	witch.	Monk,	nun.
Hart,	roe.	Sir,	madam.
Sloven,	slut.	Youth,	damsel.
Swain,	nymph.	Abbot,	abbess.
Actor,	actress.	Administrator,	administratrix.
Author,	authoress.	Benefactor,	benefactress.
Baron,	baroness.	Bridegroom,	bride.
Count,	countess.	Dauphin,	dauphiness.
Czar,	czarina.	Deacon,	deaconess.
Don,	donna.	Director,	directress.
Duke,	duchess.	Emperor,	empress.
Heir,	heiress.	Executor,	executrix.
Hero,	heroine.	Governor,	governess.

Host,	hostess.	Hunter,	huntress.
Jew,	Jewess.	Landgrave,	landgravine.
Poet,	poetess.	Monitor,	monitress.
Patron,	patroness.	Marquis,	marchioness.
Priest,	priestess.	Prince,	princess.
Tiger,	tigress.	Testator,	testatrix.
Tailor,	tailoress.	Shepherd,	shepherdess.
Prophet,	prophetess.	Viscount,	viscountess.
God,	goddess.	Widower,	widow.
Giant,	giantess.	Songster,	songstress.
Negro,	negress.	Sorcerer,	sorceress.
Sultan,	sultana.	Lion,	lioness.
Landlord,,	landlady.	Gentleman,	gentlewoman.
Peacock,	peahen.	Cocksparrow,	hensparrow.
Merman,	mermaid.	Englishman,	Englishwoman.

5. Exercises.

(*a.*) Select the nouns in the following sentences, tell whether they are common or proper, and give their number and gender. Correct all mistakes.

1. The lost ponys were found in the valley, feeding among the Turnips and potatos.

2. Three vollies were fired upon our enemys, and the echos went ringing through the forest.

3. Uncle John told a tale of elfs that ride by night?

4. Her parents dwelt beside a glen

5. The frost makes white flowers, with crystal leaf and stem, that grow in clear november nights.

6. The fairys buried the earth in snow, as Autumn winds bury the forest floor in heaps of leafs.

(*b.*) Change the number of all the common nouns in the above sentences, and the gender of all the gender-nouns.

6. Seat Work.

Study past lessons so as to be able to answer the questions of Lesson 17.

LESSON 17.

Review.

1. Questions.

1. What is language?
2. When do we use spoken language?
3. When do we use written language?
4. What class of words is indispensable in language?
5. Why are names so important?
6. What are all names called?
7. Give examples of nouns used to name parts of objects.
8. Give examples of nouns used to name persons; places.
9. What do we call a noun that may be applied to any one of a class of things?
10. Give examples.
11. What do we call a noun that is used to distinguish a particular thing from all others of the same kind?
12. Give examples.
13. With what kind of letter should common nouns begin? Proper nouns?
14. Give examples of proper names consisting of more than one word; such as, George Washington, Staten Island, Lake of the Woods.
15. Write these names upon the blackboard, giving them their proper initials.
16. What is an initial letter?
17. What kind of initial should be given to the names of the months? The seasons? The days of the week? Political parties? Religious sects; such as, *Methodists, Baptists, Presbyterians?*
18. How should the first word of a sentence begin?
19. What mark should be put at the close of a sentence?

20. What mark should be put after a question?

21. Write a sentence that should have a period after it.

22. Write one that should have a question-mark after it.

23. Give examples of nouns in the singular number. In the plural number.

24. What is commonly done to the singular noun to make it plural?

25. What do we do when *s* will not unite with the last sound of the singular noun?

26. With what sounds will the sound of *s* not unite?

27. Give examples of singular nouns that add *es* to form their plural.

28. How do we form the plural of nouns ending in *o*?

29. If a noun ending in *o* is one that has been taken from some other language, how does it commonly form its plural?

30. How do we form the plural of nouns ending in *y*?

2. Seat Work.

Prepare to answer the questions in the next lesson.

———— • ————

LESSON 18.

Review.—Continued.

1. Questions.

1. How do we form the plural of *wolf? knife? chief? shelf? leaf? fife? roof?*

2. What is the plural of *ox? foot? goose?*

3. Give some nouns that have no plural form. Some that always have the plural form.

4. What word would you use in speaking of more than one *sheep?* Of more than one *yoke* of oxen? Of a number of *cattle* of different kinds?

5. What is the singular number of *species? series? means? mathematics?*

6. What is the plural number of *apparatus ? couple ? gallows ?*

7. How many plurals has penny ?

8. When do you use each ?

9. What are the plural forms of brother ?

10. When do we use each ?

11. How do most compound words form their plural ?

12. What is the plural of *tooth-brush ? hand-ful ? apple-tree ? brother-in-law ? man-servant ?*

13. How would you form the plural of *Mrs. Clark ? Miss Johnson ?*

14. How is the plural of *solo* commonly spelled ? *zero ? stiletto ?*

15. What is the plural of *oasis ? focus ? genus ?*

16. Why do these nouns form their plural in such unusual ways ?

17. In what three ways are nouns changed to show their gender ?

18. Give examples of each.

2. Exercise.

Correct all mistakes in the following words and sentences :—

(*a.*) Heros, navys, lynxs, pullies, dutys, folioes, gnus.

(*b.*) 1. Most of the oranges sold in the united states are from the west india islands, and from the countrys bordering on the mediterranean sea.

2. The states which border on the gulf of Mexico yield large quantities of cotton.

LESSON 19.

Qualities.

1. Instruction.

(*a.*) Name things that are white; things that are smooth ; things that are cold.

Name something that is both white and cold; something that is both smooth and white; something that is cold and smooth.

(*b.*) When you said, "Chalk is white," you told a **quality** of the chalk. When you told me that ice is both smooth and cold, you told *two of the qualities of ice.*

2. Exercises.

(*a.*) Tell a quality of *iron*, of *glass*, of *lead, sugar, flowers, gold, clouds, grass, trees, John, Mary, savages.*

(*b.*) I will now write on the board some of the sentences which you have just made.

1. Iron is strong.	7. Clouds are fleecy.
2. Glass is transparent.	8. Grass is green.
3. Lead is heavy.	9. Trees are tall.
4. Sugar is sweet.	10. John is kind.
5. Flowers are beautiful.	11. Mary is modest.
6. Gold is valuable.	12. Savages are warlike.

Answer the following questions in regard to each of the above sentences :—

1. Which word names the thing that has the quality?
2. Which word shows the quality?

(*c.*) Treat the nouns as in Lesson 16.

3. Seat Work.

Make *twenty sentences*, and in each of them name something and tell a quality of it, just as we have done to-day.

LESSON 20.

Classifying the Qualities of Objects.

1. Exercises.

(*a.*) 1. Tell me what qualities apples may have, while I write the quality-words on the blackboard.

2. Which of these quality-words tell something about the *size* of apples?

3

3. Which of them describe the shape ?

4. Which tell about the taste, or flavor ?

5. Which describe the *surface ?* Which, the color ? Which, the condition ?

(*b.*) We will now arrange these words according to their use.

SIZE.—Large, small, medium.

SHAPE.—Round, conical, flattish.

SURFACE.—Rough, smooth, glossy, shining.

COLOR.—Red, green, yellow, streaked, russet.

CONDITION.—Ripe, unripe, mellow, hard, crisp, raw, cooked, sound.

FLAVOR.—Juicy, sweet, sour, spicy, tart, mild, rich, mealy, bitter.

(*c.*) Classify the qualities of horses as we have just classified the qualities of apples.

2. Seat Work.

Classify the qualities that men may have, giving qualities of size, color, character, etc.

LESSON 21.

Showing How to Write a Composition.

1. Exercises.

(*a.*) After giving me the paper that you have written about the qualities of men, you may each *tell* me some of those qualities, and I will write the quality-words on the blackboard.

QUALITY-WORDS.

Large,   small,   tall,   strong,   skillful,
     wise,   noted,   good,
happy,   poor,   cruel,   angry,
     selfish,   useful,   kind,
sober,   noble,   cheerful,   generous,
     prosperous,   industrious,   bad.

(*b.*) We will now try to write something about these qualities; and first we must have a **heading**. What shall it be? .... Very well. Every *chief word* of a heading must, in writing, begin with a capital letter.

Qualities of Men.

Some men are large, and some are small. Goliah was a large man, but David killed him with a stone. Zaccheus was a small man, and had to climb a tree to see the Saviour among the crowd.

Saul was a very tall man. He could look right over the heads of all his countrymen.

Samson was very strong. He carried away the gates of the city of Gaza.

David was skillful in war; but Solomon was noted for his wisdom. He was the wisest man living.

Samuel was a good man. He served God all his days.

Bad men are apt to be cruel, and often angry. Selfish men are not happy men.

Generous men help the poor, and care for the sick.

We love to see men noble, kind, useful, and happy. Men who are sober and industrious are apt to be cheerful and prosperous.

2. Seat Work.

Each write a *composition* about the qualities and uses of horses.

LESSON 22.

Predicating and Assuming Qualities.

1. Examples in which Qualities are Predicated.

1. Silver is bright.
2. Spring is pleasant.
3. Cherries are sour.
4. Mountains are grand.
5. Rivers are long.
6. Wells are deep.

7. Thomas is cheerful.	10. Lucy is obedient.
8. Vegetables are nutritious.	11. Berries are abundant.
9. Blossoms are fragrant.	12. Napoleon was ambitious.

2. Questions and Instruction.

1. In each of the above sentences, what word names the thing? 2. What word shows the quality of it? 3. What word stands between them? 4. Would there be any positive statement of the quality without this word?

5. In the sentence, *Grass is green*, what word names the object—the thing? 6. What word shows the quality? 7. What word stands between them? 8. Could we affirm that the *grass is green* without this word? (*No.*)

9. If the quality-word alone were placed before the noun, would it make sense? (*Yes.*) 10. Would any thought be expressed? (*Yes.*) 11. Would we understand that the *grass is green?* (*Yes.*) 12. Would there be any positive statement to that effect? (*No.*)

13. When *no statement* is made, but the quality is merely mentioned as something already known to exist in the thing, we say it is **assumed.** When there is a *positive statement* of the fact, we say it is **predicated.**

3. Exercise.

In which of the following examples is the quality assumed? In which predicated?

1. Lilies are white.	11. Ice is slippery.
2. Birds are joyous.	12. Bees are busy.
3. Clouds are black.	13. Tender vines.
4. Happy children.	14. Quiet evening.
5. Clover is fragrant.	15. Bears are clumsy.
6. Peaches are downy.	16. Enormous elephants.
7. Tumultuous seas.	17. Fruit is wholesome.
8. Snow is cold.	18. Temperate habits.
9. Dreary weather.	19. Indolent people.
10. Fruitful seasons.	20. Prairies are fertile.

4. Written Exercises ; for Seat Work.

(*a.*) Predicate qualities of the following objects :—

Sun, sky, meadows, desk, trees, house, water, brooks, stairs, pines, fire, soldiers.

(*b.*) Assume qualities of the following objects :—

Breezes, study, streets, harvests, night, echoes, life, lanes, pastures, ocean, berries, hills.

LESSON 23.

Subject and Predicate.

1. Instruction.

When we wish to tell a quality of anything, we must *name the thing.* This is necessary in order that the one to whom we speak may know what it is that has the quality.

Having named the thing, we use other words to predicate the quality of it.

2. Questions and Exercises.

(*a.*) If I say,—

Peaches are ripe,

1. What word names the things that I wish to talk about ?

2. What words predicate a quality of the peaches ?

(*b.*) In each of the following sentences, what word names a thing, and what words predicate a quality of it?

EXAMPLES.

1. Autumn is delightful.
2. Breezes are mild.
3. Skies are blue.
4. Men are mortal.
5. Abraham was faithful.
6. Tyrants are cruel.
7. God is good.
8. Fields are green.
9. Water is clear.
10. Showers are refreshing.
11. Books are valuable.
12. Great is Diana.
13. Life is short.
14. Patience is powerful.

3. Instruction Resumed.

Each of these groups of words is called a **sentence,** because it *names a thing and predicates something of it.*

The name-word tells the *subject of our thoughts*, and when we speak, it becomes the *subject of our remark;* so it is called the **subject** of the **sentence.**

1. What is the subject in each of the foregoing sentences ?

2. What is the predicate ?

3. Which is the quality-word ?

4. Which word shows that the quality is predicated ?

4. Seat Work.

Select the nouns in the examples of this lesson, tell whether they are common or proper, and give their number and gender.

LESSON 24.

The Copula.

1. Instruction.

Truth is mighty.

1. Is this group of words a sentence ? why ?

2. What is the subject ? why ?

3. What is the predicate ? why ?

4. Which is the quality-word ?

5. What word shows that the quality is predicated ?

This word which shows that the quality is predicated is called the **copula.**

2. Exercises.

(*a.*) Which of the following groups are sentences ? why ? What is the subject of each ? why ? The predicate ? why ? The quality-word ? The copula ? why ?

1. Lions are strong.	10. Lanes are narrow.
2. Butterflies are gaudy.	11. Shadows are weird.
3. Iron is tenacious.	12. Squirrels are sprightly.
4. Gold is valuable.	13. Cunning foxes.
5. Cumbersome loads.	14. Rocks are gray.
6. Angels are pure.	15. Love is eternal.
7. Cold winds.	16. Happy birds.
8. Winter is cold.	17. Heaven is glorious.
9. Scholars are studious.	18. Blue skies.

(*b.*) Assume the same qualities that are predicated in the sentences above.

REMARK.—When we assume a quality of an object, we have to *name that object* just as we do when we wish to predicate something of it; but since in this case nothing *is* predicated, the name is *not called the subject.*

(*c.*) Select the nouns in the examples given above, tell which are common and which are proper, and give the number and gender of each.

3. Seat Work.

Tell, in writing, what you have learned about predicating and assuming quality; what a sentence is, and what the subject and predicate are.

LESSON 25.

Analysis.

1. Exercise.

Analyze according to the models and directions given below.

EXAMPLES.

1. Lions are ferocious.	4. Lilacs are sweet.
2. Clouds are dark.	5. Roses are red.
3. Rivulets are small.	6. Pebbles are smooth.

7. Buttercups are yellow.	11. Indians are treacherous.
8. Saul was tall.	12. Cataracts are grand.
9. Meadows are brown.	13. Boys are noisy.
10. Summer is warm.	14. Ethan Allen was bold.

To the Teacher.—Ask the same questions as in Lesson 24. After the pupil has answered the questions on every sentence of the lesson, encourage him to make an effort to state the *same facts* in a connected manner *without questions*, first setting him an example.

MODEL FOR PARTIAL ANALYSIS.

Ex.—Rocks are grand.

1. This is a sentence.

2. **Rocks** is the subject.

3. **Are grand** is the predicate; it predicates a quality of the subject.

Suggestions.—Perhaps it will be best not to attempt any formal analysis further than to tell the subject and predicate, until the class is a little farther advanced, especially if its members are young.

This partial analysis should be followed by questions that will bring out the remaining points.

Continue to do in this way until the pupil can analyze readily without your aid. The questions may then be omitted, except in occasional instances, as the pupil will be able to give the complete analysis without them.

MODEL FOR COMPLETE ANALYSIS.

Ex.—Rocks are grand.

1. This group of words is a sentence, because it names objects, and predicates something of them.

2. **Rocks** is the subject; it names objects that have something predicated of them.

3. **Are grand** is the predicate; it predicates a quality of the rocks.

4. **Grand** denotes the quality.

5. **Are** is the copula, and shows that the quality is predicated.

2. Seat Work.

Study the next lesson; copy the examples; draw one line under the subject of each sentence, and two lines under the predicate. Then write the parsing of each noun.

LESSON 26.

Analysis of Sentences in which One Quality is Assumed and Another Predicated.

1. Exercises.

(*a.*) Predicate quality of the following objects :—

Fields, gardens, valleys, forests, hills, horses, lessons, men, children.

(*b.*) Assume some other quality of each of the objects named above.

(*c.*) Predicate one quality and assume another.

ILLUSTRATION.—*Fertile fields are pleasant. Large forests are gloomy.*

(*d.*) So change each of these sentences that the quality which is now predicated will be assumed, and the one which is now assumed will be predicated. Thus :—

> Noble men are kind.
> Kind men are noble.

(*e.*) Analyze the following sentences:—

1. Ripe peaches are delicious.
2. Good people are happy.
3. Weary children are fretful.
4. Young people are giddy.
5. Wild flowers are pretty.
6. Brown meadows were bare.
7. White lilies are beautiful.
8. Quiet waters are deep.
9. Ripe fruit is nutritious.

MODEL.

Ex.—Ripe peaches are delicious.

1. This is a sentence, because it names objects and predicates something of them.

2. *Peaches* is the subject.

3. *Are delicious* is the predicate ; it predicates a quality of the peaches.

4. *Delicious* denotes the quality.

5. *Are* shows that the quality is predicated.

6. **Ripe** describes the *peaches* by *assuming* a quality of them.

2. Seat Work.

Make two sentences like those in this lesson, and write the analysis of them.

LESSON 27.

Abstract Nouns.

1. Exercises.

(*a.*) Analyze,—

1. Harsh words are cruel.
2. Wild grapes are sour.
3. Young plants are tender.
4. Soft voices are pleasant.
5. Wild beasts are fierce.
6. Sultry days are oppressive.
7. Rainy days are dreary.
8. Wicked men are deceitful.
9. Green timber is heavy.
10. Large animals are clumsy.

(*b.*) What quality is predicated in the first sentence ? — *Cruelty.* What is assumed ?—*Harshness.*

Name all the qualities mentioned in the sentences above.

2. Instruction.

Names of qualities are called **abstract nouns.** Words that simply denote qualities are called **adjectives.**

3. Written Exercise; for Seat Work.

Change the following adjectives to abstract nouns:—

Examples.—Mild, faithful, cruel, good, powerful, mighty, pure, valuable, gaudy, tenacious, glorious, strong, sprightly, eternal, ferocious, happy, dark, warm, grand, nutritious, beautiful.

LESSON 28.

Parsing Nouns and Adjectives.

1. Exercises.

(*a.*) Parse all the *nouns* in Lessons 25 and 26.

MODEL.

Ex.—Young men are strong.

Men is a noun, common, plural number, masculine gender, and subject of the sentence.

(*b.*) Parse all the *adjectives*, noticing whether they denote a quality that is predicated, or one that is only assumed.

MODELS.

Young is an *adjective*, added to the noun *men* to assume a quality of the men.

Strong is an adjective, and denotes a quality that is *predicated* of the men.

2. Seat Work.

Write the analysis of the following sentences :—

1. Long stories are tedious.
2. Red cherries are ripe.
3. Mossy stones are beautiful.
4. Young birds are helpless.

LESSON 29.

Parsing.—Continued.

1. Exercises.

(*a.*) Parse all the *nouns*, *adjectives*, and *copulas* in Lesson 27.

MODEL FOR THE COPULA.

Ex.—Wild grapes are sour.

Are is a *copula;* it is used with *sour* to show that the thought is predicated.

(*b.*) Parse the words in sentences composed extemporaneously by pupils and teacher.

2. Seat Work.

Write out the parsing of the words in the following sentences :—

1. Green meadows are beautiful.
2. Young leaves are fresh.
3. Red clover is fragrant.
4. Little ants are industrious.

MODEL FOR WRITTEN PARSING.

Ex.— Green meadows are beautiful.

Green.—Adj., added to the noun *meadows* to assume a quality of the meadows.

Meadows.—Noun, com., pl., neu. g., and subject.

Beautiful.—Adj., and denotes a quality that is predicated of the meadows.

LESSON 30.

Actions Performed and Received.

1. Instruction.

1. *New ropes are strong.*   3. *Ropes were broken.*
2. *Horses are prancing.*   4. *Children are playing.*
5. *Fruit is gathered.*

1. What is predicated in the first sentence ?
2. What is predicated in the second ?
3. What word denotes the action ?
4. What word shows that the action is predicated ?
5. By what is the action preformed ?
6. What is predicated in the third sentence ?
7. Do the ropes perform the action, or receive it ?
8. What is predicated in the fourth sentence ?
9. Do the children perform the action, or receive it ?
10. What is predicated in the fifth sentence ?
11. Is the action performed by the subject, or received by it ?

2. Exercises.

(*a.*) Predicate other actions of —

Children, horses, fruit, ropes.

Which of these actions are performed by the subject? Which received by it?

(*b.*) Predicate actions of —

Men, boys, trees, birds, rain, clouds, grass, rivers, ships, lions, fire, water.

(*c.*) Predicate action performed by —

Dew, soldiers, stars, fountains, leaves, James, seeds, torrents, Indians, flocks, bells.

(*d.*) Predicate actions received by —

Gold, cities, food, ships, seeds, soldiers, friends, ice, lemons, houses.

3. Written Exercises; for Seat Work.

(*a.*) Use the following predicates in sentences of your own :—

EXAMPLES.—Is falling, were burned, were sold, was left, is eating, are writing, are playing, was caught, were punished, was elected, is traveling, are roaring.

(*b.*) Make five sentences predicating quality.

(*c.*) Make ten sentences predicating action.

LESSON 31.

Action Predicated.

1. Exercises.

(*a.*) Analyze the following—

EXAMPLES.

1. Ships were destroyed.
2. Bells were tolling.
3. Fish are caught.
4. Food was eaten.
5. Time is passing.
6. Diamonds are brilliant.

7. Grass was mowed.
8. Winds are blowing.
9. Dews are falling.
10. Boys were punished.
11. Rocks were rent.
12. Stars are shining.
13. Soldiers were killed.

MODEL.

Ex.—Better days are coming.

1. This is a sentence, because it names objects and predicates something of them.

2. *Days* is the subject.

3. **Are coming** is the predicate; it predicates an action performed by the subject.

4. **Coming** denotes the action, and

5. **Are** shows that the action is predicated.

6. *Better* describes the days by assuming a quality of them.

(*b.*) Parse the nouns as in Lesson 28.

2. Seat Work.

(*a.*) Write the analysis of,—

1. Beautiful fountains are playing.
2. Tiny fishes are swimming.
3. Fleecy clouds were floating.

(*b.*) Write the parsing of the nouns and adjectives.

LESSON 32.

Subject of Last Lesson Continued.

1. Exercises.

(*a.*) Analyze the following—

EXAMPLES.

1. Clouds are changing.
2. Fruit was stolen.
3. Birds are singing.
4. Fountains were opened.
5. Thrifty evergreens are ornamental.
6. Sick men were healed.
7. Cities were burned.

8. Fresh snow is light.
9. Leaves are unfolding.
10. Summer is coming.
11. Vows were broken.

12. Iron is melted.
13. Meteors are bright.
14. Nuts were gathered.
15. Gold was discovered.

(*b.*) Parse the nouns.

(*c.*) Distinguish the copula and the action-word.

MODEL.

Ex.— Cities were burned.

Cities is a noun, common, plural number, neuter gender, and subject of the sentence.

Were is the copula; used with *burned* to show that the action is predicated.

Burned is an action-word; it denotes an action that is *predicated* of the cities.

2. Seat Work.

Study the next lesson; write the analysis of sentences 1 and 2, and the parsing of the words in sentences 12 and 13.

LESSON 33.

Quality and Action.

To the Teacher.—Whenever the exercise becomes monotonous, vary it in some way. For example, question the whole class on a sentence or two, allowing them to answer in concert. The exercise should be cheerful, animated, and at the same time thoughtful. It is one of the highest accomplishments of the teacher to understand the thoughts and feelings of his class, and to control and guide them properly.

Let there be no listless, drawling reciting. Throw life and strength into it; and while you attempt to do this, let no tone or look of sarcasm, contempt, or despair, strike terror through your class. *Let in the sunshine!* Be *earnest, hopeful, happy*, and your class will catch your spirit.

1. Exercises.

(*a.*) Analyze the following—

EXAMPLES.

1. Dark clouds are gathering.
2. James was whipped.
3. Seeds were sown.

4. Cold winds are blowing.
5. Happy children were singing.
6. Heavy seas are dangerous.

7. White roses are beautiful. 11. Brave soldiers were slain.
8. Warm weather is coming. 12. Green wood was burned.
9. Children are quarreling. 13. Wild torrents are roaring.
10. Indians are treacherous. 14. Deep caverns are damp.

(*b.*) Parse all the words as shown in former lessons.

2. Seat Work.

(*a.*) Analyze and parse the examples given in the next lesson.

(*b.*) Write the analysis of sentence 3, and the parsing of all the words in sentences 9 and 12.

LESSON 34.

Quality and Action.—Continued.

1. Exercise.

Analyze and parse as in the preceding lesson.

EXAMPLES.

1. Gentle dews are falling.
2. Old men were weeping.
3. Attentive congregations are listening.
4. Noble Milton was blind.
5. Drums were beating.
6. Grandfather is old.
7. Haughty queens are cruel.
8. Strong ships were sunk.
9. Valuable buildings were destroyed.
10. Hard lessons were learned.
11. Large, red apples were gathered.
12. Cold winter is coming.

2. Seat Work.

Write a composition on *Birds*, and in writing it, answer the following questions :—

1. What qualities have birds ?
2. What can birds do ?
3. What can be done to them ?

4. What birds are useful ?

5. In what ways are they useful?

6. What other name is often given to some kinds of birds ?

7. What birds are called domestic fowls ?

8. What water-fowls can you name ?

To the Teacher.—This composition should be short and simple. It will be best to insist on the answering of the above questions in every composition.

LESSON 35.

Review.

Questions and Requirements.

1. What class of words do we use for naming objects ?

2. What class of words do we use to show the qualities of things ?

3. What do we use when we wish to show that a quality is predicated ?

4. Name things and predicate qualities of them.

5. Name things and assume qualities of them.

6. What do you call a group of words that names a thing and predicates something of it ?

7. In such a group, which word is called the *subject?*

8. Why is such a noun called the subject ?—*Because something is predicated of the thing named by that noun.*

9. In the group, *Dark clouds,* what office does each word perform ?

10. Is the name-word called the subject ?

11. Why not ?—*Because nothing is predicated of the thing named by that noun.*

12. Give sentences in which one quality is predicated and another assumed.

13. In talking of things do we always wish to speak of their qualities ? .

4

14. Of what else do we often speak ?

15. Give sentences that predicate action.

16. Give sentences that assume a quality and predicate an action.

17. Give examples of common nouns.

18. Why is such a noun called common ?—*It belongs to all the members of the class in common; for it can be applied to any one of them as well as to another.*

19. Give examples of proper nouns.

20. Why is such a noun called proper ?—*Because it names a particular individual, while a common noun can name only a class, or one of a class.*

21. Give examples of proper names consisting of two or more words, and tell which of the words should have the capital initial.

22. Give examples of common nouns that take the capital initial.

23. Why should *Democrat* begin with a capital ? *Methodist? Choctaw ?*

24. Write a sentence containing the name of a day of the week, of a month, and of a season of the year.

25. Why should the word *Englishman* begin with a capital letter ?—*Because it is derived from the proper noun "England."*

LESSON 36.

Objects Alluded To.

1. Instruction.

1. *Ellen is singing.*
2. *She is happy.*

In the first sentence, *Ellen* names a person, and *is singing* predicates something of her.

In the second sentence, we are talking of the same person as in the first, but we do not use her name. Since she has just been mentioned (*named*) we allude to her by using the word *she*. Every one knows who is meant as well as he would if I should say, "Ellen is happy."

2. Exercises.

1. *Andrew is studying.*
2. *Andrew is industrious.*

(*a.*) How may we speak of Andrew in the second sentence without using his name?

Answer similar questions in regard to the following sentences :—

1. Young trees are flourishing.
2. Young trees are fruitful.

1. Chalk is white.
2. Chalk is useful.

(*b.*) Analyze the following—

EXAMPLES.

1. He is writing.
2. They were discharged.
3. She is forgetful.
4. It is good.
5. He is haughty.
6. They were kind.
7. He was arrested.
8. She was deserted.
9. They were accused.
10. It is falling.

MODEL.

Ex.—She was glad.

1. This group of words is a sentence; it *alludes* to a person, and predicates something of her.

2. **She** is the subject; it alludes to some one previously named.

3. *Was glad* is the predicate.

3. Seat Work.

(*a.*) Study examples given for next recitation.

(*b.*) Write the following sentences correctly :—

EXAMPLES.

1. Buffalos live on the Prairies in the western part of the mississippi valley.

2. The boxs contained candys, buns, ruskes, cookys, and oranges *l*

3. The mosque of omar is built on mount moriah, where solomon's temple once stood.

4. The republicans were victorious last Autumn.

5. Oasises cheer the weary Traveler in the Desert.

6. The college term began on tuesday, Dec. 23.

7. How soon will peachs ripen.

----- • -----

LESSON 37.

Subject of the Last Lesson Continued.

1. Exercise.

Analyze,—

1. She is calling
2. It is strange.
3. They are waiting.
4. He was punished.
5. She is industrious.

6. They were angry.
7. It is treacherous.
8. They are singing.
9. He is sad.
10. It is grand.

2. Instruction.

(*a.*) 1. If my name were Clara, and I should say, "*Clara is happy*," would you think I spoke of *myself*, or of some other Clara ?

2. How would I have to speak in order that you might know that I was speaking of myself?

3. What word must I use, then, when I wish to predicate something of myself ?

(*b.*) 1. If your name were James, and I should say, "*James is welcome*," would you think I meant *you*, or some other James ?

2. What would I say if I meant you to understand that I was speaking to you of yourself ?

3. Then what word must I use when I wish to predicate something of the person I am speaking to ?

3. Exercise.

Analyze,—

1. I was entertained.
2. You are impatient.
3. We are waiting.

4. We are delayed.
5. You are kind.
6. I am coming.

MODEL.

Analyze as before, but say,—

I alludes to the speaker;

We, to the speaker and those associated with him;

You, to the person or persons spoken to;

He, she, it, to a person or thing previously mentioned;

They, to persons or things previously mentioned.

4. Instruction Resumed.

Words that represent objects by *alluding* to them instead of *naming* them, are called **pronouns.**

A pronoun that alludes to the speaker is said to be in the **first person;** one that alludes to the person spoken to, in the **second person;** and one that alludes to a person or thing spoken of, in the **third person.**

5. Seat Work.

Study the next lesson; write the analysis of the first three sentences, and the parsing of the pronouns in all.

LESSON 38.

Parsing Pronouns.

1. Exercises.

(*a.*) Analyze,—

1. He is coming.
2. You are kind.
3. I am grieved.
4. She is displeased.
5. It was beautiful.
6. They are invited.

7. It is admired.
8. They are abundant.
9. You were reciting.
10. I am busy.
11. He is generous.
12. She is conceited.

(*b.*) Parse the pronouns in the above examples, and also in Lessons 36 and 37.

MODELS.

Ex.— We are waiting.

We is a pronoun, first person, plural number, and subject of the sentence. (This word does not distinguish sex, but may allude to persons of either sex, or of both sexes.)

Ex.—He is forgetful.

He is a pronoun, third person, singular number, masculine gender, and subject of the sentence.

2. Seat Work.

Write a short composition on *Dogs.*

————•———

LESSON 39.
Mere Limitations.

1. Instruction.

1. *Men are strong.*	4. *Those men are happy.*
2. *Good men are happy.*	5. *This book is new.*
3. *These men are kind.*	6. *That land is fruitful.*

In the first sentence, *men* may mean *any* men or *all* men.

In the second sentence, *men*, with the word *good* before it, can mean only such men as are good. The word *good* shows what men are meant, by telling a quality of them.

In the third sentence, *men*, with the word *these* before it, must mean some men that are near by, or that have just been mentioned. The word *these* shows what men are meant, without telling any of their qualities.

In the fourth sentence, the word *those* tells what men are meant, without showing any quality of them. It denotes men farther away, or that were mentioned some time in the past.

In the fifth sentence, *this* shows that I mean a book that is in hand, near by, or just mentioned.

This means the same as *these;* and *that* the same as *those:* only *this* and *that* are used when but one thing is meant; and *these* and *those,* when more than one is meant.

2. Exercise.

Analyze,—

    1. Those lofty walls are crumbling.
    2. That forest is beautiful.
    3. This book is interesting.
    4. These long days are tiresome.
    5. Those great trees are majestic.
    6. This poor man is generous.

MODEL.

Ex.—That tree is fruitful.

1. *Tree* is the subject of the sentence.

2. *Is fruitful* is the predicate; it predicates a quality of the subject.

3. *Fruitful* denotes the quality.

4. *Is* shows that the quality is predicated.

5. **That** tells what tree is meant. It shows that we mean a tree that is somewhat distant, or that was mentioned in the past.

3. Instruction Resumed.

(*a.*) Words added to nouns to show quality are called **qualifying adjectives.**

(*b.*) Words like *this* and *that,* added to nouns to tell what one or which one is meant, without showing any quality of the thing, are called **limiting adjectives.**

4. Exercises.

(*a.*) Point out all the adjectives in the sentences above, and tell which are qualifying, and which limiting.

(*b.*) Parse the adjectives according to the following—

MODEL.

Ex.—Those lofty walls are crumbling.

(*a.*) **Those** is an adjective, limiting; it is added to the noun *walls* to tell what walls are meant.

(*b.*) **Lofty** is an adjective, qualifying; it is added to the noun *walls* to denote an assumed quality. (To show how high they are.)

5. Seat Work.

(*a.*) Study examples given for the next recitation.

(*b.*) Write ten sentences, each containing one of the words, *this, that, these,* or *those.*

LESSON 40.

Limiting Adjectives.

1. Exercise.

After analyzing each sentence, parse the words in it.

EXAMPLES.

1. That gloomy cave was explored.
2. Those broad valleys are productive.
3. These men are needy.
4. That house is large.
5. Those things were forgotten.
6. This water is clear.
7. That man was arrested.
8. Those lions are ferocious.
9. This lesson is short.
10. Virtuous rulers are honored.
11. Beautiful icebergs were passing.
12. Those faithful men were rewarded.

2. Seat Work.

(*a.*) Analyze and parse the sentences given for the next recitation.

(*b.*) Make sentences that will bring into use all the limiting adjectives found in the preceding lessons.

LESSON 41.

Limiting Adjectives Used to Tell How Many.

1. Instruction.

1. *Two men were drowned.*
2. *Few passengers were saved.*
3. *Several letters were received.*
4. *Many people are unhappy.*

In the first sentence, *two* tells *how many* men were drowned, so that *men*, as here used, applies to *just two* men, and cannot mean fewer or more than that number.

In the second sentence, *few* shows that a very *small* number of passengers is meant, but does not denote any *definite* number.

In the third sentence, *several* denotes an indefinite number of letters, more than a few, yet not many.

In the fourth sentence, *many* shows that a great number of people is meant, but does not make the number definite; we cannot tell just how many.

2. Exercise.

Analyze and parse,—

1. Many good men are poor.
2. That choice was bad.
3. These precious days are passing.
4. Many bright lights are burning.
5. Few buildings were occupied.
6. Several valuable ships were lost.
7. Four costly watches were stolen.
8. This book is useful.
9. One day is lost.
10. They were forgotten.
11. We are traveling.
12. You were expected.

REMARK.—In parsing *four*, say that it is added to the noun *watches* to tell how many. In parsing such an adjective as *few* or *many*, say it is added to the noun to tell indefinitely how many.

3. Seat Work.

Write a composition on what you have learned about adjectives.

LESSON 42.

Articles.

1. Instruction.

1. *The young lion was playful.*
2. *A good man is honored.*
3. *No harsh words were spoken.*
4. *An eagle is strong.*
5. *Some children are disobedient.*

In the first sentence, *the* shows that some particular lion is meant.

In the second sentence, *a* denotes *one*, but no particular one.

In the third sentence, *no* is used to give a negative meaning to the sentence. It makes it mean just the opposite of what it would without this word.

An means the same as *a;* but is used before a word that begins with a vowel sound, while *a* is used before a word that begins with a consonant sound, as may be seen in the following examples :—

A lady.	An oak.
A mountain.	An ornament.
A house.	An heir.
A eunuch.	An enemy.
A useful article.	An undertone.

In the fifth sentence, *some* shows that *children*, as here used, does not mean *all* children, but only a part of them, probably not a great many.

2. Exercise.

Analyze and parse,—

1. The leaves are fading.
2. An interesting story was read.
3. Some dread object is passing.
4. A rusty tomahawk was found.
5. No worthy effort is lost.
6. The distant sea is murmuring.
7. Few rich men are generous.
8. Many stars are shining.
9. The gentle dews are falling.
10. Three large ships were sunk.

MODELS FOR PARSING.

Sentence 1.

The is that kind of limiting adjective called a *definite article;* it is added to the noun *leaves* to show that some definite leaves are meant.

Sentence 2.

An is that kind of limiting adjective called an *indefinite article;* it is added to the noun *story,* and denotes *one* but no *definite* one.

REMARK.—In sentence 3, *some* seems to be added to the noun *object* to show that *no definite* object is meant. The speaker cannot distinguish the object.

3. Seat Work.

(*a.*) Study the sentences given for the next recitation.

(*b.*) Write the analysis of the 6th sentence, and the parsing of the adjectives in all the sentences.

LESSON 43.

Subject of the Last Lesson Continued.

1. Exercise.

Analyze and parse,—

1. Many excellent opportunities were lost.
2. Several rich mines were discovered.

3. Few people are happy.
4. Six veteran soldiers were sent.
5. No sound was heard.
6. The great change is approaching.
7. The pale moon is shining.
8. All scripture is profitable.
9. An important question was settled.
10. A hot climate is unhealthful.
11. Some strange implements were found.
12. Many delightful rambles were taken.

2. Seat Work.

(*a.*) Study the next lesson.

(*b.*) Correct the following words and sentences:—

EXAMPLES.

Follys, vollies, potatos, folioes, lifes.

1. The shipes brought Oranges from new mexico, negros from africa, and monkies from brazil !
2. I saw six deers, and three Ostrich, in my uncle's Park
3. learn the 10es and 12es for your next lesson.
4. The thiefs lay down on the leafs under the trees.

LESSON 44.

State, or Condition.

1. Instruction.

1. *Mother is weary.*
2. *The sick child is worse.*

In the first sentence, we predicate a state of mother. She is not *always* weary, but is in that state now. *Weary* denotes the condition, and *is* shows that it is predicated.

In the second sentence, we assume one condition, and predicate another. *Sick* denotes the assumed condition, and *worse*, the predicated condition.

2. Exercise.

Analyze and parse,—

1. I am sad.
2. The lonely pilgrim is worn.
3. The sick soldiers were removed.
4. The weary child is sleeping.
5. Many sad hearts were cheered.
6. Those withered leaves are dead.
7. A dreadful hurricane was described.
8. The cloudless sky is beautiful.

3. Written Exercise; for Seat Work.

1. Give a sentence that predicates quality.

2. Give a sentence that assumes one quality and predicates another.

3. Give a sentence that predicates action.

4. One that assumes quality and predicates action.

5. One that predicates state.

6. One that assumes one state and predicates another.

7. One that assumes state, and predicates action.

LESSON 45.

Review.

1. Questions and Requirements.

1. What class of words do we use when we wish to allude to things that have just been mentioned ?

2. Give several examples.

3. What word must the speaker use when he wishes to predicate something of himself ?

4. What word must he use when he wishes to predicate something of himself and those associated with him ?

5. What word do we use when we wish to speak to some one in regard to himself ?

6. Give examples of the proper use of all these pronouns.

7. What kind of adjectives are used to describe objects by telling their qualities, their condition, or their kind ? Give examples.

8. What kind of adjectives point out things, without showing their qualities, condition, or kind ?

9. What adjective is used to show that the thing we are talking about is one that is near by, or lately mentioned ?

10. What do we use when the thing is farther off in time or place ?

11. When should *these* and *those* be used in preference to *this* and *that ?*

12. Give examples of words used to tell just how many things are meant.

13. Give examples in which words are used to tell indefinitely how many.

14. What word is used to show that a very small number is meant ?

15. What word is used to denote a very large number?

16. What word denotes a number greater than a few, and not so great as is denoted by the word *many ?*

17. What adjective is sometimes used to give a sentence just the opposite meaning from what it would have without that word ?

18. Give examples of this use of the word.

19. For what purpose is *the* generally used ?

20. What does *a* denote ?

21. What do we call a noun used to name a quality ?

22. What do we call a noun that is used to name a collection of objects ?

23. When do nouns ending in *o* form their plural regularly ; that is, by adding *s ?*

24. In what other way do they form their plural ?

25. When do nouns ending in *y* form their plural regularly ?

26. How do they form the plural when the next letter before the *y* is not a vowel ?

27. Give examples of nouns that change final *f* to *ve* before adding *s*.

28. Give examples of nouns that do not change final *f* in this way.

29. Give examples of nouns that end in *fe*, and in forming the plural, change the *f* to *v* before adding *s*.

30. Give examples of nouns that, although they end in *fe*, do not change the *f* to *v* in forming the plural.

LESSON 46.

Action Denoted and Predicated in One Word.

1. Instruction.

1. *The wind is blowing.*
2. *The wind blows.*

These two sentences are alike in meaning; they both predicate the same action of the wind.

In the first sentence, *blowing* denotes the action, and *is* shows that the action is predicated; but in the second sentence, the word *blows* denotes the action and predicates it. It does the work of both the action-word and the copula.

Compare the following sentences in the same way:—

1. The rain is falling.   1. The sun is shining.
2. The rain falls.   2. The sun shines.

1. The ocean is roaring.
2. The ocean roars.

2. Exercise.

Analyze and parse,—

1. The heavy thunders roll.
2. The vivid lightnings flash.
3. The sea is rough.
4. Gay young soldiers march.
5. The hoarse torrents roar.
6. The nights were dark.
7. The precious moments fly.
8. Those wicked men are angry.
9. The light snow falls.
10. Many anxious friends wept.
11. The cold winds blew.
12. The sad rain is dripping.
13. Bright waves dance.

MODEL FOR ANALYSIS.

Ex.—The unwelcome guest departed.

1. This group of words is a sentence.
2. *Guest* is the subject.
3. **Departed** is the predicate; it predicates action.
4. *The* shows that some definite guest is meant.
5. *Unwelcome* describes the guest by assuming a quality of him.

MODELS FOR PARSING.

Ex.—The dead leaves rustle.

1. *The* is that kind of limiting adjective called a definite article. It is added to the noun *leaves* to show that some definite leaves are meant.

2. *Dead* is an adjective, qualifying, added to the noun *leaves* to show their condition.

3. **Rustle** is a verb; it denotes an action, and predicates it.

3. Seat Work.

(*a.*) Study the next lesson.

(*b.*) Write the following sentences correctly :—

1. Certain marks, such as *s, †s, etc., are used to refer to notes in the margin.
2. His slate was covered with +es, —es, ahes, nos, and mys.
3. Village creek, washington prairie, new Lisbon, and oak center, are names of places.

LESSON 47.
Parsing the Verb.

1. Exercise.

Analyze and parse,—

1. Dark clouds gather.	5. The ground is cold.
2. The weather is stormy.	6. Flowers fade.
3. The sad winds moan.	7. The old man listened.
4. The gloomy days are coming.	8. They were speechless.

9. The silent stranger retired.   12. Merry squirrels frisk.
10. The moist earth is soft.   13. We are glad.
11. The fresh young leaves unfold. 14. You are delighted.
15. I am waiting.

REMARK.—*I am waiting* means the same as *I wait;* and *am waiting*, since it means the same as *wait*, is called a verb and parsed like the others.

2. Seat Work.

(*a.*) Study the examples given for the next recitation.

(*b.*) Write the following sentences correctly :—

1. It is said that Colonel clark, who visited the Holy Land last Summer, will be in cedar springs on monday the 17th of february, and in grand rapids on tuesday.

2. Knifes, loafs, laces, brushes, cameoes, spools, and pulleies lay upon the table in endless confusion.

LESSON 48.

Action Modified by a Single Word.

1. Instruction.

1. *Winter is coming soon.*
2. *God rules above.*
3. *Gently falls the dew.*

In the first sentence, *soon* tells *when* winter is coming.
In the second sentence, *above* tells *where* God rules.
In the third sentence, *gently* tells *how* the dew falls.

2. Exercise.

Analyze and parse,—

1. Those slender branches wave gracefully.
2. The hunter rose early.
3. The bees fled precipitately.
4. The happy birds sing sweetly.
5. That voice is silent now.
6. The huge iceberg steadily approached.

5

7. The angry tempest loudly roars.
8. The eve is drawing on.
9. Slowly droops the gentle twilight.
10. The call was frequently repeated.

MODELS FOR PARSING THE ADVERB.

Ex.— Winter is coming soon.

Soon is an adverb; added to the verb *is coming* to tell *when.*

Ex.— God rules above.

Above is an adverb; added to the verb *rules* to tell *where* God rules.

Ex.—Branches wave gracefully.

Gracefully is an adverb; added to the verb *wave* to tell *how* the branches wave.

3. Seat Work.

(*a.*) Write what you know about *adverbs.*

(*b.*) Study the examples of the next lesson.

LESSON 49.
Parsing Adverbs.

1. Exercise.

Analyze and parse,—

1. The night is softly dying.
2. The beautiful stranger never returned.
3. No sad faces were seen there.
4. That foolish promise was rashly made.
5. Old friends are always kindly remembered.
6. Good men sometimes err.
7. The two friends walked on silently.
8. He pressed eagerly forward.
9. His books were carefully selected.
10. We firmly resisted.
11. Our pursuers came furiously on.

2. Seat Work.

Write a composition on *Berry-picking.*

LESSON 50.

Action Modified by Groups of Words.

1. Instruction.

1. *Peace ever reigns **there**.*
2. *Peace ever reigns **in heaven**.*
3. *Flowers bloom **in summer**.*

In the first sentence, *there* tells *where* peace reigns.

In the second sentence, *in heaven* tells where peace reigns. *Heaven* names the place, and *in* shows the relation of the place to the act of reigning.

In the third sentence, *in summer* tells *when* the flowers bloom. *Summer* names the season of the year, and *in* shows the relation of the season to the blooming of the flowers.

2. Exercises.

(*a.*) Fill the blanks in the following sentences with a group of words that will tell *where* the action is done :—

1. The sun shines——.
2. My uncle resides——.
3. Fishes live——.
4. Birds fly——.
5. Clouds float——.
6. Rabbits burrow——.
7. Wild beasts roam——.
8. Ships sail——.
9. Boys skate——.
10. Grass grows——.
11. Rain beats——.
12. Fire burns——.
13. The clock ticks——.
14. The book lies——.
15. The chair stands——.
16. Jane sits——.
17. The children play——.
18. The kitten sleeps——.
19. The cattle feed——.
20. Moses stood——.

(*b.*) Use each of the following groups in a sentence :—

1. In the house.
2. In the trees.
3. On the roof.
4. In the sky.
5. On the ground.
6. On paper.
7. By the window.
8. In the meadow.
9. Through the forest.
10. In the corner.
11. On the piano.
12. In Boston.

13. On the blackboard.	17. At the falls.
14. In the kitchen.	18. On the cars.
15. In the sea.	19. In a boat.
16. On the ocean.	20. By the fire.

21. In a chair.

(*c.*) Analyze according to the model below, and answer questions similar to those that follow it.

1. The ship sunk in the harbor.
2. The clear water trickled down the rock.
3 The horses ran furiously across the bridge.
4. Happy birds are singing in the forest.
5. The sun is peeping over the hills.

MODEL.

Sentence 1.

1. *Ship* is the subject.
2. *Sunk* is the predicate.
3. *The* shows that a particular ship is meant.
4. **In the harbor** tells *where* the ship sunk.

1. Which word of the group names the place where the ship sunk ?
2. Which word shows the relation between the place and the sinking of the ship ?

3. Seat Work.

(*a.*) Study the next lesson.

(*b.*) Write the analysis of the first three sentences.

LESSON 51.

Phrases Denoting Place and Time.

1. Exercises.

(*a.*) Analyze the following sentences, and parse such words as you have been taught to parse :—

1. Silently the twilight creeps over the valleys.
2. Pegasus strayed into a quiet village.

3. Loud the clamorous bell was ringing from its belfry grim.
4. Noisily the cocks crowed from a neighboring farm-yard.
5. A pure fountain flowed from the greensward.
6. The wigwam stood by the shining Big-Sea-Water.

(*b.*) Fill the blanks in each of the following sentences by a group of words that will tell *when*:—

1. The sun shines——.
2. My friend came——.
3. The sun is hot——.
4. The air is cool——.
5. Roses bloom——.
6. Shadows lengthen——.
7. Fruit is abundant——.
8. The birds return——.
9. Wild beasts prowl——.
10. Men sleep——.
11. They work——.
12. Cocks crow——.
13. He was rational——.
14. They came——.
15. It was completed——.
16. Snow falls——.
17. We retire——.
18. Men plow——.

(*c.*) Use each of the following phrases in a sentence of your own. Thus :—

Laborers return in the evening.

1. In the evening.
2. At noon.
3. In the morning.
4. In the winter.
5. In the spring.
6. In the twilight.
7. In autumn.
8. In the daytime.
9. In summer.
10. In the night.
11. Before breakfast.
12. Before daybreak.
13. Through the day.
14. At night.
15. At daybreak.
16. At evening.
17. After dark.
18. After dinner.
19. After sunset.
20. Before night.
21. Before noon.
22. Before morning.
23. Before midnight.
24. During the night.
25. By noon.
26. At times.

27. At last.

2. Seat Work.

(*a.*) Study the next lesson.

(*b.*) Write the parsing of all the words in sentences 1 and 2, and the analysis of sentences 4 and 5.

LESSON 52.

Subject of the Last Lesson Continued.

1. Instruction.

We have seen that a *word* added to a verb to tell *how, when,* or *where,* is called an adverb; and so a **group** of words added to a verb to tell how, when, or where, must also be an adverb. But in order to distinguish between a *single word* and a *group,* we call the single word an *adverb,* and the group an **adverbial phrase.**

REQUIREMENT.—Point out the adverbial phrases in the last two lessons, and tell why each is used.

ILLUSTRATION.—*Flowers bloom in summer.*

In summer is an adverbial phrase; it is added to the verb *bloom* to tell **when** the flowers bloom.

Notice that each of these phrases has a noun in it; and that *before* the noun there is a little word that shows relation. Now since this relation-word goes before the noun, we call it a **preposition;** for the word *preposition* [pre-position] means going before in position.

The preposition always shows the relation between the object named by the noun that follows it, and something else; so the noun is said to be the object of the relation shown by the preposition, or, for the sake of brevity, the *object of the preposition.*

2. Exercises.

(*a.*) Analyze and parse,—

1. He returned in the evening.
2. Flowers bloom in summer.
3. The leaves fall in autumn.
4. Before midnight the heavy clouds cleared away.
5. Few words were spoken during the exercises.

MODEL FOR ANALYSIS.
Sentence 1.

He is the subject, and *returned* is the predicate.

In the evening tells when he returned; *evening* names a portion of the day, and *in* shows the relation of the evening to the act of returning.

To the Teacher.—The latter portion of this analysis should be omitted after being used a short time.

MODEL FOR PARSING THE PREPOSITION AND ITS OBJECT.

In is a preposition; it shows the relation of the evening to the act of returning.

Evening is a noun, common, third person, singular number, neuter gender, and object of the preposition *in.*

(*b.*) Parse the prepositions and objects in Lesson 50.

3. Seat Work.

Study the examples in the next lesson, and write the parsing of all the prepositions and their objects.

LESSON 53.
Parsing the Preposition and its Object.

1. Exercise.

Analyze and parse the following sentences, and then parse the prepositions and objects in Lesson 51.

EXAMPLES.

1. At day-break we were suddenly awakened.
2. An incessant tumult was heard throughout the night.
3 In the morning a few fleecy clouds floated in the calm, blue sky.
4. He stood by the desk.
5. An old man died in the night.
6. They are abundant in the forest.

2. Seat Work.

Write a composition on *Wild Flowers.*

LESSON 54.

Phrases Denoting Manner.

1. Instruction.

1. *The two friends walked on in silence.*
2. *She arranged everything with care.*
3. *He listened with patience.*

In the first sentence, *in silence* tells *how* the friends walked. *Silence* names the *state* which they maintained while walking, and *in* shows the relation between that state and their walking. *In silence* means the same as *silently.*

In the second sentence, *with care* tells *how* she arranged everything, and means the same as *carefully.* *Care* names the quality which she manifested in the work of *arranging*, and *with* shows the relation of that quality to the action.

In the third sentence, *with patience* means the same as *patiently.* *Patience* names the quality manifested in the act of *listening*, and *with* shows the relation of the quality to the action.

2. Exercises.

(*a.*) In each of the following sentences, fill the blank with a group of words that tells *how* the action was done:—

1. We waited——.
2. He read——.
3. The general proceeded——.
4. The storm raged——.
5. He fought——.
6. He spoke——.
7. They dwelt——.
8. She studied——.
9. The dying man wrote——.
10. He listened——.

(*b.*) Introduce each of the following groups of words into a sentence predicating action:—

1. In patience.
2. In peace.
3. With diligence.
4. In silence.
5. With fury.
6. With deliberation.

(*c.*) Analyze and parse,—

1. He moved with caution.
2. They recited with remarkable promptness.
3. We lived in constant fear.
4. The brave men fought with unfaltering courage.
5. Comets move with great rapidity.
6. The audience listened with attention.

3. Seat Work.

Study the examples in the next lesson, explaining the phrases according to instruction given at the beginning of Lesson 55, and writing out the explanation of those in sentences 1 and 3.

LESSON 55.

Phrases Denoting Cause or Purpose.

1. Instruction.

1. *Soldiers fight for fame.*
2. *The poor man died of hunger.*

In the first sentence, *for fame* tells *why* the soldiers fight.

In the second sentence, *of hunger* tells the *cause* of the man's dying.

2. Exercise.

Analyze and parse,—

1. They studied for examination.
2. They ran for the prize.
3. He blushed for shame.
4. They wept for gladness.
5. They were treated with cruelty.
6. The two young friends talked with great earnestness.
7. The gift was accepted with gratitude.
8. The warm spring days were hailed with pleasure.

3. Seat Work.

Study the next lesson, and select sentences that will show all the uses of the adverbial phrase.

LESSON 56.

Subject of the Last Lesson Continued.

1. Exercise.

Analyze and parse,—

1. The woman fainted from fright.
2. The party were traveling for pleasure.
3. They walked for exercise.
4. He worked for a living.
5. They fought for liberty.
6. The young man came for advice.
7. They sang for joy.
8. They shouted for help.
9. The bell rang for tea.
10. The vegetables were raised for the market.

2. Seat Work.

Study the next lesson, and write the analysis of the first three sentences.

———•——

LESSON 57.

Promiscuous Examples in Adverbial Phrases.

1. Exercise.

Analyze and parse,—

1. The steamer left on Friday.
2. Some birds remain throughout the year.
3. She behaved with propriety on every occasion.
4. Burgoyne surrendered at Saratoga.
5. A strange sound issued from the cave.
6. The anchor clung to the rocks with tenacity.
7. Men endure many hardships for money.
8. She died of sorrow.
9. He sailed toward the sunset.

2. Seat Work.

Write sentences containing adverbial phrases that tell (1) when, (2) how long, (3) how often, (4) where, (5) whither, (6) whence, (7) how, (8) why, or for what purpose, (9) from what cause.

LESSON 58.

Promiscuous Examples.—Continued.

1. Exercise.

Analyze and parse,—

1. The president stayed till Monday
2. The church stands by the river.
3. He returned in September.
4. It obeyed with alacrity.
5. We are sailing down the Mississippi River.
6. He speaks of the Lord on all suitable occasions.
7. After tea the captain went on deck.
8. Across the sea the white man came.
9. He plays for amusement.
10. He failed through inattention.

2. Seat Work.

Write sentences bringing into use all the limiting adjectives found in preceding lessons.

LESSON 59.

Promiscuous Examples.—Continued.

1. Exercise.

Analyze and parse,—

1. In a lone valley the chieftain was buried.
2. There I lingered till sunrise.
3. The sound floated over the hills.
4. Soon the drowsy bees were humming among the clover-tops.

5. In the gray old towers the bells were merrily ringing.
6. He is pursuing the work with diligence.
7. Many strange people came in from the country.
8. The dam was swept away during the night.
9. The weary soldier leaned against the wall.
10. The woods are wrapped in deeper brown.
11. The owl awakens from her dell.
12. The fox is heard upon the fell.

2. Seat Work.

Study the next lesson.

LESSON 60.

Qualities and Limitations Shown by Groups of Words.

1. Instruction.

1. *Able* men are needed.
2. *Men of ability* are needed.

In the first sentence, *able* tells what kind of men are needed. It describes the men here meant, by assuming a quality of them.

In the second sentence, *of ability* does the same that is done by *able* in the first sentence. *Ability* names the quality that the men have, and *of* shows the relation of that quality to the men,—*that it exists in them.*

2. Exercises.

(*a.*) Compare the following expressions in the same way :—

1. Sad thoughts.	1. Sorrowful days.
2. Thoughts of sadness.	2. Days of sorrow.
1. Joyful moments.	1. Perilous times.
2. Moments of joy.	2. Times of peril.

The two forms of expression do not always have exactly the same meaning, as will be seen from the following examples :—

1. Troublesome waves.
2. Waves of trouble.

1. Peevish children.
2. Children of peevishness.

1. Free thoughts.
2. Thoughts of freedom.

(*b.*) Analyze, according to the model below, the following—

EXAMPLES.

1. Men of industrious habits are prosperous.
2. A young man of good morals is respected.
3. A timid deer, with white feet, fed by moonlight in the meadow.
4. A cloud of darkness settled over us.
5. Scenes of glory opened before him.

MODEL FOR ANALYSIS.

Ex.—Men of true refinement are always modest.

1. The subject of this sentence is *men.*
2. *Are modest* is the predicate; it predicates quality.
3. **Of true refinement** describes the men by assuming a quality of them.
4. **Refinement** names the quality, and **of** shows the relation of the quality to the men.
5. **True** assumes a quality of the refinement here meant.
6. *Always* tells *when* the men are modest.

3. Instruction Resumed.

The phrase that takes the place of an adjective is called an **adjective phrase ;** and, in general, a group added to a noun to limit it *in any way* is said to be an **adjective element.**

4. Seat Work.

Study the next lesson, and select other sentences containing adjective phrases that can be changed to adjectives.

LESSON 61.
Adjective Phrases.

1. Exercise.

Analyze and parse,—

1. Men of great wisdom seldom err.
2. Habits of industry are important.
3. Such deeds of kindness are appreciated.
4. Words of tenderness are precious.
5. Her tones of sympathy were unheeded.
6. Men of ability are needed in such an enterprise.
7. Songs of devotion were heard in the camp.
8. The surly chief spoke in tones of anger.
9. Thoughts of sadness pressed upon me.

2. Seat Work.

(*a.*) Write sentences that will show by example how nouns ending in *o* form their plural ; nouns ending in *y*.

(*b.*) In like manner show what nouns add the syllable *es* to form the plural.

LESSON 62.
Nouns Denoting Ownership.

1. Exercise.

Make each of the following expressions a part of a sentence :—

1. John's knife.	10. Judge Graves's farm.
2. Philip's kite.	11. General Washington's sword.
3. Julia's glove.	12. Bonaparte's dress.
4. Ellen's new book.	13. The children's toys.
5. Father's cane.	14. The men's overcoats.
6. Mother's spectacles.	15. A nation's wealth.
7. Uncle John's white horses.	16. The Marquis's mantle.
8. Aunt Mary's blue dishes.	17. The ladies' hats.
9. Jacob's cattle.	18. The boy's sled.

19. Laban's images.	24. The boys' hats.
20. Jones's mill.	25. The robbers' pistols.
21. Perkins's store.	26. The hunter's dog.
22. Mr. Knox's shop.	27. The scholar's task.
23. The old man's garden.	28. The poor man's sorrow.

2. Instruction.

In the first example, *John's* tells *whose* knife; in the second, *Philip's* tells *whose* kite; etc.

Each of these words tells who owns, or who possesses, something, and is therefore said to denote possession. You will notice that each of the words used in this way is changed by adding to it the apostrophe and *s* ('s). This addition is called the **possessive sign,** because it is a sign that the word denotes possession.

Notice that in the 17th example, *ladies'* has only an apostrophe added to it. This is all we add to any plural noun ending in *s*, as will be seen in examples 24 and 25.

When the plural noun ends in any other letter than *s*, we add to it both the apostrophe and *s*, as in examples 13 and 14.

3. Exercise.

Analyze the following—

EXAMPLES.

1. The captain's watch was stolen.
2. Charles's ring was found in Mary's box.
3. Ellen's bird escaped from the cage.
4. The flour was bought at Jones's mill.
5. Frank's boat was overturned.
6. Mr. Smith's farm is productive.

MODEL.

Ex.—John's knife is dull.

1. The subject of this sentence is *knife.*

2. *Is dull* is the predicate; it predicates a condition of the knife.

3. **John's** tells *whose* knife is meant. It names the owner.

4. Seat Work.

(*a.*) Study the next lesson.

(*b.*) Add the possessive sign to the following names, and then use them in sentences:—

EXAMPLES.—Joseph, Silas, Cæsar, Mr. Barnes, Gen. Knox, men, women, teachers, farmers, Professor Richards.

LESSON 63.

Case,—Nominative and Possessive.

1. Instruction.

1. *The captain is a brave man.*
2. *The captain's watch was stolen.*

Captain, in the first sentence, is used as subject, and has the ordinary *name form.*

In the second sentence, it is used to tell *whose watch* is meant.

When used to tell *whose,*—to denote possession,—it changes its form as noticed in the last lesson.

The ordinary form, which it has when used as subject, is called the **nominative case.**

The changed form which it has when used to denote possession, is called the **possessive case.**

2. Exercise.

Analyze and parse,—

1. The governor's elegant mansion is much admired.
2. Mr. Bliss's fruit was stolen by some roguish boys.
3. That boy's sled was bought at Wright's store.
4. Cyrus's campaign was successful.
5. Columbus's third voyage was made in 1498.
6. The book was burned in the martyr's hand.
7. The Romans landed on Albion's shore.
8. The young man's attention was fixed on the monster.

MODELS.

Ex.—Ellen's bird escaped.

Ellen's is a noun, proper, third person, singular number, feminine gender; it is used to tell *whose* bird is meant, and is therefore put in the possessive case.

Bird is a noun, com., 3d., sing.; it is used as the subject of the sentence, and is therefore put in the nominative case.

Note.—Those who prefer to do so can put the word *form* in the place of *case* in the models given above. This seems more consistent, for the definition commonly given to case does not agree with the use of the word *case* in the rules. For instance, case is defined as the *relation* of the noun or pronoun to other words in the sentence.

Then we are told by the rule that the subject of a sentence must be in the nominative case; and since case means relation, the rule virtually says that the subject of a sentence must be in the nominative *relation*, or, in other words, the subject of a sentence must be *the subject of a sentence!!*

But if we say that the subject of a sentence must be in the nominative *form*, all is consistent. It is plain that if we use the word *case* in the rule, it must be used in the sense of *form*.

3. Seat Work.

(*a.*) Study the next lesson.

(*b.*) Write the possessive of the following nouns, and then use each in a sentence :—

EXAMPLES.—Larks, Dr. Lucas, sisters, mountain, merchants, curfew, battle, Col. Church, Mr. Fish, J. Marks.

LESSON 64.

Parsing Nouns in the Possessive Case.

1. Exercise.

Analyze and parse,—

1. The children's toys are expensive.
2. The queen's barge was already proceeding up the river.
3. On Esek Harden's oaken floor, lay the ears of unhusked corn.
4. The rook's nest was destroyed.
5. William's farm is small.

6

6. Rufus's garden is well watered.

7. Philip's dwelling fronted on the street.

8. The captives' plaintive cries were heard throughout the night.

2. Seat Work.

Study the next lesson; write the analysis of sentence 12, and the parsing of the possessive nouns in sentences 4 to 11.

--------*--------

LESSON 65.

Possessive Nouns Denoting Kindred or Authorship.

1. Instruction.

1. *Frank's brother is sick.*

2. *Webster's dictionary is much used.*

In the first sentence, the word *Frank's* tells whose brother is meant, but does not show possession; for Frank does not own his brother—his brother is not his property. It is not possession, really, that is here shown, but *kindred*.

In the second sentence, *Webster's* names the *author* of the dictionary, and not the owner, for Webster has long been dead.

These words that denote kindred, authorship, etc., take the possessive sign because they answer the question *whose*, just as words do that denote real possesion.

2. Exercise in Analysis and Parsing.

EXAMPLES.

1. Moody's sermons are much admired.
2. Greene's Grammar is used in this school.
3. George's father resides in Boston.
4. Ellen's uncle went to India.
5. Scott's poems are read with delight.
6. The mat was braided by the chieftain's daughter.
7. James's mother was reading thoughtfully.
8. The young Hebrew rode in Pharaoh's chariot.
9. The article was published in Harper's Magazine.
10. Mr. Ellis's farm was sold on a mortgage.
11. Joseph's brothers were cruel.
12. The article was found in Quackenbos's Rhetoric.

MODEL FOR ANALYSIS.

Sentence 1.

1. *Sermons* is the subject.

2. *Are admired* is the predicate.

3. **Moody's** tells whose sermons are meant, by naming the author.

4. *Much* tells to what degree the sermons are admired.

MODEL FOR PARSING.

Moody's is a noun, pr., 3d., sing., masc.; added to the noun *sermons* to tell *whose,* and therefore put in the *possessive case.*

4. Seat Work.

Study next lesson, and review.

LESSON 66.

Possessive Nouns Denoting Origin or Fitness.

1. Instruction.

1. *The sun's rays.*
2. *Children's shoes.*

By the *sun's* rays we mean rays that come from the sun. *Children's* shoes are shoes of the proper size and shape for children. They may never be owned or worn by them.

Possessive nouns are often used in this way to denote the *origin, adaptation,* or *fitness,* of things.

2. Exercise in Analysis and Parsing.

EXAMPLES.

1. Gentlemen's clothing is substantial.
2. Ladies' gloves are expensive.
3. The moon's pale light fell on the lonely grave.
4. The bird's song echoed through the vale.
5. The old man's thoughts were suddenly interrupted.
6. Henrietta's sister is coming in July.
7. The ruddy camp-fire's glow was mirrored in the stream.

8. The fond mother's prayers ascended to heaven.

9. From the distant grove comes the cuckoo's song.

10. The merry skaters were distinctly seen by the bonfire's glowing light.

11. Carpenter's tools are indispensable in such work.

12. The whole earth is enlivened by the sun's radiant beams.

3. Seat Work.

Study the next lesson.

LESSON 67.

Possessive Nouns Denoting Time, Weight, Measure.

1. Instruction.

A month's pay was advanced.

In this sentence, *month's*, although it has the possessive sign, is not used to tell whose pay was advanced, but the *time* required for earning the amount paid.

Month's is said to be in the possessive case, because it has the possessive sign, and because it denotes something a little like possession, for a month's pay is the pay *belonging* to a month of labor.

2. Exercise in Analysis and Parsing.

EXAMPLES.

1. He was held at arm's length.

2. That sketch was drawn by a painter's hand.

3. American independence was gained by a seven years' war.

4. A ten miles' ride was taken before breakfast.

5. A lion's roar was heard in the forest.

6. The child's arm was crushed.

7. Twenty pounds' weight was added to each captive's burden.

8. The cattle are feeding on the hill's gentle slope.

REMARKS.—In the first sentence, *arm's* denotes the measure of the length; it is the measure of an arm.

In sentence **3**. *years'* denotes measures of time, and

seven tells how many such measures are required to measure the length of the war.

In sentence **4,** *miles'* denotes measures of distance, and *ten* shows how many such measures are required to measure the length of the ride.

In sentence **7,** *pounds'* denotes measures of weight, and *twenty* tells how many such measures are required to equal the weight of the burden.

3. Seat Work.

Write a composition on *Food.*

QUESTIONS.

1. What are the chief articles of food in our country?

2. What articles of food do we get from other parts of the world?

3. The people of foreign lands use what kinds of food that are not used here?

4. How do savages obtain their food?

5. How did Adam and Eve obtain their food before they sinned?

6. Did they have any work to do?

7. How do people obtain their food in very cold countries?

8. How easily can people get food in some very hot countries?

9. What evils do people have to suffer in hot countries?

10. Tell some of the different ways in which food is prepared in various parts of the world.

LESSON 68.

Possessive Pronouns.

1. Instruction.

1. *My path is lost.*
2. *Your kindness is appreciated.*
3. *His father is dead.*

In the first sentence above, *my* alludes to the speaker, and shows *whose* path is lost.

In the second sentence, *your* alludes to the person spoken to, and shows whose kindness is meant. Etc.

1. If I want to represent a home as belonging to myself, what pronoun must I employ?

2. How would I represent it as belonging to myself and others associated with me?

3. How would I represent it as belonging to some person spoken to? To several persons spoken to?

4. What pronoun would you use in showing that the home belongs to a man? To a woman?

5. What pronoun would you use in showing that it belongs to two or more men? To two or more women? To a man and a woman? To men and women?

6. When we wish to represent anything as belonging to an object that has no sex, we use the pronoun **its.**

ILLUSTRATION.—*The tree is gigantic; its diameter is over ten feet, and its top towers far above the steeple.*

7. Sometimes the name of the thing possessed is *understood;* as,—

I took his umbrella, and left *mine* [i. e., *my umbrella*].

When the noun is understood, we use *mine* instead of *my; ours* instead of *our; yours* instead of *your;* and *theirs* instead of *their.*

So we have a complete set of words [pronouns] used to allude to the possessor.

They are,—

My or mine,	Our or ours,
Thy or thine,	Your or yours,
His,	Her or hers,
Its,	Their or theirs.

Since these words always denote possession, they need no possessive sign, so the 's is never added to them.

2. Exercises.

(*a.*) Make each of the preceding words a part of a sentence, and tell whether it denotes ownership, authorship, origin, fitness, a part, kindred, etc.

(*b.*) Analyze a few of the sentences thus formed.

QUESTIONS.

1. What words may be used to allude to the speaker?
2. Which of these should be used as the subject of a sentence?
3. Which to denote possession?
4. Which as the object of a preposition?
5. Can *I* be used as the object of a preposition?
6. Can it denote possession?
7. Can *me* be used as subject?
8. Can *my* be used as subject?
9. Can *me* denote possession?

I is called the **Nominative Case,** or *Nominative Form,* because it is used as subject.

Since *my* is used to denote possession, it is called the **Possessive Case,** or *Possessive Form.*

Since *me* is used as the object of a preposition, it is called the **Objective Case,** or *Objective Form.*

3. Seat Work.

Study the sentences given in the next lesson, and write the parsing of the nouns and pronouns.

LESSON 69.

Parsing Possessive Pronouns.

1. Questions.

1. What words may allude to a person spoken of?
2. Which of these words may be used as the subject of a sentence?

3. Which may be used to show possession ?
4. Which may be used as the object of a preposition ?
5. In what case is *he? him? his? her? she?*

2. Exercise.

Analyze and parse,—

1. My house is small.
2. His eyes were swollen.
3. Her thoughts were vain.
4. Milton's writings are extensively read.
5. The farmer's cattle are quietly resti..g.
6. My mother's Bible is lying on her lap.
7. I rode through the forest.
8. Their joy was clearly shown in their faces.
9. The mountain is proud of its snowy wreath.
10. We are often deceived by our desires.

MODELS.

Ex.— Our days are numbered.

Our is a pronoun, first person, plural number, and includes both sexes; it is used to tell whose days are numbered, and is therefore put in the the possessive case.

Abbreviated form to be used in writing.

Our.—Pro., 1st per., plu. n.; tells whose days, poss. c.

Ex.— Your kind offer is gratefully accepted.

Your.— Pro., 2d per., sing. or plu. n.; tells whose offer, poss. c.

3. Seat Work.

Write what you have learned of the different forms of pronouns, and their uses.

——— - • - ———

LESSON 70.

Pronouns.—Continued.

1. Exercise.

Analyze and parse,—

1. My father's traits of character are repeated in me.
2. Your writings are received with uncommon favor.
3. Our good resolutions are often broken.

4. A father's blessing rested on his child.
5. For days he wandered by the river's brink.
6. On its margin the great forest stood.
7. Our harps were left by Babel's stream.

2. Seat Work.

Write the analysis and parsing of the following sentence :—

They protected their father's grave with jealous care.

MODEL FOR WRITING THE PARSING OF ADJECTIVES.

Sentence 6.

Great.—Adj., q., added to *forest* to show its extent.

LESSON 71.

Possession Denoted by a Phrase.

1. Instruction.

1. *Solomon's wisdom is proverbial.*
2. *The wisdom of Solomon is proverbial.*

These two sentences are exactly alike in meaning. In the first, *Solomon's* tells whose wisdom is meant, and in the second, *of Solomon* tells the same thing. *Solomon* names the possessor ; and the *possessive sign* in the first sentence, and the word *of* in the second, show the relation of Solomon to wisdom,—the relation of possession.

2. Exercises.

(*a.*) In the following sentences change the possessive sign from *'s* to *of*, or from *of* to *'s :*—

1. The governor's elegant mansion is much admired.
2. Childhood's happy days are remembered with pleasure.
3. The farm of Mr. Smith is very productive.
4. The word of the Lord came to the prophet.
5. Solomon's temple was built on Mount Moriah.
6. The troops of Washington were poorly clad.
7. An eagle's nest was found near the place.
8. The barge of the queen was already proceeding up the river.

(*b.*) Analyze the sentences given above.

MODELS.

1. **Of the Lord** tells whose word is meant. *Lord* names the being who spoke the word, and *of* shows the relation of the Lord to the word.

2. **Of the queen** tells whose barge was moving up the river. *Queen* names the person for whom the barge was especially intended, etc.

3. **Of Washington** tells whose troops are meant. *Washington* names the man who commanded the troops, etc.

Suggestion.—Those who prefer to do so can shorten the analysis, and only say, "*Of the Lord* tells whose word is meant;" and so with other phrases.

3. Seat Work.

(*a.*) Study the next lesson with reference to the thoughts expressed, the analysis of the sentences, and the parsing of the words.

(*b.*) Change the adjective phrases to nouns in the possessive case.

LESSON 72.

Subject of the Last Lesson Continued.

1. Exercise.

Analyze and parse,—

1. The ripples of the rivulet are flashing in the light.
2. Into the valley of Death rode the six hundred.
3. 'Tis written in the book of fate.
4. The curious ways of birds were well known to him.
5. The attention of the tavern politicians was soon attracted by the appearance of Rip.
6. The fruit of the hawthorn, black and red, was gathered in those autumn days.

2. Seat Work.

Study the next lesson, and review Lessons 65 and 66.

LESSON 73.

Phrases Denoting Origin or Authorship.

1. Exercise.

Analyze and parse,—

1. The rays of the sun are reflected by the moon.
2. The smoke of the battle is clearing away.
3. The twitter of birds was heard in the grove.
4. Softly came the murmur of distant music.
5. The writings of Milton are sublime.
6. Midst the roar of the storm a faint cry was heard
7. The arguments of Locke were clearly stated.

MODELS.

Of the sun tells what rays are meant, by denoting *origin*. *Sun* names the body that produces the rays, and *of* shows the relation of the sun to the rays.

Of Milton tells whose writings are meant. *Milton* names the author, and *of* shows the relation of Milton to the writings.

2. Seat Work.

(*a.*) Study the next lesson.

(*b.*) Tell for what different purposes nouns in the possessive case are used, and give examples.

LESSON 74.

Phrases Denoting Material; or the Whole, of which Something is a Part.

1. Exercise.

Analyze and parse,—

1. The curtains were supported by pillars of brass.
2. The mouth of the Amazon is broad.
3. A wedge of gold was found in Achan's tent.

4. The rising sun was seen upon the mountain's brow.

5. A pillar of fire stood over the tabernacle.

6. The advance guard of the British army encamped near the river.

7. The mast-head of the vessel was seen above the waves.

MODELS.

Of brass tells what kind of pillars supported the curtains. *Brass* names the material of which the pillars were made, and *of* shows the relation of the brass to the pillars.

Of the Amazon tells to what the mouth belongs. *Amazon* names the river of which the mouth is a part, and *of* shows the relation between the Amazon and the mouth.

2. Seat Work.

(*a.*) Study the next lesson.

(*b.*) Explain the different cases, or forms, of pronouns; tell when they are used, and give examples.

LESSON 75.

Phrases Denoting Time, Measure, Weight, etc.

1. Exercise.

Analyze and parse,—

1. By a pleasant ride of twelve miles, we were brought to the beautiful residence of my friend.

2. They were prepared for a stay of several weeks.

3. Their freedom was purchased by a war of thirty long years.

4. A channel of five hundred feet was cut through a bed of rock.

5. A weight of ten pounds was attached to the end of the lever.

6. We were equipped for a journey of a thousand miles.

7. The children of Israel were doomed to a journey of forty years in the wilderness.

MODELS.

Of ten pounds tells how heavy the weight was. **Pounds** names the kind of measure employed in estimating the weight. **Ten** shows how many such measures of weight equal the weight attached to the end of the lever. **Of** shows the relation between the pounds and the weight.

Of five hundred feet tells how long the channel was. **Feet** names the kind of measure. **Five hundred** shows how many such measures are required to equal the length of the channel. **Hundred** names one of the great orders of numbers, and **five** tells how many of these must be taken. **Of** shows the relation between the feet and the channel.

2. Seat Work.

Study the next lesson.

--------- ►•◄ ---------

LESSON 76.

Promiscuous Examples.

1. Exercise.

Analyze and parse,—

1. The dews of night descended on the lonely grave.
2. The winds of autumn wail sadly through the naked trees.
3. The graves of the warriors were dug in the vale.
4. The bright flowers of summer are faded and dead.
5. The sweet songs of birds were heard in the grove.
6. The fruit of that land was good.
7. On the third day of September, we arrived at our new home in the fertile valley of this beautiful stream.

MODEL.

Sentence 4.

1. *Flowers* is the subject.

2. **Are faded and dead** is the predicate; it predicates two conditions of the flowers. **Faded** and **dead**

denote the conditions, and *and* shows that they are alike related to the subject.

3. Etc.

MODEL FOR THE WRITTEN PARSING OF THE NOUN.

Sentence 4.

Flowers.—N., c., 3, pl., n., Sub., Nom. c.

Summer.—N., c., 3, s., n., Obj. of prep., Obj. c.

2. Seat Work.

Study the next lesson.

LESSON 77.

Promiscuous Examples.—Continued.

1. Exercise.

Analyze and parse,—

1. The lay of the minstrel was heard in the bower.
2. In the pride of his strength came the proud Briton on.
3. Two large ships were sunk in the harbor.
4. A box of children's shoes was sent to the destitute settlers.
5. The philosophers of that day excelled in wisdom.
6. Morning's rosy light is dawning upon the mountain's brow.
7. A line of breakers stretched across the entrance to the bay.

REMARKS.—In sentence **2,** *in the pride of his strength* tells how the Briton came on, by telling what quality he manifested in coming. *Pride* names the quality, and *in* shows its relation to the act of coming.

Of his strength tells what kind of pride he manifested. *Strength* names the quality in which he took pride, and *of* shows the relation between strength and pride.

In sentence **5,** *of that day* tells what philosophers were meant. *Day* names a definite portion of time, but is here used figuratively to denote a period in the world's history.

2. Seat Work.

(*a.*) Study the next lesson.

(*b.*) Write out what you know about *adverbs* and *adverbial phrases.*

LESSON 78.

Qualities Modified.

1. Exercise.

Analyze and parse,—

1. Those tones are wonderfully clear.
2. The redwood trees of California are very tall.
3. The tones of the old violin were charmingly sweet.
4. Cyrus was wonderfully expert in the chase.
5. The beast was great, and terrible, and strong exceedingly.
6. The kingdom is partly strong and partly broken.
7. The young chief of the Onondagas was fleet in the chase and strong in battle.

REMARKS.—The examples given in this lesson show how qualities are modified.

Analyze as in preceding lessons, and say that *wonderfully* tells how clear the tones were; *very* tells how tall the trees were, showing that they possess the quality of tallness (height) in a remarkable degree; etc.

These words are classed as *adverbs*, and parsed the same as those that modify actions, except that they are added to adjectives instead of being added to verbs.

In sentence **6**, *partly* tells in what way the kingdom was strong,—it is strong in some parts and broken in others.

In sentence **7**, *in the chase* tells where the chief was fleet. *Chase* names the exercise in which his fleetness was especially manifested, etc. *In battle* tells where his strength was especially manifested. *Battle* names a conflict between armies, and *in* shows the relation between the battle and the strength of the chief.

2. Seat Work.

Write a Composition.

LESSON 79.

Action Performed by the Subject and Received by an Object.

1. Instruction.

1. *The child is eating an apple.*
2. *John saws wood.*
3. *Helen studies grammar.*

1. What is predicated in the first sentence?
2. Who performs the action?
3. What receives it?
4. What receives the action predicated in the second sentence?
5. What receives the action predicated in the third sentence?

2. Exercises.

(*a.*) Fill the blank in each of the following sentences with a word showing what receives the action:—

1. Carpenters build——.
2. I hear——.
3. I like——.
4. Good children obey——.
5. Merchants sell——.
6. Snow covers——.
7. The hunters killed——.
8. The waves washed——.
9. Indolent people hate——.
10. Mary studies——.
11. Farmers raise——.
12. Boys write——.
13. The sun warms——.
14. Lucy reads——.
15. The idler wastes——.
16. My father bought——.

(*b.*) Change each of the foregoing sentences so that the word showing what receives the action will be made the subject of the sentence.

(*c.*) Analyze,—

1. Some birds build their nests on the ground.
2. Moses received the tables of stone on Mount Sinai.
3. The bright waves washed the pebbly shore.
4. Abraham left the land of his fathers.

5. The merry songs of birds filled the air.
6. The pages of thy book I read.
7. They clasped his neck.
8. He saw the fire of the midnight camp.

MODEL.

Ex.—Some birds build their nests on the ground.

1. *Birds* is the subject of this sentence.

2. *Build* is the predicate.

3. *Some* shows that *birds*, as used in this sentence, does not mean *all* birds, but only a certain class, probably not very numerous.

4. **Nests** shows *what* the birds build. It tells what receives the action.

5. *Their* alludes to birds, and thus tells whose nests are meant.

6. *On the ground* tells *where* the nests are built.

3. Seat Work.

Study the next lesson.

LESSON 80.

Subject of the Last Lesson Continued.

1. Exercise.

Analyze,—

1. He saw once more his dark-eyed queen.
2. Odors of orange-flowers reached him.
3. Loud he sang the psalm of David.
4. The voice of his devotion
Filled my soul with strange emotion.
5. An earthquake's arm of might
Broke their dungeon-gates at night.
6. He heard at times a horse's tramp
And a blood-hound's distant bay.
7. In happy homes he saw the light
Of household fires, so warm and bright.

7

REMARKS.—Parse *once more* together as an adverb. It probably comes from the adverbial phrase *for one more time.*

In sentence **5,** the earthquake is represented as having an arm of might, and breaking with it the gate of the dungeoñ. We speak of the earthquake as though it were a person. This is called a figure of **personification.** We say that it has an arm of might because it has such great power, shaking the earth as it does, rending rocks asunder, and upheaving islands in the sea. The meaning is that the earthquake so shook the prison that the doors flew open.

In sentence **6,** *at times* tells when he heard the horse's tramp and the blood-hound's bay. *Times* names certain points, or short periods, with intervals between. If he had heard the sounds all the while, continuously, there would have been only *one* time of hearing them; but since there were intervals, short spaces of time, when he did not hear them, he heard them *at times.*

A capital letter should begin the first word of every line of poetry.

2. Seat Work.

Write—

(*a.*) Five sentences that predicate quality.

(*b.*) Five that predicate action not received by anything.

(*c.*) Five that predicate action received by the subject.

(*d.*) Five that predicate action performed by the subject and received by something else.

LESSON 81.

Regular and Irregular Verbs.

1. Instruction.

Lightnings flash.

What is predicated in this sentence? Is the action represented as present or past at the time of mentioning it?

Lightnings flashed.

In this sentence, is the action represented as present or past at the time of mentioning it ?

Which verbs in the following sentences represent the action as present ? Which represent it as past ?

1. Torrents roared.
2. Thunders roll.
3. Waves dash.
4. Trees fell.
5. People fled.
6. Birds seek shelter.
7. The storm beats.
8. The eagle screamed
9. The wind blows.
10. The ocean roars.

A verb that represents action as present at the time of mentioning it, is said to be in the **present tense.**

A verb that represents action as past at the time of mentioning it, is said to be in the **past tense.**

2. Exercises.

(*a.*) Tell the tense of the verb in each of the following sentences :—

1. The fox-gloves stand in a long black row.
2. The slender swallows fly joyously about the eaves of the old barn.
3. The snow fell fast.
4. The sheep are feeding on the hillside.
5. The children swung on the old gate.
6. Across the stepping stones we passed.
7. A graveled walk led to the door.
8. The full creek rushes noisily along.
9. Here a row of doves sit from morn till night.
10. We sat down in the chimney nook.

(*b.*) 1. What is the past tense of *walk ? look ? burn ? help ?*

2. Write each of these verbs in the present tense.

3. Write each in the past tense. What have you added to the present tense in changing it to the past ?

3. Instruction Resumed.

(*a.*) A verb that forms its past tense by adding *ed* to the present, is called **a regular verb.**

(*b.*) 1. What is the past tense of *go? ride? see? feel? sing? find? write?*

2. Does there seem to be any regular way of forming the past tense of these verbs?

3. Such verbs are called **irregular** because they do not form their past tense in the regular way, that is, by adding *ed* to the present.

4. Exercise.

Which of the following verbs are regular? Which irregular?

Do,	seek,	fill,	rest,	call,	swim,
climb,	sit,	fling,	chirp,	fly,	stand,
fight,	fall,	freeze,	flee,	play,	whisper,
wait,	wander,	think,	fold,	sleep,	search.

5. Seat Work.

(*a.*) Select ten sentences each having a regular verb in the present tense.

(*b.*) Select ten sentences each having an irregular verb in the past tense.

LESSON 82.

Transitive and Intransitive Verbs; Voice.

To the Teacher.—Whenever a lesson is too long for a single recitation, divide it.

1. Instruction.

Birds build nests.

What is predicated in this sentence?

By what is the action performed?

By what is it received?

Answer the same questions in regard to the following sentences:—

1. Julia writes letters.
2. Bees make honey.
3. Cannibals eat men.
4. Farmers till the ground.
5. Mills grind wheat.

A verb that represents an action as *performed by the subject* and *received by something else*, is a **transitive verb,** in the **active voice.** It is called *transitive*, because the act *passes* from the one who performs it to some person or thing that receives it, and *transitive* means *passing*. It is said to be in the *active voice* because the subject performs the action.

The letter was written by Julia.

In this sentence, Julia *performs* the act of writing, and the letter *receives* it, just as in sentence 1 above; but in this sentence the name of the thing that receives the action is the subject, while in the former sentence, the name of the one who performs the action is the subject.

When the action is received by the subject, the verb is said to be **transitive** and in the **passive voice.** It is said to be *transitive* because the action *passes* from the one who performs it to something which receives it. It is said to be in the *passive voice* because the subject receives the action.

. We see, then, that a verb is *transitive* whenever it represents the action as *passing to anything*, or received by anything; and that a *transitive verb* is in the *active voice* when the subject *performs* the action, and in the *passive voice* when the subject *receives* the action.

When the subject performs the action and something else receives it, the name of the thing that receives the action is said to be the *object of the verb*.

2. Exercises.

(*a.*) Make each of the following verbs the predicate of a sentence in which the action shall be performed by the subject and received by an object:—

EXAMPLES.—Take, seek, strike, build, buy, cultivate, study, till, leave, deceive, kill, punish, send, open, rend, break, gather, discover.

(*b.*) Make each of these verbs the predicate of a sentence in which the action shall be received by the subject.

Suggestion.—Of course the *form* of the verb will have to be changed and the copula used before it.

3. Instruction Resumed.

The bird sings in the tree.
The flowers bloom in the garden.
Beasts roam in the forest.

1. What is predicated by the verb in each of these sentences ?

2. Is the action received by an object ?

3. Is the action received by the subject ?

When the action is not represented as being received by anything, the verb is said to be **intransitive,** that is, *not* transitive.

4. Exercise.

Make ten sentences, each having an intransitive verb as predicate.

1. When is a verb transitive ?

2. When intransitive ?

3. When is a transitive verb in the active voice ?

4. When in the passive voice ?

5. Seat Work.

Select fifteen sentences; five with an intransitive verb, five with a transitive verb in the passive voice, and five with a transitive verb in the active voice.

LESSON 83.

Parsing of Verbs.

To the Teacher.—Be thorough. Review, question, and cross-question, every day.

1. Exercise.

Analyze and parse,—

1. They gathered ripe nuts in autumn.
2. The waysides are fringed with flowers.
3. Many a green old sycamore shaded in summer the creek.
4. Oft they watched with wondering eye the swallow.
5. Brightly the morning sunshine glowed.

6. The barns are filled to the full with grain.
7. Through the autumn leaves the ripe fruit gleamed.
8. The orchard trees of their load complain.
9. The dull, red sun shines through the soft, smoky haze.
10. The oaten sheaves in autumn were piled to the very eaves.

MODELS.

Ex.— Cortez conquered Mexico.

1. **Conquered** is a verb, regular, transitive, active voice, and past tense.

2. **Mexico** is a noun, proper, 3d, sing., neu.; *object* of the verb *conquered*, and therefore put in the objective case.

Ex.—Foot-prints were found in the solid rock.

1. **Were found** is a verb, irregular, transitive, passive voice, and past tense.

2. **In** is a preposition; it shows the relation of the rock to the finding of the foot-prints.

3. **Rock** is a noun, com., 3d, sing., neu.; it is the *object* of the prep. *in*, and is therefore put in the objective case.

Ex.— Clouds float in the sky.

Float is a verb, reg., intransitive, present tense.

REMARKS.—When we say that a word is the *object of a verb*, we mean that the object represented by that word receives the action expressed by the verb.

In sentence **6**, *full* may be parsed as a noun, although it is generally an adjective.—*See Dictionary.*

In sentence **10**, *very* is an adjective, added to the noun *eaves* for emphasis. We mean the *true* eaves, the *real* eaves, the eaves *themselves*.

2. Seat Work.

Study the next lesson, and write the parsing of the verbs.

LESSON 84.

Verbs.

1. Exercise.

Analyze and parse,—

1. All the signs foretold a long winter.
2. Filled was the air with a dreamy, magical light.
3. Glasses with horn bows sat astride on his nose.
4. Basil knocked from his pipe the ashes.
5. All his thoughts were congealed into lines on his face.
6. Then the smoke rose slowly, slowly, through the tranquil air of morning.
7. All the tribes beheld the signal.
8. Then the warriors washed the war-paint from their faces.

2. Seat Work.

Write sentences showing all the different uses of adjective and adverbial phrases.

LESSON 85.

Verbs.—Continued.

1. Exercise.

Analyze and parse,—

1. On the banks their clubs they buried.
2. Two good friends had Hiawatha.
3. All the coals were white with ashes.
4. From his pouch he drew his peace-pipe.
5. Made of red stone was the pipe-head.
6. All the land with snow was covered.
7. Homeward shoots the arrowy swallow.
8. A scent of growing grasses through the lodge was gently wafted.
9. From his eyes the tears were flowing.

2. Seat Work.

Write sentences that will bring into use all the pronouns given below.

I, we, our, my, me, ours, mine, us, you, your, yours, he, his, him, she, her, hers, it, its, they, their, theirs, them.

LESSON 86.

Review.

1. Questions and Requirements.

1. Give a sentence whose verb denotes action and predicates it in one word.

2. Give a sentence whose verb employs one word to denote action and another to show its predication.

3. Parse the verb in each of these sentences.

4. Make sentences that will show how the adverb is employed to tell *how, when, where,* actions are performed.

5. Parse the adverbs.

6. Make sentences that will show how *groups* of words are employed for the same purposes.

7. Give an example of an adverbial phrase, denoting purpose. One denoting cause.

8. Give an example of an adjective phrase used to denote quality. One used to denote possession.

9. How do we change the form of nouns to make them denote possession? Give examples.

10. How do we form the possessive case of singular nouns ending in **s**? Of plural nouns ending in **s**?

11. Give a list of the possessive pronouns.

2. Seat Work.

(*a.*) Write sentences containing all the possessive pronouns.

(*b.*) Study the next lesson.

LESSON 87.

Review.—Continued.

1. Questions and Requirements.

1. For what different purposes do we use nouns in the possessive case ? Give examples.

2. What pronouns of the *first person* may be used in the *nominative case ?* What in the *possessive case ?* What in the *objective case ?*

3. What pronouns of the *second person* may be used in the *nominative case ?* What in the *possessive ?* What in the *objective ?*

4. What pronouns of the *third person, masculine gender*, may be used in each of the cases ? What in the *feminine gender ?* What in the *neuter ?*

5. Give sentences containing a transitive verb in the active voice.

6. Give sentences containing a transitive verb in the passive voice.

7. Give sentences containing an intransitive verb.

8. When is a verb said to be regular, and when irregular ? Give examples of both kinds.

9. When is a verb in the present tense ?

10. When in the past tense ?

11. Give sentences containing an irregular transitive verb in the passive voice and past tense.

12. Give sentences containing a regular transitive· verb in the active voice and present tense.

2. Seat Work.

Write what you know of the formation of the plural.

LESSON 88.

Person and Number of the Verb.

1. Instruction.

I *work.*	He *works.*
We *work.*	She *works.*
You *work.*	It *works.*
They *work.*	Thou *workest.*

From the above, we see that the verb *work* has three forms in the present tense. When any one of the words *I, we, you,* or *they,* is used as subject, the verb is **work.** When any one of the words, *he, she,* or *it,* is used as subject, the verb is **works.** When *thou* is used as subject, the verb is **workest.**

This change in the form of the verb is called its **person and number.**

He, she, and *it* are each in the third person, singular number; so we see that when the subject is in the third person, singular number, *s* is added to the verb. The verb is then said to be in the third person singular number.

It is *really* the *subject* that has the person and number, and the *verb changes its form to agree with it.*

When the subject is a *noun* in the 3d, sing., the verb is changed in form just as it is when the subject is a pronoun; as,—

Men work.	The boys play.
Man works.	The boy plays.

Thou is never used in common language. It is sometimes found in poetry, and is much used in the Bible and other ancient books. When used, it requires *t, st,* or *est* to be added to the verb, unless the verb already ends in *st.*

From the following, it will be seen that the verb does not change its form in the past tense, except for *thou*.

I *worked.*	He *worked.*
We *worked.*	She *worked.*
You *worked.*	It *worked.*
They *worked.*	Thou *worked***st***.

2. Exercises.

(*a.*) Employ the following verbs in sentences of your own :—

Forsake, reach, stand, descend, approach, defends, forsakes, stands, defend, approaches, watches, reaches, make, descends, write, tells, watch, fall, falls, come, comes.

(*b.*) Make each of the following words the subject of a sentence :—

Nathan, mountains, city, sea, queens, soldier, landscape, castles, oceans, we, they, she, I, you, he, sky, books, fountains, ostrich, piano, pictures.

(*c.*) Change the number of each noun-subject, and the number and person of each pronoun-subject, and see what change will be required in the verb.

3. Seat Work.

(*a.*) Fill the blanks in the following sentences :—

1. The —— contains many people.
2. The —— falls heavily on the roof.
3. The priest-like —— reads the sacred page.
4. Softly now the ————————
   Fades upon my sight away.
5. How regally the —— look down.
6. The summer —— lie pitched like tents.
7. And yet once more the —— sing.
8. And the ——, dark and lonely,
   Move through all their depths of darkness.
9. The gray-haired —— kneels beside the bier.

(*b.*) Correct all errors in the following sentences, giving reasons :—

1. The heavens looks down with angry frown.
2. The waves makes moan.

3. The wild winds roars.
4. The tempest rage.
5. Across the deck the huge waves dashes.
6. The forest leaves falls like flakes to the ground.
7. "The lion eat flesh," says I.
8. A robe of leaves cover all the trees.
9. The violets peeps from beneath the leaves.
10. A dish of nuts stand on the table.
11. The stars shines through the rents of ruin.
12. The tree wave in the blue midnight.
13. How sweet the moonlight sleep upon the bank.
14. The wild waters leaps on the crags.
15. Thou worked with ease.
16. The Jordan rush to the Dead Sea.
17. He praisedst the singer.

LESSON 89.

Person and Number of the Verb To Be.

1. Instruction.

The verb BE is different from other verbs in many respects. It has more forms in the present tense than other verbs have, as will be seen by the following:—

I **am.**	We *are.*
Thou ***art.***	You *are.*
He **is.**	They *are.*

It also has more forms in the past tense, as seen below.

I **was.**	We *were.*
Thou ***wast.***	You *were.*
He **was.**	They *were.*

When the predicate consists of a copula and some other word, the *copula is changed* to show the person and number, but the other word remains unchanged.

MODELS FOR PARSING THE VERB.

Ex.—Sad-voiced Autumn grieves.

Grieves is a verb, regular, intransitive, present tense, third person singular number, to agree with its subject *Autumn.*

Ex.—Below me roar the rocking pines.

Roar is a verb, regular, intransitive, present tense, third person plural number, to agree with its subject *pines.*

Ex.—Glossy leaves are twinkling in the sun.

Are twinkling is a verb, regular, intransitive, present tense, third person plural number, to agree with its subject *leaves.*

Ex.—The wind is heard among the mountains.

Is heard is a verb, irregular, transitive, passive voice, present tense, third person singular number, to agree with its subject *wind.*

Ex.—I am sad.

Am is a verb, irregular, copula, present tense, first person singular number, to agree with its subject *I.*

Ex.—He trod the dark valley alone.

Trod is a verb, irregular, transitive, active voice, past tense. This verb does not change its past tense for the person and number of its subject.

2. Exercise.

Parse the verbs in the following—

EXAMPLES.

1. The torrent pours down the rock.
2. The tree-tops faintly rustle.
3. Silence reigned in the streets.
4. Your eyes are dim.
5. Thou art welcome.
6. That star now holds the top of heaven.
7. The sun shoots his upward beam against the dusky pole.

8. My brothers stepped to the next thicket.
9. Was I deceived ?
10. A sable cloud turns forth her silvery lining.
11. I saw them under a green mantling vine.
12. I am content.
13. Thou art free.
14. The ploughman is whistling o'er the furrowed land.

3. Seat Work.

Correct all errors in the following sentences, giving reasons :—

1. They was smitten with blindness.
2. Adown the glen rides armed men.
3. Deep, fiery clouds o'er-spread the sky.
4. Dread stillness reign in air.
5. They keeps time to the music.
6. We was invited.
7. The mountain tower above the sky.
8. The tickets was all taken before noon.
9. Them is pretty.
10. I were sadly disappointed.
11. Them boys write letters in school.
12. Flowers is prettiest in the morning.
13. The books was found in the thief's trunk.
14. A load of boys are passing.
15. A vase of flowers were presented to the teacher.
16. A crown of thorns was placed upon his brow.
17. A confusion of sounds strike on my ear.

LESSON 90.

Interrogative Sentences.

1. Exercises.

(*a.*) Change each of the following sentences so as to make it *inquire* for the quality, action, or state :—

1. Joseph is industrious.
2. Those buildings were new.
3. The soil is productive.

4. The wind is blowing.
5. Those trees are fruitful.
6. They were improving.
7. Good resolutions are often forgotten.

What change has been made in each sentence, in order to make it inquire for the action or quality?

(*b.*) After the above sentences have been changed to the interrogative form, analyze them according to the following—

MODELS.

Ex.—Are you weary?

You is the subject.

Are weary is the predicate; it inquires for a condition of the subject.

Ex.—Is the dew falling?

Is falling is the predicate; it inquires for an action of the dew.

(*c.*) Analyze and parse,—

1. Why are you so sad?
2. Where is she going?
3. Were you present at the opening of the session?
4. Was Cromwell destitute of private virtues?
5. Art thou alone in this dreary wood?
6. Hear you that distant murmur?

2. Seat Work.

Study the next lesson, and select five sentences each containing a verb in the imperative mode.

LESSON 91.

Commands, Exhortations, etc.

1. Instruction.

Hear me.

(*a.*) These words are addressed to some one who is supposed to be present. If the person spoken to is younger than the speaker, or inferior in rank, the words will be understood as a *command;* if he is equal in age and rank, they will be understood as an *exhortation;* but if he is a superior, they will be regarded as a *petition,* or an *entreaty.*

If they are addressed to God, they will be understood as a *prayer* or *supplication.* So the same words may express a *command,* an *exhortation,* a *petition,* or a *prayer.*

(*b.*) The expression, *hear me,* is regarded as a sentence. The subject is *thou* or *you* understood. If the subject were written, the sentence might stand thus: *Hear thou me.* The subject *thou* would allude to the person spoken to; but since that person is present, the subject may be dropped.

2. Exercise.

Analyze the following sentences :—

1. Rise up to thy full height.
2. Listen to the advice of the godly.
3. Be wise.
4. Be encouraged by your success.
5. Be guided in all things by the Word of God.

MODELS FOR ANALYSIS.

Ex.—Come in the morning bright.

1. The subject is **thou, you,** or **ye**, understood. If the subject were given, it would allude to the person spoken to; but since that person is present, it is unnecessary to allude to him, therefore the subject is omitted.

2. **Come** is the predicate; it exhorts or invites the person addressed to perform an act.

3. *In the morning* shows *when* he is invited to come.

4. Etc.

Ex.—Be quiet.

1. The subject is **thou, you,** or **ye,** understood, etc.

2. The predicate is **be quiet;** it commands some one to assume a state and remain in it.

3. **Quiet** denotes the state, and **be** shows that it is predicated.

8

Ex.—Be not deceived.

1. **Thou** or **you**, understood, is the subject.

2. **Be deceived** is the predicate; it exhorts some one to receive an action.

3. **Deceived** denotes the action, and **be** shows it to be predicated.

4. **Not** makes the sentence mean just the opposite of what it would mean without that word.

3. Remarks on Mode.

The verb in such sentences as those given above is said to be in the **imperative mode;** for *imperative* means *commanding,* and the leading use of such sentences is to give commands.

The verbs in all the sentences that we have had heretofore, are said to be in the **indicative mode.** They simply *indicate* or *declare* an act, being, or state, or *inquire* for it.

4. Exercise.

Parse several of the verbs in Lesson 89, and also in the following sentences:—

1. Moses was instructed by the Lord.
2. Spring is coming.
3. Tears fell.

MODELS FOR PARSING.

Sentence 1.

Was instructed is a verb, regular, transitive, passive voice, indicative mode, past tense, third person singular number, to agree with its subject *Moses.*

Sentence 2.

Is coming is a verb, irregular, intransitive, indicative mode, present tense, third person singular number, to agree with its subject *spring.*

5. Seat Work.

Study the next lesson, and write the parsing of the verbs.

LESSON 92.

Imperative Mode.

1. Exercise.

Analyze and parse,—

1. Trust in the Lord with all thy heart.
2. Get wisdom.
3. Honor the Lord with thy substance.
4. In all thy ways acknowledge him.
5. Hear the instruction of thy father.
6. Enter not into the path of the wicked.
7. Learn to guard the temper.
8. The floors of the taverns are strewn with fragrant tips of fir-boughs.
9. Receive my instruction.
10. Keep thy heart with all diligence.

MODEL FOR PARSING.
Sentence 2.

Get is a verb, irregular, transitive, active voice, imperative mode, present tense, second person singular or plural number, to agree with its subject *thou, ye,* or *you,* understood.

2. Seat Work.

Write the parsing of the verbs in the next lesson.

LESSON 93.

Declarative, Interrogative, and Imperative Sentences.

1. Exercise in Analysis and Parsing.

EXAMPLES.

1. Go not in the way of evil men.
2. Ponder the ways of thy feet.
3. In the first watch of the night,
    Without a signal's sound,
   Out of the sea, mysteriously,
    The fleet of Death rose all around.

4. Whence comes that murmur?
5. Whither goest thou?
6. Put away from thee a froward mouth.
7. When was the independence of the United States acknowledged by Great Britain?
8. There in close covert by some brook
   Hide me from day's garish eye.
9. With speeches fair she wooes the gentle air.
10. She hides her guilty front with innocent snow.

REMARKS.—In sentence **3,** parse the two words *out of* together as a preposition.

Around, although it would be a preposition if the ellipsis were supplied, is better parsed as an adverb, representing an adverbial phrase in which the object of the preposition is understood. The meaning is that the fleet of Death rose all around the ship.

All is an adverb, added to the adverb *around.* It seems to convey the idea that every part of the sea around this ship was covered with the fleet of Death.

2. Seat Work.

Tell, in writing, how all kinds of nouns form their plural.

LESSON 94.

Class Predicated.

1. Instruction.

Things that are alike are said to be of the same class.
Men that build houses and barns are called *carpenters;* men that till the soil are called *farmers;* men that study law, and plead cases in court, are called *lawyers;* men that work in iron are called *blacksmiths.*

QUESTIONS.

1. Men that make flour are called what? 2. Men that weave cloth? 3. Men that dig minerals from the

earth? 4. Men that build walls and houses of brick and stone? 5. Men that spend their lives upon the sea? 6. Men that roam the forests in search of game?

7. What other classes of men can you name?

In this way we classify men in respect to their employment in life.

Those of the same employment may be very different in other respects. For instance, some farmers are very industrious, others are indolent; some are temperate, others are intemperate; some are honest, and others are dishonest. Yet all these men belong to the class called farmers; for they are following farming as an employment.

2. Exercise.

Analyze and parse,—

1. Tennyson is a poet.
2. His father was a minister.
3. Locke was a philosopher.
4. My brother is a musician.
5. Bonaparte was a general.
6. Gold is a metal.
7. He was a Samaritan.
8. The captain was a Spaniard.
9. That tall, gray man was a general in the rebel army.
10. The inventor of the magnetic telegraph was an American.

MODEL FOR ANALYSIS.

Ex.—My uncle is a merchant.

1. *Uncle* is the subject of this sentence.

2. **Is merchant** is the predicate; it predicates that my uncle belongs to a class of men called merchants.

3. **Merchant** names one of a class.

4. **Is** shows that the thought is predicated.

5. *My* alludes to the speaker, and shows whose uncle is meant.

6. *A* denotes one, but no particular one.

Merchant is a noun, common, third person, singular number, masculine gender; used with the copula to form the predicate, and therefore put in the nominative case.

3. Seat Work.

Study the next lesson; write the analysis of the first sentence, and the parsing of all the nouns used in predicate.

LESSON 95.

Subject of the Last Lesson Continued.

1. Exercise in Analysis and Parsing.

EXAMPLES.

1. Demosthenes was an orator.
2. His son was a lawyer.
3. John was an apostle.
4. Bryant was a poet.
5. That man is a sailor.
6. My neighbor is a painter.
7. Water is a liquid.
8. The earth is a planet.
9. Good people are always generous.
10. That body of land is an island.
11. This plant is a perennial.
12. That dark building is a prison.

Ex.—Demosthenes was an orator.

Was is a verb, irregular, copula, indicative mode, past tense, third person singular number, to agree with its subject *Demosthenes.*

2. Seat Work.

Study the next lesson. Write the analysis of the first sentence, and the parsing of all the words in it.

LESSON 96.

Class Assumed.

1. Exercise in Analysis and Parsing.

EXAMPLES.

1. Demosthenes the orator was remarkably eloquent.
2. Booth the assassin shot Lincoln.
3. Raphael the artist was very industrious.
4. The sentinel stars set their watch in the sky.
5. John the apostle was much beloved by his Lord.
6. Bryant the poet is dead.
7. At the dead of the night a sweet vision I saw.
8. Sweetly the founts of that valley fall.
9. Bright are the waters of Sing-su-hay.

Note.—For models see next lesson.

2. Seat Work.

Study the next lesson, and write four sentences that assume one class and predicate another. Write out the analysis of your first sentence, and the parsing of the nouns in all of them.

LESSON 97.

Assuming One Class and Predicating Another.

1. Instruction.

Considering him with respect to his occupation, or business in life, I might say, "Mr. Jones is a lawyer;" but considering him in regard to his religious views, I might say, "Mr. Jones is a Baptist." By this we see that Mr. Jones might belong to two classes at the same time. If we wished to predicate that he belongs to both the classes noticed above, we would say, "Mr. Jones is a lawyer and a Baptist."

If we wished to predicate that he belongs to one class, and assume that he belongs to another, we would say, "Mr. Jones, the lawyer, is a Baptist;" or "Mr. Jones, the Baptist, is a lawyer."

2. Exercise in Analysis and Parsing.

EXAMPLES.

1. Arnold the traitor was false to his country.
2. Simon the tanner dwelt by the sea.
3. Tecumseh the "Prophet" was a warrior.
4. Saul the king was slain.
5. Spencer the poet was a recluse.
6. Luther the reformer exposed the errors of the Romish church.
7. Bonaparte the Corsican commanded the armies of France.

MODEL FOR ANALYSIS.

Ex.—Paul the apostle was a martyr.

1. *Paul* is the subject.

2. *Was martyr* is the predicate; it predicates that Paul belonged to a class of men called martyrs.

3. *Martyr* names one of that class, and

4. *Was* shows that the thought is predicated.

5. **The apostle** assumes that Paul belonged to a class of men called apostles.

6. **Apostle** names one of that class, and *the* shows that some particular apostle is meant.

MODEL FOR PARSING.

Ex.—Spencer the poet was a recluse.

Poet is a noun, common, third person, singular number, masculine gender; it describes Spencer by naming one of a class to which he belonged. A noun so used is said to be in *apposition* with the noun it describes, and is therefore put in the same case.

3. Seat Work.

Study the next lesson; write the analysis of sentences 1 and 9, and the parsing of the words in sentences 4 and 8.

LESSON 98.

Class.—Continued.

1. Exercise in Analysis and Parsing.

EXAMPLES.

1. The Indians were brave warriors.
2. The Northmen were bold adventurers.
3. Cactuses are hardy plants.
4. Why are you so careless in your work?
5. The Spaniards are treacherous foes.
6. Bonaparte was a successful general.
7. That horse is a beautiful animal.
8. Reprove not a scorner.
9. Those houses with stone fronts are beautiful buildings.

MODEL FOR ANALYSIS.

Ex.—The young Italians are excellent musicians.

1. *Italians* is the subject.

2. **Are excellent* musicians** is the predicate; it predicates that these Italians belong to a class of musicians called *excellent*.

3. **Musicians** names a class; **excellent** describes the kind of musicians here meant, by assuming a quality of them; and **are** shows that the thought is predicated.

4. *Young* describes the Italians by telling their age, and *the* shows that some particular young Italians are meant.

---

*NOTE.—**Are musicians** is the *grammatical* predicate, but does not express the thought that is predicated; and so, in this instance, we give the *logical* predicate. A closer analysis may be drawn out from the following remarks:—

We classify men, not only by their employments, but by the qualities they possess. When we consider men in regard to their stature, we find that some are *larger* than most men are, and that others are *smaller* than the average. All men of great size are called *large* men, and those of less than the ordinary size, *small* men.

The word *men*, taken alone, means *any* men, or *all* men; but if we say *large* men, *large* assumes a quality of the men here meant, and shows that they belong to a class of men who are great in stature.

If we speak of honest men, *honest* assumes a quality of the men, and shows that they belong to a class of men that are upright in their dealing.

Other things, as well as men, are classified by their qualities. We classify

Ex.—Booth was a good actor.

1. *Booth* is the subject.

2. *Was a good actor* is the predicate; it predicates that Booth belonged to a class of actors called *good*.

---

trees as tall trees. low trees, large trees, small trees. stately trees, scraggy trees. forest trees. fruit trees, ornamental trees, etc. One class of fruits is called apples. another pears, another peaches, etc. Apples are distinguished as sour apples. sweet apples, ripe apples. good apples. poor apples. mellow apples, tart apples, etc.

Among days, we have long days. short days. hot days. cold days. fair days, rainy days, cloudy days, dry days, sultry days, autumn days. wintry days, etc.

The word *days*, taken alone, means *any* days, or *all* days; but *long days* means a class of days that are remarkable for the *quality* of *length*. *Long* assumes the quality, and shows that the days here meant belong to the class that possesses this quality. All long days are said to belong to the same class because they are alike in this one thing,—they have a common quality.

ILLUSTRATION.

Ex.—My brothers are farmers.

In this sentence we predicate that my brothers belong to a class of men called farmers; but there are different classes among farmers, and if we wish to show to which of these classes the brothers belong, we must have a word to denote that particular class.

If I say, "My brothers are *thrifty* farmers," *farmers* names a class of men, and *thrifty*, by assuming a quality of the farmers here meant, shows to what particular class of farmers they belong.

The word *farmers*, taken alone, means *any* farmers, *all* farmers,—the *entire* class; but the word *thrifty* assumes a quality of the farmers here meant, and shows that they belong to the class that possess this quality.

MODELS FOR ANALYSIS.

Ex.—The young Italians are excellent musicians.

1. *Italians* is the subject.

2. **Are excellent musicians** is the predicate; it predicates that these Italians belong to a certain class of musicians.

3. **Musicians** names a general class that includes the one to which these Italians belong.

4. **Excellent,** by assuming a quality of the musicians here meant, shows to what particular class of musicians they belong.

5. **Are** shows that the thought is predicated.

Ex.—Gibson the old hunter was a noted guide.

1. **The old hunter** assumes that Gibson belonged to a certain class of hunters.

2. **Hunter** names one of a general class.

3. **Old,** by assuming a quality of the hunter here meant, shows to what particular class of hunters he belonged.

3. **Actor** names one of a class; **good** describes the kind of actor here meant, by assuming a quality of him; and **was** shows that the thought is predicated.

Suggestion.—Those who prefer to do so can tell what the predicate does as a whole, without noticing the office of its separate words.

2. Seat Work.

Study the next lesson; write the analysis of the first four sentences, and the parsing of the predicate-nouns in the remaining sentences.

————→•←————

LESSON 99.

Class.—Continued.

1. Exercise in Analysis and Parsing.

EXAMPLES.

1. The Cabots were successful discoverers.
2. The lark is a sweet singer.
3. Cortez was a cruel invader.
4. The Richardsons are good neighbors.
5. The Scandinavians are hardy mariners.
6. Keep thy father's commandment.
7. He was, assuredly, an excellent solicitor.
8. With the neighboring gentry, however, he was no favorite.
9. Hang a lantern aloft in the belfry arch of the North Church tower.
10. Our uncle, innocent of books,
    Was rich in lore of fields and brooks.
    　　　　　—*Whittier.*
11. The mellow light of sunset shone sweetly on the wood-girt town.
12. And above, in the light
    Of the star-lit night,
    Swift birds of passage wing their flight
    Through the dewy atmosphere.
    　　　—*Longfellow, p.* 131.

2. Seat Work.

Study the next lesson; write the analysis of sentences 7 and 8, and the parsing of the words in sentence 7.

LESSON 100.

Class.—Continued.

1. Exercise in Analysis and Parsing.

EXAMPLES.

1. Milton the great poet was a devout man.
2. Wednesday was a stormy day.
3. The Reformers were earnest Christians.
4. Newton was a great mathematician.
5. These substances are pure metals.
6. The orange is a delicious fruit.
7. Iagoo, the great boaster, was a marvelous story-teller.
8. Keep your mind upon worthy subjects.
9. Why were you tardy?
10. Wake the song of jubilee.
11. Beside the river's tranquil flood
    The dark and low-walled dwelling stood.
12. The skirts of a heavy thunder-cloud hung over the western hill.

MODEL FOR ANALYSIS.

Ex.—Gibson, the old hunter, was a noted guide.

1. *Gibson* is the subject.

2. *Was a noted guide* is the predicate; it predicates that Gibson belonged to a class of men called *noted guides*, etc.

3. **The old hunter** describes Gibson by *assuming* that he belonged to a certain class of men; **hunter** *names* one of a class, and **old** describes the kind of hunter here meant by assuming a quality.

REMARK.—This sentence predicates that Gibson belonged to one class, and assumes that he belonged to another.

2. Seat Work.

Select or compose seven sentences like the one given in the model above; write the analysis of the first one, the parsing of the nouns in the second, and the parsing of the verbs in the others.

LESSON 101.

Class.—Continued.

1. Exercise in Analysis and Parsing.

1. Miles Standish, the Puritan captain, was a little man.
2. Nauhaught, the Indian deacon, was a poor man.
3. A hearty man was Benedict, the wealthy farmer of Grand Pre'.
4. The landlady's son, a tall viking, went with us.
5. Dr. Franklin, the great philosopher, was the son of a poor man.
6. Fear not the icy fingers of Death.
7. Why is seven a perfect number?
8. Alden, the taciturn stripling, was a fair-haired Anglo-Saxon.

REMARKS.—In sentence **1**, *Miles Standish* may be parsed as one word. *Puritan* is a noun, com., 3d., sing., masc.; used here as an adjective. It describes the captain by naming the religious sect to which he belonged. It takes the capital initial, not because it is a proper noun, but because it is the name of a sect. It cannot be a proper noun; for it may be applied to any one of a large class.

Puritan is sometimes wholly an adjective, as when we speak of Puritan principles; or it may be wholly a noun, as when we say a man is a Puritan.

In sentence **2**, Indian is a common noun, and used in very much the same way as Puritan in the sentence above. It takes the capital initial because it is derived from the proper noun *India*.

Viking means a *pirate chief;* but this young man is probably called a viking on account of his commanding appearance. He looks as though he might be strong and courageous enough for a viking.

In sentence **6,** Death is represented as being a person. He is said to have icy fingers, because when people die, their fingers become very cold.

Fair-haired is one word—an adjective.

Note.—These *remarks* are meant especially for those who study without a teacher.

2. Seat Work.

Study the next lesson; write the parsing of all the nouns used to show identity, and the analysis of sentences 3 and 6.

LESSON 102.

Assuming and Predicating Identity.

1. Instruction.

1. *That tall man is Abraham Lincoln.*
2. *Israel's wisest king was Solomon.*
3. *The boy Henry fell into the sea.*
4. *The brig Rover was sunk.*
5. *That wise king, Solomon, built the temple.*

In sentence **1,** the subject names one of a class, and the predicate identifies him by giving his individual name.

In sentence **2,** *Israel's wisest king* names and describes one of a class, and *was Solomon* predicates his identity.

In sentence **3,** the subject, *boy,* names one of a class, and *Henry,* his individual name, assumes his identity.

In the fourth sentence, *brig* names one of a class of vessels, and *Rover* names the particular one here meant.

In the fifth sentence, *wise king* names and describes one of a class; and *Solomon,* his proper name, identifies the *wise king* here meant.

Note.—When we wish to make the *person* or *thing* more prominent, we put the individual-name for the subject, and the class-name in the predicate; as,—

Benedict Arnold was a most noted traitor.

But when we wish to make the *class* more prominent, we put the class-name for subject, and the individual name in the predicate; as,—

This noted traitor was Benedict Arnold.

Just so it is in *assuming* the same thought. Corresponding with the first sentence above, we have,—

> *Benedict Arnold, a most noted traitor, etc.*

Corresponding to the second sentence, we have,—

> *That most noted traitor, Benedict Arnold, etc.*

So, too, in briefer form we have,—

> 1. *Arnold the traitor.*
> 2. *The traitor Arnold.*

In sentences **3** and **4**, the words *Henry* and *Rover* are so closely connected in sense with the words just before them that it is not proper to set them off by any mark of punctuation; but in sentence **5**, the word *Solomon* is not so closely connected with the word before it. We would be almost certain that Solomon was the king meant, if the word *Solomon* were left out; but to remove all doubt, we insert the word by way of explanation, putting a comma before it and another after it, and thus separating it from other parts of the sentence. This is what we call "setting off" a word by the comma.

Notice, with regard to punctuation, the appositional nouns and phrases in preceding lessons.

Note.—A noun in apposition, taken together with the words which belong to it, may, for convenience, be called an **appositional phrase.**

2. Exercise in Analysis and Parsing.

EXAMPLES.

1. The schooner Melrose was wrecked.
2. The orator Webster was a great man.
3. The poet Wordsworth possessed a noble spirit.
4. The river Ganges is worshiped by the Hindoos.
5. The emperor Augustus was a patron of the fine arts.
6. The old man in the white-skin wrapper was Peboan, the winter.

MODELS FOR ANALYSIS.

Ex.—The brig Rover was sunk.

1. *Brig* is the subject; it names one of a class of vessels.
2. *Was sunk* is the predicate.

3. **Rover** identifies the brig here meant, by giving its individual name.

Ex.—That tall man is Lincoln.

1. **Man** is the subject : it names one of a class.

2. **Is Lincoln** is the predicate ; it predicates the identity of the man here meant.

MODEL FOR PARSING.

In the first sentence above, *Rover* is a noun, pr., 3d, sing., neu.; it identifies the brig here meant by giving its individual name. A noun so used is said to be in *apposition* with the noun it identifies, and is therefore put in the same case.

3. Seat Work.

Study the next lesson. Write the analysis of the first two sentences, and the parsing of the nouns and verbs in the next four.

LESSON 103.

Class.—Continued.

1. Exercise in Analysis and Parsing.

EXAMPLES.

1. The apostle John was particularly beloved by his Master.
2. His father-in-law Jethro came unto him.
3. Milton, the author of Paradise Lost, was a noble man.
4. The emperor Antoninus wrote an excellent work on morals.
5. Pau-Puk-Keewis, the handsome Indian, was a gambler.
6. Alph, the sacred river, ran through caverns measureless, down to a sunless sea.
7. That youthful stranger at the door is Segwun, the spring-time.

2. Seat Work.

Select all kinds of examples assuming and predicating class.

LESSON 104.
Promiscuous Examples.
1. Exercise.

Analyze and parse, and explain punctuation and figures.

1. Round their necks were suspended their knives, in scabbards of wampum.

2. Then Evangeline lighted the brazen lamp on the table.

3. Meanwhile the stalwart Miles Standish was marching steadily northward along the trend of the sea-shore.

4. After a three days' march he came to an Indian encampment.

5. Then the Black-Robe chief, the prophet, told his message to the people.

6. They hung on the headstones garlands of autumn leaves, and evergreens from the forests.

2. Seat Work.

Study the next lesson, and review on the verb.

LESSON 105.
Promiscuous Examples.—Continued.
1. Exercise.

Analyze, etc.,—

1. In the infinite meadows of heaven, blossomed the lovely stars, the forget-me-nots of the angels.

2. Soon with a soundless step the foot of Evangeline followed.

3. Art thou afraid?

4. Gather the host together for battle.

5. Take thou this holy sword, a gift from God.

6 The morning sun is shining on their shields of gold.

7. Send before us a good angel.

8.   A flush of shame
Over the face of the leader came.

9. Silently over that house the blessing of slumber descended.

2. Seat Work.

Study the next lesson.

9

LESSON 106.

Review.

Direction.—Give examples of everything brought out in the questions.

Questions and Requirements.

1. What is a common noun? A proper noun? A collective noun? An abstract noun?

2. What classes of common nouns take the capital initial?

3. Write the following words and expressions correctly :—

EXAMPLES.—The cape of good hope, columbia river, alps mountains, Smiths' sound, the bay of biscay, Washington city, the great city of london, Washington was a federalist, mr. bailey, the Missionary to south africa, the methodist minister, tuesday, nov. 5th, autumn.

4. How do most nouns form their plural?

5. How do we form the plural of nouns whose final sound will not unite with the sound of *s?*

6. What nouns belong to this class?

7. What nouns form their plural by adding *es* without increasing the number of their syllables?

8. How do nouns ending in *y* form their plural?

9. How should we form the plural of nouns ending in *f?* Of nouns ending in *fe?*

10. How do qualifying adjectives limit nouns?

11. How do limiting adjectives differ from qualifying adjectives?

12. Give examples of limiting adjectives that show *what* or *which ones* are meant.

13. Give examples of limiting adjectives that show indefinitely *how many* are meant.

14. Give examples of adjectives that tell *definitely* how many.

15. What pronouns may be used to represent the speaker?

16. Which of these may be used as subject? Which as object?

17. Which of them may be used to denote ownership, origin, etc.?

18. What four pronouns may be used to represent the speaker and those associated with him?

19. How must each of them be used?

20. What pronouns may be used to represent the person or persons spoken to?

21. How is each of them employed?

22. What pronouns may be employed in speaking of a person of the male sex?

23. In speaking of a person of the female sex?

24. In speaking of something that has no sex?

25. What four pronouns are used in speaking of things without regard to sex?

26. How must each be used?

27. Give examples of the incorrect use of pronouns.

LESSON 107.

Review.—Continued.

Direction.—Illustrate by *examples*, as in the last lesson.

1. Questions and Requirements.

1. In what four ways are adverbial phrases used?

2. For what different purposes are nouns in the possessive case used?

3. Tell some of the different uses of adjective phrases.

4. How do singular nouns form the possessive case? Plural nouns?

5. When is a verb called a copula?

6. When is it said to be intransitive?

7. When is it transitive?

8. When is a transitive verb in the active voice?

9. When is it in the passive voice?

10. When is a verb said to be regular?

11. Give examples of irregular verbs.

12. Give examples of verbs in the *imperative mode*. In the *indicative mode*.

13. Give examples of interrogative sentences.

14. Give examples of verbs in the present tense. In the past tense.

15. Make a sentence with the verb in the present tense, third person singular number.

16. One with the verb in the third person plural number. First person singular number. First person plural number. Second person singular. Second person plural.

17. Change these verbs to the past tense.

18. How does the verb BE differ in person and number from other verbs?

19. Show this difference by examples.

20. Predicate that a person or object belongs to a class of persons or things.

21. Express the same thought without predicating it.

22. Parse, in each sentence, the noun that names the class.

23. Predicate identity. Assume identity.

24. Assume one class and predicate another in the same sentence.

25. Analyze the sentence thus formed.

2. Seat Work.

Study next lesson, and write the analysis of the last three sentences.

LESSON 108.

Action Assumed.

1. Instruction.

1. *Beautiful insects dancing in the air.*
2. *Bright flowers growing by the wayside.*
3. *Walking by the beach, I saw a huge sea-lion, playing in the water.*

The first group of words above is not a sentence; for although it names objects, it does not predicate anything of them.

Dancing denotes an action, but we do not say that the insects *are* dancing. We mention the action *incidentally*, as though it were not the chief thought which we wish to express. The action is not predicated, but merely *assumed*.

In the second group, *growing* assumes an action of the flowers.

The third example is a sentence; it predicates one action, and assumes two others.

Saw predicates an action of the speaker, and *walking* assumes an action of the same person.

Sea-lion names what I saw.

Playing assumes an action of the sea-lion.

A word that merely *assumes* an action, but does not predicate it, is called a **Participle.**

2. Exercises.

(*a.*) Write ten sentences in which action is assumed.

(*b.*) Analyze the following sentences :—

1. Trusting in his own strength, he failed.
.2. The stream flowing from that lake empties into the bay near the old fort.
3. That tall man standing by the wheel is the captain of the vessel.

4. Those fleecy clouds, sailing slowly through the sky, are lovely.

5. Going to the blazing fire, she held out her hand.

6. He hears the tread of the grenadiers, marching down to their boats on the shore.

7. Thus came the lovely spring, flooding the earth with flowers.

MODEL FOR ANALYSIS.

Ex.—Rapidly crossing the stream, the spy plunged into the forest.

1. **Crossing the stream** describes the spy by assuming an action of him.

2. **Crossing** denotes the action.

3. **The stream** tells what he crossed.

3. Seat Work.

When no seat work is given, it is always understood that the next lesson is to be studied; and the teacher may give such written exercises as seem best suited to the wants of the class.

LESSON 109.

Participles, Present Active.

1. Instruction.

A participle is *present* when it represents the act as taking place at the time denoted by the predicate, whether that time be past, present, or future.

A participle is *active* when the thing described by it performs the action.

2. Exercise in Analysis and Parsing.

EXAMPLES.

1. Hearing a sharp cry from the thicket, I stopped my horse.

2. Following the stream, we soon came to a beautiful waterfall.

3. Coming suddenly upon a trapper's hut, we uttered a cry of joy.

4. Our lives are rivers, gliding to that boundless sea, the silent grave.

5. Leaving there his offering, he turned his feet toward his long-deserted home.

6. Across the ocean came a gallant bark, bearing a precious cargo.

7. He sat down by his sunny doorway, murmuring there unto himself.

MODELS FOR PARSING.

Sentence 6.

Bearing is a participle, present active, transitive, added to the noun *bark* to denote an assumed action performed by the bark.

Cargo is a noun, com., 3d, sing., neu.; object of the participle *bearing*, and therefore put in the objective case.

REMARK.—In sentence **7**, *himself* is a pronoun, object of the preposition *unto*. *Self* is added to *him* merely for emphasis. Such pronouns have the same form whether used as subject or object, and should never be used in the possessive case.

3. Seat Work.

Study the next lesson; write the analysis of the first two examples, and the parsing of the participles in all the others.

————— ▸•◂ —————

LESSON 110.

Punctuation of Participial Phrases.

1. Instruction.

The participle is usually accompanied by other words, that tell *what* receives the action, or *how, why, when,* or *where* the action was performed, thus forming a *group* called a **participial phrase.**

In the first example below, *fearing an attack* is a participial phrase.

Point out the participial phrases in the other examples

of this lesson, and in the examples of the two preceding lessons.

The participial phrase is commonly set off by the comma; but sometimes it is used to tell *what one* or *which one*, as it does in sentences **4** and **5** of this lesson. The phrase is then said to be **restrictive,** and should *not* be *set off*.

In sentence **4,** *which* man is the emperor? In sentence **5,** *which* lady is the governor's wife? Notice that in each case the participial phrase answers the question. But in sentences **1,** **2, 3,** no such question can be answered by the participial phrase.

2. Exercise in Analysis and Parsing.

EXAMPLES.

1. Fearing an attack, the general set a double guard.
2. Fording the stream, we were soon threading our way through the winding ravines leading up the mountain's side.
3. My friend, losing his way, spent the night in the forest.
4. That man looking through an opera-glass is the Emperor of Brazil.
5. That lady standing by the window is the governor's wife.
6. From his wigwam he departed, leading Laughing Water with him.

3. Seat Work.

Write five sentences each containing a participial phrase that is *restrictive*, and five other sentences each containing a participial phrase that is *not restrictive*.

LESSON 111.

Passive Participles.

1. Instruction and Exercise.

A participle is **passive** when the thing described by it receives the action.

EXAMPLES.

1. Smiling Nature is seen, clad in garments green.
2. A net made of thongs was used by the natives.

3. The captives taken by the savages were tortured.

4. Walking through the camp at daybreak, I met a spy in disguise.

5. Guarded by thy protection, we sink to rest.

6. He looked down on the sunlight flowing over all the landscape.

7. The fruit raised in that region is exported to many countries.

8. Bearing the body to a thick grove of cedars, she covered it with dry leaves.

MODEL FOR ANALYSIS.

Ex.—Grain sown in spring is harvested in autumn.

1. *Grain* is the subject.

2. *Is harvested* is the predicate; it predicates action received by the subject.

3. **Sown in spring** describes the grain by assuming that it receives an action.

4. **Sown** denotes the action, and **in spring** tells when it was performed.

5. *In autumn* tells when the grain was harvested.

MODELS FOR PARSING.

Sown is a participle, past passive, added to the noun *grain* to denote an assumed action received by the grain.

Sentence 5.

Guarded is a participle, present passive, added to the pronoun *we* to denote an assumed action received by the speaker and those associated with him.

REMARK.—In sentence 5, *rest* is a noun, object of the preposition *to*.

2. Seat Work.

Write the parsing of all the participles in the next lesson.

LESSON 112.

Participles.—Continued.

1. Exercise in Analysis and Parsing.

Suggestions.—From this point onward, let it be understood that, unless special directions are given, the Examples in every lesson are to be—

1. Corrected, if any errors can be found.
2. Analyzed with special reference to the thought.
3. Explained with regard to punctuation and the use of capital letters.
4. Explained in regard to the origin and meaning of the figures, if any occur.
5. Parsed, so far as may be necessary in order to keep up complete familiarity with the parsing of words in all conditions and relations.

EXAMPLES.

1. The cottage he sees, embowered upon the banks of Tees.
2. Patiently sat Hiawatha, listening to his father's boasting.
3. A fragment of rock, torn from the brow of the cliff, was precipitated into the abyss below.
4. At the doorway of his wigwam sat the ancient arrow-maker, making arrow-heads of jasper.
5. Sat his daughter, Laughing Water, plaiting mats of rushes.
6. A carriage drawn by eight horses was overturned near the bridge.
7. Far away in the briny ocean
      There rolled a turbulent wave,
   Now singing along the sea-beach,
   Now howling along the cave.
                              —*Longfellow.*

Remarks.—In sentence **3**, *below* is an adjective, added to *abyss* to show its condition in regard to place. It takes the place of the adjective phrase *below us*, or *below the brow of the cliff*, and means the same as the adjective clause, *which was below*, etc.

In sentence **7**, the word *there* is used merely to give smoothness to the expression, and is sometimes called a **word of euphony.** Some call it an *expletive*, since it performs no part in expressing the thought, and is therefore not really needed.

The two words *far away* seem to be used together to tell where the wave rolled, and may be parsed as an adverb.

2. Seat Work.

Write the analysis of the first sentence in the next lesson, and the parsing of all the words in the second sentence.

LESSON 113.

Participles.—Continued.

1. Examples.

1. In her wigwam, Laughing Water sat with old Nokomis, waiting for the steps of Hiawatha homeward from the hunt returning.

2. So saying, he walked away, followed by Walter.

3. The ground-pine curled its pretty wreath, running over the club-moss burs.

4. Silently he laid his hand on the head of the maiden, raising his tearful eyes to the silent stars above them.

5. The brooklet came from the mountain, running with feet of silver over the sands of gold.

REMARKS.—Sentence **5** contains some beautiful figures. As animals run with feet, so the brook is said to run with feet. The feet are said to be silver, because the water, as it runs over pebbles in shallow places, looks white and glistening, in the sunlight, like polished silver.

The sands are said to be gold, because they are yellow and shining like gold.

So we sometimes give to one thing the name of another when they are strikingly alike in some one quality which we wish to make prominent.

When we wish to call particular attention to some quality of a thing, we give to it the name of something else that is remarkable for that quality. This is what is called a *figure of* **metaphor.**

2. Seat Work.

Whether mentioned or not, the seat work of each day should include the careful study of the next lesson. In studying the lesson, each sentence should be analyzed and each word parsed, at least once, and the difficult parts should be studied until they are entirely familiar.

LESSON 114.

Participles.—Continued.

1. Examples.

1. In the pastures decked with flowers, lambs are frisking everywhere.

2. The skeleton found near my house was exhibited at the museum.

3. Leaving the military in the lobby, Cromwell entered the House.

4. He is standing on the ocean-beach, watching the crested billows.

5. The broad valley, stretching away toward the sea, was dotted with beautiful villages.

6. A strange fish caught in the China Sea was exhibited in Boston.

7. Words spoken in jest are often taken in earnest.

REMARKS.—In sentence **3**, *House* means the room where Parliament meets; the *lobby* is a waiting-room; the *military* means the soldiers.

In sentence **5**, *stretching* means the same as extending, or spreading.

2. Seat Work.

Write the analysis of the first sentence, and the parsing of all the words in the second.

LESSON 115.

Participles.—Continued.

1. Examples.

1. Noiselessly throwing the oars from the canoe, she quickly swung it round into the rapidly rolling current.

2. The dress worn by the president's wife was made in France.

3. The young chief, seeing the peril of his situation, leaped from the bark.

4. The region traversed by that mighty stream is very productive.

5. Following time down through its various windings, we are led from the death of Cain to the flood.

6. The precepts contained in that Holy Book were given by the Creator of the universe.

REMARKS.—We have seen that participles describe things by assuming *action* of them just as adjectives do by assuming *quality* or *condition*. On the other hand, participles denote *action* just like verbs, and would be verbs if they had the power to predicate the action which they denote.

Now it is because these words participate in the nature of both the verb and the adjective that they are called *participles.*

When the participle is used just before the noun which it limits, its adjective nature greatly predominates, and we almost lose sight of the action denoted by it. It is then called a **participial adjective.** The first sentence of this lesson affords an example of a participial adjective.

In sentence **3,** *peril* names a condition of danger. *Situation* names that to which the peril pertained.

In sentence **5,** *time* is compared to a stream.

2. Seat Work.

Write a composition.

LESSON 116.

Actions and Qualities Named.

1. Instruction.

1. *Walking* is a healthful exercise.
2. Nathan was condemned for *stealing*.
3. *Gentleness* is becoming.

In the first sentence above, we predicate something of the act of walking; and the word *walking* names that action.

In the second sentence, *stealing* names the action for which Nathan was condemned, and *for* shows the relation of the act of stealing to the act of being condemned.

In the third sentence, we predicate something of the quality called gentleness; and the word *gentleness* names the quality.

2. Exercises.

(*a.*) Name the actions and qualities denoted by the following words :—

EXAMPLES.—Walk, think, write, talk, select, array, destroy, fulfill, rapid, sublime, weak, timid, accomplish, great, grand, true, strong, high, delicate, mighty.

Participles used to name actions are called **participial nouns.**

(*b.*) Analyze and parse the following—

EXAMPLES.

1. Wisdom is the principal thing.
2. The sighing of the wind among the branches makes mournful music.
3. Arnold is despised for betraying his country.
4. We heard the roaring of the cataract.
5. Bonaparte was noted for his indomitable perseverance.
6. They dropped their lines in the lazy tide,
   Drawing up haddock and mottled cod.
   —*Whittier.*
7. All the woodland's voices meet,
   Mingled with its murmurs sweet.

MODELS FOR PARSING.

Sentence 1.

Wisdom.—N., com., abstract, 3d, s., n.; subject of the sentence, and therefore put in the nominative case.

Sentence 2.

Sighing.—N., com., participial, 3d, s., n.; subject of the sentence, and therefore put in the nominative case.

Sentence 3.

Betraying.—N., com., participial, 3d, s., n.; object of the preposition *for*, and therefore put in the objective case.

Country.—N., com., 3d, s., n.; object of the action expressed by the participial noun *betraying*, and therefore put in the objective case.

Sentence 4.

Roaring.—N., com., participial, 3d, s., n.; object of the action denoted by the verb *heard*, and therefore put in the objective case.

3. Seat Work.

Write five sentences, each containing a *participial noun;* and five, each containing an *abstract noun.*

LESSON 117.

Participial and Abstract Nouns.

1. Examples.

1. Earnestness always gives promise of success.
2. Barnstable well understood the captain's reason for adopting this course.
3. Goodness is necessary to true greatness.
4. Eating too often is injurious to health.
5. Writing letters employs his leisure hours.
6. He employs his leisure hours in writing letters.

7. The rivalry between Edom and Israel began with Esau and Jacob, the ancestral founders of the two nations.

8. And then in a twinkling I heard on the roof
The prancing and pawing of each little hoof.

2. Seat Work.

Write the parsing of the verbs and participial nouns in the next lesson.

LESSON 118.

Participial and Abstract Nouns.—Continued.

1. Examples.

1. My friend is engaged in collecting botanical specimens.

2. A net made of thongs was employed in capturing game.

3. Was it the wind above the smoke-flue, muttering down into the wigwam?

4. Kindly caring for the sick is a noble work.

5. The sudden sinking of the mercury betokened a storm.

6. Hastening to the window, I was startled at the approach of twenty armed men, bearing a litter with a crimson cloth spread over it.

7. Turning to my friend, I chided him for deceiving me.

2. Seat Work.

Write the analysis of sentence 6 in the next lesson, and the parsing of all the participles and participial nouns.

LESSON 119.

Participial and Abstract Nouns.—Continued.

1. Examples.

1. Goodness is a virtue.

2. Singing in the open air expands the lungs.

3. Why are you so careless in studying these lessons?

4. Suddenly comes the darkness down, with hardly a pause in its coming.

5. Her courage arrested the king's fury.

6. Supporting his rude civilization by hunting, the Red Man waited for the coming of the pale-faced races.

7. He looked up from his writing.

8. Jerusalem, the city of the great king, is glorious for situation.

2. Seat Work.

Write seven sentences each containing a participial noun that has an object.

LESSON 120.

Participial and Abstract Nouns.—Continued.

1. Examples.

1. The beauty of holiness rests over it, softening his features.

2. The Captain continued his reading.

3. I wait with a thrill in every vein
For the coming of the hurricane.

4. I hear the rushing of the blast.

5. He felt the breath of the morning breeze, blowing over the meadows brown.

6. Turning southward, and galloping over a narrow plain encircled by hills, we soon came in sight of Bethlehem.

7. He heard the barking of the farmer's dog.

8. You are an excellent scholar, having skill in the turning of phrases.

9. Through each branch-enwoven skylight,
Speaks He in the breeze.

2. Seat Work.

Write the parsing of all the verbal nouns in the next lesson.

LESSON 121.

Second Form of Naming Action.

1. Instruction.

In the preceding lessons, the names of actions all end in *ing;* but names of actions frequently take another form. We may say, "*Singing* is pleasant," or "*To sing* is pleasant." The latter form is called the **infinitive.** When the infinitive is used to name an action, it is called a **verbal noun.** The participial noun is also a verbal noun.

A verbal noun is a participle or infinitive used to name an action.

1. *Skating by moonlight is enchanting.*
2. *To skate by moonlight is enchanting.*
3. *It is enchanting to skate by moonlight.*

These sentences all express the same thought. In the first, the *participial form* of the verbal noun is used as the subject; in the second, the *infinitive form* is used in the same way, and with the same meaning. In the third sentence, the pronoun *it* is made the subject, and the verbal noun is put in apposition, to explain what is meant by *it*.

2. Examples.

1. To forgive is divine.
2. To err is human.
3. It is human to err.
4. It is wrong to excite false hopes.
5. To do good is a privilege.
6. It is natural to shrink from danger.
7. It grieves me much to see this quarrel.
8. Use your knowledge by gratuitously instructing some humble friend.
9. It is not wise to spend too much time in amusement.

MODELS FOR PARSING.
Sentence 2.

To err is a noun, com., verbal, infinitive form, 3d, sing., neu.; subject of the sentence, and therefore put in the nominative case.

Sentence 3.

To err is a noun, com., verbal, infinitive form, 3d, sing., neu.; used to explain what is meant by *it*, and therefore put in the same case.

3. Seat Work.

Write seven sentences each containing an infinitive verbal noun and a noun in apposition.

LESSON 122.

Verbal Nouns.

1. Examples.

1. It is our duty to love our enemies.
2. To write under such circumstances is discouraging.
3. Always to give vent to our feelings is ruinous to happiness.
4. It is wrong to cherish hatred.
5. Sings the blackened log a tune,
   Learned in some forgotten June
     From a school-boy at his play.
6. To make new discoveries was the universal passion.
7. The prophets accused the Edomites of cherishing toward their brethren the Israelites a perpetual hatred, and of rejoicing in their calamity.
8. To die in such a cause is glorious.
9. The employment of some poor mortals is to cultivate a bad temper.

2. Seat Work.

Study the next lesson.

————— •◄► —————

LESSON 123.

Review.

1. Questions and Requirements.

1. What do we call a word that denotes action and predicates it?
2. What do we call a word that assumes action, but has no power to predicate it?
3. Give sentences containing both these kinds of words.
4. When is a participle said to be present?
5. When is it said to be past?
6. When is it said to be active?
7. When is it passive?

8. Give five sentences containing present active participles.

9. Give five sentences containing present passive participles.

10. Give a sentence containing a past passive participle.

· 11. Participles commonly participate in the nature of what two parts of speech ?

12. How is a participle like an adjective ?

13. How is it like a verb ?

14. Give a sentence containing a participle that participates in the nature of a verb and a noun.

15. What are such participles called ?

16. Make sentences that shall contain the words *walking*, *parsing*, *writing*, used as participial nouns.

17. Give sentences in which the same words shall be used as ordinary participles ; that is, to limit nouns.

18. Give sentences each containing a transitive participle and its object.

19. Give sentences each containing a participial noun and its object.

20. Parse the noun and its object.

21. Select or make sentences each containing a phrase that has a transitive participial noun for the object of its preposition.

22. Parse the preposition, the participial noun, and its object.

23. What two kinds of verbal nouns are there ?

24. Show how a *participial verbal noun* may be changed to an *infinitive verbal noun.*

25. Give sentences that have a participial verbal noun for subject.

26. So change these sentences that the infinitive verbal noun shall be in apposition with the subject.

27. What are abstract nouns ?

28. Give examples.

2. Seat Work.

Write a composition telling what you have learned about participles, abstract nouns, and verbal nouns.

LESSON 124.

Coördinate Words.

1. Instruction.

1. *Charles **is a musician.***
2. *Joseph **is a musician.***

In the examples above, the same thing is predicated of two different persons; so the predicates in the two sentences are just alike.

Now we may express both these thoughts in one sentence, by putting the subjects one after the other with *and* between them, and using the predicate only once. Thus :—

> *Charles and Joseph **are musicians.***

In what person and number is the subject of each sentence as given at first?

How many separate subjects has the sentence that we have formed by uniting the first two into one?

Of how many persons are we talking in this last sentence?

What pronoun might be put in place of these subjects?

So we see that two subjects taken together are the same as a plural subject, and must be represented by a pronoun in the plural number. Since this is so, we change *is* to *are* when we combine the two sentences into one.

In what person and number is *is?*

In what person and number is *are?*

Why do we drop the word *a* in combining the sentences?

In the sentence, *Charles and Joseph are musicians,*

the subjects are equal in rank. The same thought is predicated of both. They have the same relation to the predicate; it is their common property, for it belongs to one as much as to the other. So these subjects, and all other words used in a similar way, are said to be **coördinate.**

Two coördinate words make **a couplet,** and three or more make a **series.**

The word **and** placed between the terms of a couplet or series shows that the terms are *coördinate,* and is therefore called a **coördinate conjunction,** that is, a *joiner* of terms that are of the same order, and in the same office.

2. Exercises.

(*a.*) Make seven sentences each having two subjects.

(*b.*) Combine the following sentences into one, supposing the young women to be sisters.

  1. Constance is traveling in Europe with her father.
  2. Gertrude is traveling in Europe with her father.
  3. Eleanor is traveling in Europe with her father.

(*c.*) Separate the following sentences into others that will express the same thoughts, and yet have but one subject each.

  1. Chaucer, Spenser, Shakspeare, and Milton were eminent English poets.
  2. Europe, Asia, and Africa are the grand divisions of the eastern continent.
  3. Fruits, grains, and grasses are produced in abundance.

(*d.*) Analyze the following—

EXAMPLES.

  1. France and England are rival nations.
  2. Russia, Prussia, Sweden, and Denmark border on the Baltic Sea.
  3. Peter and James and John went up with Christ into the Mount of Transfiguration.
  4. Cool shades and dews refresh my lonely way.

MODEL FOR ANALYSIS.

Ex.—Mountain and moor were buried in snow.

1. **Mountain** and **moor** are the subjects.
2. *Were buried* is the predicate.
3. **And** shows that *mountain* and *moor* are equal in rank and alike related to the predicate.
4. *In snow* tells what covers mountain and moor. *Snow* names the substance employed, and *in* shows its relation to the act of burying.

3. Seat Work.

Study the next lesson, and fulfill its requirements.

LESSON 125.

Coördinate Conjunctions.

1. Instruction.

When we wish to predicate two or more things of the same person or object, we use the subject but once, and combine the predicates as we did the subjects in the last lesson. Thus :—

1. *Mountains are lofty and grand.*
2. *James reads, writes, and ciphers.*
3. *The horse is a kind and faithful animal.*

Convert the first and third sentences each into two, and the second into three.

Make other sentences each having more than one predicate.

Select sentences having coördinate terms in the predicate.

So, also, a verb or a preposition may have a couplet or series of objects; and a verb may be limited by a couplet of adverbs, as seen below.

1. *The sun gives light and heat.*
2. *He lectured in New York, Pittsburg, and Albany.*
3. *Hendrick writes easily and rapidly.*

2. Examples.

1. We admired the beautiful landscape, plucked the bright autumn leaves, and rested under the great oak.

2. The goodness of God calls for gratitude, love, and obedience.

3. We crossed mountain, lake, and river.

4. From the chimney-top, ascending and slowly expanding into the evening air, a thin, blue column of smoke arose.

5. Is it a good practice to wake at night and sleep by day?

6. Heard ye the crashing, long and loud,
Of the chariot of God in the thunder-cloud?

MODEL FOR PARSING.

Ex.—He wandered through forest, glade, and glen.

1. **And** is a conjunction, *coördinate;* it is said to join *forest, glade,* and *glen,* because it shows them to be in the same office. They are all objects of the preposition *through.*

3. Seat Work.

Study the next lesson, and select couplets and series whose terms are joined by the different conjunctions explained in that lesson.

LESSON 126.

Special Signification of And, But, Yet, Or, and Nor.

1. Instruction.

These conjunctions are all alike in their general office of showing that the terms joined by them are coördinate; but each has a special signification of its own.

1. *And* implies that what follows is additional to what has gone before.

2. *But* implies that what follows it, is opposed to what has gone before, or that it is in some way adverse to it in meaning.

3. *Yet* suggests that what follows it, is contrary to what would be expected from that which has gone before.

4. *Or* shows that the parts joined by it are to be considered separately.

5. *Nor* is equivalent to *and not*, and is usually employed to prevent the repetition of a negative word.

2. Examples.

1. The twilight deepened and darkened around.
2. He was tall and thin, but not ill-made.
3. The thing is not impossible nor improbable.
4. The laborers turn the crumbling ground,
   Or drop the yellow seed.
5. I marked his firm yet weary tread.
6. No welcome greeted our return, nor clang of martial tread.
7. 'Tis a bleak, wild hill, but green and bright
   In the summer warmth and the midday light.
   —*Bryant, p.* 109.
8. Long they looked and feared and wept within his distant home.

REMARKS.—In analyzing sentence **2**, say that **but** shows that *ill-made* is equal in rank with *tall* and *thin*, and in the same office. It also shows that what follows it, is opposed in meaning to what goes before,—the qualities denoted by *tall* and *thin* exist in the person, while that denoted by *ill-made* does *not* exist in him.

In sentence **3**, **nor** shows that *impossible* and *improbable* are equal in rank, and have the same relation to the subject. It also gives a negative meaning to the second term, just as *not* does to the first.

In sentence **4**, **or** shows that *turn* and *drop* are equal in rank and alike related to the subject. It also shows that the two actions are to be considered separately: the actions either occurred at different times, or a part of the laborers were performing one action, while the other part were performing the other.

In sentence **5**, **yet** shows that *firm* and *weary* are equal in rank, and alike related to *tread;* it also intimates that the quality denoted by *weary* would not be expected to exist in connection with the quality denoted by *firm*.

In sentence **6, nor** joins the two subjects, *welcome* and *clang*, and shows them to be alike related to the predicate; it also gives a negative meaning to the second, as *no* does to the first.

In sentence **7, and** is understood between *bleak* and *wild*. **But** shows that the two adjectives following it are equal in rank with *bleak* and *wild*, and in the same relation to *hill*. It also shows that the qualities denoted by the adjectives following it are opposed in nature to the qualities denoted by the adjectives preceding it, or, at least, that they are very different.

3. Seat Work.

Study the next lesson *thoroughly*.

LESSON 127.

Punctuation of the Couplet and Series.

1. Instruction.

THE COUPLET.

1. *Flake after flake they sink in the **dark** and **silent** lake.*
2. ***Faintly, slowly,** the bells for vespers rung.*
3. *Then they **retired,** and **sank** into the deep*
   And helpless imbecility of sleep.
4. *Rivers have small **beginnings, or sources.***
5. *He could **write,** and **cipher** too.*

Each of the above sentences contains a couplet.

In the *first sentence,* the terms of the couplet are joined by the conjunction, and are not limited by other words; so no mark of punctuation is required.

In the *second sentence,* the conjunction is omitted, and so the terms are separated by the comma.

In the *third sentence,* the conjunction is not omitted,

but the limitations of the two verbs are very different, both in form and meaning. *Retired* is limited only by *then*, a simple adverb of time ; while *sank*, the other term of the couplet, is limited by a long, complex phrase, denoting place; hence the terms are separated by the comma.

In the *fourth sentence*, the terms of the couplet are alike in meaning. *Sources* is only another name for *beginnings ;* for the source of a river is its beginning. In all such cases, the terms of the couplet should be separated by the comma, and another comma should be placed after the second term, unless some other mark of punctuation is required in that place.

In the *fifth sentence*, the second term of the couplet is *emphatically distinguished*, and for this reason the terms are separated by the comma.

THE SERIES.

1. ***Dreamlike,*** *and* ***indistinct,*** *and* ***strange*** *were all things around them.*

2. *Ever unmoved they stand,*
   Solemn, eternal, *and* ***proud.***

3. *The silence was* ***vast, measureless, complete.***

4. ***Loud*** *and* ***sudden*** *and* ***near*** *the note of the whip-poor-will sounded.*

Each of the above sentences contains a series.

In the *first sentence*, the conjunction occurs between the terms throughout; in the *second*, it occurs between the last two only ; while in the *third*, it is omitted altogether. It may be noticed, however, that in all these cases, the terms of the series are separated by the comma. But when the conjunction occurs between the terms throughout, the comma may sometimes be omitted, as seen in the fourth sentence.

In the *second sentence*, the adjectives, *solemn, eternal,* and *proud*, taken together, make an adjective element that is not restrictive, and so the whole group is set off from the rest of the sentence by a comma.

2. Examples.

1. His affections were high, and pure, and generous.

2. The banks of the lovely basin, at its outlet, or southern end, were steep but not high.

3. They are few, but memorable.

4. Studies serve for delight, for ornament, and for ability.

5. A hearty, hale old man was Benedict Bellefontaine, the wealthiest farmer of Grand-Pre'.

6. Here he paused, and against the trunk
   Of a tall, gray linden leant.

3. Questions and Remarks.

1. Why are the terms of the first couplet in the second sentence separated by the comma ?

2. Why is the second term followed by the comma ?

3. Why are the terms of the couplet separated in the third sentence ?

4. In sentence **4,** each term of the series is a phrase.

5. What appositional phrase is found in the fifth sentence ?

6. Why is it set off ?

7. What couplet is found in the same sentence ?

8. Why are its terms separated ?

9. *Hearty, hale,* and *old* are adjectives, added to the noun *man;* but *old* is more intimately related to the noun *man* than the other two are. This may be proved by supplying the conjunction. If we should say, "A hearty *and* hale *and* old man," the sentence would seem very awkward. It would not express the thought intended. But we may say, "A hearty *and* hale old man," and it seems all right. The mind first applies the quality denoted by *old,* and then the conception of an *old man* is modified by the qualities denoted by the other adjectives. So in the punctuation, we do not regard the three adjectives as a series. But the first two are taken as a couplet limiting the conception, already formed, of an old man.

10. How many couplets in the sixth sentence ?

11. What is the first ?
12. Why are its terms separated ?
13. What is the second couplet ?
14. Why are its terms separated ?

4. Seat Work.

Study the next lesson very carefully, especially the remarks.

LESSON 128.

Coördinate Terms.

Suggestion.—Do not forget to give reasons for the punctuation of each sentence in all the lessons from this point onward.

1. Examples.

1. His hand was ready and willing.
2. His solemn manner and his words touched the deep, mysterious chords.
3. Meek meadow-sweet and violet of the ground
   Lean lovingly against the humble stone.
4. A good lad and cheerful was Joseph.
5. A calm and lovely paradise is Italy.
6. He started from his seat, and gazed around.

REMARKS.—In sentence **1,** we say that his *hands* are ready and willing, when we mean that the *man* is ready and willing to work with his hands. The hands are made to mean the whole man. This taking a part to represent the whole is called a figure of **Synecdoche.**

In sentence **2,** we compare the emotions to the chords of a musical instrument, and the agitation of feeling produced by the solemn words and manner, to the trembling of the chords when they are touched, or when the wind passes over them.

The chords are called deep, mysterious chords, because they produce deep, mysterious sounds.

Deep, mysterious sounds must mean those that are low

and long,—such as we could imagine might come from some deep place, like a cave, full of mystery because so deep, dark, and winding that we know not what mysteries may be concealed there.

In sentence **3**, the flowers are called *meek* because they grow close to the ground and appear by their drooping to avoid notice, just as meek people, by their quiet ways, avoid attention.

They are said to ·lean *lovingly*, because they assume an attitude that would indicate love in beings that can exercise affection.

The stone is *humble*, because it is cheap and plain, and suited to humble people.

In sentence **5**, Italy is called a paradise, because it is beautiful like paradise.

2. Seat Work.

Select sentences like those given for instruction in Lesson 127.

LESSON 129.

Subject of the Last Lesson Continued.

1. Examples.

1. His noontide glory fell on the corn-fields, and the orchards, and the softly-pictured wood.

2. At last a gleam of sudden fire shot up behind the walls of snow, and tipped each icy spire.

3. I am poor and old and blind.

4. Through a thin, dry mist the sun rose, broad and red.

5. On bright streams and into deep wells shone the high midsummer sun.

6. In such a home, beside the Schuylkill's wave, he dwelt in peace with God and man.

REMARKS.—In analyzing sentence **5**, say, *On bright streams and into deep wells* tells where the sun shone. *On bright streams* tells one place, and *into deep wells* tells another.

And shows that these two phrases are equal in rank and alike in their use, each being used to tell where the sun shines.

In analyzing sentence **6**, say, *with God and man* tells to whom the peace relates. *God* and *man* name those with whom he is at peace. *And* shows that God and man are alike related to peace, and *with* shows what that relation is.

2. Seat Work.

Select sentences containing couplets and series of phrases.

LESSON 130.

Coördinate Phrases.

1. Examples.

1. The notes of the robin and blue-bird are sweet upon wold and in wood.

2. The grass is still verdant on the hills and in the valleys.

3. The flowers are abundant along the margin of rivers, and in hedge-rows, and among the woods.

4. In taste, in grace, in facility, in happy invention, and in the richness and harmony of coloring, he was equal to the great masters of the renowned ages.

5. Steep is the western side, shaggy and wild with mossy trees, and pinnacles of flint, and many a hanging crag.

—*Bryant, p.* 63.

REMARK.—Coördinate phrases are punctuated in the same way as coördinate words.

2. Seat Work.

Study the next lesson, and select five sentences containing coördinate clauses.

LESSON 131.

Coördinate Clauses.

1. Examples.

1. Sudden and swift a whistling ball came out of a wood, and the voice was still.

2. The boughs in the morning wind are stirred, and the woods their songs renew.

3. The spice-lamps in the alabaster urns burned dimly, and the white and fragrant smoke curled indolently on the chamber walls.

4. Freshly the cool breath of the coming eve stole through the lattice, and the dying girl felt it upon her forehead.

5. Sorrow and silence are strong, and patient endurance is godlike.

6. The hay appeareth, and the tender grass showeth itself, and herbs of the mountains are gathered.

—*Prov.* 27:25.

7. But in the fisherman's cottage
There shines a ruddier light,
And a little face at the window
Peers out into the night.
—*Longfellow,* p. 127.

MODEL FOR ANALYSIS.

Sentence 1.

1. This sentence consists of two clauses, joined by *and* to show that they are equal in rank.

2. Since they are closely related in sense, and joined by a conjunction, they are separated by the comma.

3. The subject of the first clause, etc.

MODEL FOR PARSING.

And is a conjunction, *coördinate;* it is said to join the two clauses, because it shows them to be in the same rank, or order; they are both principal clauses.

REMARKS.—When two or more clauses are closely connected in thought, and joined by a conjunction, they are separated by the comma; unless the clauses themselves, one or more of them, contain important divisions that are separated by the comma. When the clauses are thus subdivided, the semicolon instead of the comma is placed between them.

In sentence **1,** *sudden* and *swift* are adverbs, telling how the ball came. They mean the same as *suddenly* and *swiftly,* but the poet's license allows him to leave off the *ly*.

In sentence **2,** the woods are said to renew their songs, when the meaning is that the birds renew their songs in the woods.

In sentence **3,** the smoke is said to curl indolently, because it moves slowly, like an indolent person.

In sentence **4,** the gentle breeze of evening is compared to breath, because it strikes one softly, as the breath does. It is called the breath of *evening,* because it comes with the evening—the evening produces it.

2. Seat Work.

Select sentences each containing one of the conjunctions, *and, or, nor, but, yet.*

LESSON 132.

Coördinate Constructions.

1. Examples.

1. Gentle but firm were his words of reproof.
2. They hear not, nor see, nor know.
3. Of mass or prayer there was no need.
4. Uttered not, yet comprehended,
   Is the spirit's voiceless prayer.
5. Thou changest not, but I am changed.
6. No other voice nor sound was heard.
7. Is it night, or is a storm coming on ?
8. They shouted long and loud, yet no answer came.
9. They conquered, but Bozzaris fell, bleeding at every vein.
10. Go not forth in the morning, nor in the evening.

REMARK.—In sentence **5,** the thought expressed in the second clause is adverse to that expressed in the first; for in the first the action is denied, while in the second it is affirmed.

2. Seat Work.

Select other sentences like those required in the last lesson.

LESSON 133.

Coördinate Constructions.—Continued.

1. Examples.

1. She breathes, but she speaks not.
2. Few were his words of rebuke, but deep in the hearts of his people
   Sank they, and sobs of contrition succeeded the passionate outbreak.
              —*Longfellow, p.* 104.
3. The day brought no food nor shelter for him.
4. So came the autumn, and passed, and the winter; yet Gabriel came not.
5. No more thou sittest on thy tawny hills
   In indolent repose,
   Or pour'st the crystal of a thousand rills
   Down from thy house of snows.
              —*Bayard Taylor.*
6. Speech is silvern, but silence is golden.
7. Deep is the sleep of the dead;
   Low is their pillow of dust.

REMARKS.—In sentence **2,** the writer uses the word *hearts* to denote the feelings of the people. He says that the words sank into their hearts, when he means that the sentiments expressed by the words affected their feelings to such a degree as not to be easily forgotten, just as anything that sinks deeply into a body, is not easily removed.

In sentence **3,** the day is said to bring no food nor shelter, because none was found on that day.

Sentence **4** has two subjects in the first clause, and the two actions denoted by *came* and *passed* are predicated of both of them. The meaning is that autumn and winter came and passed.

In sentence **5,** the writer speaks to California as he would to a person. In a preceding stanza, he says,—

> "O fair young land! the youngest, fairest far
> Of which our world can boast."

And in the next,—

> "How art thou conquered, tamed in all the pride
> Of savage beauty still!
> How brought, O panther of the splendid hide,
> To know thy master's will!"

Then follows the sentence which forms the subject of this remark.

In sentence **6,** *speech* is called silvern because it is valuable—a precious gift; and *silence* is said to be golden because in some instances it is better than speech.

In sentence **7,** the conjunction is omitted between the two clauses, and so they are separated by the semicolon.

2. Seat Work.

Study the next lesson, and select sentences containing *associated conjunctions.*

----•----

LESSON 134.

Associated Conjunctions.

1. Instruction.

It is midsummer, but yet the air is cold.

The clauses of this sentence are joined by *but yet.* *But* shows them to be equal in rank and adverse in meaning. *Yet* is added to show that what follows would not be expected from what has gone before.

Still, notwithstanding, nevertheless, else, and some other words are used in a similar way, either for emphasis, or to suggest the nature of the thought that is to follow.

Some of these associated conjunctions seem much like adverbs; but these words are employed chiefly to show the *relation* of thoughts rather than to modify them.

2. Examples.

1. They were silenced, but yet they yielded not.

2. Not a breath crept through the rosy air, and yet the forest leaves were stirred with prayer.

3. I never knew thee nor thy peers;
    And yet my eyes are filled with tears.

4. Every pine, and fir, and hemlock
    Wore ermine too dear for an earl,
    And the poorest twig on the elm-tree
    Was ridged inch deep with pearl.
                     —*James Russell Lowell.*

5. It was a lodge of ample size,
    But strange of structure and device.
                     —*Scott, p.* 193.

6. Now from the stream the rocks recede,
    But leave between no sunny mead.
                     —*Ib.. p.* 308.

MODEL FOR ANALYSIS.

Sentence 1.

This sentence consists of two clauses.

But yet shows them to be equal in rank, somewhat adverse in meaning, and that the thought expressed in the second is not what would be expected from the statement made in the first.

MODEL FOR PARSING.

But is a conjunction, coördinate, it shows that the clauses are equal in rank, and somewhat adverse in meaning. **Yet** is a conjunction, coördinate, associated with *but* to show that the thought which follows would not be expected from what goes before.

3. Seat Work.

Select sentences containing *correlative conjunctions.*

LESSON 135.

Correlative Conjunctions.

1. Instruction.

1. **Both** Jane **and** Lucy *were present.*
2. **Either** Philip **or** his brother *is going to Europe.*

In sentence **1**, *both* is used with *and* to show that *Jane* and *Lucy* are alike related to the predicate. The meaning would be the same if the word *both* were omitted; but *both* seems to strengthen the word *and*, and make the idea of the relation more prominent.

In sentence **2**, *either* is used as *both* is in sentence **1**. *Either* gives emphasis to the idea that Philip and his brother are to be regarded separately with respect to the action predicated.

Such words are called **correlative conjunctions.**

The introductory correlative gives emphasis to the relation expressed by the principal one, by awakening an expectation of such a relation.

2. Examples.

1. He is either sick or fatigued.
2. Neither the Austrians nor the French were victorious.
3. He either left the key in the door, or else the robber had a false key.
4. Not only the prime minister but also the king was expected.
5. Not only am I instructed by this exercise, but I am also invigorated.
6. Both religion and reason condemn us.
7. Not only the wise and the learned but also the common people heard him gladly.
8. For Romans in Rome's quarrel spared neither land nor gold,
   Nor son nor wife, nor limb nor life, in the brave days of old.

MODELS FOR PARSING.

Ex.—Neither truthfulness nor elegance was sacrificed.

Neither is a conjunction, coördinate, correlative to *nor*, and used to give emphasis to the relation expressed by that word.

Nor is a conjunction, coördinate, correlative to *neither;* it shows that *truthfulness* and *elegance* are equal in rank, and alike related to the predicate. It also gives a negative meaning to the second term as *neither* does to the first.

Ex.—Not only is energy required but perseverance also.

Not only is a conjunction, coördinate; it is correlative to *but also*, and awakens an expectation of the relation denoted by those words.

But also is a conjunction, coördinate, correlative to *not only*. *But* is the principal conjunction and *also* is associated with it.

Note.—This method of parsing these words is based upon the best of authority, and seems to be, on the whole, most consistent and profitable. The attempt to dispose of some of them as adverbs has not been very satisfactory, as it leads into a minute and puzzling analysis, which seems to be not only perplexing and doubtful, but practically useless.

Ex.—Both energy and perseverance are required.

Both is a conjunction, coördinate; correlative to *and*, and used to give emphasis to the relation expressed by that word.

And is a conjunction, coördinate, correlative to *both;* it is used to show that *energy* and *perseverance* are equal in rank and alike related to the predicate.

2. Seat Work.

Study for review.

.LESSON 136.

Review.

1. Questions and Requirements.

1. What way have we of shortening the expression when we wish to predicate the same thought of two or more persons or things?

2. Give examples.

3. In what way may we sometimes shorten the expression when we .wish to predicate several thoughts of the same person or thing?

4. Give examples.

5. Give other examples of coördinate words.

6. Why are these words said to be coördinate?

7. What term is applied to two coördinate words taken together? To more than two?

8. What class of words is employed to show that the terms of a couplet or series are equal in rank and in the same office?

9. Give a list of the words most commonly employed in this way.

10. In what respect are they all alike in their use?

11. What is the special signification of each?

12. When should the terms of the couplet be separated by the comma?

13. How should the terms of a series be separated?

14. What exception sometimes occurs?

15. What kind of adjective elements are set off by the comma?—*Those that are not restrictive.*

2. Seat Work.

(*a.*) Select two adjective elements of each of the following kinds :—

1. An adjective phrase consisting of adjectives joined coördinately.

2. An adjective phrase introduced by a preposition that has a couplet or series of nouns for its object.

3. An adjective phrase that consists of an adjective word having other words or phrases limiting it.

4. A participial phrase.

5. An appositional phrase.

(*b.*) Notice how these phrases are punctuated, and tell why they are so punctuated.

LESSON 137.

Review.

1. Questions and Requirements.

1. Give sentences each containing a couplet of phrases.

2. Give a sentence containing a series of phrases.

3. Give sentences each containing two coördinate clauses.

4. When are coördinate clauses separated by the comma ?

5. When one or more of the coördinate clauses are separated into important divisions by the comma, what mark is used to separate the clauses from one another ?

6. When coördinate clauses have no conjunction between them, what mark is commonly used to separate them ?

7. How are coördinate phrases punctuated ?

8. Give sentences that will illustrate the use of associated conjunctions.

9. Analyze such a sentence, and parse the conjunctions.

10. Give sentences that will illustrate the use of correlative conjunctions.

11. Analyze such a sentence, and parse the conjunctions.

12. Give a sentence in which correlative and associated conjunctions are used together.

13. Parse all the words in the following examples.

2. Examples.

1.   Looking down,
  I behold the shadowy crown
  Of the dark and haunted wood.

2. Is it changed, or am I changed?

3. Neither highway nor human habitation appeared, but still we pressed on through biting cold and blinding storm.

3. Seat Work.

Write a *composition* on what you have learned about verbs.

LESSON 138.

Adjectives Limiting a Noun Understood.

1. Instruction.

1. *Many* were hurt by the accident.
2. *Some* said one thing, and *some another.*

1. In the first sentence, the thought is that many *people* were hurt by the accident. We omit the word people, because the meaning is just as clear without it. The omitted word is said to be *understood,* and the omission of such words is called **ellipsis.** Restoring the omitted word is what we call *supplying the ellipsis.*

2. What words are understood in the second sentence?

3. Supply the ellipses.

4. In the first sentence, the real subject is the noun *persons* or *people* understood; but sometimes the word *many* is called the subject, because it seems to *represent* the noun understood. For the present, at least, we will say that the noun understood is the subject.

5. How many clauses are there in the second sentence?

6. How are these clauses joined?

7. What is the subject of each ?

8. What is the verb in the second clause ?

9. What is the object of that verb ?

2. Examples.

1. One was killed, and several were injured.

2. Eternal life is offered to all men, yet few accept it.

3. Two were excused, and three were punished.

4. Many are called, but few are chosen.

5. This is a bright day.

6. This book is valuable, but that is worthless.

7. Allured by hope, or driven by fear, all crowded to the altar-rail.

MODEL FOR PARSING.
Sentence 1.

One is an adjective, limiting; added to a noun understood, to tell *how many.*

Those who prefer it can use the following—

MODEL.

One is an·adjective, limiting; added to a noun understood, to tell how many. In representing the noun understood, it becomes a *substantive,* and may be regarded as the *subject* of the sentence.

REMARKS.—A *substantive* is a noun or anything that has the office of a noun. All pronouns are substantives, and sometimes even clauses become so, as will be seen hereafter.

Whenever the second model for parsing is used, the analysis should be made to harmonize with it. Whether we should use this model or the first, depends upon whether we regard the adjective as representing its noun or not. It is more commonly taken *to represent* the noun understood; but this view involves some inconsistencies, as will be seen from remarks on sentence **1,** of Lesson 140.

Practically, it makes very little difference which view we take. The first is more simple, but the second is more common.

3. Seat Work.

Select ten sentences each containing an adjective or a possessive pronoun limiting a noun understood.

LESSON 139.

Possessive Pronouns Limiting a Noun Understood.

1. Instruction.

1. *He refused my offer, but accepted* ***John's.***
2. *Both my child and thy child are lost.*
3. *The fault is not only* ***mine*** *but* ***thine*** *also.*
4. ***His*** *was a checkered life.*

Supply the ellipsis in the first sentence above.

Point out the possessive pronouns in the second sentence, and notice how they are spelled.

Re-write the third sentence, supplying the ellipses.

On supplying the ellipses, what change did you have to make in the possessive pronouns?

By this, we see that *my* and *thy* are changed to *mine* and *thine* when used to limit a noun understood.

Anciently, *mine* and *thine* were used when the noun was expressed, as may be seen in the Bible.

The possessive noun does not change its form when used to limit a noun understood, as may be seen in sentence 1 above; and by supplying the ellipsis in sentence 4, it appears that the same is true of the pronoun *his*.

Make sentences in which the possessive case of the pronouns *we, you, her,* and *they* shall be used to limit nouns understood.

Supply the ellipses, and see what change will be required in the possessive pronouns.

The adjective **other,** when used to limit a plural noun understood, changes its form by adding *s.* Thus :—

He saved ***others,*** *himself he cannot save.*

None is seldom used to limit a noun expressed. It is peculiar in other respects; for, although it seems to be made up of *no* and *one*, it requires a plural verb after it; as,—

None ***are*** *free from sin.*

But whenever the noun is expressed, it is singular, and is followed by a singular verb, as seen in the example below.

He swam the Eske River, where **ford** *there was* **none.**

—*Scott.*

Note.—In this example *there* is merely a word of euphony. and *none* limits *ford;* but if it came immediately before its noun it would be changed to *no.* Thus: *There was no ford.*

One and **other** take the possessive sign whenever a noun in the possessive case is understood after them. Thus :—

    1. *It is hard to control* **one's** *thoughts.*

    2. *Each strove to take the* **other's** *life.*

Either and *neither* should be used with reference to *two* things *only.* *Any* or *none* should be used when more that two things are referred to.

2. Examples.

1. You took mine and left yours.
2. The cattle upon a thousand hills are mine.
3. I feel his icy fingers, clasping mine amid the darkness.
4. The lark's bold song comes from the skies, but hers comes from the earth.
5. His, not mine, are the gifts.
6. Those men are fishermen, and the boats on the beach are theirs. Ours are moored in the shadow of that great rock.

In sentence **5,** we may transpose, and supply the ellipsis, thus :—

The gifts are his, **and are** *not mine.*

But it seems as well to regard the copula already expressed as showing that both thoughts are predicated, and the negative adverb *not* as having the power to cause it to predicate a denial of the second condition.

MODEL FOR PARSING.
Sentence 1.

Mine is a pronoun, personal, first per., sing. num. It does not distinguish sex. By alluding to the speaker, it tells to whom the thing belongs that would be named by the noun understood, and is therefore put in the possessive case.

REMARKS.—In sentence **2**, *a thousand* tells how many hills are meant. *Thousand* names one of the great orders of numbers, and *a* shows, that just *one* thousand is meant.

Thousand is here used, not to denote a definite number, but a *great many.*

Note.—A pronoun is said to be **personal** when we can tell by its form whether it denotes the speaker, the person spoken to, or the person spoken of. None but personal pronouns have thus far been used in the examples of these lessons. Relative and interrogative pronouns will be introduced hereafter.

3. Seat Work.

Write out the parsing of the nouns and pronouns in the next lesson.

LESSON 140.

Subject of the Last Two Lessons Continued.

1. Examples.

1. These books are mine, those are yours, the others are Luther's.

2. This is the forest primeval.

3. On their knees they received the queen's blessing, some kissing her hands, others her mantle.

4. There is a monk in Melrose tower,
    He speaketh word to none.

5. These and many more with king Olaf sailed the seas.

6. Many run well for a season, but few persevere to the end.

7. The gray mist left the mountain side,
    The torrent show'd its glistening pride ;
    Invisible in fleckéd sky,
    The lark sent down her revelry ;
    The blackbird and the speckled thrush

Good-morrow gave from brake and bush;
In answer cooed the cushat dove
Her notes of peace, and rest, and love.
                              —*Scott*, p. 202.

REMARKS.—Some parse such pronouns as *mine*, *yours*, etc., as compound in their office, representing both the possessor and the thing possessed. Such parsing is not a little awkward and inconvenient, as may be seen by parsing the word *mine* in sentence **1.** Thus:—

Representing the *possessor*, it is in the 1st person; representing the *things possessed*, it is in the 3d person: representing the *possessor*, it is in the singular number; representing the *things possessed*, it is in the plural number: and again, representing the *possessor*, it is masculine or feminine gender; representing the *things possessed*, it is in the neuter gender: representing the *possessor*, it is in the possessive case; and representing the *things possessed*, it is in the nominative case.

A close study of sentence **1,** will also make this method of parsing appear *inconsistent;* for if *mine* and *yours* represent the noun understood after them, *Luther's* must do the same, and must be parsed as *mine* is, above. This would probably be carrying the matter a little farther than any would wish to carry it, even for the sake of avoiding ellipses.

Again: if the pronouns *mine* and *yours* do not represent the nouns understood after them, why should the adjectives *those* and *others* be regarded as representing the nouns understood after them?

2. Seat Work.

Select ten sentences containing nouns independent by address.

LESSON 141.

Nouns Independent by Address.

1. Instruction.

1. Sometimes we use a person's name for the sake of getting his attention. Thus :—

James, you are too bold.

2. Not unfrequently we use the name of the person with whom we are conversing, not so much 'for the purpose of gaining his attention, as for giving earnestness to what we are saying.

3. In the sentence,—

You are wrong, Julia,

the word *Julia* names the person spoken to, and tells who is meant by *you.* It is probable that several persons are present, and that the speaker wishes to show *which* one he is addressing, and so speaks her name.

4. Since it has no part in bringing out the thought expressed in the sentence, a noun thus used in addressing a person, is said to be **independent by address.**

2. Examples.

1. Thou speakest truly, poet.
2. Come hither, my little daughter.
3. Your coming, friends, revives me.
4. Fight on, brave, true heart, through dark fortune and through bright.
5. Come, gentle dreams.
6. Spare me, dread angel of reproof.
7. Stay, rivulet, nor haste so soon from the lovely vale.
8. Mary, be a good girl.
9. I greet thee, bonny boat!
10. England, with all thy faults, I love thee still.
11. Weep, Albin! to death and captivity led.
12. Roll on, thou deep and dark blue Ocean—roll!
13. Come back, come back, Horatius!

MODELS FOR ANALYSIS.

Ex.—John, you are wanted at the office.

1. *You* is the subject.
2. *Are wanted* is the predicate.
3. *At the office* tells where you are wanted.
4. **John** is used to gain the attention of the person addressed.

Ex.—Philip, come here.

1. *Thou* or *you* understood is the subject.
2. *Come* is the predicate.
3. **Philip** is used to gain the attention of the person addressed.
4. *Here* tells where he is requested to come.

MODEL FOR PARSING.

Philip is a noun, proper, 2d, s., mas.; independent by address, and therefore put in the nominative case.

REMARKS.—This lesson contains several examples in which inanimate objects are addressed as though they had intelligence, and could understand language. Since we speak to them as though they were persons, they are said to be **personified.**

In sentence **4,** the heart is taken to represent the whole person.

A noun independent by address should, together with its limiting words, be set off by the comma, and when exclamatory, should be followed by an exclamation point.

3. Seat Work.

Study the next lesson, and select ten sentences each containing a noun independent by address, and accompanied by an interjection.

LESSON 142.

Address Accompanied by Emotion.

1. Instruction.

A noun independent by address is often accompanied by a word used to express deep feeling or sudden emotion. Thus:—

O Lord, thou art very great!

A word so used wholly to express emotion is called an **interjection.**

2. Examples.

1. O dread and cruel deep, reveal the secret concealed beneath thy waves!

2. O brothers! pray for me.

3. Fear not, O little flock!

4. Your voiceless lips, O flowers! are living preachers.

5. Keep, O pleasant Melvin stream,
Thy sweet laugh, in shade and gleam!
—Whittier, p. 301.

6. O Rivermouth Rocks, how sad a sight
Ye saw in the light of breaking day!

7. Ah, brother! only I and thou
Are left of all that circle now.

MODEL FOR ANALYSIS.

Ex.—O Lord, thou art very great!

1. *Thou* is the subject.
2. *Art great* is the predicate.
3. *Very* tells how great.
4. **Lord** invokes the attention of God.
5. **O** is used to denote an emotion of reverence and awe.

MODEL FOR PARSING.

O is an interjection, and is used to express emotion. It has no part in bringing out the thought expressed in the sentence, and is therefore said to be independent.

12

REMARKS.—In sentence **6,** *how* is an adverb, added to *sad* to denote án unusual degree of the quality. The sadness is so great as to cause deep emotion.

In sentence **7,** *I* and *thou,* taken together, represent the speaker and the one associated with him. Thus they become nearly equivalent to *we,* so the verb takes the same form as it would if the subject were *we.*

3. Seat Work.

Study the next lesson, and select sentences containing adverbial phrases that have no preposition.

LESSON 143.

Adverbial Phrases without a Preposition.

1. Instruction.

The adverbial phrase is often used without a preposition. The preposition is understood, or at least a relation similar to that commonly expressed by a preposition, but the relation word cannot always be supplied; for, in some instances, there seems to be no word that is exactly suited to express the relation.

Some of the most common omissions of the preposition may be illustrated as follows :—

1. *He came to his home on the Tweed on the seventh day of April, and died on the third day of May.*

2. *He came home April 7th, and died May 3d.*

It is plain that the relation of the man's home to the act of his coming is the same in the second sentence as it is in the first; and that the word *home* in the second sentence tells where he came, just as *to his home* does in the first, the preposition *to* being understood before it.

It is also plain that *April 7th* is equivalent to *on the seventh day of April;* and *May 3d,* to *on the third day of May.*

In the analysis we say that *home* is used to tell whither he came.

Home names the place, and the relation of the place to the act of coming is understood to be the same as would be denoted by the word *to*. *April 7th* tells when he came, and *May 3d* when he died.

We parse *home, April, May*, as nouns, each the object of a preposition; and *seventh*, and *third*, as adjectives, each limiting a noun understood.

2. Examples.

1. My friend came in the evening.
2. The general arrived last evening.
3. Maria taught school last summer.
4. The meeting continued two weeks.
5. We traveled forty miles a day.
6. My brother spent six months in Europe.
7. He remained three months in Paris.
8. The wall was six feet high.
9. The cloth was thirty inches wide.
10. I came home yesterday.
11. To-day thy Saviour calls.

REMARKS.—In sentence **5,** *forty miles* is an adverbial phrase telling how far we traveled. *A day* means the same as *in a day*, and tells how long it took us to travel forty miles.

In sentence **6,** *months* is the object of the transitive verb *spent;* but in sentence **7,** *months* is the object of a preposition understood; for *remained* is an intransitive verb, and *three months* is a phrase telling *how long* the man remained.

The meaning of sentences 8 and 9 may be expressed thus:—

The wall was high *unto* six feet.
The cloth was wide *unto* thirty inches.

In sentence **10,** *yesterday* is a noun, 3d, s., n., and object of a preposition understood. It tells when I came home, for it is what remains of an adverbial phrase. *To-day* is used in sentence 11 just as *yesterday* is in sentence 10.

3. Seat Work.

Study the next lesson, and select comparisons introduced by *like*.

---•---

LESSON 144.

Comparison Introduced by Like.

1. Instruction.

Not unfrequently the best way to describe a thing with which our hearers are not familiar is to compare it with something well known to them. Such comparisons are often introduced by the word *like*, as shown by the sentence given in the following—

MODEL FOR ANALYSIS.

Ex.—The masts shake like quivering reeds.

1. **Like quivering reeds** tells by comparison how the masts shake.

2. **Like** *introduces* the comparison,

3. **Masts** is the first term, and

4. **Reeds** is the second term.

5. *Masts* and *reeds* are compared in regard to an action,—the act of shaking.

Like is parsed by some authors as a *preposition;* and by others as an *adjective* or an *adverb*, with the preposition *to* or *unto* understood after it.

2. Examples.

1. Through woods and mountain passes,
   The winds, like anthems, roll.

2. Like the wings of sea-birds,
   Flash the white-caps of the sea.

3. Forest leaves are bright,
   And fall like flakes of light,
     To the ground.
                         —*Bryant.*

4. Like a demon of the night
   He passed, and vanished from my sight

5. Scattered were they like flakes of snow.

6. They fought like brave men, long and well.

7. A solemn fear on the listening crowd
   Fell like the shadow of a cloud.
                         --*Whittier.*

8. Straight there arose from the forest the awful sound of
     the war-whoop,
       And, like a flurry of snow on the whistling wind of
       December,
   Swift and sudden and keen came a flight of feathery arrows.
                         —*Longfellow.*

MODEL FOR PARSING.
Sentence 1.

Like is a preposition; it shows the relation between
the *anthems* and the *rolling* of the winds.

REMARK.—Describing things by formal comparison, as
in the sentences of this lesson, is called a figure of **Simile.**

3.   Seat Work.

Review Lessons 138-144.

———•—

LESSON 145.
Review.

1. Questions and Requirements.

1. Give three examples of the ellipsis of a noun after
an adjective.

2. Analyze such a sentence and parse the adjective.

3. What peculiarity has the adjective *other*, when used
to limit a noun understood?

4. When does it take the possessive sign?

5. What other adjective takes the possessive sign in the same way?

6. Give some of the peculiarities of the adjective *none*.

7. Give an example of a possessive noun used to limit a noun understood.

8. Show by example how each of the possessive pronouns may be used in the same way.

9. Parse the possessive noun and pronouns in these sentences.

10. What change is required in the possessive pronouns when they limit a noun understood?

11. Does the possessive noun require any change when used in a similar way?

12. Show from the Bible how *mine* and *thine* were once used to limit a noun expressed.

13. In such words as *ours, yours, theirs*, should the apostrophe be used before the *s?*

14. What caution must be observed in regard to the adjectives *either* and *neither.*

15. What expression should be used in speaking of reciprocal action between two persons?—*Each other.*

16. What expression should be used to denote reciprocal action among a greater number than two?

17. Is it right to say, "The three boys divided the melon between themselves"?

18. Is it right to say, "Theron and Anson divided the melon among themselves"?

19. For what three leading purposes do we use a person's name without giving it any office in the sentence?

20. Give examples.

21. What do we say of a noun thus used? Why?

22. Give examples of a noun independent by address, and accompanied by a word denoting emotion.

23. What do we call a word that is used wholly to express emotion?

24. Parse the independent noun and the interjection in one of the examples just given?

25. Give examples of adverbial phrases without a connective.

26. Parse the italicised words in the following—

EXAMPLES.

1. *Yesterday* he wept, *but to-day* he rejoices.
2. *Ah! sir,* the lake is three hundred miles long.
3. The bullets fell *like* hail.

27. Analyze the third sentence.

28. What figure is employed in this sentence?

29. When do we use a figure of simile?

2. Seat Work.

Look over the first seventy-five lessons of this book, and notice what is taught in them.

LESSON 146.
Compound Sentences.

Suggestions.—When certain words, or parts of speech in certain uses, occur so frequently that the class have become entirely familiar with their parsing, it is better in most cases to pass them by, parsing only such words as the class may need to drill upon.

So, also, it is better to omit the more minute parts of the analysis whenever the pupil has become so familiar with them that they give his mind no suitable exercise. In this way he will be led to observe the more important groups, or constructions, that make up language.

1. Examples.

1. The sun is dim in the thickened sky, and the clouds in sullen darkness rest.

2. With even strokes their scythes they swing,
   In tune their merry whetstones ring.
   —*J. T. Trowbridge.*

3. The pine is bending his proud top, and now among the nearer groves, the chestnut and oak are tossing their green boughs about.

4. The splendor falls on castle walls,
   And snowy summits old in story;
   The long light shakes across the lakes,
   And the wild cataract leaps in glory.
   —*Tennyson.*

5. I sift the snow on the mountains below,
   And the great pines groan aghast.
                                   —*Shelley.*

REMARKS.—In sentence **1**, the *darkness* is called *sullen*, because it is gloomy, like the countenance of a sullen person.

In sentence **2,** the *whetstones* are said to be *merry*, because the sound they produce upon the scythes is such as people who are merry would be likely to make. The *mowers* are the ones who really possess the quality.

In sentence **3,** the top of the pine is said to be *proud*, because it rises so high above the other trees of the forest, just as proud people try to exalt themselves above their fellows.

In sentence **5,** the *pines* are said to *groan*, because men or beasts would groan if they had to bear so heavy a load of snow.

2. Seat Work.

Look over Lessons 76 to 145, and notice what is taught in them.

LESSON 147.

Coördinate Clauses.—Continued.

1. Examples.

1. The tall maize rolls up its long green leaves ; the clover droops its tender foliage and declines its blooms.

2. And prancing steeds, in trappings gay,
   Whirl the bright chariot o'er the way.

3. Sweet woodland music sinks and swells;
   The brooklet rings its tinkling bells;
   The swarming insects drone and hum;
   The partridge beats his throbbing drum.
                                   —*J. T. Trowbridge.*

4. But, silent, sinew-bows were strung,
   And, sudden, heavy quivers hung,
   And, swiftly, to the battle sprung
   Tall, painted braves, with tufted hair,
   Like death-black banners in the air.
                                   —*Joaquin Miller.*

REMARKS.—In sentence **1,** the two clauses have no conjunction between them; and for this reason, they are separated by the semicolon instead of the comma.

In sentence **2,** *and* shows that this sentence is equal in rank with what has gone before, and that it expresses an additional thought.

Sentence **3** consists of four clauses. The conjunction is omitted between them; so they are separated by the semicolon.

Sentence **4** consists of three clauses, joined by *and,* and closely related in sense; so they are separated by the comma.

Silent, sudden, and *swiftly* are all adverbs, the *ly* being dropped from the first two to perserve the rhythm of the poetry.

2.   Seat Work.

Write examples illustrating the chief points brought out in the next lesson.

LESSON 148.

Synoptical Review.

To the Teacher.—If Lessons 148 and 149 are too long for single recitations, divide them according to the ability of the class and the time that can be given to each recitation.

1.   Distinguishing Objects.—(Nouns.)

In language, we need a multitude of names to distinguish the great variety of objects of which we wish to speak.

We need, **1.** Names for things regarded *as a whole,* and names for their *parts;* **2.** Names for one or more things belonging to the *same class,* and names for *individual* persons or objects; **3.** Names for *single* things, names for *two or more* things of the same kind, and names for *collections* of objects; **4.** Names for *males,* names for *females,* and names for things that have *no sex.*

2. Qualities and Conditions of Objects.—(Qualifying Adjectives.)

In talking of objects, we often wish to speak of their *qualities* and *conditions;* so we must have *words* to *denote* those qualities and conditions.

Sometimes we wish to *state positively* that the quality exists in a thing; but at other times we wish merely to *mention it incidentally,* as though it were a quality already known to exist in the thing under consideration.

Sometimes we wish to talk of the *quality itself;* and for this purpose we need *names* for qualities.

Qualities are commonly expressed by *single words,* but in many instances by *groups of words.*

3. Actions Predicated.—(Verbs.)

We also need a great number of words to denote the *actions* of persons and things; for we speak of actions oftener than of qualities.

Sometimes we wish to speak of an action *performed* by a thing, and sometimes of an action *received* by it.

Sometimes we wish to speak of both the *qualities* and the *actions* of a thing, and then we make use of *action-words* and *quality-words* in the same sentence.

4. Alluding to Objects.—(Pronouns.)

When any one wishes to speak of *himself,* or of any one that he is *talking to,* there is need of special words to represent the *speaker* or the person *spoken to;* for if the *name* were used, it might be taken to mean *another person* of the same name. It is also convenient *to allude* to a person that has already been spoken of, without repeating his name. So we have a set of words for the express purpose of *alluding* to the *speaker,* or to the *speaker* and *those associated with him;* to the person or persons *spoken to;* and to the person or persons *spoken of.*

QUESTIONS.

1. Why do we need a multitude of names in language?
2. What are these names called?
3. Give examples of nouns used to name whole things. Nouns used to name parts of things.

4. Why do we need the two kinds of nouns called *common* and *proper?*

5. Why do we need nouns in both the singular and the plural number ?

6. Why must we have nouns in the three different genders ?

7. How are singular nouns commonly changed to plural nouns ?

8. When does the syllable *es* have to be added ?

9. In what different ways do nouns ending in *y* form their plural ? Nouns ending in *o?* In *f?* In *fe?*

10. How are the different genders distinguished ?

11. Why do we need qualifying adjectives ?

12. In what two different ways are they used ? Give examples.

13. In what two ways are qualities expressed ?

14. Why do we need verbs in language ?

15. Give examples of verbs consisting each of a single word.

16. Give examples of verbs each consisting of two words.

17. Why do we need two words in the last case ?

18. Give examples of verbs which represent the action as received by the subject. Performed by the subject.

19. Give a sentence that assumes a quality of some thing, and predicates an action of the same thing.

20. When are verbs said to be regular ? When irregular ?

21. What is the difference between a transitive verb and an intransitive verb ?

22. What is the difference between an intransitive verb and a copula ?

23. When do we employ a transitive verb in the active voice ?

24. When do we employ a transitive verb in the passive voice ?

25. When do we employ the past tense ? When the present ?

26. For what different purposes do we use a verb in the imperative mode ?

27. What do we call the different forms that a verb takes to agree with its subject ?

28. What is the only verb that has person and number in the past tense ?

29. What change do ordinary verbs have in the present tense ? In the past tense ?

30. What different forms does the verb *to be* have in the present tense ? In the past tense ?

31. Why do we need pronouns in language ?

32. What four forms of the pronoun are used to represent the speaker ?

33. What four are used to represent the speaker and those associated with him ?

34. What three are used to represent the person or persons spoken to ?

35. What three are used to represent a male that is spoken of ?

36. What three to represent a female that is spoken of ?

37. What two to represent a thing that has no sex ?

38. What four are used to represent two or more persons or things spoken of ?

39. Which of these forms are said to be in the first person ? Which in the second ? Which in the third ? Why ?

LESSON 149.

Subject of the Last Lesson Continued.

5. Distinguishing Objects of the Same Kind.—(Limiting Adjectives.)

In talking of objects of the same kind, we often need words to tell just *which one*, or *which ones*, are meant.

Sometimes we need words to tell *definitely how many* are meant, and at other times, when we do not know the definite number, or knowing, do not wish to tell it, we need words that will tell *indefinitely how many,*—words that will show whether the number is large or small.

6. Actions and Qualities Modified.—(Adverbs and Adverbial Phrases.)

It often becomes necessary to tell *when* a thing happened, or *where* it happened; *how* it was done, or *why* it was done. Sometimes, too, we wish to tell how much of the quality a thing has, or just how it applies.

This may be done by *single words*, or by *groups of words*.

7. Ownership, Authorship, Origin, Fitness, etc.—(Possessive Case and Adjective Phrase.)

Sometimes we wish to tell *who owns* a thing, *who* or *what produced* it, or to *what* it is *adapted.* For this purpose, we sometimes employ *words* of a *peculiar form;* and at other times, *groups of words.*

8. Describing Objects by Referring them to a Class.—(Apposition, and Nouns in the Predicate.)

Sometimes we describe an object, not by telling its qualities directly, but by saying that it is *one of a class of things* whose qualities are well known. We may *state positively* that it belongs to the class; or we may *mention* the fact *incidentally*, as a thing already known.

9. Assuming Action.—(Participles.)

Sometimes we wish merely to *attribute* an action to an object, without stating positively that the person or thing either performs the act or receives it. This calls for a class of words especially adapted to such a use.

10. Relations.—(Prepositions and Conjunctions.)

We also need to show the relation of objects, qualities, actions, and thoughts, to one another; so we have a set of words for this purpose.

11. Emotions.—(Interjections.)

Sometimes a person's feelings are so deep, so sudden, or of such a nature, that they cannot be expressed by ordinary forms of speech. This leads to the use of a set of words that express *emotion*, but *no thought*.

QUESTIONS.

1. How do we distinguish objects ?

2. How do we distinguish a particular person or place from all others ?

3. How do we distinguish a class of persons or things from those that do not belong to that class ?

4. How do we distinguish males from females ?

5. How do we distinguish males and females from things that have no sex ?

6. How do we distinguish one from more than one ?

7. What do we call words that are used to name collections of objects ?

8. What do we call words used to name qualities ?

9. What do we call words that merely *denote* quality without naming it ?

10. What do we call those words that tell *what* ones, *which* ones, or *how many ?*

11. Give examples of words that tell *definitely* how many. Of those that tell *indefinitely* how many. Of those that tell *what* ones or *which* ones without telling how many.

12. What words denote *one* but no definite one ?

13. When should *a* be used in preference to *an ?*

14. What word is employed to show that some definite one is meant ?

15. For what different purposes, then, do we need *limiting adjectives ?*

16. What does it often become necessary to tell in regard to actions ?

17. Show by example how single words are employed to tell the *time* of an action. The *place.* The *manner.* The *purpose.* The *cause.*

18. Show by example how phrases are used for all these purposes.

19. For what different purposes is the possessive case used ?

20. Give examples.

21. Show by examples how the adjective phrase may be used for the same purposes.

22. When do we use a noun in the predicate ?

23. When do we use a noun in apposition ?

24. Give examples of both.

25. Give sentences that predicate identity.

26. Give sentences in which identity is assumed.

27. Why do we need participles ?

28. Give examples of their use.

29. Give sentences in which participles are used to name action.

30. Give sentences in which a peculiar form of the verb is used to name action.

31. What do we call participles and infinitives when they are used to name action ?

32. What two classes of words are used merely to show relation ?

33. Show by examples how a preposition may be used to show the relation between two objects. Between an object and an action. Between two actions.

34. How do we show that two or more terms are equal in rank, and alike in relation ?

35. What name do we give to a group consisting of two coördinate terms ? Of three or more ?

36. Give sentences that have a couplet or series of subjects. Predicates. Objects. Adjectives. Adverbs.

37. Give examples of coördinate phrases. Coördinate clauses.

38. What words are most commonly used as coördinate conjunctions ?

39. In what respect are these words alike in their use ?

40. In addition to this general use, what peculiar relation of thoughts does each suggest?

41. Why do we need interjections?

42. Give examples of their use.

LESSON 150.

Adverbial Clauses.

1. Instruction.

1. *Men make hay in fair weather.*
2. *Men make hay when the sun shines.*

1. In the first sentence above, *in fair weather* is added to the verb *make* to tell *when* the hay is made. It is therefore an *adverb*, and since it consists of a group of words, it is called an *adverbial phrase*.

2. In the second sentence, *while the sun shines* is added to the verb *make* to tell *when* the act of making was performed. It must therefore be an *adverb*. It consists of a *group* of words; but unlike the adverbial phrase, it has a *subject* and *predicate;* so we call it an **adverbial clause.**

3. In an *adverbial clause,* the subject and predicate, and all the words that limit them, are analyzed and parsed just as they are in an ordinary simple sentence; but in addition to these parts, every adverbial clause must have a word to show its relation to other parts of the sentence. This word is called a *connective,* or *introductory* word.

4. It will be remembered that principal clauses are sometimes joined in one sentence, with a connecting word between them to show that they are equal, or coördinate, in rank. This connecting word, since it shows the clauses to be coördinate in rank, is called a *coördinate conjunction.*

5. But the adverbial clause is *not* equal in rank with the principal clause,—is not coördinate,—but merely an *adverb,* used to modify a word in the principal clause. It is of a *lower rank* than the principal clause, or the word which

it limits,—and since *sub* means *under*, or *lower*, we call such a clause a **subordinate clause;** and the word that introduces it, and shows it to be subordinate, we call a **subordinate conjunction.**

6. In the analysis of a subordinate clause, we first notice *its use as a whole*, and afterward take up its *parts*, beginning with its introductory word, subject, and predicate.

2. Examples.

1. We wept while we listened.
2. He came when darkness curtained the hills.
3. When the sun rose, we pursued our journey.
4. Full of wrath was Hiawatha when he came into the village.
5. When they ceased, a sudden darkness fell, and filled the silent wigwam.
6. When he awoke, it was already night.

MODEL FOR ANALYSIS.
Sentence 1.

1. *We* is the subject.
2. *Wept* is the predicate.
3. **While we listened** tells *when* we wept.
4. **While** introduces this clause, and indicates its use.
5. *We* is the subject, and *listened* is the predicate.

MODEL FOR PARSING.

While is a *conjunction*, **subordinate;** it shows its clause to be an adverb of time, and subordinate to *wept*.

REMARK.—In sentence **2,** darkness is said to curtain the hills because it hides them from view, as curtains conceal the objects that are behind them.

3. Seat Work.

Study the next lesson; write the analysis of the first two sentences, and the parsing of the subordinate conjunctions in the first four.

13

LESSON 151.

Adverbial Clauses.—Continued.

1. Instruction.

Adverbial clauses, like other adverbial elements, are used to tell, not only *when*, but also *where*, *why*, *how*, for what *purpose*, and by what *cause*, actions take place. All these uses will be shown in the lessons that follow.

PUNCTUATION.—In some of the examples of this lesson, and in several of the preceding lesson, the adverbial clause comes before the word it limits. When it is so arranged, it is said to be *transposed*, and should be set off by the comma, as seen in the examples referred to.

2. Examples.

1. When the world is dark with tempests, thou lookest in thy beauty from the clouds.

2. Three friends, the guests of summer-time, pitched their white tents where sea-winds blew.
—Whittier, p. 294.

3. When I blow my breath about me,
   When I breathe upon the landscape,
   Flowers spring up o'er all the meadows,
   Singing, onward rush the rivers.
—Longfellow, p. 187.

4. I watched him as he went.

5. I calmly stand and wait till the hinges turn for me.

6. The battle was lost before reënforcements arrived.

3. Seat Work.

Study the next lesson; write the analysis of the first two sentences, and the parsing of the subordinate conjunctions in all the sentences.

LESSON 152.

Adverbial Clauses.—Continued.

1. Examples.

1. Heavily sank he, as a stone sinks.

2. Two angels passed o'er our village as the morning broke.

3. Pleasant it is to roam about the lettered world as the traveler roams.

4. And bright where summer breezes break,
   The green wheat crinkles like a lake.
   —*Trowbridge.*

5.. A thousand recollections weave their bright hues into woof,
   As I listen to the patter of the soft rain on the roof.

6. As they bend to the soft winds, the sun looks in, and sheds a blessing on the scene.

REMARKS.—In sentences **1** and **3,** the subordinate clause is an abverb of manner.

In the other sentences it denotes time, place, or circumstance.

In sentence **1,** *as a stone sinks* tells by comparison how he sinks. The sinking of a person is compared to the sinking of a stone. This is called a figure of **simile.**

In sentence **4,** *bright* is an adjective; it describes the appearance of the wheat as it crinkles. Notice the beautiful simile in this sentence.

In sentence **5,** our life is compared to a web of cloth. The *warp* must be *time,* or the regular train of acts and events in life, and into this, memory is represented as weaving recollections of particularly pleasant occurrences, just as the weaver interlaces the *woof* [*filling*] with the warp; and as the woof hides the warp, and gives color and general appearance to the cloth, so these pleasant recollections are uppermost in our memory, and give character to all our past life.

2. Seat Work.

Study the next lesson, and select sentences containing adverbial clauses like those in preceding lessons.

LESSON 153.

Adverbial Clauses.—Continued.

1. Examples.

1. When she awoke from the trance, she beheld a multitude near her.

2. Flowers peep from the ground where'er I pass.

3. We paused at last where home-bound cows
　　Brought down the pasture's treasure,
And in the barn the rhythmic flails
　　Beat out a harvest measure.
　　　　　　　　—*Whittier, p.* 328.

4. When the repast was ended, they arose and went into the garden.

5. 'Tis a dangerous adventure; but as he puts his feet and hands into those gains, and draws himself carefully up to his full length, he finds himself a foot above every name chronicled in that mighty wall.

2. Instruction.

A sentence made up of coördinate clauses is called a **compound sentence.**

A sentence that has one principal clause, and one or more subordinate clauses, is called a **complex sentence.**

A sentence made up of principal clauses, with one or more subordinate clauses, is both compound and complex. Sentence **5** of this lesson affords an example. Adverbial clauses may be coördinate with one another, and at the same time subordinate to the word they limit. See sentence **3,** of this lesson.

Remarks.—In sentence **2,** do the flowers literally peep? What is it to peep? Why are the flowers said to peep?

In sentence **3,** what is meant by the pasture's treasure? Why is it called the pasture's treasure, since the cows produce it? Why are the flails said to be rhythmic? What is meant by a harvest measure?

In this case the name of the thing that is filled by the grain is put for the grain itself. This is called a figure of **metonymy.**

3. Seat Work.

In addition to studying the next lesson, select two adverbial clauses denoting time, two denoting manner, and two denoting place.

LESSON 154.

Adverbial Clauses.—Continued.

1. Examples.

1. Between the dark and the daylight,
     When the night is beginning to lower,
   Comes a pause in the day's occupations.
   —Longfellow, p. 225.

2. As I look and listen, the sadness wears away.

3. But e'er he touched the latchet, from within a whisper came.

4. The cheerful rivulet sang and gossiped as it hastened ocean-ward.

5. I watch the mowers as they go
   Through the tall grass, a white-sleeved row.
   —Trowbridge.

6. I saw him when he fell.

7. The silver moon at midnight cold and still,
   Looks, sad and silent, o'er yon western hill.

8. Where the wave is tinged with red,
     And the russet sea-leaves grow,
   Mariners, with prudent tread,
     Shun the shelving reefs below.
   —John Leyden.

REMARKS.—In sentence **4,** how could the rivulet sing? How could it gossip?—Perhaps some of the noises made by the rivulet in its flowing, reminded the poet of the chattering of people who gossip.

In sentence **3**, *within* seems to be a noun. Perhaps, however, *from within* would better be parsed as an adverb representing a phrase whose noun is understood.

2. Seat Work.

Select three sentences containing transposed adverbial clauses; three containing adverbial clauses that are not set off, because so closely connected in thought; and three that contain adverbial clauses so slightly connected in thought as to be set off by the comma.

LESSON 155.

Adverbial Clauses.—Continued.

1. Examples.

1. We hate some persons because we are not acquainted with them.

2. Since retreat was now impossible, Colter turned the head of the canoe.

3. A poet, as he paces to and fro, murmurs his sounding lines.

4. Thou comest not when violets lean
O'er wandering brooks, and springs unseen,
Or columbines, in purple dressed,
Nod o'er the ground-bird's hidden nest.
—*Bryant, p. 128.*

5. The castle-bell, with backward clang,
Sent forth the larum peal;
Was frequent heard the heavy jar,
Where massy stone and iron bar
Were piled on echoing keep and tower.
—*Scott.*

REMARK.—In sentence **2**, what is meant by the head of the canoe? Why is this part called the head?—Animals always move with the head forward, and this may be the reason why the part of the boat that goes forward is called the head.

PUNCTUATION.—We have already seen that transposed adverbial clauses are set off by the comma. Those that are not transposed, are also set off when not very closely connected in sense with the word they limit, but when closely connected, they are not set off. These latter clauses correspond, in their relation, to restrictive participial phrases; while those that are not closely related, correspond to phrases that are not restrictive.

2. Seat Work.

Study the next lesson, and write the analysis of sentence 4.

LESSON 156.

Adverbial Clauses.—Continued.

1. Examples.

1. For them the early violet no more
   Opens upon thy bank, nor, for their eyes,
   Glitter the crimson pictures of the clouds
   Upon thy bosom when the sun goes down.
   —*Bryant, p.* 238.

2. But when the hymn was sung, and the daily lesson completed,
   Swiftly they hurried away to the forge of Basil the black-smith. —*Evangeline.*

3. Wild with the winds of September,
   Wrestled the trees of the forest, as Jacob of old with the angel. —*Ibid.*

4. And southerly, when the tide is down,
   'Twixt white sea-waves and sand-hills brown,
   The beach birds dance and the gray gulls wheel
   Over a floor of burnished steel.
   —*Whittier, p.* 207.

REMARKS.—In sentence **2,** *but* shows the relation of this sentence to one that has gone before.

In sentence **3,** the trees are said to wrestle with the wind, because the wind seems to be trying to throw them down, and they writhe about as men do in wrestling.

In sentence **4,** the " floor of burnished steel " is the surface of the water. It is called a " floor " because the birds as they dart about so rapidly close to its surface, remind the poet of people dancing on a floor. It is called a floor of " burnished steel " because it glistens like burnished steel.

2. Seat Work.

Study the next lesson, and write the analysis of sentence **1.**

LESSON 157.

Adverbial Clauses.—Continued.

1. Examples.

1. When beechen buds begin to swell,
    And woods the blue-bird's warble know,
    The yellow violet's modest bell
    Peeps from the last year's leaves below.
    —*Bryant. p. 23.*

2. When the showering vapors gather
    Over all the starry spheres,
    And the melancholy darkness
    Gently weeps in rainy tears,
    'Tis a joy to press the pillow
    Of the cottage chamber bed,
    And listen to the patter
    Of the soft rain overhead.
    —*Coates Kinney.*

3. But their voices sank yet lower, sank to husky tones of fear,
    As they spake of present tokens of the powers of evil near.   —*Whittier. p. 222.*

REMARKS.—In sentence **1,** *from below* may be parsed as a preposition, showing the relation of the leaves to the peeping of the violet's modest bell.

In sentence **3,** *near* is an adjective, added to *evil* to show its condition in regard to proximity. It represents the adjective phrase *near them.*

In sentence **2,** the darkness is said to be melancholy; and then, to carry out the figure, it is said to weep, the raindrops being taken for tears.

2. Seat Work.

Study the next lesson, and write out the parsing of all the conjunctions, both coördinate and subordinate.

LESSON 158.

Adverbial Clauses.—Continued.

1. Examples.

1.   Suddenly,
As on his words entrancedly they hung,
The crowd divided, and among them stood
   Jairus the Ruler.
                    —*Willis.*

2. Witlaf, a king of the Saxons,
   E'er yet his last he breathed,
To the merry monks of Croyland
   His drinking-horn bequeathed.
                    —*Longfellow, p.* 132.

3.   And when the herbs
Of summer drooped beneath the mid-day sun,
She sat within the shade of a great rock,
Dreamily listening to the streamlet's song.
                    —*Bryant, p.* 268.

4. Lies a calm along the deep,
   Like a mirror sleeps the ocean,
And the anxious steersman sees
   Round him neither stir nor motion.
                    —*Goethe.*

REMARKS.—In sentence **1**, the people "hung" on his words; i. e., they let none escape them, but listened with eagerness, trying to remember all they heard.

In sentence **2**, *ere yet* is a subordinate conjunction, and means the same as *before*.

2. Seat Work.

Study the next lesson, and write the analysis of the fourth example.

LESSON 159.

Adverbial Clauses.—Continued.

1. Examples.

1.   The arrowy beam
Of moonlight, slanting to the marble floor,
Lay like a spell of silence in the rooms,
As Jairus led them on.
                                        —*Willis.*

2. I hear the beat
Of their pinions fleet,
As from the land of snow and sleet,
  They seek a southern lea.
                                        —*Longfellow. p.* 131.

3. Only the long waves, as they broke
In ripples on the pebbly beach,
Interrupted the old man's speech.

4. Strange domes and towers
Rose up where sty or corn-crib stood,
Or garden wall, or belt of wood.
                                        —*Snow-bound.*

5. There is no glory in star or blossom
  Till looked upon by a loving eye;
There is no fragrance in April breezes
  Till breathed with joy as they wander by.
                                        —*Bryant.*

REMARK.—In sentence **4**, *stood* has four subjects,— *sty, corn-crib, wall,* and *belt.*

2. Seat Work.

Study the next lesson; write the analysis of the first stanza, and the parsing of the conjunctions.

LESSON 160.

Adverbial Clauses.—Continued.

1. Examples.

1. I wield the flail of the lashing hail,
    And whiten the green plains under;
   And then, again, I dissolve it in rain,
    And laugh as I pass in thunder.
    —Shelley.

2. We wandered where the sun never shines.

3. My friend came yesterday, and returned to-day.

4. This is the unkindest cut of all.

5. Yours was a life of suffering, mine, of exquisite delight.

6. I am going, O my people,
    On a long and distant journey.
    —Hiawatha.

7. Down the coast of Norway,
   Like a flock of sea-gulls,
   Sailed the fleet of Olaf
   Through the Danish Sound.
   —Longfellow, p. 259.

2. Questions and Requirements.

1. In what are the adverbial word, phrase, and clause alike?

2. Give an example of a word, phrase, and clause, each used to tell when something happened.

3. In what respect are the adverbial phrase and clause alike?

4. In what respect are they unlike?

5. How do they differ in form?

6. In analyzing an adverbial clause, what should first be noticed?

7. What should next receive attention?

8. In what respects are an adverbial clause and a principal clause alike?

9. In what do they differ?

10. What must be prefixed to a clause before it can be used as an adverb?

11. Give principal clauses, and change them to adverbial clauses.

12. Give adverbial clauses, and change them to principal clauses.

13. When should an adverbial clause be set off by the comma?

14. When is a sentence said to be compound? When complex?

3. Seat Work.

Study the next lesson, and write the analysis of sentences 5–7.

LESSON 161.

Adjective Clauses.

1. Instruction.

1. *We respect an **industrious** man.*
2. *We respect a man **of industry**.*
3. *We respect a man **who is industrious**.*

In the first sentence, we describe the man by the use of the word *industrious*, which assumes a quality of him. In the second sentence, we describe him by the phrase *of industry*, which means the same as *industrious*. In the third sentence, we bring out the same thought by the use of the clause *who is industrious*.

"Industrious" is an *adjective;* "of industry" is an *adjective phrase;* "Who is industrious" is an *adjective clause.* The word, the phrase, and the clause all describe the man by attributing to him the quality of industry. The word and the phrase *assume* the quality; the clause *predicates* it, but represents it as a subordinate thought, secondary in importance to the thought predicated in the principal clause.

The adjective clause is subordinate to a noun just as the adverbial clause is to a verb. As with the adverbial, so with the adjective clause; we first speak of its use *as a whole*, then of its introductory or relation word, its subject, predicate, etc.

2. Examples.

1. Happy is the man that findeth wisdom.
2. We see not the hand which is guiding us.
3. God honors the man who walks uprightly.
4. Mr. Austin has a clock that marks the changes of the moon.
5. My friend sailed on the ship that left port yesterday.
6. The poet Bryant was a man who loved the forest.
7. He that winneth souls is wise.

MODEL FOR ANALYSIS.

Ex.—We respect a man who is industrious.

1. *We* is the subject.
2. *Respect* is the predicate.
3. **A man who is industrious** tells whom we respect.
4. **Man** names a person.
5. *A* denotes one but no definite one.
6. **Who is industrious** describes the kind of man here meant, by predicating a quality of him.
7. **Who** alludes to the man, to show who is described by this clause.
8. **Who** is the subject of the clause, and **is industrious** is the predicate.

REMARKS.—In sentence **2,** God's providence is called a "hand" because he guides us by it as we lead the weak by the hand. In sentence **3,** a man's course of conduct in life is compared to walking. One who is in the full vigor of health, and has a clear conscience, walks uprightly; so one who obeys God in all things is morally healthy and vigorous, is never turned aside by temptation, and never yields to wrong; he is therefore said to walk uprightly.

3. Seat Work.

Study the next lesson, and write the analysis of sentences 1, 3, and 5.

LESSON 162.

The Relative Pronoun as Subject.

1. Instruction.

A pronoun that shows a clause to be in a subordinate relation to some noun, is called a **relative pronoun**.

The noun which the pronoun represents is called its **antecedent.** A pronoun always means the same **person** or thing as its antecedent, and therefore must have the same person, number, and gender; but it may represent that person or thing in a different relation, and hence is not necessarily put in the same case.

PUNCTUATION.—When the adjective clause is **not** restrictive, it must be set off by the comma. Notice the difference between the restrictive and non-restrictive clauses in this lesson.

1. Does the adjective clause in the first sentence tell *what* Jane or *which* Jane is meant?

2. In the fifth sentence, does the adjective clause tell *what* Voltaire is meant?

3. In the sixth sentence, does the adjective clause tell *which* man or what *particular kind* of man is meant?

4. In the third sentence, does the adjective clause tell what particular kind of persons have great influence in society?

5. Which of these clauses, then, are restrictive, and which are not?

2. Examples.

1. The child was much attached to Jane, who loved her dearly.

2. Death is the season that tries our affections.

3. Those who are wealthy frequently have great influence in society.

4. The eye, that sees all things, sees not itself.

5. Voltaire, who saw him, speaks repeatedly of his majestic appearance.

6. The man who trusts in God is blessed.

7. Oh, a dainty plant is the ivy green,
   That creepeth o'er ruins old.
   —*Dickens.*

3. Seat Work.

Write the parsing of the relative pronouns in the next lesson.

LESSON 163.

The Relative Pronoun as Object.

1. Examples.

Was it the chime of a tiny bell
   That came so sweet to my dreaming ear,
Like the silvery tones of a fairy's shell,
   That he winds on the beach, so mellow and clear?
   —*John Pierpont.*

2. The evil that men do lives after them.

3. The hills which our feet climbed in childhood are dear.

4. He that gathereth in summer is a wise son.

5. He liveth long who liveth well.

6. The book of poems which I lent you was a present.

7. He prayeth best who leaves unguessed
   The mystery of another's breast.

MODELS FOR PARSING THE RELATIVE PRONOUN.

Ex.—We mourn for the heroes who fell.

Who is a relative pronoun. As a relative, it shows its clause to be in a *subordinate relation* to the noun *heroes*. As a pronoun, it is third per., plu. num., mas. gen., because it means the same as *heroes*. It is subject of the clause, and is therefore put in the nominative case.

Ex.—I found the pen which you lost.

Which is a relative pronoun. As a relative, it shows its clause to be in a subordinate relation to the noun *pen*. As a pronoun, it is third per., sing. num., neu. gen., because it means the same as *pen*. It is object of the verb *lost*, and is therefore put in the objective case.

Ex.—He that walketh uprightly walketh surely.

That is a relative pronoun. As a relative, it shows its clause to be in a subordinate relation to the pronoun *he*. As a pronoun, it is third per., sing. num., mas. gen., because it means the same as *he*. It is subject of the clause, and is therefore put in the nominative case.

REMARKS.—In sentence **4,** middle life is compared to summer. In summer, everything is favorable to the raising of grains and fruits ; and he who improves the opportunity and gathers in an abundant store, will not want when winter comes. So middle life, when all the powers are vigorous and active, is a favorable time for acquiring knowledge and wealth ; so, too, we should improve the present life in laying up treasure in heaven.

Sentence **5,** contains a significant figure. He lives long who lives well, because he accomplishes more, even in a few years, than others do in a long life.

The meaning of sentence **7** may seem at first a little obscure. To be prying into the secret thoughts and feelings of others is displeasing to God, and hinders communication with him.

2. Seat Work.

Study the next lesson; write the parsing of the relative pronouns in sentences 1, 2, and 3, and the analysis of sentence 6.

LESSON 164.

Relative Pronoun in the Possessive Case.

1. Examples.

1. I venerate the man whose heart is warm.

2. They came to the chief man of the island, whose name was Publius.

3. Contemplate him whose yoke is easy, and whose burden is light.

4. None knew the burden that she bore.

5. This plain was dotted with lovely lakes, whose waters shone in the slanting rays of the declining sun.

6. Under the boughs of Wachita willows, that grew by the margin,
Safely their boat was moored; and scattered about on the greensward,
Tired with their midnight toil, the weary travelers slumbered.

Suggestion.—In parsing *whose*, say, at the last, *it is used to tell whose heart is meant, and is therefore put in the possessive case.*

REMARKS.—*Sentence 1.*—The man has a warm heart who has kind and sympathetic feelings. Tender plants and flowers shrink and die in the cold, but give them warmth, and they thrive; so selfishness and unkindness blight the tender buds of affection and hope in the human heart. But under the genial influence of kindness and sympathy they unfold into purity, beauty, and usefulness.

Sentence 3.—The service which Christ requires of us is here compared to the service that kind men require of beasts of burden. The yoke is so made that they can

14

work easily in it, and they are not overloaded; so the service required of us is never hard when we perform it willingly.

2. Seat Work.

Write the parsing of the pronouns and prepositions in sentences 5 and 6.

———— • ————

LESSON 165.

Relative Pronoun as Object of a Preposition.

1. Examples.

1. The streams at which our young lips drank are sweet.

2. Every good man loves the country in which he was born.

3. The flowers that bloom in early spring are generally small and delicate.

4. It is a maxim whose truth many have realized.

5. It is a maxim the truth of which many have realized.

6. One long bar of purple cloud, on which the evening star shone like a jewel on a scimitar, held the sky's golden gateway.

7. The valley stream is frozen,
       The hills are cold and bare,
    And the wild white bees of winter
       Swarm in the darkened air.
                    —*Bayard Taylor.*

MODEL FOR ANALYSIS.
Sentence 1.

1. *Streams* is the subject, and *are sweet* is the predicate.

2. *At which our young lips drank* tells what streams are meant.

3. *Lips* is the subject of the clause, and *drank* is the predicate.

4. **At which,** meaning *at the streams*, tells where our lips drank.

5. **Which** alludes to the streams to show what this clause describes.

MODEL FOR PARSING.

Which is a *relative pronoun.* As a relative, it shows its clause to be in a *subordinate relation* to the noun *streams.* As a pronoun, it is in the 3d per., plu. num., neu. gen., because it means the same as *streams.* It is object of the preposition *at,* and is therefore put in the *objective case.*

REMARKS.—In sentence **1,** the streams are said to be sweet to our young lips because in youth we have a keener relish than in after years; but the real meaning is that, as we have a keener relish for food, so we have a livelier appreciation of all the enjoyments of life, hence they seem dearer to us.

Sentence **6** contains two beautiful figures. In the first, it is clearly stated that the star on the cloud shines like a jewel on a scimitar. This is called a *Simile.* In the second, the comparison is not stated, but merely implied. That part of the sky where the sun has just gone out of sight is called heaven's gateway, because the sun has seemed to go out at it, as one would go out through a gateway. It is called golden, because it is bright and yellow like gold. Such a figure is called a *Metaphor.*

2. Seat Work.

Select three sentences each containing a relative pronoun as subject; two, with a relative pronoun as object of a transitive verb; one, with a relative pronoun in the possessive case; and one, with a relative pronoun as object of a preposition.

LESSON 166.

Adjective Clauses.—Continued.

1. Examples.

1. Before me spreads the lake,
   Whose long and solemn-sounding waves
   Against the sunset break.

2. The laws which govern the world are universal.

3. The laws by which the world is governed are universal.

4. He it was whose hand in autumn
   Painted all the trees with scarlet,
   Stained the leaves with red and yellow;
   He it was who sent the snow-flakes,
   Sifting, hissing through the forest,
   Froze the ponds, the lakes, the rivers,
   Drove the loon and sea-gull southward,
   Drove the cormorant and curlew
   To their nests of sedge and sea-tang
   In the realms of Shawondasee.
   —*Longfellow. p.* 145.

2. Seat Work.

Study the next lesson, and write the parsing of the pronouns.

LESSON 167.

Adjective Clauses.—Continued.

1. Examples.

1. The prince that wanteth understanding is also a great oppressor.

2. She is a tree of life to them that lay hold upon her, and happy is every one that retaineth her.

3. Within, in the wide old kitchen,
   The old folks sit in the sun,
   That creeps through the sheltering woodbine,
   Till the day is almost done.

4. O mountain friends! with mine
   Your solemn spirit blends.

5.   He whose presence fills
   With light the space of these hills
   No evil to his creatures wills.

REMARK.—Sentence **2** speaks of wisdom as a tree of life. By eating of the tree of life, men may perpetuate their existence forever; so by following the dictates of true wisdom they may secure eternal life, for it will make them wise unto salvation. Therefore, wisdom is said to be a tree of life to them that lay hold upon her.

2. Seat Work.

Study the next lesson, and write the analysis of sentence 2.

LESSON 168.

Adjective Clauses.—Continued.

1. Examples.

1. Sometimes along the wheel-deep sand
   A one-horse wagon slowly crawled,
   Deep laden with a youthful band,
   Whose look some homestead old recalled.
   —*Whittier, p. 296.*

2. Slowly lifting the horn that hung at his side, and expanding
   Fully his broad, deep chest, he blew a blast, that resounded
   Wildly and sweet and far, through the still, damp air of the evening.   —*Longfellow, p. 112.*

3. Long and thin and gray were the locks that shaded his temples.

4. He that only rules by terror
   Doeth grievous wrong.
   —*Tennyson.*

5. The woodlands wore a gloomy green,
   The tawny stubble clad the hill;
   And August hung her smoky screen
   Above the valleys, hot and still.
   —*Bayard Taylor.*

2. Seat Work.

Study the next lesson, and write the analysis of sentence 3.

LESSON 169.

Adjective Clauses.—Continued.

1. Examples.

1. Late, with the rising moon, returned the wains from the
      marshes,
   Laden with briny hay, that filled the air with its odor;
   Cheerily neighed the steeds, with dew on their manes
      and their fetlocks,
   While aloft on their shoulders the wooden and ponderous
      saddles,
   Painted with brilliant dyes, and adorned with tassels of
      crimson,
   Nodded in bright array, like hollyhocks heavy with
      blossoms.   —*Longfellow*, *p.* 98.

2. Under a towering oak, that stood in the midst of the
      village,
   Knelt the Black Robe chief with his children.
                                        —*Ibid. p.* 117.

3. Yet, 'twas a pleasant toil to trace and beat
   Among the glowing trees this winding way,
   While the sweet autumn sunshine, doubly sweet,
      Flushed with the ruddy foliage, round us lay,
   As if some gorgeous cloud of morning stood
   In glory mid the arches of the wood.
                                        —*Bryant p.* 308.

REMARKS.—In sentence **1**, *while* is a coördinate conjunction, as may be proved by putting *and* in its place.
It is slightly different in meaning from *and*, but not more
so than *yet*. It is in some respects like *nor;* for while
nor is exactly equivalent to *and* and the negative adverb
not, *while* seems to be equivalent to *and* and an adverbial
phrase denoting simultaneous time. "*And at the same time*"
might take the place of *while* in sentence **1**. *While*, when
used in this way, seems also to imply that the clause
following it, although coördinate with the one before it,
is slightly secondary to it in importance.

In sentence **3,** at the beginning of the fifth line, are two conjunctions—*as* and *if*. *As* is all that remains of a clause whose predicate is modified by the clause introduced by *if*. Supplying the ellipsis, it would read, "As *it would lie* if some gorgeous cloud," etc. For the sake of brevity, however, it is as well, after having explained as above, to parse *as if* together as a conjunction introducing the clause that follows.

2. Seat Work.

Study the next lesson, and write the analysis of sentences 1, **4,** and 5.

LESSON 170.

Adjective Clauses Introduced by When and Where.

1. Instruction.

1. *I remember the day* **when I first left home.**
2. *We passed the house* **where the murder was committed.**

In sentence **1,** *when I first left home* is added to the noun *day* to show what particular day is meant; it must therefore be an *adjective clause*. We may give further proof of its being an adjective clause by putting in its place an adjective phrase, or an adjective clause of the ordinary form. Thus:—

1. I remember the day *of my first leaving home.*
2. I remember the day **on which I first left home.**

By noticing the last sentence it will be seen that *when*, as used in the example at the head of this lesson, is just equivalent to *on which*. Now *on which* is an adverbial phrase modifying the verb in the subordinate clause; but *which*, the object of the preposition in that phrase, is a *relative pronoun*, and alludes to the *day*, to show what is described or pointed out by the subordinate clause.

1. Repeat the subordinate clause found in the second sentence at the head of this lesson.

2. For what purpose is it used?

3. Put in its place an adjective clause containing a relative pronoun.

4. What relation is shown by the relative pronoun?

5. Then what relation is shown by the word *where?*

6. What would be the use, or office, of the phrase *in which?*

7. Then what two purposes are served by the word *where*, since it is equivalent to the phrase *in which?*

8. Are the words *when* and *where* commonly used as they are in these sentences?

9. Give sentences in which these words are used as conjunctions.

10. Give sentences in which they are used as adverbs.

2. Examples.

1. The rootlets of the trees found the prison where she lay.

2. We visited the place where the old chief was buried.

3. We know not the time when he cometh.

4. They emerged into broad lagoons where silvery sand-bars lay in the stream.

5. So, with aching limbs and head,
   Plod I to a quiet glade,
   Where a miniature cascade,
   Fashioned by some artist's cunning,
   Over shells and stones is running.
   —*Goethe.*

MODEL FOR ANALYSIS.

Ex.—I know the rock whence those waters flow.

1. *I* is the subject, *know* is the predicate, and *rock* names the thing that I know.

2. **Whence those waters flow** tells what particular rock is meant.

3. **Whence** alludes to the rock here meant, in order to show what this clause describes.

4. *Waters* is the subject of the clause, and *flow* is the predicate.

MODEL FOR PARSING.

Whence is a relative adverb.

As a *relative*, it shows its clause to be subordinate to the noun *rock*.

As an *adverb*, it modifies the verb *flow*.

3. Seat Work.

Study the next lesson; write the analysis of sentences 2 and 4, and the parsing of the relative adverbs in all the sentences.

LESSON 171.

Subject of the Last Lesson Continued.

1. Examples.

1. They reached a spot where the narrow road descended to the river through deep and gloomy woods.

2. There come moments in life when our feelings find expression both in smiles and in tears.

3. In the leafy tree-tops, where no fears intrude, merry birds are singing.

4. Open now the crystal fountain
   Whence the healing waters flow.

5. Toward the south end of the plateáu are many shapeless ruins, that probably indicate the site of Herod's palace.

6. The entire locality now presents a scene of indescribable desolation, and all who visit it are impressed with the mournful though magnificent outlook over the Dead Sea, and the picturesque, wild, and worn mountains of Moab and Edom beyond.

—*Land and Book*, p. 295.

REMARKS.—In sentence **3**, *where no fears intrude* is not used to tell what tree-tops are meant, but rather to describe them as a safe retreat for the birds.

In sentence **4**, *whence* means *from which*, and performs the same office as *where.* In sentence **6,** *though* is a coördinate conjunction, nearly equivalent to *yet.*

2. Seat Work.

Study the next lesson, and write the analysis of sentences 2 and 4.

LESSON 172.

Clauses Introduced by Relative Adverbs.

1. Examples.

1. We are told of a home where sorrow never comes.
2. In that hour when night is calmest,
   Sang he from the Hebrew psalmist.
3. After a day of cloud and wind and rain,
   Sometimes the setting sun breaks out again,
       And, touching all the darksome woods with light,
   Smiles on the fields, until they laugh and sing;
   Then, like a ruby from the horizon's ring,
       Drops down into the night.
                              —*Longfellow, p. 353.*
4. Pass on to homes where cheerful voices sound, and cheerful looks are cast.
5. The marble flags of the corridor
   Through open windows meet the floor,
   And Moorish arches in darkness rise
   Against the gleam of the silver skies;
   Beyond, in flakes of starry light,
   A fountain prattles to the night,
   And dusky cypresses, withdrawn
   In silent conclave, stud the lawn;
   While mystic woodlands, more remote,
   In seas of airy silver float.
                              —*Bayard Taylor.*

MODEL FOR THE ANALYSIS OF A LONG SENTENCE.

Sentence 3.

1. *Sun* is the subject.
2. *Breaks, smiles,* and *drops* are the predicates.

3. *And* shows that *breaks* and *smiles* are coördinate, but the connective is omitted between *smiles* and *drops*.

4. *Touching all the darksome woods with light* describes the sun by assuming an action of it.

5. *On the fields* tells where the sun smiles, and *until they laugh and sing* shows the effect of that action.

6. *Then* tells when the sun drops ; *like a ruby from the horizon's ring* tells by comparison how it drops, *down* tells which way, and *into the night,* where.

7. *After a day of cloud and wind and rain* tells when the sun does all these things.

8. *Sometimes* shows that these actions do not commonly take place under such circumstances, but only occasionally.

2. Seat Work.

Select—

(*a.*) Two adjective clauses, one introduced by *when* and the other by *where*.

(*b.*) Four adverbial clauses, two introduced by *when* and two by *where*.

LESSON 173.

Subject of the Last Lesson Continued.

1. Examples.

1. Alden went into the tranquil woods, where blue-birds and robins were building towns in the populous trees.
—Longfellow, in Miles Standish.

2. Each heart has its haunted chamber, where the silent moonlight falls. *Longfellow, p. 228.*

3. Into the mirror of the brook,
Where the vain blue-bird trims his coat,
Two tiny feathers fall and float.
—J. T. Trowbridge.

4. And he thought on the days that were long since by,
When his limbs were strong, and his courage was high.
—Scott.

5. I love the garden wild and wide,
  Where oaks have plum-trees by their side ;
  Where woodbines and the twisting vine
  Clip round the pear-tree and the pine.
                              —*Allan Ramsay.*

REMARKS.—In sentence **1**, the adjective clause does not tell *what* woods are meant, but describes them by telling what was going on there.

In sentence **2,** the heart is taken to represent the feelings, and the thought seems to be that there are moments in every one's life, when, by certain trains of thought, he is brought into a state of feeling similar to what one might be supposed to have in a haunted chamber where the silent moonlight falls ; and at such moments, absent or departed friends are seen in imagination, as clearly as ghosts are said to be seen.

2. Seat Work.

Study the next lesson; write the parsing of all the relative pronouns, and the analysis of sentence 3.

LESSON 174.

Relative Pronoun used also as an Adjective.

1. Instruction.

1. *I accept* **any** *terms* **which** *you propose.*
2. *I accept* **whatever** *terms you propose.*

By comparing these sentences it will be seen that they are alike in meaning, and that *whatever* is exactly equivalent to the two words *any* and *which*. Now *any* is a limiting adjective, and *which* is a relative pronoun; and since *whatever* does the work of these two words, it is plain that it should be parsed both as a limiting adjective, and as a relative pronoun.

2. Examples.

1. Take whatever course suits you.
2. I obtained what help I needed.
3. Whatever alms were received were given to the poor.
4. Make what preparations are necessary.
5. I sent what money I had.
6. Bear patiently whatever misfortunes fall to your lot.
7. I bought whatever provisions were needed.

MODEL FOR ANALYSIS.
Sentence 1.

1. *Thou* or *you,* understood, is the subject.
2. *Take* is the predicate.
3. *Course* is the object of the verb.
4. **Whatever suits you** points out the course here meant.
5. **Whatever** alludes to the course, to show what the clause describes.
6. *Whatever* is the subject of the clause, and *suits* is the predicate.

MODEL FOR PARSING.

Whatever is a *relative pronoun,* used also as an adjective. As a relative, it shows its clause to be in a subordinate relation to the noun *course.* As a pronoun, it is 3d, sing., neu., because it means the same as *course.* It is subject of the clause, and is therefore put in the nominative case. As an adjective, it is equivalent to *any,* and limits the noun *course.*

REMARK.—In sentences **2, 4,** and **7,** the relative pronoun, in its adjective use, is nearly equivalent to *the.* In some sentences it is (in its adjective use) equivalent to *any,* and in others, to *all.*

3. Seat Work.

Study the next lesson, and write the parsing of the relative pronouns.

LESSON 175.

Relative Pronoun Representing a Noun Understood.

1. Instruction.

1. *I accept* **whatever terms** *you propose.*
2. *I accept* **whatever** . . . . *you propose.*

By comparing these sentences, it will be seen that in the second, the relative pronoun represents some noun (like *terms*) understood; and that, in all respects, it sustains the same relation to that noun *understood* that it would to the same noun *expressed*.

2. Examples.

1. Buy what books you need.
2. Buy what you need.
3. Remember what hardships they endured.
4. Practice what you teach.
5. He fails in whatever enterprise he undertakes.
6. Observe what you are taught.
7. Whene'er a noble deed is wrought,
   Whene'er is spoken a noble thought,
   Our hearts, in glad surprise,
   To higher levels rise.
   —*Longfellow, p. 222.*

MODEL FOR ANALYSIS.
Sentence 2.

1. *Thou* or *you*, understood, is the subject.
2. *Buy* is the predicate.
3. *Some noun understood* is the object of *buy*.
4. **What you need** describes the thing, or things, named by the noun understood.
5. **What** alludes to that noun to show what the clause describes.
6. *You* is the subject of the clause, *need* is the predicate, and *what* is the object of *need*.

MODEL FOR PARSING.

What is a relative pronoun, used also as an adjective. As a relative, it shows its clause to be in a subordinate relation to *some noun understood*. As a pronoun, it represents the noun understood, and must therefore have the same person, number, and gender. It is object of the verb *need*, and is therefore put in the objective case. As an adjective, it is equivalent to *the,* and limits the noun understood.

REMARKS.—If the sentence analyzed and parsed above has reference to the *quantity* of anything; such as, wheat, hay, flour, or sugar, *what*, in its adjective use, would be equivalent to *all the;* for the meaning would be, "Buy all the flour which you need."

Who is sometimes used instead of *whoever;* as, "*Who steals my purse, steals trash*," meaning "*Whoever steals*," or "*Any person who steals*," etc.

Note.—Teachers who prefer to do so may use the models given below instead of those above. Those above are more thorough and complete; those below, more common.

MODEL FOR ANALYSIS.

Ex.—Buy what you need.

1. *Thou* or *you* is the subject; *buy* is the predicate; and *what*, as antecedent, is object of the verb.
2. **What,** as antecedent, is limited by the adjective clause *what you need.*
3. *You* is the subject of the clause; *need* is the predicate, and *what*, as relative, is its object.

MODEL FOR PARSING.

What is a pronoun, and since it performs the office of both antecedent and relative, it is said to be compound. It is 3d, sing. or plu., neu.; as antecedent, it is object of the verb *buy*, and as relative, it is object of the verb *need.*

3. Seat Work.

Study the next lesson, and select sentences that will exemplify the adjective clause introduced in all the different ways that have been noticed.

LESSON 176.

Subject of the Last Lesson Continued.

1. Examples.

1. I sent what I had.
2. Take whichever picture you prefer.
3. Whoever commits sin dishonors God.
4. He records whatever discoveries are made.
5. I saw what you had in your hand.
6. Perform faithfully whatever duties are required of you.
7. There was a considerable breeze, yet the water was calm and motionless.

REMARK.—Much difference of opinion prevails among authors in regard to *as* and *than* in such sentences as the following :—

    1. He hired as much help *as* was needed.
    2. He hired more help *than* was needed.

Some contend that *as* and *than*, as here used, are relative pronouns; others, supposing the sentences to be highly elliptical, regard them as conjunctions. Those who regard the sentences as elliptical, supply the ellipsis something as follows :—

    1. He hired as much help as was the help that was needed.
    2. He hired more help than was the help that was needed.

These words can be better explained after we have studied correlative clauses.

2. Seat Work.

Study the next lesson, and write the analysis of sentence 5.

LESSON 177.

Adjective Clauses.—Continued.

1. Examples.

1. We obeyed whatever orders were given.

2. We learned what you assigned us.

3. The high wall, on the top of which ran the aqueducts, was faced with small stones, neatly cut, and fitted into it in patterns like tessellated pavement.—*Land and Book.*

4. He bore patiently whatever fell to his lot.

5. Along the roadside, like the flowers of gold
That tawny Incas for their gardens wrought,
Heavy with sunshine droops the golden-rod.
—*Whittier, p.* 325.

6. I have a part of what you sent me.

2. Seat Work.

Study the next lesson.

LESSON 178.

Review.

1. Questions and Requirements.

1. When should adjective elements be set off by the comma ?

2. How may we make a distinction between adjective phrases introduced by a preposition, and those consisting of an adjective with its modifiers, or of two or more adjectives joined coördinately ?—The former class may be called simply *adjective phrases*, and the latter **adjectival phrases.**

3. Give an example of an adjective phrase that is set off by the comma because it is not restrictive.

4. Give an example of an adjectival phrase that is set off for the same reason.

15

5. Give a sentence containing an appositional phrase that should be set off by the comma.

6. Give a sentence containing a restrictive participial phrase.

7. Give a sentence containing a participial phrase that is not restrictive.

8. Give a sentence containing an adjective clause that is not restrictive.

9. Give a sentence containing a restrictive adjective clause.

10. Change your adjective clauses to participial phrases, and your participial phrases to adjective clauses, without changing the meaning of the sentences.

11. When should adverbial clauses be set off by the comma ?

12. Give an adverbial clause that should not be set off.

13. Give an example of an adverbial clause that should be set off because not closely connected in sense with the word it modifies.

2. Seat Work.

Study the next lesson, and write the changed forms of the constructions.

LESSON 179.

Changing Constructions.

1. Exercises.

(*a.*) Change the form, so far as possible, of all the *adjective elements* in the sentences below; changing words to phrases, phrases to clauses, and *vice versa*. In like manner change the phrases from one form to another.

EXAMPLES.

1. But Time, the old sailor, tugged away at his oar and kept steadily on.

2. There is no place which is too humble for the glories of heaven to shine in.

3. His work, finished in good time, showed his diligence.

4. In the production and preservation of order, all men recognize something that is sacred.

5. Every teacher loves a pupil who is attentive and docile.

6. And when the moonrise flooded coast and bay,
He climbed the headland stretching far away.

7. Now came the brilliant mornings, kindling all
The woody hills with pinnacles of fire.

8. Cradled in the camp, Napoleon was the darling of his army.

9. She, the mother of thy boys, will talk of thy doom without a sigh.

10. It was a grove of date-trees, clustering close about a tiny spring.

11. The bright flowers, living, fading, dying, are fit emblems of human life.

12. The best sermon which was ever preached upon modern society is "Vanity Fair."

13. A ship, sailing across the channel, struck a hidden rock.

14.   Upstood
The hoar, unconscious walls, bisson and bare,
Like an old man, deaf, blind, and gray.

15.   From the trees
That shook down pulpy dates, and from the spring,
The quiet author of that happy grove,
My wants were sated.

16. A man of calm and equable temper commands the respect of all who associate with him.

17. Among them is standing Sandalphon, the angel of glory, Sandalphon, the angel of prayer.

(*b.*) Look over past lessons, and change the constructions as you have been changing those of this lesson.

2. Seat Work.

Study next lesson, and write the parsing of all the pronouns.

LESSON 180.

Pronouns used in Asking Questions.

1. Instruction.

From the examples in the exercise below, it will be seen that the pronouns *who*, *which*, and *what* are often employed to represent the person or thing inquired for; and since they are thus used in asking questions (interrogating), they are called **interrogative pronouns.**

Interrogative pronouns have some peculiarities. They are the same words that are so often used as relative pronouns; but, unlike the relative pronouns, they have no antecedent expressed, and do not show the clause to be in a subordinate relation to any word.

The interrogative pronoun can have no antecedent expressed, for, if the speaker or writer could name the person or thing inquired for, the inquiry would be unnecessary, and no interrogative pronoun would be used. For this reason the number and gender of an interrogative pronoun are often indefinite.

2. Examples.

1. Who comes there?
2. What grieves you?
3. What is his name?
4. What is he doing?
5. Which suits you best?
6. Whom was he calling?
7. Whose horse ran away?
8. For whom were you inquiring?
9. Whose house was burned last night?—Mr. Joy's.
10. Who is sitting under the tree?—Joseph.

MODELS FOR ANALYSIS.

Ex.—Who came with you?

Who is the subject; it alludes to the person inquired for; *came* is the predicate; etc.

Ex.—Whom seek ye?

Whom alludes to the person inquired for as the one sought.

Ex.—Whose book have you?—Clara's.

1. **Whose** alludes to the person inquired for as the owner of the book.

2. **Clara's** answers the question by representing the elliptical clause, "I have Clara's book."

MODELS FOR PARSING.

Ex.—Who are you?

Who is a pronoun, interrogative, third person, number and gender indefinite; it is used with the copula to form the predicate, and is therefore put in the nominative case.

Ex.—Whose child is that?

Whose is a pronoun, interrogative, third per., sing. num., gender unknown; used to inquire for the possessor, and therefore put in the possessive case.

Ex.—Whose grammar do you use?—Greene's.

Whose is a pronoun, interrog., 3d., sing., gender unknown; it inquires for the author, and is therefore put in the possessive case.

Greene's is a noun, proper, 3d, sing., masc.; it limits the noun *grammar*, understood, by denoting authorship, and is therefore put in the possessive case.

3. Seat Work.

Study the next lesson; select three interrogative sentences introduced respectively by the interrogative pronouns *who*, *which*, and *what;* and four interrogative sentences introduced respectively by the adverbs *when, why, how,* and *where.*

LESSON 181.

Adjectives Used Interrogatively.

1. Examples.

1. What noise is that?
2. Which State has the greatest population?
3. What man lived longest?
4. Beneath, terrific caverns gave
   Dark welcome to each stormy wave
   That dashed, like midnight revellers, in.
   —*Moore.*
5. Which is the lesson?
6. For whom were you waiting?
7. What I learned I remember.
8. Who cares for him?
9. I think of thee whene'er the sun is glowing
       Upon the lake;
   Of thee, when in the crystal fountain flowing
       The moonbeams shake.
   —*Goethe.*

REMARKS.—In sentence **1**, the subject is *noise*, understood, or the word *that* representing *noise*. *Is what noise* is the predicate; it inquires for the particular noise—perhaps we might say the identity of it. If I say, "What man is that," *is what man* inquires for the identity of the man denoted by the subject; *man* names one of a class, and *what* inquires for his individual name. *That* should be parsed as a limiting adjective, belonging to the noun *man* understood; and if it is regarded as representing that noun, it is a substantive, subject of the sentence, and therefore put in the nominative case. **What** should be parsed as an adjective, limiting, added to the noun *man* to inquire for his identity—his proper name.

In trying to determine the subject in such sentences, remember that whenever the interrogative pronoun is used with the copula to inquire for the identity of a thing, it must be a part of the predicate, instead of being the subject. For instance, in sentence **5**, *is which* is the predicate, for it inquires for the particular kind of lesson here meant.

The interrogative pronouns *which* and *what* might be regarded as interrogative adjectives limiting a noun understood, but they are commonly parsed as pronouns whenever the noun is not expressed.

2. Seat Work.

Study the next lesson, and select three sentences introduced by interrogative adverbs; three introduced by interrogative adjectives; and three, by interrogative pronouns.

LESSON 182.

Interrogative Adjectives.—Continued.

1. Examples.

1. What is his name?
2. What studies are you pursuing?
3. Always seek for what you most need.
4. Who fell on that bloody field where heroes bled?
5. Which horse is yours?
6. What implement is that which you hold in your hand?
7. Which is the largest ocean?
8. Whose rod was kept in the ark?
9. I see thee when the wanton wind is busy,
   　　And dust-clouds rise;
   In the deep night, when o'er the bridge so dizzy
   　　The wanderer hies.
   　　　　　—Goethe.

2. Seat Work.

Study the next lesson, and write the parsing of all the conjunctions, and the analysis of sentences 7 and 8.

LESSON 183.

Substantive Clause as Object.

1. Instruction.

I hear that you are going to Europe.

In this sentence, *that you are going to Europe* tells what I hear. It is a clause, for it has a subject and predicate,' and since it is the object of the transitive verb *hear*, it does the work of a noun; for nouns and pronouns are the words commonly used in that office. Nouns and pronouns are called *substantives;* and since this clause does the work of a noun or pronoun, it is called a **substantive clause.**

2. Examples.

1. I know that my Redeemer liveth.
2. I believe that the Bible is a sacred book.
3. We found that he was prepared.
4. I deny that I deceived you.
5. What wicked man murdered all his brothers?
6. We admit that we were wrong.
7. They acknowledged that they were defeated.
8. Our happiness depends on what we desire.
9. I fear that I weary you.
10. Some deny that Bonaparte was a great man.

MODEL FOR ANALYSIS.
Sentence 1.

1. *I* is the subject.
2. *Know* is the predicate.
3. **That my Redeemer liveth** tells what I know.
4. **That** shows the clause to be subordinate in rank.
5. *Redeemer* is the subject; *liveth* is the predicate; and *my*, by alluding to the person speaking, tells whose Redeemer is meant.

MODEL FOR PARSING.

That is a conjunction, subordinate; it introduces a substantive clause which is object of the verb *know.*

3. Seat Work.

Study next lesson; write the parsing of the interrogative and relative pronouns, and the analysis of sentence 7.

LESSON 184.

Substantive Clauses Introduced by Interrogative Pronouns.

1. Instruction.

*I know **who took the melons.***

In this sentence, *who took the melons* is a substantive clause, object of the verb *know.* If this clause stood alone, it would be interrogative; so the pronoun *who,* which introduces it, is called an interrogative pronoun. It seems best to call these pronouns interrogative from the following considerations :—

1. Such a pronoun cannot be personal, for its person cannot be determined from its form.

2. It cannot be a relative pronoun, for it does not show its clause to be in a subordinate relation to any word.

3. It agrees with the interrogative pronoun in the following particulars :—

(*a.*) Its number and gender are often indefinite.

(*b.*) It has no antecedent expressed.

(*c.*) It introduces a clause which would, in most cases, ask a question if it stood alone.

2. Examples.

1. We heard who was elected.

2. He knows who burned the building.

3. He said, "Lord, who is it?"

4. What next befell me then and there
   I know not well.   —*Byron.*

5. I know who you are.

6. I know who took the books that lay on the table.

7. Scatter the wheat for shipwrecked men,
   Who, hunger-worn, rejoice again
   In the sweet safety of the shore.
   —*Bryant, p.* 247.

MODEL FOR ANALYSIS.
Sentence 1.

1. *We* is the subject.

2. *Heard* is the predicate.

3. **Who was elected** tells what we heard.

4. *Who* is the subject of the subordinate clause; *was elected* is the predicate.

MODEL FOR PARSING.

Who is a pronoun, interrogative, 3d., sing., gender indefinite; it is subject of the clause, and is therefore put in the nominative case.

3. Seat Work.

Study the next lesson; write the parsing of the conjunctive adverbs, and the analysis of sentence **7.**

LESSON 185.

Substantive Clauses Introduced by Conjunctive Adverbs.

1. Instruction.

We heard
{
that he hid the money.
who hid the money.
why he hid the money.
how he hid the money.
when he hid the money.
where he hid the money.
}

By studying this diagram, it may be seen that a substantive clause used as object of a transitive verb may be introduced by the conjunction *that*, by an *interrogative pronoun*, or by one of the adverbs *why, how, when,* or *where.* Each of these words has its peculiar signification. *That* directs attention to the *action*—the fact of his *hiding* the money; *who* directs attention not so much to the action as to the *person* that performs the action; *why* intimates that attention is called chiefly to the person's *motive* or *purpose* in hiding the money; *how* calls attention to the *manner* of the action, rather than to the action itself; *when*, to the *time;* and *where*, to the *place.*

2. Examples.

1. He told how the ship was managed.
2. The Indian knows where his friends are buried.
3. We know not when his life departed.
4. I heard why he declined the office.
5. I guessed how the box was opened.
6. No man ever heard how the conflict ended.
7. We never knew why he concealed his left hand.
8. At his death he told where the body was hidden.

MODEL FOR ANALYSIS.

Sentence 2.

1. *Indian* is the subject.
2. *Knows* is the predicate.
3. **Where his friends are buried** tells what the Indian knows.
4. **Where** shows the clause to be subordinate in rank.
5. *Friends* is the subject; *are buried* is the predicate; and *his*, by alluding to the Indian, tells whose friends are meant.

MODEL FOR PARSING.

Where is a **conjunctive adverb.** As a conjunction, it introduces a substantive clause that is object of the verb *knows;* as an adverb of place, it modifies the verb *are buried.*

REMARK.--Some may think that *how* as an introductory

word does not show its clause to be subordinate in rank, since a clause with this word at its head may be an *exclamatory sentence.* But exclamatory sentences are used in expressing strong emotion, and when such a clause is made the object of a transitive verb, it becomes a **direct quotation**, the word *how* begins with a capital letter, **does** not show its clause to be subordinate, and should be parsed merely as an adverb. But in the ordinary expression of thought, the case is different. Drop the word *how* from the subordinate clause in the first sentence of this lesson, and see if it will be a subordinate clause without that word. Could it in that form be used as object of the verb *told?*

3. Seat Work.

Study the next lesson; write the analysis of sentences 2 and 3, and the parsing of the conjunctive adverbs in the remaining sentences.

LESSON 186.

The Substantive Clause as Subject.

1. Instruction.

1. *That you are studious appears from your recitations.*

This sentence has a subordinate clause for its subject. *That* introduces the clause, and shows it to be subordinate in rank. True, the clause as subject cannot be subordinate to any particular word; but it is not a principal clause, for it would not make complete sense if it stood alone; and since it is an element in a sentence, and could not constitute a sentence in itself, it is called subordinate. It is shown to be subordinate by the word *that*, for if this word were removed, the clause would make complete sense standing alone, and would therefore be a principal clause.

2. Examples.

1. That the prisoner is guilty was proved by many witnesses.

2. How you obtained the money so soon is a mystery to me.

3. That the man confessed his guilt when no evidence was found against him, surprised the court.

4. How he made his escape is a mystery.

5. When he gave the fatal blow is a matter of uncertainty.

6. Where he concealed the body is a subject that is much discussed.

7. A pale yellow glow on the horizon told us where the lights of Edinburgh were afire.

8. He knew by the streamers that shot so bright,
That spirits were riding the northern light.

MODEL FOR ANALYSIS.
Sentence 1.

1. *That the prisoner is guilty* is the subject.

2. *Was proved* is the predicate.

3. The subject is itself a clause, and is introduced by *that,* which shows it to be subordinate in rank.

4. *Prisoner* is the subject of the subordinate clause, and *is guilty* is the predicate.

5. *By many witnesses* tells how the prisoner was proved guilty.

MODEL FOR PARSING.

That is a conjunction, subordinate; it introduces a substantive clause that is subject of the sentence.

3. Seat Work.

Study the next lesson, and write the analysis of sentences 2, 8, and 9.

LESSON 187.

Substantive Clauses in Predicate and in Apposition.

1. Examples.

1. The report is that the ship sailed yesterday.

2. The decision was that the prisoner is guilty.

3. My position is that negroes are men.

4. The general opinion is that Morgan was murdered.

5. The truth is that you are guilty.

6. It is surprising that you care so little for the improvement of your mind.

7. It is the general opinion that Morgan was murdered.

8. It is probable that the money was taken by a servant.

9. The question, "Are we a nation?" is now answered.

10. Bursts the moon through glade and greenwood,
  Soft the herald zephyrs play,
And the waving birches sprinkle
  Sweetest incense on my way.
         —Goethe.

MODELS FOR ANALYSIS.
Sentence 1.

1. *Report* is the subject.

2. *Is that the ship sailed yesterday* is the predicate.

3. *That the ship sailed yesterday* explains the nature of the report, and *is* shows that the thought is predicated.

4. *That* shows the clause to be subordinate in rank.

5. *Ship* is the subject, and *sailed* is the predicate.

Sentence 7.

1. *It* is the subject, and *is opinion* is the predicate.

2. *That Morgan was murdered* explains what is meant by *it.*

3. *That* shows the clause to be subordinate in rank.

4. *Morgan* is the subject, and *was murdered* is the predicate.

MODELS FOR PARSING.
Sentence 1.

That is a conjunction, subordinate ; it introduces a substantive clause that is used with the copula to form a predicate.

Sentence 7.

That is a conj., subor.; it introduces a substantive clause that is in apposition with *it.*

2. Seat Work.

Study the next lesson, and write the analysis of sentences 1, 2, and 4.

LESSON 188.

Substantive Clauses.—Continued.

1. Examples.

1. It is reported that the governor is coming to this place next week.

2. I hear that the young prince is an excellent scholar.

3. I fear that you are careless in studying your lesson.

4. He told how he escaped from the Indians.

5. To see you here on such a day surprises me.

6. Animals know who love them.

7. We know whom we worship.

8. The aquilegia sprinkled on the rocks
A scarlet rain; the yellow violet
Sat in the chariot of its leaves; the phlox
Held spikes of purple flame in meadows wet,
And all the streams with vernal-scented reed
Were fringed; and streaky bells of miskodeed.
—*Bayard Taylor.*

2. Seat Work.

Study the next lesson, and write the parsing of the pronouns and adverbs.

LESSON 189.

Miscellaneous Exercise.

1. Examples.

1. Who is the old man that came into meeting yesterday with his hat on?

2. Why are you spending so much time in an enterprise that gives no promise of success?

3. Blessed is the man whose God is the Lord.

4. He accepts what others reject.

5. Be honest in whatever business you engage.

6. A large building stands over the cave where Abraham was buried.

7. Sing me about the wild waste shore,
 Where, long and long ago, with me
You watched the silver sails that bore
 The great, strong ships across the sea,—
 The blue, the bright, the boundless sea.
        —*Alice Cary.*

REMARK.—Sentence **7** contains a case of apposition in which a word is repeated for rhetorical effect. The word *sea* in the last line becomes explanatory of the word *sea* in the preceding line, because in the last line it is limited by the adjectives *blue*, *bright*, and *boundless*. These adjectives might be added to the noun without repeating it, but the thought would not be so forcibly expressed.

Such a case of rhetorical apposition is called an **echo**, and requires the addition of a dash to the comma used to set it off.

2. Seat Work.

Write the analysis of sentence 5, and the parsing of the relative pronouns in all the sentences.

LESSON 190.

Miscellaneous Exercise.—Continued.

1. Examples.

1. We ascended the hill on which the battle was fought.

2. He builds a palace of ice where his torrent falls.

3. A kind boy avoids doing whatever annoys others.

4. He did what was right.

5. Closing the book, and turning toward the fire, he sat for a long time, gazing at the dying embers, and meditating on the strange events recorded in the book which was lying before him.

6. Thus we are marking on all our work whatever we have of grace.

7. And ever and anon came on the still air the soft, eternal pulsations of the distant sea,—sound mournfulest, most mysterious, of all the harpings of nature.—*Mrs. Stowe.*

REMARK.—Sentence **7** contains an echo, not of a *word*, but of a *thought*. It is punctuated like the ordinary echo. This sentence also contains two examples of what is called the **superlative form** of the adjective. It is the form which we use, when, in comparing one object or group of objects with several others, we wish to represent it as possessing more or less of the quality than any other with which it is compared. This form is commonly made by adding *est* to short words, and by prefixing the words *most* or *least* to longer ones. Both methods are illustrated in sentence 7.

2. Seat Work.

Write the analysis of sentence 2, and the parsing of the participles in the other sentences.

LESSON 191.

Miscellaneous Exercise.—Continued.

1. Examples.

1. They came to masses and fragments of naked rock, heaped confusedly together, like a cairn reared by giants in memory of a giant chief.

2. On returning from Portmoak church-yard, where Bruce is buried, I, attended by my venerable guide, visited the lowly dwelling where the parents of the poet resided.

3. Ascending a narrow lane, we reached, near its center, the house in which Bruce was born.

4. The moon arose: the bosom of the lawn
Whitened beneath her silent snow of light,
Save where the trees made isles of mystic night,
Dark blots against the rising splendor drawn.
—*Bayard Taylor, p.* 31.

16

5. It is a good divine that follows his own instructions.
—*Shakspeare.*

6. Mislike me not for my complexion,
The shadowed livery of the burnished sun
To whom I am a neighbor, and near bred.
—*Ibid.*

REMARK.—Sentence **4** contains a substantive clause that is object of the preposition *save*, and sentence **5**, an adjective clause that limits *it*, or the noun *divine* represented by *it;* for the meaning is, "The divine that follows his own instructions. is a good divine."

2. Seat Work.

Write the analysis of sentence 3, and the parsing of the relative pronouns in all the sentences.

LESSON 192.

Miscellaneous Exercise.—Continued.

1. Examples.

1. Then Evangeline lighted the brazen lamp on the table,
Filled, till it overflowed, the pewter tankard with home-brewed,
Nut-brown ale, that was famed for its strength in the village of Grand Pre'. *Longfellow, p.* 101.

2. On the dam stood Paw-puk-keewis,
On the dam of trunks and branches,
Through whose chinks the water spouted,
O'er whose summit flowed the streamlet.
—*Ibid., in Hiawatha.*

3. The wild, untraveled forest spreads
Back to those mountains white and cold,
Of which the Indian trapper told,
Upon whose summits never yet
Was mortal foot in safety set.

2. Seat Work.

Write the parsing of the participles in the next lesson, and the analysis of sentence 4.

LESSON 193.

Review on Participles.

1. Examples.

1. Leisurely we moved along, gazing all day on the grandeur and beauty of the wild scenery around us.

2. He heard the plaintive Nubian songs again,
And mule-bells, tinkling down the mountain-paths of Spain.
—*Whittier, p.* 296.

3. Hidden in the alder-bushes,
There he waited till the deer came.
—*Longfellow, p.* 148.

4. From his lodge went Hiawatha,
Dressed for travel, armed for hunting;
Dressed in deer-skin shirt and leggings,
Richly wrought with quills and wampum.
—*Ibid.*

5. It was the sea,—the deep, eternal sea,—the treacherous, soft, dreadful, inexplicable sea.—*Stowe.*

6. Moan, ye wild winds! around the pane,
And fall, thou drear December rain!
Fill with your gusts the sullen day,
Tear the last clinging leaves away!
—*Bayard Taylor.*

2. Questions and Requirements.

1. How do participles differ from verbs?

2. Give an example of a participle used as an adjective.

3. Give a sentence containing a participle used as a noun.

4. Explain the difference between passive participles and active participles, and illustrate by examples.

5. How do we determine whether a participle should be called past or present?

3. Seat Work.

Write sentences containing transitive and intransitive verbal nouns of both forms,—participial and infinitive.

LESSON 194.

Review on Verbal Nouns.

1. Examples.

1. To-morrow morning, with the rising sun,
   Go back unto your convent, nor refrain
   From fasting and from scourging.

2. The prisoner attempted to escape.

3. They laid plans for undermining the walls of the prison.

4. Sometimes a cloud, with thunder black,
   Stooped low upon the darkening main,
   Piercing the waves along its track
   With the slant javelins of rain.

5. His trying to evade our question proved his guilt.

6. Worn out by watching for the coming of the secret foe, he sought to arouse himself by thinking of the dangers of his situation.

7. The moonlight falls in a misty flood
   Adown on my chamber roof,
   And a thousand thoughts in my busy brain
   Soon are woven into woof.
   I think I stand on Italia's shore,
   And muse as the moonbeams fall
   On the glassy sea, and the ivied fanes,
   And many a ruined wall.—*Sara Genevra Chafa.*

REMARK.—The expression *many a ruined wall* is nearly equivalent to *many ruined walls.* It seems inconsistent that *many* and *a* should limit the same noun, since the former is always used with a plural noun, and the latter with a singular. But the expression seems to mean about the same as *many times a ruined wall,* or at least the mind is led to consider the walls *separately,* and thus they appear more distinct and more numerous.

2. Seat Work.

Write out the analysis of sentence 5, and the parsing of the nouns in apposition.

LESSON 195.

Review on Class.

1. Examples.

1. The original draft was penned by Mr. Jefferson, the chairman of the committee.

2. The autumnal tints already decorated the shores of that queen of rivers, the Ohio.

3. What are ye, O pallid phantoms!
   That haunt my troubled brain?
   That vanish when day approaches,
   And at night return again?
   —*Longfellow, p.* 228.

4. The Duchess, a very tall and very handsome woman, with a smile of the most winning sweetness, received me at the door.—*Willis.*

5. He appeared on this occasion in great state, accompanied by his household and his kinsmen, the heads of the noblest families in Spain.

2. Seat Work.

Write the analysis of sentences 1, 2, and 4.

LESSON 196.

Review on Interrogative Sentences.

1. Examples.

1. Is that a being of life, that moves
   Where the crystal battlements rise?
   —*Bryant.*

2. Is there neither spirit nor motion of thought
   In forms so lovely, and hues so bright?
   —*Ibid.*

3. There is a reaper whose name is Death,
   And with his sickle keen,
   He reaps the bearded grain at a breath,
   And the flowers that grow between.
   —*Longfellow.*

4. For whom are those glorious chambers wrought,
   In the cold and cloudless night?
   —*Bryant.*

5. Whither now·are fled those dreams of greatness?

6. Again I track its footsteps,
   To a far Egyptian plain,
   Where it falls in liquid glory
   Like a shower of silver rain.
   And it haloes the grand old pyramids
   In their mighty, solemn state,
   And it calls up within my spirit
   The dead, and the ancient great.
   —*Chafa.*

2. Seat Work.

Write the analysis of sentence 4, and the parsing of the conjunctions in all the sentences.

LESSON 197.

Review on Coördinate Clauses.

1. Examples.

1. I was oppressed by such unexpected kindness, and sleep fled from my eyes.

2. The snows of age fell, but he was not chilled by them.

3. O'er the frozen earth, the loud winds run,
   Or snows are sifted o'er the meadows bare.

4. Vainly, but well, the chieftain fought;
   He is a captive now,
   Yet pride, that fortune humbles not,
   Is written on his brow.

5. And virtue never dwells with slaves, nor reigns
   O'er those, who, cowering, take a tyrant's yoke.

6. But trees, and rivulets whose rapid course
   Defies the check of winter, haunts of deer,
   And sheep-walks populous with bleating lambs,
   And lanes in which the primrose, ere her time,

Peeps through the moss that clothes the hawthorn root,
Deceive no student.   Wisdom there and truth,
    .   .   .   .   seize at once
The roving thought, and fix it on themselves.
—Cowper.

2. Seat Work.

Write the analysis of sentence 3, and the parsing of all the subordinate conjunctions.

LESSON 198.

Review on Substantive Clauses.

1. Examples.

1. I fear that some are deceiving themselves.

2. I learned with sorrow that my old friend was dead.

3. Of all beasts he learned the language,
    Learned their names and all their secrets,
    How the beavers built their lodges,
    Where the squirrels hid their acorns,
    How the reindeer ran so swiftly,
    Why the rabbit was so timid,
    Talked with them whene'er he met them.
    —Hiawatha.

4. Who revealed the secret was never known.

5. That he was an impostor is probable from his disappearing so suddenly.

6. It is plain that they are striving for the honor and glory which this world gives.

7. Some believe that man is immortal.

2. Seat Work.

Write the parsing of the relative pronouns in the next lesson.

LESSON 199.

Review on Relative Pronouns.

1. Examples.

1. Blessed are they whose iniquities are forgiven.

2. Blessed is the man to whom the Lord imputeth not iniquity.

3. Encounter bravely whatever difficulties you meet.

4. Where are they now? What lands and skies
    Paint pictures in their friendly eyes?
    What hope deludes, what promise cheers,
    What pleasant voices fill their ears?
                                        —*Tales of a Wayside Inn.*

5. He gave me what he had.

6. There is a tide in the affairs of men,
    Which, taken at its flood, leads on to fortune.

REMARKS.—In example **4**, *they* is the subject of the first sentence, and *are where* is the predicate. It inquires for condition in regard to locality. *Where*, then, must be an adjective, just like *here* and *there* when used with the copula to predicate condition in regard to locality. These words are so generally used as adverbs, that it seems hard to recognize them in any other office; but "John is *here*" means exactly the same as, "John is *present*," and no one doubts that *present* is an adjective. These adverbs appear to become adjectives by representing some participle which they would limit as adverbs if it were expressed; but in many instances it seems impossible to find a participle that will exactly express the thought, and so we have to make the adverb do the work of an adjective. In the same way, phrases originally adverbial become adjective by the omission of the participle. Thus :—

The rich valley *lying* at our feet was beautiful in the extreme.
The rich valley *at our feet* was beautiful in the extreme.

In the first sentence, *lying at our feet* is a participial phrase, and as a whole, an adjective element; but *at our feet* is, in that sentence, an adverbial phrase limiting a participle. In the second sentence, however, *at our feet* seems to do the same work that the entire participial phrase does in the first, and so becomes an adjective element.

2. Seat Work.

Write the parsing of the relative adverbs and relative pronouns in the next lesson.

LESSON 200.

Review on Relative Adverbs.

1. Examples.

1. We came to a place where the stream was crowded into a narrow channel between two perpendicular walls of solid rock.

2. This is a time when all men are looking for some great event in the world's history.

3. It is reported that the general is visiting among his friends.

4. We carefully preserved whatever records were entrusted to our care.

5. That is the room where my father died.

6. We all remember the bright May morning when he closed his eyes, and passed away so peacefully.

7. Then, seizing a staff in his eager hand,
He hurried over the burning sand,
To a cell where a holy brother lay,
Wasting and dying day by day.
—Phebe Cary.

8. But peaceful was the night
Wherein the Prince of Light
His reign of peace upon the earth began.
—Milton.

2. Seat Work.

Study the next lesson.

LESSON 201.

Synoptical Review.

1. Outline.

In past lessons we have noticed :—

1. **Names** of things, and how, by change of form and position, they are adapted to the different circumstances of their use.

2. **Qualities** of things : how denoted ; how predicated ; and how assumed.

3. The convenience of **alluding to** the speaker, a person spoken to, or a person or thing that has been named.

4. Our need for **pointing out particular things,** or for telling **how many,** without giving any of their qualities.

5. **Actions :** how denoted ; how predicated.

6. The **modifying** of actions and qualities by single words and by groups of words.

7. How groups called adjective phrases are sometimes employed instead of single words to denote quality ; and also how these phrases, as well as possessive nouns and pronouns, are used to denote ownership, origin, authorship, adaptation, etc.

8. How the **verb** by certain **changes of form,** is adapted to the various circumstances of its use.

9. How sentences are made to ask questions, or to express commands, exhortations, entreaties, etc.

10. How things are described by assuming or predicating that they belong to a class whose qualities are well known, and how we assume or predicate the identity of things already known to belong to a certain class.

11. How actions are assumed, and the different ways in which they are named.

12. How words, phrases, and clauses are shown to be equal in rank, and alike in relation.

13. How adjectives and possessive pronouns are employed to limit nouns understood.

14. How nouns may be independent by address, and sometimes accompanied by words denoting emotion.

15. How adverbial phrases may be used without a preposition.

16. How things may be described by comparing them with other things whose qualities are well known.

17. How clauses may be employed as adverbs, to modify actions or qualities; as adjectives, to point out or describe objects; or like nouns, as the subject of a sentence, the object of a verb or preposition, with the copula in predicate, or in apposition.

2. Requirements.

1. Show by examples how nouns are adapted to the various circumstances of their use.

2. Exemplify the various forms and uses of the personal pronouns.

3. Show by examples the various uses of the verb.

4. Show how sentences are made to ask questions, and how they are made to express commands.

5. Show how things are described by assuming or predicating that they belong to a class.

6. Give examples of assuming and predicating identity.

7. Show by examples how actions are assumed.

8. Illustrate by examples the different ways of naming actions.

9. Show how words, phrases, and clauses are made coördinate.

10. Give examples of adjectives and possessive pronouns used to limit a noun understood.

11. Give examples of nouns independent by address; of adverbial phrases used without a preposition.

12. Show how things may be described by comparing them with other things whose qualities and actions are known.

13. Give examples of clauses used as adverbs.

14. Give examples of clauses used as adjectives.

15. Give examples of clauses used as nouns in all the offices mentioned in 17 above.

Suggestion.—How to keep up a profitable exercise in composition has long been a perplexing question. The following plan has proved to be very practical and successful:—

Prepare cards for all the members of the class, marking them Monday, Tuesday, Wednesday, Thursday, Friday; Monday', Tuesday', etc., till you have enough. Then, putting them blank side up, let the members of the class each draw a card. Ask each to write his name on the card he has drawn, then, collecting them, take a record that will show on what day each is to present a composition, according to his lot. This done, the cards may be returned to the members who drew them.

By this arrangement you will get a composition every day. Each composition should be handed in at least a day before the time for reading it, in order that the teacher may have time to look it over. The teacher should then read one composition every day before the class, criticising it for the benefit of all, but withholding the name of the writer.

If the compositions are poorly written, the teacher should not point out all the errors in them, for this might discourage the writers. It is better to point out only the commonest errors until the writer has learned to avoid them, and then to notice others.

By this plan, those who have had the best advantages, and can write with fewest errors, will be likely to have as many corrections made in their work as those who cannot do so well; for the object of criticism is not to show who has made most mistakes, but to help every one to write better.

The teacher must not forget to notice excellences, as well as defects, and to give to every pupil that meed of praise which may be indispensable to his success: for a discouraged pupil can hardly succeed. It is the *effort made* that should claim the teacher's approbation, rather than the proficiency attained. Do not forget to notice every indication of improvement, as well as every evidence of painstaking. Thus treated, pupils will soon come to love the exercise which they commonly dread.

The compositions should be very short, not occupying over two pages of note-paper.

LESSON 202.

Future Tense Predicating Action.

1. Instruction.

Sometimes we wish to *predict* a *future action*, and sometimes to *express our determination* to perform an action, or that some one else shall perform it. For this purpose we have a peculiar form of the verb called the **future tense.**

We have seen that there are two ways of naming actions. We may say—

> *Running* tires me,
> *To run* tires me, or
> *It tires me to run.*

In the first sentence, *running* names the action that tires me, and in the other two sentences, *to run* names the same action.

Running and *to run* are both verbal nouns, one in the participial form, and the other in the infinitive form. The word *run* is used when we wish to predicate the action; but *to run* is called the **name-form** of the verb; for it is used to name the verb itself, and also the action or state denoted by the verb.

In forming the future tense we use the *name-form* of the verb, leaving off the *to*, and prefix to it the word *shall* or *will*. The *name-form without to* denotes the action, and *shall* or *will* shows it to be future.

Verbs in the future tense do not change their form on account of the person and number of their subject, except for *thou*, which requires *shalt* and *wilt* in place of *shall* and *will*.

Form the future tense of—

To sing,	to succeed,	to persevere,	to try,
to talk,	to believe,	to descend,	to obey,
to think,	to remain,	to follow,	to travel.

1. When do we employ the future tense?

2. In making this tense, what do we use to denote the action?

3. What to show the time?

2. Examples.

1. He will come in an hour when some least expect him.

2. Here shall I rest with my friends by the sounding rock.

3. The stars of heaven shall guide us,
   The breath of heaven shall speed.

4. He never knew what hurt him.

5. I shall one day stand by the river cold,
    And list for the sound of the boatman's oar.

6. Back will I go o'er the ocean.

7. Turn, gentle hermit of the dale,
    And guide my lonely way,
    To where yon taper cheers the vale
    With hospitable ray.
    —*Oliver Goldsmith.*

8. No flocks that range the valley free,
    To slaughter I condemn;
    Taught by that power that pities me,
    I learn to pity them.
    —*Ibid.*

3. Seat Work.

Write the parsing of the verbs in the next lesson, and the analysis of sentences 4 and 5.

LESSON 203.

Future Tense Predicating Quality, Condition, or Class.

1. Instruction.

When we wish to predict future quality or condition, we put the future tense of the copula before the adjective that denotes the quality or condition.

The future tense of the copula is formed by the rule already given. The name-form of the copula is *to be.* Dropping the *to,* and prefixing *shall* or *will,* we have *shall be* or *will be* as the future tense of the copula.

When we wish to predict that some person or thing will be a member of a class at some future time, we put the future tense of the copula before the noun that names the class.

Change the verbs in the following sentences to the future tense :—

1. James is faithful.
2. Andrew is a good scholar.
3. Arthur is ready.
4. I am satisfied.
5. The task was difficult.
6. He was an excellent guide.

REMARK.—In all these cases the copula is parsed by itself as a verb. The adjective and the noun form a part of the predicate, but not a part of the verb.

2. Examples.

1. Cold will be the winter, for thick is the fur of the foxes.
2. By silent river, by moaning sea,
   Long and vain shall thy watching be.
3. Who will be a hero in the strife?
4. We learned where it was obtained.
5. No more shall he hear thy voice;
   No more awake at thy call.
6. I shall be cold in death before the morning breaks.
7. Ye shall be a peculiar treasure unto me.
8. When o'er their boughs the squirrels run,
   And through their leaves the robins call,
   And, ripening in the autumn's sun,
   The acorns and the chestnuts fall,
   Doubt not that she will heed them all.
   —*Oliver Wendell Holmes.*

3. Seat Work.
Select—
Four sentences predicating future action.
Two sentences predicating future condition or quality.
Two sentences predicating future class.

———•——

LESSON 204.

The Present Perfect Tense.

1. Instruction.
Sometimes we wish to show that the action is in a completed state at the time of mentioning it. For the purpose of showing the completed, or finished, state of the

action, we have what is called the **past participle.** In regular verbs this past participle is spelled the same as the past tense, but the past participle of irregular verbs usually differs from the past tense, as will be seen by the following table :—

Name-Form.	Pres. Tense.	Past Tense.	Past Participle.
To walk,	walk *or* walks,	walked,	walked.
To write,	write *or* writes,	wrote,	written.
To go,	go *or* goes,	went,	gone.
To fly,	fly *or* flies,	flew,	flown.
To see,	see *or* sees,	saw,	seen.
To leave,	leave *or* leaves,	left,	left.
To be,	am, is, *or* are,	was *or* were,	been.

This past participle cannot in itself predicate anything. When we wish to predicate an action and represent it as completed at the time of mentioning it, we use the past participle to denote the completed state of the action, and put before it the verb "to have" to show that the act is predicated. We use the *present tense* of "to have" (*have* or *has*) to show that the act is in a completed state *at the time of mentioning it.*

The tense thus formed is called the **present perfect tense,** because it shows the action to be in a completed (perfect) state at the *present time.* The act is *perfect* in the sense of being *completed.*

2. Questions.

1. What do we have for the purpose of denoting action, and representing it as being in a completed state ?

2. What class of verbs always have their past tense and past participle formed alike ? Give verbs whose past tense and past participle are not alike.

3. When we wish to predicate an action, and show that it is completed, what do we use to denote the action?

4. Does this word do anything more than merely to *denote* the action ? What ?

5. Can it *predicate* the action ?

6. Can it show the *time* of the action?

7. What is employed to show the *time* of the action, and that it is predicated?

8. What do we call that form of the verb that predicates that an action is complete (finished) at the present time?

9. Of what two parts does this tense consist?

10. What two purposes does the past participle serve?

11. What two purposes are served by the auxiliary verb *to have?*

In common language, the present perfect tense has but one change for the person and number of its subject. Whenever the subject is in the third person, singular number, we use *has* in place of *have.*

Thou changes *have* to *hast.*

3. Exercises.

(*a.*) Form the present perfect tense of every verb in the list given above.

(*b.*) Tell, in every case, why you use the *past participle*, and why the verb *to have.*

(*c.*) Tell what is wrong in each of the following sentences, why it is wrong, and how it can be made right :—

1. I have broke my slate.
2. Ellen has tore her dress.
3. I have eat my dinner.
4. Ben has went to town.
5. I have ran all the way.
6. We have wrote our compositions.
7. The young birds have flew away.
8. I have saw a man walk on a rope.
9. I seen Sarah tear that book.
10. I run all the way to school yesterday.

MODEL FOR CORRECTING TENSE FORMS.

Sentence 1.

Have broke should be **have broken,** for the *past participle* should be used with *have* or *has* to form the *present perfect tense.*

17

Sentence 9.

In this sentence, **seen** should be **saw;** for *seen* is the past participle, and can neither show time nor predicate action.

4. Seat Work.

Write the analysis of sentences 1, 4, and 6.

LESSON 205.

The Present Perfect Tense.—Continued.

1. Examples.

1. O have ye seen the young Kathleen, the flower of Ireland?
2. We have come across the sea.
3. Thou hast brought comfort to our dwelling.
4. I shall watch for a gleam of the flapping sail;
   I shall hear the boat as it gains the strand.
                                          —*Miss Priest.*
5. The wind and the waves their work have done;
   We shall see him no more beneath the sun.
                                          —*Whittier.*
6. Who has not dreamed of a world of bliss
   On a bright, sunny day like this?
7. Now every hovering insect to his place beneath the leaves hath flown.
8. Sweet smiling village, loveliest of the lawn,
   Thy sports are fled, and all thy charms withdrawn;
   Amidst thy bowers the tyrant's hand is seen,
   And desolation saddens all thy green.
                       —*Goldsmith, in Deserted Village.*

REMARK.—**Are fled,** in sentence **8,** means *have fled;* it is a relic of an old conjugation, now nearly obsolete, in which *to be* was used in place of *to have* in the perfect tenses. It should be parsed as the present perfect tense.

MODEL FOR ANALYSIS.

Ex.—I have given some attention to farming.

1. *I* is the subject.
2. **Have given** is the predicate; it predicates action. and represents it as completed at the time of mentioning it.

3. **Given** denotes the action, and represents it as completed.

4. **Have** shows that the action is predicated, and denotes present time.

5. Etc.

2. Seat Work.

Write the analysis of sentences 4 and 6 of the next lesson; correct all errors in the other examples, writing reasons for the changes made.

LESSON 206.

Subject of the Last Lesson Continued.

1. Examples.

1. The wind has blew furiously all night.

2. I give two dollars for that book, and afterward sold it for ninety cents.

3. We never knew who released the prisoners.

4. Since then, the winter blasts have piled the white pagodas of the snow on these rough slopes.

5. My grandfather come over in a ship that was built in Holland.

6. And over those gray fields, then green and gold,
The summer corn has waved, the thunder's organ rolled.

7. The price of wheat has fell ten cents on a dollar.

8. I knowed him when he first come in.

MODELS FOR CORRECTING TENSE FORMS.

Knowed should be *knew;* for *know* is an irregular verb, and does not form its past tense by adding *ed* to the present.

Come should be *came;* for *come* is the present tense and also the past participle, but should never be used as the past tense.

2. Seat Work.

Write out the analysis of sentences 4 and 6 of the next lesson.

LESSON 207.

The Past Perfect Tense.

1. Instruction.

We often wish to represent an act as having been completed at some time in the past. We then use the past participle to denote the action and show it to be in a completed state, and the past tense of "to have," to show that the act is predicated, and to denote the time in which it was completed.

In this case we want to predicate an action, and represent it as completed, just as we do in the present perfect tense ; but we wish to show that it was completed *in the past*, so we use the *past tense* of "to have" instead of its *present tense*. This tense is called the **past perfect tense**, and differs from the present perfect only in time. It consists of the past participle, and the *past* tense of "to have," just as the present perfect consists of the past participle, and the *present* tense of "to have."

The past perfect tense has no change for person and number ; so in parsing verbs in this tense, we do not give person and number, but say, "*Verbs in this tense do not change their form for the person and number of their subject.*"

Change the present perfect tenses in the two preceding lessons to past perfect tenses.

2. Examples.

1. They had waited by the sea till he came o'er from Gadara.

2. Many a weary year had passed since the burning of Grand Pre'.

3. The evening gun had sounded from gray Fort Mary's walls.

4. The night cloud had lowered, and the sentinel stars set their watch in the sky.

5. I will still trust in him.

6. He had taken refuge in a cave, the entrance of which was hid from observation by a thick clump of cedars.

3. Seat Work.

Study the next lesson, and write out the parsing of the verbs.

LESSON 208.

Miscellaneous Exercise in the Tenses.

1. Examples.

1. The lowliest bush that by the waste is seen
   Hath changed its dusky for a golden green.

2. When night comes on the hill, and when the loud winds arise, my ghost shall stand in the blast, and mourn the death of my friends.

3. She had lain since noontide in a breathless trance.

4. "Here I remain!" he exclaimed, as he looked at the
   heavens above him,
   Thanking the Lord, whose breath had scattered the mist
   and the madness,
   Wherein, blind and lost, to death he was staggering
   headlong.   —*Longfellow.*

5. Those dusky foragers, the noisy rooks,
   Have from their green high city-gates rushed out.
   Thomas Miller.

REMARK.—**Hath,** in sentence **1,** belongs to what is called the *solemn style.* It is seldom used except in the Bible, in poetry, and in the conversation of the Friends.

2. Seat Work.

Study the next lesson; write the parsing of the verbs, and the analysis of sentence 5.

LESSON 209.

The Future Perfect Tense.

1. Instruction.

Sometimes we wish to predict that an action will be completed at some point of time in the future. This creates a demand for what is called the **future perfect tense.** This tense is just like the other perfect tenses, except in time. It consists of the past participle and the *future* tense of "to have," just as the *past* perfect consists of the past participle and the *past* tense of "to have"; the past participle being used to show the completed state of the action, and the future tense of "to have" to show that it is to be completed in future time.

The future tense of "to have" is formed just like the future tense of any other verb. Dropping *to* from the name-form, and then prefixing *shall* or *will*, gives us *shall have* or *will have* as the future tense, and prefixing this to the past participle of any verb gives us the *future perfect tense* of that verb.

The future perfect tense, like the past perfect, never changes its form for the person and number of its subject.

Adapt the questions in Lesson 204 to the future perfect tense, and give proper answers.

Form all the perfect tenses of the following verbs :—

Fear,   stay,   wear,   smite,   shake,   write,
throw,   steal,   sing,   weave,   take,   rise.

2. Examples.

1. I shall have completed the work before the appointed time.

2. Before you receive this letter, he will have met his fate.

3. Three nights by its quiet side had greatly endeared to us the associations of its waves and shores.

4. By the time I see him again, he will have lost all these qualities; he will have acquired some knowledge of the world.

5. For weeks the clouds had raked the hills,
   And vexed the vales with raining;
   And all the woods were sad with mist,
   And all the brooks complaining.
                        —*Whittier, p.* 327.

6. By that time he will have reached his destination.

3. Seat Work.

Study next lesson, and write out the analysis of sentence 2.

LESSON 210.

Miscellaneous Exercise.

1. Examples.

1. Dikes, that the hands of the farmers had raised with
      labor incessant,
   Shut out the turbulent tides.

2. All day the darkness and the cold
      Upon my heart have lain,
   Like shadows on the winter sky,
      Like frost upon the pane.

3. We shall have pleasant walks with your friends.

4. Before he reaches his victim, he will have met the fate
he so richly deserves.

5. I have seen him to-day.

6. Painter, paint me a sycamore,
      A spreading and snowy-limbed tree,
      Making cool shelter for three,
   And, like a green quilt at the door
      Of the cabin near the tree,
      Picture the grass for me,
   With a winding and dusty road before,
      Not far from the group of three
      And the silver sycamore-tree.—*Alice Cary.*

2. Seat Work.

Write sentences containing all the tenses of the verb
to be.

LESSON 211.

Tenses of the Verb To Be.

1. Instruction.

All the tenses of the verb *to be* are employed as *copula;* and all alike show that some thought is predicated,—some action, quality, condition, or class, denoted by a word used with the copula to form the predicate. But, like *have* in the perfect tenses, the verb *to be,* as copula, not only shows that the thought is predicated, but also the *time* when that quality, condition, or class pertains to the subject. Some of these uses are shown in the examples below.

The verb *to be* is sometimes used to denote simply the existence of the subject. It is not then a copula, but may be parsed as an intransitive verb. This use is illustrated in the third example.

2. Examples.

1. It is twenty long years since that old ship went out of the bay.

2. The leaves of the elm-tree were dusty and brown.

3. The joys that have been are joys still.

4. It had been a happy morning's work.

5. That old house was our home.

6. My brother has been sick for several days.

7. They had been students at the university.

8. I shall have been a teacher thirty years next autumn.

9. It will be delightful to meet the friends whom we have loved in this life.

10. Yes, we're boys,—always playing with tongue or with pen;
And I sometimes have asked, Shall we ever be men?
Shall we always be youthful, and laughing, and gay,
Till the last dear companion drops smiling away?

- Oliver Wendell Holmes.

3. Seat Work.

Write out all the tenses of the verbs—

To sit, to set, to lie, to lay.

LESSON 212.

The Verbs, Sit, Set, Lie, and Lay.

1. Instruction.

To sit and **to lie** are intransitive verbs, and should not be used when the action is represented as being received by something.

To set and **to lay** are transitive verbs, and should be used when the action is represented as being received by something.

The *examples* of this lesson afford several instances of the improper use of these verbs.

2. Examples.

1. After I had laid down, I remembered that I had left my pistols on the table.

2. I have lain your book on the shelf.

3. Will you sit the pitcher on the table?

4. I was setting by her bedside.

5. I counted thirteen vessels lying at anchor in the stream.

6. He laid down at night, but rose not again.

7. I will lie on the sofa.

8. The vessel lays in St. Katherine's docks.

9. We often set traps for mice, and gardeners set cabbage-plants.

10. I laid down under the first tree I came to.

11. I shall go and lie down.

12. We had set in the shade of that tree many times.

3. Seat Work.

Put each of the following verbs in all the tenses, progressive form :—

| Hope, | strive, | think, | expect, | look, |
| write, | work, | endeavor, | watch, | wait. |

Note.—For the sake of brevity we often omit the *to* in speaking of verbs, as above.

--- --- • --- ---

LESSON 213.

Progressive Form.

1. Instruction.

Sometimes we wish to predicate an action, and at the same time show that it is *continuing.* For the purpose of showing that the action is continuing, we have the **present active participle.** This participle is formed by dropping *to* from the name-form, and then adding *ing.* It cannot be used alone as a verb, for it can neither predicate action, nor show time. So when we wish to predicate an act and represent it as progressing at the time referred to, we use the *present active participle* to denote the action, and put before it the *copula* to denote the time and to show that the act is predicated.

This makes what is called the **progressive form** of the verb. We have already used this form many times in our lessons, without explaining it.

Ex.—Snow is falling. Grass is growing. Winds are blowing.

The progressive form consists of two parts,—the *present active participle* and the *copula.* The participle does two things,—it denotes the action, and represents it as progressing. The copula does two things,—it shows that the act is predicated, and also the time when the act is represented as progressing.

The progressive form represents the action as being

incomplete, just as the perfect tenses of the common form represent it as being *complete.*

If we wish to represent an action as progressing at the present time, we join the participle to the *present* tense of the copula. Thus :—

am writing, is writing, or *are writing.*

If we wish to represent an action as progressing in past time, we join the participle to the *past* tense of the copula. Thus :—

was writing or *were writing.*

If we wish to predict that an action will be continuing in the future, we join the participle to the *future* tense of the copula. Thus :—

shall be writing.

If we wish to show that an action has been progressing in what we regard as the present period, but that it is now completed, we join the participle to the *present perfect* tense of the copula. Thus :—

have been writing or *has been writing.*

If we wish to show that an action was continuing in a past period, but was completed at a specified time in the past, we join the participle to the *past perfect* tense of the copula. Thus :—

had been writing.

If we wish to predict that the action will be progressing in the future, and that it will be completed before a specified time in the future, we join the participle to the *future perfect* tense of the copula. Thus :—

shall have been writing.

2. Questions.

1. When do we use the past progressive ?

2. When do we use the present progressive ?

3. When do we use the future progressive ? The present perfect progressive ? The future perfect progressive ?

4. When do we use the past perfect progressive?

5. Of what two parts does the progressive form consist?

6. What two things does each part do?

7. Can the participle predicate action?

8. Can it show the time of the action?

9. What do we employ for these purposes?

10. Which part shows the state of the action?

11. Which determines the tense?

12. In what are all the tenses of the progressive form alike?

13. In what are they different?

3. Examples.

1. I shall have been attending school two years when this term closes.

2. One night he had been thinking of his mother and her picture in the drawing-room down stairs.

3. My friend is studying French.

4. She will be sleeping under the daisies.

5. Will you be coming this way again!

6. The night was winter in its roughest mood;
The morning sharp and clear. But now at noon,
Upon the southern side of the slant hills,
And where the woods fence off the northern blast,
The season smiles, resigning all its rage,
And has the warmth of May. The vault is blue
Without a cloud, and white without a speck
The dazzling splendor of the scene below.
—Cowper.

MODEL FOR ANALYSIS.
Sentence 1.

1. *I* is the subject.

2. **Shall have been attending** is the predicate.

3. **Attending** denotes the action and represents it as progressing.

4. **Shall have been,** the future perfect tense of the copula, shows that the progressive action is to be completed before some future time specified.

5. *School* tells what I am attending; *two years* tells how long; and *when this term closes* tells when the two years will expire, or when I shall have attended school two years.

4. Seat Work.

Study the next lesson, and write the analysis of sentences 3 and 4.

LESSON 214.

Subject of the Last Lesson Continued.

1. Examples.

1. As they were working hard at the building, a frightful scream was heard.

2. He saw that the floor was sinking.

3. I am expecting my friend Thornton, who has been an officer in the army, and is soon going to Europe.

4. She had been writing to her mother, and was just folding the letter when Ruth came in.

5. The ghost of what was once a ship is sailing up the bay.

6. The sun was now setting upon one of the rich, glassy glades of this forest.

7. They had been fishing all night, but had caught nothing.

8. All day the low-hung clouds have dropped
    Their garnered fullness down;
All day that soft gray mist hath wrapped
    Hill, valley, grove, and town.

2. Seat Work.

Write all the tenses, *passive form*, of the following verbs :—

Forget, strike, see, forsake, wrap, steal, disturb.

LESSON 215.

. The Passive Form.

1. Instruction.

The *passive voice* of the verb may be called the **passive form.** It is used when we wish to predicate an action, and show that it is received by the subject.

The passive form consists of the **passive** *participle* and the *copula*, just as the progressive form consists of the **present active** *participle* and the *copula*.

The *passive participle* denotes the action, and shows that the subject receives it.

The copula does just what it does in the progressive form.

Look over the examples of Lessons 213 and 214, and change the transitive verbs to the passive form.

2. Examples.

1. On the shores, meanwhile, the evening fires had been kindled, built of drift-wood thrown on the sands from the wrecks of the tempest.

2. And the names he loved to hear
   Have been carved for many a year
     On the tomb.

3. Many centuries have been numbered
   Since in death the baron slumbered
   By the convent's sculptured portal,
   Mingling with the common dust.

4. Before another sun shall set, the tidings of victory will have been borne to every hamlet in the land.

5. By the majestic rivers, and in the depths of the solitary woods, the feeble sons of the bow and arrow will be seen no more.

6. A vessel had been wrecked on that lonely island many years before.

REMARKS.—The model for analyzing verbs in the progressive form will, with slight changes, apply as well to the analysis of verbs in the passive form. When this careful analysis of the tense-forms has become entirely familiar, it need be given only occasionally.

In sentence **5,** the Indians are called the sons of the bow and arrow on account of their close relation to these implements as their chief means of defense in time of war, and of support in time of peace.

3. Seat Work.

Select sentences containing the passive form of the verb in all its tenses.

LESSON 216.

Promiscuous Exercise.

1. Examples.

1. Cool airs are murmuring that the night is near.

2. The town had drifted behind us, and we were entering among the groups of islands.

3. I have been watching for you since early morning.

4. I had been detained, in the course of a journey, by a slight illness, from which I soon recovered.

5. I am gazing into the twilight
    Where the dim-seen meadows lie,
And the wind of night is swaying
    The trees with a heavy sigh.

6. Nevermore shall her voice be heard in our happy throng.

7. Long will he have been sleeping the sleep of death.

2. Seat Work.

Write the tenses of the verbs *hear*, *sing*, *speak*, in all the forms.

LESSON 217.

Emphatic Form.

1. Instruction!

Sometimes we wish to predicate an action with more than usual earnestness; and for the purpose of doing this, we have what is called the **emphatic form.**

EXAMPLES.

Common form.	*Emphatic Form.*
I *believe.*	I *do believe.*
I *went.*	I *did go.*

This form is found only in two tenses; the present and the past. It consists of two parts; the *name-form without to,* and the verb *to do.*

This form is frequently used in the present and past indicative for the purpose of asking questions, since the ordinary form consists of but one word, and in asking a question we have to put the first word of the verb before the subject. Thus:— .

Do you *believe?*   ***Did*** you *go?*

In denying a thing we usually put the negative word after the first word of the verb, and so have use for the emphatic form just as we do in asking questions. Thus:—

I *do* not *believe* it.   I *did* not *go.*

2. Examples.

1. We do not insist upon any arbitrary forms.

2. He did not believe there was any such thing, because he had never seen it.

3. What city do we inhabit!

4. I thought of a mound in sweet Auburn
   Where a little headstone stood;
   How the flakes were folding it gently,
   As did robins the babes in the wood.

—James Russell Lowell.

5. She did not set a high value upon herself, but when others valued her, she was glad.

6. "I do believe you," said Alice.

7. Everything was hers, but what did it avail now?

8. After this visit I did not see her again till the day of Alice's funeral.

9. And then in my dream we stood alone
   On a forest path where the shadows fell;
   And I heard again the tremulous tone,
   And the tender words of his last farewell.
   —*Sarah T. Bolton.*

3. Seat Work.

Give the tenses of the following verbs in all the forms, writing out the tenses of the first:—

To steal, to subdue, to defend.

MODEL FOR WRITING TENSE-FORMS.
Tense-forms of the verb *To Drive.*

COMMON FORM.
PRESENT TENSE.

With a subject in the 3d, sing., *drives;*
With any other subject (except *thou*), *drive.*

PAST TENSE.
Drove.

FUTURE TENSE.
Shall drive or *will drive.*

PRESENT PERFECT TENSE.

With a subject in the 3d, sing., *has driven.*
With any other subject, *have driven.*

PAST PERFECT TENSE.
Had driven.

FUTURE PERFECT TENSE.
Shall have driven or *will have driven.*

18

PROGRESSIVE FORM.

PRESENT TENSE.

With a subject in the 1st, sing., *am driving;*
With a subject in the 3d, sing., *is driving;*
With any other subject, *are driving.*

PAST TENSE.

With a subject in the 1st or 3d, sing., *was driving.*
With any other subject, *were driving.*

FUTURE TENSE.

Shall be driving or *will be driving.*

PRESENT PERFECT TENSE.

With a subject in the 3d, sing., *has been driving.*
With any other subject, *have been driving.*

PAST PERFECT TENSE.

Had been driving.

FUTURE PERFECT TENSE.

Shall have been driving or *will have been driving.*

PASSIVE FORM.

This form differs from the progressive only in substituting the passive participle for the present active, and should be written out accordingly.

EMPHATIC FORM.

PRESENT TENSE.

With a subject in the 3d, sing., *does drive.*
With any other subject, *do drive.*

PAST TENSE.

Did drive.

(Used for Inquiry.)

Do I *drive?*   *Does* he *drive?*

(Used for Denial.)

I *do* not *drive.*   He *does* not *drive.*

TENSE-FORMS REQUIRED FOR "THOU."

	Common Form.	Progressive Form.
Present Tense,	drivest,	*art* driving.
Past Tense,	drovest,	*wast* driving.
Future Tense,	shalt drive,	*shalt be* driving.
Pres. Perf. Tense,	hast driven,	*hast been* driving.
Past Perf. Tense,	hadst driven,	*hadst been* driving.
Fut. Perf. Tense,	shalt have driven,	*shalt have been* driving.

The passive form merely substitutes the passive participle for the present active of the progressive.

LESSON 218.

Perfect Participles.

1. Instruction.

Common Form.

Perf. Tense,	**Have** *called.*
Perf. Participle,	**Having** *called.*

Progressive Form.

Perf. Tense,	**Have** *been calling.*
Perf. Participle,	**Having** *been calling.*

Passive Form.

Perf. Tense,	**Have** *been called.*
Perf. Participle,	**Having** *been called.*

1. What is the difference between a participle and a verb?

2. What participle assumes an action and represents it as present at the time of a past action predicated by the verb?

3. What participle assumes an action and represents it as present at the time of a future action predicated by the verb? See Lesson 109.

4. When is a participle said to be active?

5. When passive?

6. What tense predicates action, and represents it as completed at the time of mentioning it?

7. What tense predicates action, and represents it as completed at some time in the past? In the future?

Sometimes, instead of *predicating,* we wish to *assume* an action and represent it as completed. The *tenses* that *predicate* action and represent it as completed are called *perfect tenses;* so the participle that assumes action and represents it as completed is called the **perfect participle.** As we need only one participle to represent action as being *present* at any time denoted by the verb, so we need only one perfect participle to represent action as *completed* at any time denoted by the verb; and as the perfect tenses have three forms,—common, progressive, and passive,—the perfect participle has the same; for the perfect participle may be used to assume anything that a perfect tense can predicate.

The perfect tenses and the perfect participle are alike in representing the action as completed; so they both employ the same word, *the past participle,* to denote the action. The perfect tenses employ the verb *to have* as auxiliary, to show that the act is predicated, and to show *when* it is completed; but the perfect participle must not *predicate* the action, and its *time* depends upon the predicate verb; so instead of employing the *tense-forms* of "to have" as auxiliaries, it takes the *present active participle* of that verb, as seen in the illustrations at the head of this lesson. In the progressive and passive forms, the perfect tenses of any verb take the perfect tenses of the copula as auxiliaries; so, in the corresponding forms, the perfect participle of any verb takes the perfect participle of the copula as auxiliary, as illustrated above.

Make the perfect participles of the following verbs, in the three forms,—common, progressive, and passive :—

Choose, hide, speak, take, weave.

2. Examples.

1. Having been riding all day in the rain, I was completely drenched and extremely weary.

2. The savage beast, having finished his repast, sought repose.

3. Having been reduced to extreme poverty, she wandered about from house to house, looking for work.

4. These are the gardens of the desert, these
   The unshorn fields, boundless and beautiful,
   For which the speech of England has no name—
   The prairies.   —*Bryant, p.* 130.

5. Locke was traveling on the Continent for his health when he learned that he had been deprived of his home and of his bread without a trial or even a notice.—*Macaulay.*

6. This having learned, thou hast attained the sum
   Of wisdom.   —*Milton.*

MODEL FOR ANALYSIS.
Sentence 1.

1. *I* is the subject.

2. *Was drenched* and *weary* is the predicate.

3. **Having been riding all day in the rain** describes the speaker by assuming an action of him.

4. **Riding** denotes the action, and represents it as progressing.

5. **Having been** shows that the action, which had been progressing, was completed at the time denoted by the predicate.

6. *All day* tells how long he had been riding, and

7. *In the rain* tells under what circumstances he had been riding.

MODEL FOR PARSING.

Having been riding is a participle, perfect progressive, intransitive, added to the pronoun *I* to denote an assumed action performed by the speaker.

3. Seat Work.

Write the perfect participles (common, progressive, and passive forms) of the verbs—

Hew, shake, steal, teach, write.

LESSON 219.

Subject of the Last Lesson Continued.

1. Examples.

1. Having experienced some difficulty in making my way through the jungle, I was separated from my friends, and had the pleasure of completing my journey alone.

2. Never having been initiated into this wild sport, I made many ridiculous blunders.

3. The colonists, having gained peace and security, gave their attention to the founding of a permanent government.

4. Having been driven from his home, he wandered among the mountains, subsisting on berries and wild game.

5. Moses, having led his flock to the backside of the desert, was astonished at the sight of a burning bush.

6. But he that hides a dark soul and foul thoughts,
Benighted walks under the mid-day sun;
Himself is his own dungeon.
—*Milton.*

7. Next day, within a mossy glen, 'mid moldering trunks were found
The fragments of a human form upon the bloody ground;
White bones from which the flesh was torn, and locks of glossy hair;
They laid them in the place of graves, yet wist not whose they were.
—*Bryant, p.* 173.

2. Seat Work.

Study the next lesson, and write the parsing of all the participles.

LESSON 220.

Complete Classification of Participles.

1. Instruction.

Every verb has three participles,—the present, the past, and the perfect.

The present participle represents the action as present at the time denoted by the predicate. The present participle of a transitive verb may be *active* or *passive*, as seen in the following example :—

Loving all and loved by all, he enjoys a happy life.

In this sentence, *loving* is present active, and *loved* is present passive.

The past participle (except when passive) is combined with some other word or words, as it is in the perfect tenses and perfect participles.

The past participle of a transitive verb is sometimes passive, as seen below.

A fish caught in the China Sea will be exhibited in Boston.

In this sentence, *caught* represents the action as taking place before the time denoted by the predicate, and is called the **Past Passive Participle.** The present passive participle, and the past participles, both active and passive, are written alike, and have to be distinguished by the manner in which they are used, as will be seen by comparing the following examples with the last one given above :—

1. *The fish caught in those waters are very large.*
2. *I have caught many fine fish in that lake.*

A perfect participle, as already noticed, may take the common form or the progressive ; and if transitive, the passive form also.

Give all the participles of the following verbs :—

Speak, watch, give, teach, fall, improve.

FORM FOR WRITING PARTICIPLES.

PRESENT PARTICIPLES.		PAST PARTICIPLES.	
Active.	*Passive.*	*Active.*	*Passive.*
Speaking,	spoken,	spoken,	spoken.
Watching,	watched,	watched,	watched.
Giving,	given,	given,	given.

PERFECT PARTICIPLES.		
Common Form.	*Progressive Form.*	*Passive Form.*
Having spoken,	having been speaking,	having been spoken.
Having watched,	having been watching,	having been watched.
Having given,	having been giving,	having been given.

2. Examples.

1. Having been summoned to the seat of war, he immediately departed.

2. Foiled and defeated, the British general effected a gloomy retreat.

3. Having wielded his sword with success, he retired with honest delight to his farm.

4. The Indian currency consisted of a sort of long beads cut from the inside of shells.

5. Having gathered up the dry pine branches, he kindled a fire.

6. To threats the stubborn sinner oft is hard,
  Wrapped in his crimes, against the storm prepared;
  But, when the milder beams of mercy play,
  He melts, and throws his cumbrous cloak away.
                     —*Dryden.*

3. Seat Work.

Study the next lesson; write the parsing of the participles, and give all the other participles that can be derived from the same verbs.

LESSON 221.

Miscellaneous Exercise.

1. Examples.

1. Having risen to a state of affluence, he neglected the humble friends who had aided him in former years.

2. The patient Innuit had been watching all day on the ice for the appearance of Nutchook, the seal.

3. Having failed in the object of his mission, he engaged in the better enterprise of exploring the south-western coast of America.

4. Who of us will then care for praise?

5. Some fondly imagine that they will never die.

6. You, my dear sir, have often been seen in the company of profligate men.

7.   They do not err
Who say, that when the poet dies,
Mute Nature mourns her worshiper,
And celebrates his obsequies.
—*Scott.*

2. Seat Work.

Study the next lesson, and write the analysis of sentence 6.

LESSON 222.

Miscellaneous Exercise.—Continued.

1. Examples.

1. None ever knew for whom the hut was built.

2. The cars have been running to Nelson for the last three weeks.

3. In the next town the lecturer had been making quite a stir among the people.

4. Fred was the only scholar who had been absent, so all knew who the teacher meant.

5. Have all those upon whom this disappointment falls been laboring in vain?

6. Our object will not have been accomplished till the tomahawk shall be buried forever; till the wilderness and the solitary place shall have been glad for us, and the desert shall rejoice, and blossom as a rose.—*Francis Wayland.*

7. Our object will not be accomplished until every idol temple shall have been utterly destroyed.—*Ib.*

Note.—An error has been purposely made in one of the above examples. Do not fail to correct it.

2. Seat Work.

Select sentences containing all the different kinds of participles.

LESSON 223.

Miscellaneous Exercise.—Continued.

1. Examples.

1. The gleaming swords like meteors flash.

2. We have the promise that we shall not tread the dark valley alone.

3. That he was seen elsewhere the same evening, affords no proof of his innocence.

4. Having been earnestly engaged in the duties of his profession, he was unacquainted with the current news of the day.

5. A glorious remnant linger yet,
    Whose lips are wet at Freedom's fountains,
    The coming of whose welcome feet
    Is beautiful upon our mountains.
    —*Whittier, p.* 54.

6. But not for her has spring renewed the sweet surprises of the wood.—*Ibid, p.* 371.

2. Seat Work.

Study the next lesson so as to be able to describe the different tenses and participles in all their forms.

LESSON 224.

Synopsis of the Formation and Uses of the Different Tenses and Participles.

1. Instruction.

The Indicative mode has six tenses which have been considered in all their forms. In the—

COMMON FORM,

The **present tense** is the simplest form of the verb, with such changes as may be required by the person and number of the subject. It is used when we wish to represent an action as present at the time of mentioning it.

The **past tense** of regular verbs is the simplest form of the verb, with *ed* added. Irregular verbs have no regular way of forming their past tense, hence their name. The past tense is used when we wish to represent the action as past at the time of mentioning it.

The **future tense** consists of the name-form without *to*, as chief word, or *basis*, with one of the words *shall* or *will*, prefixed as auxiliary. It has no change for the person and number of its subject, and is used whenever the speaker wishes to predict an action, state, or quality.

The **present perfect tense** consists of the *past participle* as basis, with the *present tense* of "*to have*" for auxiliary. It is used when we wish to represent an action as completed at the time of mentioning it.

The **past perfect tense** consists of the *past participle* as basis, with the *past tense* of "*to have*" for auxiliary. It is used when we wish to represent an act as completed at some point of time in the past.

The **future perfect tense** consists of the *past participle* as basis, with the *future tense* of "*to have*" for auxiliary. It is used when we wish to predict that an action will be completed at some point of time in the future.

PROGRESSIVE FORM.

In this form we employ the *present active participle* as basis in all the tenses, and for auxiliary that tense of the verb *to be* which corresponds to the tense we wish to form.

PASSIVE FORM.

This form consists of the *passive participle* as basis, with the tenses of the verb *to be* for auxiliaries.

PARTICIPLES.

The ***present active*** *participle* is made by dropping *to* from the *name-form,* and then adding *ing.* It is employed to assume an action, and represent it as continuing at the time denoted by the predicate.

The ***present passive*** *participle* of a regular verb takes the same form as its past tense. It is employed to assume an action, and represent it as being received at the time denoted by the predicate.

The ***past active*** *participle* is the same in form as the *passive,* but differs from it in its use. It is seldom, if ever, used alone, but is employed with the tenses and present active participle of *to have* in forming the perfect tenses and perfect participles.

The ***past passive*** *participle* differs from the *present passive* only in that it represents the act denoted by it as occurring *before* the act denoted by the predicate, while the present passive represents its act as taking place at the same time as that denoted by the predicate of the clause in which it is used.

The ***perfect active*** *participle* has the *past participle* as basis, and the *present active* of "*to have*" as auxiliary. It corresponds to the perfect tenses, common form, and assumes just what they predicate.

The ***perfect progressive*** *participle* has for its basis the *present active participle* of the verb whose tense we are forming, and for auxiliary the *perfect active participle* of the verb "*to be.*" It corresponds to the perfect progressive tenses, and assumes just what they predicate.

The *perfect passive* *particle* has for its basis the *passive* participle of the verb whose tense we are forming, and for auxiliary the perfect active participle of "*to be.*" It corresponds to the perfect passive tenses, and assumes just what they predicate.

2. Seat Work.

Study next lesson ; write out the parsing of the words in sentence 1, and a brief analysis of sentence 2.

LESSON 225.

Review Exercise.

1. Examples.

1. Not what we think, but what we do, makes saints of us.

2. The stag at eve had drunk his fill,
   Where danced the moon on Monan's rill,
   And deep his midnight lair had made
   In lone Glenartney's hazel shade ;
   But when the sun his beacon red
   Had kindled on Benvoirlich's head,
   The deep-mouth'd blood-hound's heavy bay
   Resounded up the rocky way,
   And faint, from farther distance borne,
   Were heard the clanging hoof and horn.
   —*Scott.*

REMARK.—In sentence 1, we may supply a predicate, but it is probably unnecessary, for *not* may be regarded as giving a negative meaning to the predicate as applied to the first subject, and *but* as showing that in its application to the second subject it has an *opposite* meaning, that is, an *affirmative.*

What are the subjects of this sentence—*things* understood, or the clauses, *What we think*, and *What we do*, taken separately ?

If *things* or some such noun understood is the subject, then why is the verb in the third person singular number?

Again: is it the *things* or the *doing* of them that makes us saints?

2. Seat Work.

Study the next lesson, and write the analysis of the first example.

--------•--------

LESSON 226.

Review Exercise.—Continued.

1. Examples.

1. Now was the winter gone, and the snow; and Robin the
   Redbreast
   Boasted on bush and tree it was he, it was he and no
   other
   That had covered with leaves the Babes in the Wood;
   and blithely
   All the birds sang with him, and little cared for his
   boasting,
   Or for his Babes in the Wood, or the Cruel Uncle, and
   only
   Sang for the mates they had chosen, and cared for the
   nests they were building.
   —*Longfellow.*

2.   The fowls of heaven,
   Tamed by the cruel season, crowd around
   The winnowing store, and claim the little boon
   Which Providence assigns them.
   —*Thomson.*

3. At length a murmur like the winds that break
   Into green waves the prairie's grassy lake,
   Deepened and swelled to music clear and loud.
   —*Whittier.*

2. Seat Work.

Study the next lesson, and write the analysis of examples 5, 7, and 8.

LESSON 227.

Potential Mode; Present and Past Tenses.

1. Instruction.

1. *He contributes generously.*　　3. *The Spartans fought bravely.*
2. *You* **can assist** *me.*　　　　4. *Henry* **could speak** *fluently.*

In the *first sentence* above, we predicate the real performance of an action, and represent it as taking place in what is regarded as the present period. But in the *second sentence*, we simply predicate the *power* to act. *Assist* denotes the action, and *can* shows that it is the *power to act* rather than the *act itself* that is predicated.

The *third sentence* predicates the actual performance of an action in the past; but the *fourth sentence* predicates, not that Henry *performed* the act in the past, but simply that he had the *power* to perform it.

In like manner we may predicate the *necessity, possibility,* or *probability* of an action; the *duty* of acting, *permission* to act, etc. Thus :—

1. *We must go to-day.*　　　3. *All men should honor God.*
2. *We may return to-morrow.*　　4. *You may remain a week.*

We have seen that the indicative mode represents the action, quality, or condition, predicated of the subject, as actually taking place or existing; that the imperative mode predicates a command or an exhortation to act; and now it is seen that we have need of *another* mode for the purpose of predicating the power to act, the necessity of acting, etc.

Potency means power; and since this mode is so often used to predicate power, it is called the **potential mode.** It has four tenses; the *present,* the *past,* the *present perfect,* and the *past perfect.* Each of these tenses consists of two parts,—the action word, or *basis,* and an auxiliary.

The present tense and the past tense have the same basis,—the *name-form* without *to*. The present tense employs one of the words, *may, can,* or *must,* as auxiliary ; and the past tense, *might, could, would, should,* or *ought.* When *ought* is used as auxiliary, the *to* of the name-form is retained.

From the illustrations given below it will be seen that the tenses of this mode do not always denote the time indicated by their names. The present tense often denotes future time, and the past may denote a present event, or even one that is to take place in the future.

1. *I may go next week.*
2. *He might become a scholar if he would.*
3. *If I could sell my place to-day, I would go to-morrow.*

2. Examples.

1. I can hear that voice yet.

2. Through the trees, we could see the waters, sparkling in the sun.

3. Two little urchins at her knee you must paint, sir.

4. The berries we gave her, she would n't eat.

5. I can hear sweet invitations
   Through the sobbing, sad vibrations
   Of the winds that follow.

6. Joys of earth on earth must pass away.

7. Beneath the hill you may see the mill
   Of wasting wood and crumbling stone.

8. The gates of the city we could not see.

MODEL FOR ANALYSIS.

Ex.—I could not go yesterday, but I must go to-day.

1. This sentence consists of two clauses.

2. *But* shows that these clauses are of equal rank, and that the second is opposed to the first in meaning ; the first saying that I *could not* go, and the second, that I *must* go.

3. *I* is the subject of the first clause.

4. **Could go** is the predicate; it predicates that I have the power to go.

5. **Go** is the "name-form without *to*," and denotes the action.

6. **Could** shows that it is the *power to act*, rather than the action itself, that is predicated; it also indicates the past tense.

7. *Not* makes the predicate deny what it would otherwise affirm.

8. *Yesterday* tells when I could not go; it is what remains of the phrase *on yesterday*.

9. *I* is the subject of the second clause.

10. **Must go** is the predicate; it predicates a necessity for an action.

11. **Go** is the "name-form without *to*," and denotes the action.

12. **Must** shows that it is the *necessity* for the action, rather than the action itself, that is predicated; it also denotes the present tense.

13. Etc.

MODEL FOR PARSING.

Could go is a verb, irreg., intr., potential mode, past tense. Verbs in this mode do not change their form for the person and number of the subject.

Must go is a verb, irreg., intr., potential mode, present tense. Verbs in this mode, etc.

3. Seat Work.

Study the next lesson; write the parsing of the verbs in sentences 1 to 6, and the analysis of sentences 7 and 8.

LESSON 228.

The Present and Past Potential of "To Have."

1. Examples.

1. He may have a message for you.

2. You might have the approval of all who know you.

3. Every man should have an interest in his country's welfare.

19

4. You can see the gap in the old wall still, and the stepping-stones in the shallow brook.

5. We must have confidence in God's providential care, or we can never have perfect peace.

6. He could have an honorable position, but he prefers the life of an idler.

7. He knew that his friends would no.longer have any confidence in his plans.

8. All who would have the approval of God must practice self-denial.

9. White blossoms are bursting
    The thickets among,
And all the gay greenwood
    Is ringing with song !
There's radiance and rapture
    That naught can destroy,
O earth, in thy sunshine,
    O heart, in thy joy !
              —*Goethe.*

2. Seat Work.

Study the next lesson.

LESSON 229.

The Perfect Tenses of the Potential Mode.

1. Instruction.

The perfect tenses of the potential mode consist of the past participle and the verb "*to have*," just as they do in the *indicative ;* but the present and past *potential* of "*to have*" are used instead of the present and past indicative. Thus :—

	Indicative.	Potential.
Present Perfect....	*Have* risen,	*may have* risen.
	Have given,	*can have* given.
	Have broken,	*must have* broken.

	Indicative.	Potential.
Past Perfect.......	Had run,	might have run.
	Had striven,	should have striven.
	Had drawn,	could have drawn.
	Had taught,	would have taught.
	Had been,	ought to have been.

The present tense of "*to have*" in the *potential mode*, as has been seen, is *may have, can have,* or *must have,* and its past tense, *might have, could have, should have, would have,* or *ought to have.*

Select verbs from the preceding lessons, and form their perfect tenses in the potential mode, telling how it is done, and why.

2. Examples.

1. All the birds by the roadside laughed at him, and told him that the hare must have reached the forest long ago.

2. You might have heard the cricket's trill,
   Or night birds, calling from the hill.

3. This elegant rose might have bloomed with its owner awhile.

4. You should have seen that long hill-range,
   With gaps of brightness riven.

5. "You should not have left the others," she said.

6. Who would have thought it was so late?

7. You would not have talked a year ago,
   As you have talked to-night.

8. He must have contemplated joining our party.

9. He can have come for no other purpose.

10. You could have gone on the evening train, and saved a day by it.

11. He may have lost his way, and some one should search for him.

MODEL FOR ANALYSIS.
Ex.—He could have written.

1. *He* is the subject.

2. **Could have written** is the predicate; it pred-

icates the possibility or the power to have completed an action in the past.

3. *Written* denotes completed action.

4. **Could have** is the past potential of *to have*, and shows that the power or possibility of completing the action existed in the past.

3. Seat Work.

Study the next lesson, and select examples of the tenses explained in this lesson.

LESSON 230.
Promiscuous Review.
1. Examples.

1. We may believe that to her lonely heart the voice of human praise was sweet.

2. Everybody who could escape had fled from the city.

3. There were some passages that would have served better for a prose pamphlet.

4. Should not the dove so white
Follow the sea-mew's flight?

5. He has gone at last, yet I could not see when he passed to his final rest.

6. Can we regain what we have lost?

7. Who can tell what may come upon us before another year shall close?

8. Then some looked up into the sky,
And all along where Lindis flows,
To where the goodly vessels lie,
And where the lordly steeple shows.
—*Jean Ingelow.*

9. It might have been the evening breeze
That whispered in the garden trees,
It might have been the sound of seas
That rose and fell.

2. Seat Work.
Select sentences like the examples in the next lesson.

LESSON 231.

Potential Mode Predicating Existence, Quality, Condition, or Class.

1. Instruction.

The different tense forms of the verb *to be*, in the potential mode, are used,—

(*a.*) To predicate that the *existence of the thing* denoted by the subject is possible; or that it was possible, or necessary, etc., as illustrated below.

1. *Such things must be.*
2. *Such things might have been.*
3. *It can not be.*

(*b.*) To predicate that the *existence of a quality* or *condition* is possible; or that it was possible, or necessary, etc. Thus :—

1. *He could be agreeable.*
2. *He might have been rich.*

(*c.*) To predicate that the possibility, etc., for the subject to belong to a *certain class*, exists, or did exist. Thus :—

1. *You must be our guide.*
2. *He might have been a scholar.*

2. Examples.

1. We should be thankful for present blessings.

2. Happiness must be lawful, or it cannot be lasting.

3. You may be faithful without being appreciated.

4. He might by this time have been an accomplished workman.

5. She must have been ninety years old.

6. He might have been famous, but he could not have been a good man.

7. Gifted must be the man who is loyal to so high a vocation.

8. Thou knowest the shadow could not be, without a light beyond.

9. His religious opinions would have been acceptable to neither party.

MODELS FOR ANALYSIS.

Ex.—He might have been rich.

1. *He* is the subject.

2. **Might have been rich** is the predicate; it predicates the possibility of a condition.

3. **Rich** is an adjective, and denotes the condition.

4. **Might have been** is the past perfect potential of the copula, and shows that the possibility of his being in this condition existed and came to an end in the past.

Ex.—He might have been a scholar.

1. *He* is the subject.

2. **Might have been a scholar** is the predicate; it predicates the possibility of his having belonged to a class called *scholars*.

3. **Scholar** names one of this class.

4. **Might have been** is the past perfect potential of the copula, and shows that the possibility of his belonging to this class existed and came to an end in the past.

Ex.—Such things must be.

1. *Things* is the subject.

2. **Must be** is the predicate; it predicates a present necessity for the existence of the things denoted by the subject.

3. *Such*, etc.

Ex.—I think that you might be useful.

1. *I* is the subject.

2. *Think* is the predicate.

3. *That you might be useful,* tells what I think, and is called the object.

4. *That* introduces the clause, and shows it to be subordinate in rank.

5. *You* is the subject.

6. **Might be useful** is the predicate; it predicates the possible existence of a quality.

7. *Useful* is an adjective, and denotes the quality.

8. **Might be** is called the past tense of the copula, but is here used to show a present possibility for the existence of the quality.

MODELS FOR PARSING.

Ex.—You should have been more cautious.

Should have been is a verb, irreg., cop., potential mode, past perfect tense. Verbs in this mode do not change their form for the person and number of the subject.

Cautious is an adjective, qual., used with the copula to form the predicate.

3. Seat Work.

Give all the tense-forms of the following verbs in the potential mode, progressive form, writing out the first two:—

Think, look, sleep, preach, wait.

LESSON 232.

Progressive Form of the Potential Mode.

1. Instruction.

Write upon your slates all the tense-forms of the verb *to be* in the potential mode.

Now add to each of these tenses the present active participle of the verb *to work*. Thus:—

PRESENT.—*May, can,* or *must* be **working.**

PAST.—*Might, could, would, should,* or *ought* (to) be **working.**

PRESENT PERFECT.—*May, can,* or *must have been* **working.**

PAST PERFECT.—*Might, could, would, should,* or *ought* (to) have been **working.**

This shows that the progressive form in the potential mode consists of the *present active participle and the copula*, just as it does in the indicative. It is used to predicate the possibility, necessity, etc., of a progressive action.

2. Examples.

1. He may have been dreaming.
2. You should have been watching.
3. He might have been earning something.
4. You must be improving your time.
5. We should be laying up treasures in Heaven.
6. I honor your judgment, dear brother, but yet can not see the propriety of taking the course which you recommend.
7. Dull would he be of soul who could pass by a sight so touching.
8. We may be learning something each hour.
9. He may have been sick, but the probability is that he was intoxicated.
10. He must have been thinking of something else, or he would not have made such a remark.
11. The ploughman that turns the sod may be a Cincinnatus or a Washington, or he may be brother to the clod he turns.

MODEL FOR ANALYSIS.
Sentence 1.

1. *He* is the subject.

2. **May have been dreaming** is the predicate; it predicates the possibility of a progressive action.

3. **Dreaming** denotes the action.

4. *May have been* is the present perfect potential of the copula, and shows that the possibility of his performing this progressive action existed and came to an end in the present period.

REMARKS.—In sentence **2,** *should have been watching* predicates a duty in regard to a progressive action. *Watching* denotes the action, and *should have been* shows that his duty to perform the action existed and came to an end in the past.

In sentence **4,** *must be* shows that the necessity for performing the action exists at the time of speaking.

In sentence **5,** *should be* is called the past potential of the copula, but here shows that our duty in regard to this progressive action exists at the present time.

3. Seat Work.

Study the next lesson, and write the analysis of sentences 7, 9, and 11.

LESSON 233.

Subject of the Last Lesson Continued.

1. Examples.

1. That star may have been shining for ages.

2. We should be making preparations for our departure.

3. It must have been a grievous offense of which Moses and Aaron were guilty.

4. Our friends must be crossing the mountains by this time.

5. That must have been a merry sight.

6. You may be copying while I am searching for examples.

7. The king will have been dead three days before you can reach the camp.

8. You should have been giving attention to the speaker.

9. Thoughts of what "might have been" never troubled him.

10. We should have been ready at ten o'clock.

11. He may have been striving to the best of his ability.

12. We should each day of our lives be stepping heavenward.

2. Seat Work.

Study the next lesson. Write the analysis of sentences 1, 4, 8, and 9.

LESSON 234.

Passive Voice of the Potential Mode.

1. Instruction and Exercises.

Write on your slates all the tense-forms of *to be* in the potential mode.

Now add to these the passive participle of any transitive verb; *to break*, for instance.

By examining these forms it will be seen that the passive voice, or passive form, of the potential mode, consists of the *passive participle* and *the copula*, just as it does in the indicative mode, except that we use the potential form of the copula instead of the indicative.

Change the transitive verbs, in this lesson and in the preceding one, to the passive form; then change them to the passive form of the indicative mode; lastly, change them to the indicative progressive.

Form the passive voice of the following verbs in all the tenses of the potential mode :—

Deceive, teach, write, astonish, convince.

2. Examples.

1. Who can tell what crimes may have been committed in that dark place?

2. Not a shadow could be seen.

3. Much valuable information may be found in Macaulay's Essays.

4. Some time should be given to extemporaneous speaking.

5. He may have been deceived in regard to duty.

6. By proper management the fort might have been taken.

7. The college can be seen for several miles.

8. It is not surprising that it should have escaped the search of strangers.

9. The war could have been brought to a close much sooner.

3. Seat Work.

Write the analysis of examples 4 and 5 of the next lesson.

LESSON 235.

Various Forms of the Potential Mode.

1. Examples.

1. The soldiers must have been thoroughly drilled, or they would have fallen into disorder under such circumstances.

2. Some may be waiting for a more favorable opportunity.

3. Why I should have been chosen, I cannot understand.

4. Whither, midst falling dew,
    While glow the heavens with the last steps of day,
    Far through their rosy depths dost thou pursue
    Thy solitary way?   —*Bryant, p. 26.*

5. Seekest thou the plashy brink
    Of weedy lake, or marge of river wide,
    Or where the rocking billows rise and sink
    On the chafed ocean-side ?   —*Ibid.*

6. For I think the affections must be sadly checked and chilled, even in the best men, by their intercourse with the world.

7. The good people feared that they might be driven away from hearth and home.

8. This is the way in which all the work might have been done.

REMARK.—In example **5**, the clause in the third line seems to limit some noun understood, such as *spot* or *shore*.

2. Seat Work.

Study the next lesson, and write the analysis of sentences 3 and 9.

LESSON 236.

Review Exercise.

1. Examples.

1. He will have been waiting for you in Paris several days before you arrive.

2. A government having at its command the armies, the fleets, and the revenues, of Great Britain, might possibly hold Ireland by the sword.

3. The maiden clasped her hands, and prayed
   That savèd she might be ;
   And she thought of Christ, who stilled the wave
   On the Lake of Galilee.

4. We are told that the Union must be preserved without regard to the means.

5. Was it a dream we dreamed?
   Or did we hear
   The harping of silver harps,
   Divinely clear?

6. I tried my voice,—'t was faint and low,
   But yet he swerved as from a blow.
   —*Byron.*

7. He wasted no time in play when he should have been studying.

8. For none return from those quiet shores
   Who cross with the boatman cold and pale.

9. Childhood is the bough, where slumbered
   Birds and blossoms many-numbered ;—
   Age, that bough with snows encumbered.
   —*Longfellow.*

2. Seat Work.

Study the next lesson, and write the parsing of all the words except those that are repeated in the same office.

LESSON 237.

Review Exercise.—Continued.

1. Examples.

1. The play's the thing
Wherein I'll catch the conscience of the king.
—*Shakspeare.*

2. Speaking of their beauty, we must not forget what useful things flowers and plants are.

3. There is a world where all are equal—
We are hurrying toward it fast—
We shall meet upon the level there
When all the gates of death are past.

4. Who has been putting this nonsense into your head?

5. I saw a famous fountain, in my dream,
Where shady pathways to a valley led;
A weeping willow lay upon that stream,
And all around the fountain brink were spread
Wide-branching trees, with dark green leaf rich clad,
Forming a doubtful twilight—desolate and sad.
—*Charles Lamb.*

6. O Liberty, can man resign thee,
Once having felt thy generous flame?

7. He would not admit me until I promised that he should have half of what I should get for my turbot.

2. Seat Work.

Write the analysis of examples 4 and 5 of the next lesson, and the parsing of the verbs in the other examples.

LESSON 238.

The Imperative Mode.

1. Instruction.

The imperative mode has but one tense—the present. It is the name-form without *to*, and differs from the present indicative only in the verb *to be*, as seen below:—

INDICATIVE.—*You **are** honest.*
IMPERATIVE.—***Be** honest.*

2. Examples.

1. Be faithful.
2. Be a gentleman.
3. Write often.
4. Be men, not beggars. Cancel all
   By one brave, generous action; trust
   Your better instincts, and be just.
5. Awake, Sir King, the gates unspar!
   Rise up and ride both fast and far!
   The sea flows over bolt and bar!
6.   'Twas our favorite dell,
   Cut by the trout-stream through a wooded ridge:
   Above, the highway on a mossy bridge
      Strode o'er it, and below, the water fell
   Through hornblende bowlders, where the dircus flung
      His pliant rods, the berried spice-wood grew,
   And tulip-trees and smooth magnolias hung
      A million leaves between us and the blue.
   —*Bayard Taylor.*
7. Long after every star came out, we paced
   The terrace, still discoursing on the themes
   The day had started, intermixed with dreams
   Born of the summer night.
   —*Ibid.*

3. Seat Work.

Write the parsing of the verbs in the last six examples of the next lesson.

LESSON 239.
The Infinitive Mode.
1. Instruction.

The infinitive mode has two tenses; the present and the present perfect. The present infinitive is the name-form, already described. Thus:—

To be, to write, to think.

The present perfect consists of the past participle, and

the *present infinitive* of "*to have*"; just as the present perfect *indicative* consists of the past participle, and the present *indicative* of "*to have*."

Observe that the past participle is used in all the perfect tenses and perfect participles to denote a completed action. With this, we use, in the common form, the present *indicative* of "*to have*," for the present perfect tense of the *indicative mode;* the present *potential* of "*to have*," for the present perfect tense of the *potential mode;* the present *infinitive* of "*to have*," for the present perfect tense of the *infinitive mode;* and the present active *participle* of "*to have*," for the *perfect active participle.* Thus :—

> PRESENT PERFECT INDICATIVE.—*Have spoken.*
> PRESENT PERFECT POTENTIAL.—*May have spoken.*
> PRESENT PERFECT INFINITIVE.—*To have spoken.*
> PERFECT ACTIVE PARTICIPLE.—*Having spoken.*

The verb in the infinitive mode, like the participle, assumes or names the action, but can never predicate it. Since it cannot predicate anything, it has no person and number. It always has the same form, regardless of the person and number of its subject, but drops *to* when used after certain verbs ; such as *make, feel, let, need, shall, see, will, may, can, must, might, could, would, should,* etc.

It differs from the participle in form, and in some of its uses.

The infinitive may be used as an adjective, or as an adverb, but it is more commonly a noun.

2. Examples.

1. The time to part has come.
2. He has come to spend the winter.
3. To feel the fresh air of a spring morning is delightful.
4. It is delightful to feel the fresh air of a spring morning.
5. His feet are swift to shed blood.
6. I hope to find it.
7. A desire to assist you prompted the proposal.

8. They remained to visit their friends.

9. To do good is the duty of all.

10. We are anxious to improve.

11. He was unable to persuade the multitude.

12. He that would be a hero must not fear to die.

13. The time to plant flowers has come.

14. I profess, sir, to have kept steadily in view the prosperity and honor of the whole country.

MODELS FOR ANALYSIS.
Sentence 1.

1. *Time* is the subject.

2. *Has come* is the predicate.

3. *The* shows that some definite time is meant.

4. **To part** tells *what* time is meant.

5. Etc.

Sentence 2.

1. *He* is the subject.

2. *Has come* is the predicate.

3. **To spend the winter** tells why he came.

4. *Winter* names the season that he came to spend.

5. Etc.

MODELS FOR PARSING.
Sentence 1.

To part is a verb, reg., intr., infinitive mode, present tense, and is used to tell what time is meant.

Sentence 2.

To spend is a verb, irreg., tr., active voice, infinitive mode, present tense, and is used to tell the purpose of his coming.

Sentence 3.

To feel is a verb, irreg., tr., active voice, infinitive mode, present tense; it is used in this sentence to name an action, and thus becomes a verbal noun; it is the subject of the sentence, and is therefore put in the nom. case.

Sentence 4.

To feel is a verb, irreg., tr., active voice, infinitive mode, present tense; it is used to name an action, and thus becomes a verbal noun; it explains what is meant by *it*, and is therefore put in the nom. case.

3. Seat Work.

Write the parsing of the words in the first example of the next lesson, and the analysis of the second example.

LESSON 240.

Subject of the Last Lesson Continued.

1. Examples.

1. Do you know what has been done to check this growing evil?

2. With such crazy vessels and such discontented crews, all his heroism would have failed to insure success.

3. My lord, I came to see your father's funeral.

4. A desire to please characterized all his actions.

5. Do you expect to complete your education this year?

6. It is useless to quarrel with nature.

7. I think I may venture to go it alone.

8. But I would like first to explain how water freezes.

9. The magpie readily learns to repeat a few words.

10. Music hath charms to soothe the savage breast.

2. Seat Work.

Select nine sentences, each containing a verb in the infinitive mode,—six in the present tense, and three in the present perfect tense.

20

LESSON 241.

Progressive and Passive Forms of the Infinitive Mode.

1. Instruction.

The infinitive, like the other modes, has the progressive and passive forms. The present infinitive, progressive form, consists of the present active participle, and the present infinitive of the copula. Thus :—

Com.—*To watch.*   Progr.—*To be watching.*

. The present perfect infinitive, progressive form, consists of the present active participle, and the present perfect infinitive of the copula. Thus:—

Com.—*To have watched.*   Progr.—*To have been watching.*

The passive form of the infinitive mode is the same as the progressive, except that the *passive* participle is used in place of the *present active.*

Put the tenses of the copula, infinitive mode, on your slates. Then add the present active participle to make the progressive form, and afterward the passive participle to make the passive form. Thus :—

	Present.	*Present Perfect.*
Com.—	*To be,*	*to have been.*
Progr.—	*To be watching,*	*to have been watching.*
Pass.—	*To be watched,*	*to have been watched.*

To be denotes existence that is present at the time referred to. *To have been* denotes existence that is past and completed [*ended*] at the time referred to.

To be watching denotes an action that is, was, or will be, progressing at the time referred to.

To have been watching denotes an action that has been progressing, but is completed at the time referred to.

To be watched denotes the reception of an action at the time referred to.

To have been watched represents an action as having been received and completed.

Give the progressive and passive forms of the following verbs in the infinitive mode:—

To reach, to strike, to drive, to teach, to write, to scold, to reprove, to try, to hear.

These forms are often used as *verbal nouns*, as seen below.

2. Examples.

1. It is our duty to be watching.

2. To have been watching would have been prudent.

3. It is not always pleasant to be watched.

4. To have been hindered at such a time must have been unpleasant.

5. It is sad to see such forgetfulness of duty.

6. To be forgetful in such a cause is sinful.

7.   Think not that thou and I
  Are here the only worshipers to-day
    Beneath this glorious sky,
  Mid the soft airs that o'er the meadows play;
    These airs, whose breathing stirs
    The fresh grass, are our fellow-worshipers.

    See, as they pass, they swing
  The censers of a thousand flowers, that bend
    O'er the young herbs of spring,
  And the sweet odors like a prayer ascend,
    While, passing thence, the breeze
    Wakes the grave anthem of the forest trees.
                    —*Bryant, p.* 349.

MODEL FOR ANALYSIS.
Sentence 1.

1. *It* is the subject.

2. *Is our duty* is the predicate; it predicates that whatever is denoted by *it* belongs to that class of objects called duties.

3. *Duty* names one of the class.

4. *Our*, by alluding to the speaker and those associated with him, shows whose duty it is.

5. *Is* shows that the thought is predicated.

6. **To be watching,** by naming an action, shows what is meant by *it*.

MODELS FOR PARSING.

To be watching is a verb, reg., intr., infinitive mode, present tense, progressive form; it is used in this sentence to name an action, and thus becomes a verbal noun; it explains what is meant by *it*, and is therefore put in the nom. case.

Sentence 2.

To have been watching is a verb, reg., intr., infinitive mode, present perfect tense, progressive form; it is used to name an action, and thus becomes a verbal noun; it is the subject of the sentence, and is therefore put in the nom. case.

Sentence 4.

To have been hindered is a verb, reg., tr., passive voice, infinitive mode, present perfect tense; it is used to name an action, and hence becomes a verbal noun; it is the subject of the sentence, and is therefore put in the nom. case.

3. Seat Work.

Write the parsing of the infinitives in the next lesson.

LESSON 242.

Subject of the Last Lesson Continued.

1. Examples.

1. Many shop-customers were waiting to be served.

2. This voyage deserves to be noted.

3. We ought to be preparing for that great change which must soon come to us all.

4. To have been living at such a time would have been a privilege.

5. Now came still evening on, and twilight gray
Had in her sober livery all things clad.
—Milton.

6. To have been sleeping at my post when the general passed by, would have cost my life.

7. It is our duty to be always seeking opportunity for doing good.

8. "The Pink Page deserves to be hung, and you too, since you knew all about it," growled the king.

9.   When summer came,
Our pastime was, on bright half-holidays,
To sweep along the plain of Windermere
With rival oars.   *—Wordsworth, p.* 483.

10. He claims to have been well instructed in the arts of war before leaving his native land.

2. Seat Work.

Write the analysis of sentences 2 and 3 of the next lesson.

LESSON 243.

Miscellaneous Exercise.

1. Examples.

1. The natives scarcely know what it is to see the gray head of an Englishman.

2. "I would like," said the Lily, "to bloom in the palace of the king; to be seen by the lords and ladies in their dresses of velvet, silk, and gold."

3. I cannot help thinking that he ought to have recollected the many fields of fight in which we have been contributors to his renown.

4. To have broken the line of battle at that point would have secured the victory.

5. Their manner of treating the dead was similar to that observed among the natives of some of the islands. Having deposited the corpse in a cavern or sepulchre, they placed a jar of water and a few eatables at its head, and then abandoned it without moan or lamentation.—*Washington Irving.*

2. Seat Work.

Select sentences illustrating the progressive and passive forms of the infinitive mode.

LESSON 244.

The Infinitive and Other Phrases in the Predicate.

1. Instruction.

The infinitive is sometimes used with the copula to form the predicate. Thus :—

1. He *is to go to-morrow.*
2. He *was to have gone yesterday.*

Is to go predicates *determination* in regard to a future action.

Is is the copula, and **to go** is the present infinitive, used with the copula to form the predicate.

Was to have gone predicates determination in regard to a past action.

Was is the copula.

To have gone is the perfect infinitive, and is used with the copula to form the predicate.

The *phrase* composed of a preposition and its object is often used with the copula to form the predicate. Thus :—

1. We *are in health.*
2. He *is without friends.*

In the first sentence, **are in health** means the same as *are well.* In the second sentence, **is without friends** means the same as *is friendless.*

2. Examples.

1. You are in fault.

2. The fiftieth anniversary of her birthday is to be celebrated next Tuesday.

3. I'm to be queen-of-the-May, mother.

4. You will be in danger of incurring the displeasure of your party.

5. I am in want of efficient help.

6. A public dinner is to be given in honor of the president's return.

7. No trace of blood was to be found.

8. The princess is to be instructed in the art of bread-making.

9. The general is to be in town to-morrow.

10. The first great object of education is to discipline the mind.

MODEL FOR ANALYSIS.

Sentence 1.

1. *You* is the subject.

2. **Are in fault** is the predicate.

3. *Are* is the copula.

4. **In fault** is used with the copula to form the predicate, and denotes a predicated condition of the one spoken to.

MODELS FOR PARSING.

Sentence 1.

Are is a verb, irreg., cop., indic. m., pres. tense, 2d per. plu. num., to agree with its subject *you*.

In is a preposition, and shows the relation of the fault to the person denoted by the subject.

Fault is a noun, abstract, 3d per., sing. num., neuter gender, object of the relation expressed by the preposition *in*, and therefore put in the objective case.

Sentence 2.

Is to be celebrated is a verb, reg., tr., pass. voice, indic. m., pres. tense, 3d per. sing. num., to agree with its subject *anniversary*.

REMARKS.—In sentence **7,** *was to be found* predicates possibility; it means the same as *could be found.*

In sentence **9,** *is to be in town* is the predicate. *In town* denotes a condition, and *is to be* predicates that that condition is expected or determined upon. *Is to be* is a verb, irregular, copula, indic. mode, pres. tense, 3d per. sing. num., to agree with its subject *general.*

In sentence **10,** *to discipline* is a verbal noun in the nominative case.

3. Seat Work.

Write the analysis of sentences 1 and 11 of the next lesson, the parsing of the participles in sentences 2 and 10, the preposition in sentence 4, and the infinitive and predicates in sentence 3.

LESSON 245.

Subject of the Last Lesson Continued.

1. Examples.

1. Certain gentlemen and mariners of Norway, having considered all that they had heard of the Earthly Paradise, set sail to find it.

2. Having been arrested and convicted, he was shut up in Bedford jail.

3. To be loitering when so much work is to be done is disgraceful.

4. They were at variance.

5. Having collected new force by its temporary suspension, the river spread devastation on every side.

6. Principles and manners are to be discussed, and not the motives or characters of those who advocate them.

7. I am in earnest.

8. He knew where they were to be had.

9. He has never been in possession of his father's estate.

10. Having declined the proposal, I determined on a course suited to my own taste.

11. The Intrepid herself was a fire ship, having been supplied with combustibles, a mass of which lay in barrels on her quarter deck, covered only with tarpaulin.

2. Seat Work.

Study the next lesson, and write the parsing of the nouns in the *absolute phrases.*

------•------

LESSON 246.

Noun Independent with a Participle.

1. Instruction.

1. *Having completed our preparations, we set out on our journey.*

2. *The morning having dawned, we resumed our journey.*

3. *The morning had dawned, and therefore we resumed our journey.*

In the first sentence above, the participle, **having completed,** assumes an action of the persons represented by *we,* and *we* is the subject of the sentence.

In the second sentence, **having dawned** assumes an action of the morning, but *morning* is not the subject of the sentence. It is no part of the clause of which *we* is the subject. It assumes just what the first clause of the third sentence predicates, and is just as independent of the clause that follows.

In the third sentence, the first clause predicates an action which was the cause of our resuming our journey.

In the second, the *phrase* tells the cause of our resuming the journey.

Note.—A noun used like *morning* in sentence 2, is sometimes said to be in the nominative case absolute, and the phrase consisting of the noun and its participle, with their limitations, if they have any, is called an absolute phrase.

PUNCTUATION.—The phrase absolute should be set off by the comma.

2. Examples.

1. Darkness coming upon us, we pitched our tents.

2. My health failing, the enterprise was abandoned.

3. The night, her task completed, stole away on lightest tiptoe.

4. Two games had been finished, the young man losing each time.

5. Topsy came up, her round, hard eyes glittering and blinking with a mixture of apprehensiveness, and their usual odd drollery.

6. Above all, towers Chimborazo, its pure white dome piercing the clear azure.

7. Still above us is a wild chaos of mountains, their sides broken into ravines.

8. Descending from the summit of the pass, we come to Ambato, a town beautifully situated in a deep ravine.

MODEL FOR ANALYSIS.

Sentence 1.

1. *We* is the subject, and *pitched* is the predicate; *our tents* tells what we pitched.

2. **Darkness coming upon us** tells the cause of our pitching tents.

3. **Darkness** names a state, and **coming** assumes an action of it; *upon us* tells where it came.

MODELS FOR PARSING.

Darkness is a noun, com., abstract; 3d, s., neu.; independent with a participle, and therefore put in the nominative case.

Coming is a participle, present active, intr.; added to the noun *darkness*. It describes the darkness by assuming an action of it.

REMARKS.—In sentence **3,** *her task completed* tells incidentally what the night had finished before she stole away, and seems to intimate that she stole away *because* that work was accomplished, and she had nothing more to do.

In sentence **4**, *the young man losing, etc.*, calls attention to an action that is associated with that of finishing the games. The act of losing is assumed of the young man, while the act of finishing the game is predicated.

In sentence **5**, *her round, hard eyes glittering, etc.*, describes Topsy's appearance at the time of coming up.

In sentence **6**, *its pure white dome piercing, etc.*, calls attention to an action that is intimately associated with the one denoted by the predicate.

In sentence **7**, *their sides broken, etc.*, gives an additional thought concerning the mountains.

In sentence **8**, *a town beautifully situated, etc.*, is appositional, not independent.

3. Seat Work.

Study next lesson, and write the analysis of the sixth example.

LESSON 247.

Subject of the Last Lesson Continued.

1. Instruction.

Sometimes the action or condition denoted by the participle or infinitive of an absolute phrase is not to be attributed to any particular person or thing, and in such cases there is, of course, no noun given on which the participle or infinitive depends. The first examples of the exercise following afford illustrations of the participle and the infinitive absolute, that is, *absolved* from all dependence upon any particular word.

For emphasis, we sometimes call attention to an object by naming it and afterward using a pronoun to represent it in the clause that follows; as,—

1. *Gad, a troop shall overtake him.*
2. *His teeth, they chatter, chatter still.*

A noun so used is said to be **independent by pleonasm.** The figure of pleonasm should never be used except when emphasis is required, otherwise, it becomes a blemish instead of an ornament in language. The fourth example below gives another illustration of its use.

2. · Examples.

1. His conduct, generally speaking, is highly honorable.

2. To be plain with you, I think you are much in fault.

3. This gentleman, taking him for all in all, possessed a wonderful variety of knowledge.

4. God, from the mount of Sinai, whose gray top
   Shall tremble, he, descending, will himself
      Ordain their laws.

5. I never sought an opportunity of meeting him, to tell the truth.

6. The maples bending o'er the gate,
     Their arch of leaves just tinted
   With yellow warmth, the golden glow
     Of coming autumn hinted.
             —*Whittier, p.* 328.

7. The sun being risen, we departed on our journey.

8. Shame being lost, all virtue is lost.

9. The danger being past, we entered the forest.

10. His father being dead, the prince succeeded to the throne.

11. Paul being a Roman, they feared to kill him.

REMARKS.—In sentences **7** to **11,** *being,* the participle of the copula, denotes the present existence of the action or condition assumed by the word that follows.

In sentence **11,** *being a Roman* assumes that Paul belonged to a class. *Roman* names one of that class, and *being,* the participle of the copula, denotes the existence of Paul's relation to that class, at the time referred to.

When *being* precedes the passive participle, the two words should be parsed together as a *passive participle,* just as the copula itself and the passive participle are parsed together as a verb in the passive voice.

When *being* precedes an adjective or a noun, it must be parsed alone. It belongs to the same noun as does the adjective or noun that follows it, and is used as described above.

3. Seat Work.

Write the analysis of sentence 4 of the next lesson.

Note.—Do not forget that the next lesson is always to be studied throughout, whether mention is made of it or not.

LESSON 248.

Participles, Nouns Independent, Etc.

1. Examples.

1. The timber is scattered in groves and strips, the whole country being one vast, illimitable prairie, ornamented by small collections of trees.

2. And the young city round whose virgin zone
The rivers like two mighty arms were thrown,
Marked by the smoke of evening fires alone,
Lay in the distance.
—*Whittier, p. 360.*

3. This tree grows to the height of a hundred feet, its slender trunk surmounted by a magnificent tuft of great fan-shaped fronds, under which grow, in large clusters, scaly fruit, resembling pine cones.

4. Why weep ye then for him, who, having won
The bound of man's appointed years, at last,
Life's blessings all enjoyed, life's labors done,
Serenely to his final rest has passed?

2. Seat Work.

Write all the tense-forms of the verb *to teach* in the four modes already given.

LESSON 249.

Subjunctive Mode.

1. Instruction.

1. *Whither thou goest, I will go.*
2. *If thou go, see thou offend not.*
3. *Though he was modest in appearance, he was brave in action.*
4. *Though he were a slave to-day, he would be free to-morrow.*
5. *He was wrong in action, but right in motive.*
6. *If thou canst govern thyself, thou mayest govern others.*
7. *Were I not your friend, I would not reprove you.*

The first clause in the second sentence above is made conditional by the conjunction *if*. Now this conditional clause and the first clause in sentence 1 have the same subject and the same verb, but the verb in the conditional clause does not change its form for the person and number of its subject.

By comparing sentences 4 and 7 with sentence 5, it will be seen that, in the conditional clauses of those sentences, the past tense of the verb *to be* differs from its ordinary form in the same person and number.

The peculiar forms which the verb often takes in conditional clauses, constitute what is called the **subjunctive mode**. This mode has only two tenses; the present and the past.

The **present tense** consists of the name-form (*present infinitive*) without *to*.

The **past tense** is, in most cases, the same as the ordinary past tense of the indicative mode; and in the verb *to be* the plural form is used with all subjects.

The peculiarities of this mode are shown in the following tables:—

TENSE-FORMS OF THE SUBJUNCTIVE MODE.

Present Tense.		*Past Tense.*	
1. If I *love*,	If we *love*,	1. If I *loved*,	If we *loved*,
2. If thou *love*,	If you *love*,	2. If thou *loved*,	If you *loved*,
3. If he *love*;	If they *love*.	3. If he *loved*;	If they *loved*.

Present Tense.		*Past Tense.*	
1. If I *be*,	If we *be*,	1. If I *were*,	If we *were*,
2. If thou *be*,	If you *be*,	2. If thou *wert*,	If you *were*,
3. If he *be*;	If they *be*.	3. If he *were*;	If they *were*.

By the above it will be seen that the subjunctive mode has no change of form except for *thou*, and none for that except in the past tense of the verb *to be*.

By comparing sentences 3 and 5, at the beginning of this lesson, and by noticing sentence 6, it will be seen that the verb in a conditional clause is not always put in the subjunctive mode. We may, indeed, have conditional clauses with a verb in any tense of the indicative or of the potential mode; but the true subjunctive mode is found only in the two tenses represented in the tables above.

The verbs in such conditional clauses as are found in sentences 3 and 6 are sometimes said to be in the *subjunctive mode, common form;* but it is probably better to say that they are in the indicative or in the potential mode, and that the *clause* is made conditional by the conjunction that introduces it.

Sometimes, however, the clause is made conditional by placing the verb, or the first word of it, before the subject, as seen in sentence 7 above.

The *present* subjunctive usually denotes future time; and the *past*, present or indefinite time.

2. Examples.

1. Had I known it, I should not have gone.
2. Were death denied, all men would wish to die.
3. Though thou wert huge as Atlas, thy efforts would be vain.
4. If he be but discreet, he will succeed.

5. If I were to write, he would not regard it.

6. If thou cast me off, I shall be miserable.

7. If thy enemy be hungry, give him bread to eat.

8. If this be enthusiasm, would that all were enthusiasts.

9.   Thy brow,
Glorious in beauty though it be, is scarred
With tokens of old wars.
                 —*Bryant, p.* 199.

MODEL FOR ANALYSIS.
Sentence 4.

1. *He* is the subject.

2. *Will succeed* is the predicate.

3. **If he be but discreet** tells the condition under which he will succeed.

4. **If** introduces the clause and shows it to be subordinate.

5. *He* is the subject of the clause, and *be discreet* is the predicate.

6. **But** makes the predicate emphatic; the condition affirmed by the predicate is the only one we care to make. The other conditions of success are already certain.

MODEL FOR PARSING.

Be is a verb, irreg., copula, subjunctive mode, present tense; verbs in this mode do not change their form for the person and number of the subject.

REMARKS.—In sentence **3,** the subordinate clause states a condition *notwithstanding which* the efforts "would be vain." The subordinate clause in sentence **9** is used in a similar way.

3. Seat Work.

Write properly the examples given for correction in the next lesson, and also write the reason for putting the verb in the form which you have chosen.

LESSON 250.

Conditional Clauses.

1. Examples.

1. If your sweet flowers remain with you,
   Fruitless your boughs must be.
2. I will await his coming, though it be a year.
3. If God required from thee an angel's deeds,
   He would have given thee an angel's powers.
4. I watched the proceedings with considerable interest, though I took no active part in them.
5. Had I the wings of a fairy,
   Up to thee would I fly.
   — *Wordsworth, p.* 139.
6. He will not be pardoned, unless he repent.

REMARKS.—When to use the subjunctive mode in conditional clauses is a perplexing question. Authors do not agree very well on this point. Perhaps Mr. Brown's rule is as safe as any. It is in substance as follows :—

1. A future contingency is best expressed by a verb in the subjunctive present.

2. A mere supposition with indefinite time is best expressed by a verb in the subjunctive past.

3. A conditional circumstance assumed as a fact, requires the indicative mode.

The following sentences illustrate the rules just given:—

1. If thou forsake him, he will cast thee off forever.
2. If it were not so, I would have told you.
3. Though he is poor, he is contented.

Correct the following examples according to the rules given above :—

1. He will not be pardoned, unless he repents.
2. They will fine thee, unless thou offerest an excuse.
3. I wish that I was at home.

21

4. He will maintain his cause, though he lose his estate.

5. I shall walk out in the afternoon, unless it is rainy.

6. Take heed lest your reputation suffers.

7. On condition that he comes, I consent to stay.

8. If he is but discreet, he will succeed.

9. If thou castest me off, I shall be miserable.

10. Watch the door of thy lips, lest thou utterest folly.

11. If thou feltest as I do, we should decide.

12. Though thou sheddest thy blood in the cause, it would but prove thee sincerely a fool.

2. Seat Work.

Write the parsing of the verbs in the next lesson.

LESSON 251.

Subject of the Last Lesson Continued.

1. Examples.

1. If this be peace, pray what is war?

2. Magellan declared that should they even be reduced to eat the leather of their shoes, he would persevere to the end.

3. She said, "Not so : but I will know
If there be any faith in man."
—Tennyson.

4. Never in the coming years,
Though he seek for it with tears,
Will he find so sweet a rest.

5. But should Providence determine otherwise, should you fall in this struggle, should the nation fall, you will have the satisfaction of having performed your part.

6. Though winter storms be nigh,
Unchecked is that harmony.
—Wordsworth.

7. Pack your thoughts close together, and though your article may be brief, it will have weight, and be more likely to make an impression.—*How to Write, p.* 149.

8. And did not pity touch my heart,
   To see how ye are all distrest,
   Till my ribs ached, I'd laugh at you.
   — *Wordsworth.*

2. Seat Work.

Study the next lesson, and illustrate it by examples.

——— • ———

LESSON 252.

Description of the Tense-Forms.

1. Common Form.

PRESENT TENSE.

INDICATIVE.—The simplest form of the verb.

POTENTIAL.—The name-form without *to*, with *may, can,* or *must* as auxiliary.

IMPERATIVE.—The name-form without *to*.

INFINITIVE.—The name-form.

SUBJUNCTIVE.—The name-form without *to*.

PAST TENSE.

INDICATIVE.—In all regular verbs, the present tense with *ed* added.

POTENTIAL.—The name-form without *to*, with *might, could, would,* or *should,* as auxiliary.

SUBJUNCTIVE.—Has the same form as the past plural indicative.

FUTURE TENSE.

INDICATIVE.—The name-form without *to*, with *shall* or *will* as auxiliary.

PRESENT PERFECT TENSE.

INDICATIVE.—Has the past active participle for basis, and the *present indicative* of "to have" as auxiliary.

POTENTIAL.—The past active participle as basis, and the present *potential* of "to have" as auxiliary.

INFINITIVE.—The past active participle as basis, and the present *infinitive* of "to have" as auxiliary.

PAST PERFECT TENSE.

INDICATIVE.—The past active participle as basis, and the *past indicative* of "to have" as auxiliary.

POTENTIAL.—The past active participle as basis, and the past *potential* of "to have" as auxiliary.

FUTURE PERFECT TENSE.

INDICATIVE.—The past active participle as basis, and the future indicative of "to have" as auxiliary.

2. Progressive Form.

INDICATIVE.—Has the present active participle for basis, and the indicative tenses of "to be" as auxiliary.

POTENTIAL.—The present active participle as basis and the potential tenses of "to be" as auxiliary.

IMPERATIVE.—The present active participle as basis, and the imperative of "to be" as auxiliary.

INFINITIVE.—The present active participle as basis, and the infinitive tenses of "to be" as auxiliary.

SUBJUNCTIVE.—The present active participle as basis, and the subjunctive tenses of "to be" as auxiliary.

3. Passive Form.

The passive form is made in the same way as the progressive form, only we use the *passive* participle as basis instead of the *present active.*

4. Emphatic Form.

PRESENT TENSE.

INDICATIVE.—The name-form without *to,* for basis, and the present indicative of "to do" as auxiliary.

IMPERATIVE.—The name-form without *to,* for basis, and the imperative of "to do" as auxiliary.

PAST TENSE.

INDICATIVE.—The name-form without *to,* and the past indicative of "to do" as auxiliary.

5. Seat Work.

Study the diagram given in the next lesson, and conjugate the verbs *choose* and *leave,* throughout the various forms of all the modes and tenses.

LESSON 253.

Condensed Conjugation of the Verb.

1. Instruction.

A systematic arrangement of all the forms of the verb in its various modes and tenses is called the **conjugation of the verb.** The diagram on page 327 is meant to show at a glance all the forms of the verb and its participles.

In each tense we give, first, the common form, and immediately below it, the progressive and the passive ; also the emphatic wherever it occurs.

There are four ways of reciting from this diagram :—

1. Following the top line through from left to right, we find all the tenses of the indicative mode, common form; and the second, third, and fourth lines followed through in the same way give in succession the progressive, passive, and emphatic forms of the same mode. Proceed in like manner with each mode, first giving all the tenses in the common form, then in the progressive, etc.

2. First give *all* the forms of the present tense, indicative mode ; then all the forms of the past tense, same mode ; thus passing on to the right until the conjugation of the verb in the indicative mode is made complete. Proceed in the same way with each successive mode until the entire conjugation has been given.

3. Give the common form of the present indicative ; then the common form of the potential present, and so down the left hand column until the common form in the

present tense of all the modes has been given. Then following down the second column, give the common form in the past tense of all the modes, and proceed in the same way with column after column throughout all the tenses. Then go back and go through the progressive form in the same way, and so on until all the forms have been given.

4. Give all the forms in the present indicative, and then all the forms in the present potential, and so on down the left hand column throughout all the modes. Proceed in the same way with each of the other tenses until the conjugation is complete.

All the tense forms of the verb *to be* may be seen in the auxiliaries of the progressive and passive forms.

Suggestion.—Every good teacher realizes the necessity of making his pupils entirely familiar with all the forms of the verb, their proper use, and the laws of their formation. But the common form of conjugation takes up so much time in the recitation, that many teachers feel compelled wholly or partially to neglect it.

It is hoped that the method here recommended will be entirely practicable; for the complete conjugation of the verb can be deliberately given by it in three minutes. A class that has become entirely familiar with the conjugation of the verb should be frequently reviewed until the entire subject has been so fastened in the mind that it can never be removed. The recitation according to the fourth method given above may be carried on as follows:—

Present tense, indicative mode, *see* or *sees; am seeing, is seeing,* or *are seeing; am seen, is seen,* or *are seen; do see* or *does see.*

Potential mode, *may see, can see,* or *must see; may be seeing, etc.*

If the recitation is deliberately made, with proper pauses, the different forms will be readily distinguished. The best way to save time is not by speaking rapidly, but by omitting unnecessary words.

By examining the diagram on the opposite page, it will also be seen that:—

1. The **past participle** is used as basis in the common form of the perfect tenses and the perfect participle.

2. The **present active participle** is used as basis in all the tenses of the progressive form, and in the perfect progressive participle.

3. The **passive participle** is used as basis in all

DIAGRAM OF TENSE FORMS AND PARTICIPLES.

TENSES—	PRESENT.	PAST.	FUTURE.	PRESENT PERFECT.	PAST PERFECT.	FUTURE PERFECT.
Indicative Mode.	*See* or *Sees.* *Am, is,* or *are seeing.* *Am, is,* or *are seen.* *Do see* or *does see.*	*Saw.* *Was* or *were seeing.* *Was* or *were seen.* *Did see.*	*Shall see.* *Shall be seeing.* *Shall be seen.*	*Have* or *has seen.* *Have* or *has been seeing.* *Have* or *has been seen.*	*Had seen.* *Had been seeing.* *Had been seen.*	*Shall have seen.* *Shall have been seeing.* *Shall have been seen.*
Potential Mode.	*May see.* *May be seeing.* *May be seen.*	*Might see.* *Might be seeing.* *Might be seen.*		*May have seen.* *May have been seeing.* *May have been seen.*	*Might have seen.* *Might have been seeing.* *Might have been seen.*	
Imperative Mode.	*See.* *Be seeing.* *Do see,* etc. *Be seen.*					
Infinitive Mode.	*To see.* *To be seeing.* *To be seen.*			*To have seen.* *To have been seeing.* *To have been seen.*		
Subjunctive Mode.	If I, he, we, you, or they— *See.* *Be seeing.* *Be seen.*	If I, he, we, you, or they— *Saw,* *Were seeing.* *Were seen.*				
Participles.	*Seeing.* *Seen.*	*Seen.* *Seen.*		*Having seen.* *Having been seeing.* *Having been seen.*		

(327)

the tenses of the passive form, and in the perfect passive participle.

4. The **name-form** without *to* is used as basis in the future indicative and in the present and past potential. It constitutes the only tense of the imperative, and the present tense of the subjunctive.

The **name-form** *complete* constitutes the present tense of the infinitive mode.

5. The verb **to have** is used as auxiliary in the perfect tenses and the perfect participle, common form.

6. The verb **to be** is used as auxiliary in the progressive and passive forms.

LIST OF IRREGULAR VERBS.

When more forms than one are given for the past tense or past participle, that which stands first is to be preferred.

Present Tense.	Past Tense.	Past Participle.
Abide	abode	abode
Am *or* be	was	been
Awake	awoke, awaked	awaked
{ Bear (to bring forth)	bore	born
{ Bear (to sustain)	bore	borne
Beat	beat	beaten, beat
Begin	began	begun
Bend, *un-*	bent, bended	bent
Bereave	bereft, bereaved	bereft, bereaved
Beseech	besought	besought
Bet	bet, betted	bet, betted
Bid	bid, bade	bidden, bid
Bind, *un-*, *re-*	bound	bound
Bite	bit	bitten, bit
Bleed	bled	bled
Blow	blew	blown
Break	broke	broken
Breed	bred	bred
Bring	brought	brought
Build, *re-*, *up-*	built, builded	built, builded
Burn	burned, burnt	burned, burnt
Burst	burst	burst
Buy	bought	bought

Present Tense.	Past Tense.	Past Participle.
Can	could	——
Cast	cast	cast
Catch	caught	caught
Chide	chid	chidden, *chid
Choose	chose	chosen
{ Cleave (to adhere)	cleaved	cleaved
{ Cleave (to split)	cleft	cleft, cleaved
Cling	clung	clung
Clothe	clothed, clad	clothed, clad
Come, *be-, over-*	came	come
Cost	cost	cost
Creep	crept	crept
Crow	crew, crowed	crowed
Cut	cut	cut
Dare (to venture)	durst, dared	dared
Deal	dealt, dealed	dealt, dealed
Dig	dug, digged	dug, digged
Do, *un-, mis-, over-*	did	done
Draw, *with-*	drew	drawn
Dream	dreamed, dreamt	dreamed, dreamt
Drink	drank	drunk, drank
Drive	drove	driven
Dwell	dwelt, dwelled	dwelt, dwelled
Eat	ate	eaten
Fall, *be-*	fell	fallen
Feed	fed	fed
Feel	felt	felt
Fight	fought	fought
Find	found	found
Flee	fled	fled
Fling	flung	flung
Fly	flew	flown
Forbear	forbore	forborne
Forbid	forbade	forbidden
Forsake	forsook	forsaken
Freeze	froze	frozen
Freight	freighted	fraught, freighted
Get, *be-, for-*	got	got, gotten
Gild	gilded, gilt	gilded, gilt
Gird, *be-, un- en-*	girded, girt	girded, girt

Present Tense.	Past Tense.	Past Participle.
Give, for-, mis-	gave	given
Go, fore-, under-	went	gone
Grave, en-	graved	graven, graved
Grind *	ground	ground
Grow	grew	grown
Hang*	hung	hung
Have	had	had
Hear, over-	heard	heard
Heave	heaved, hove	heaved, hoven
Hew	hewed	hewn, hewed
Hide	hid	hidden, hid
Hit	hit	hit
Hold, be-, with-, up-	held	held, holden
Hurt	hurt	hurt
Keep	kept	kept
Kneel	knelt, kneeled	knelt, kneeled
Knit	knit, knitted	knit, knitted
Know fore-	knew	known
Lade (to load)	laded	laden
Lay (to place), in-	laid	laid
Lead, mis-	led	led
Leave	left	left
Lend	lent	lent
Let	let	let
Lie (to recline)	lay	lain
Light	lighted, lit	lighted, lit
Load, un-, over-	loaded	loaded, laden
Lose	lost	lost
Make	made	made
May	might	——
Mean	meant	meant
Meet	met	met
Mow	mowed	mown, mowed
Must	——	——
Ought	——	——
Pay, re-	paid	paid
Pen (to inclose)	penned, pent	penned, pent
Put	put	put

*Hang, to take away life by hanging, is regular.

Present Tense.	Past Tense.	Past Participle.
Quit	quit, quitted	quit, quitted
———	quoth	———
Read	read	read
Rend	rent	rent
Rid	rid	rid
Ride	rode	rode, ridden
Ring	rang, rung	rung
Rise, *a-*	rose	risen
Rive	rived	riven, rived
Run, *out-*	ran	run
Saw	sawed	sawn, sawed
Say, *un-, gain-*	said	said
See, *fore-*	saw	seen
Seek	sought	sought
Seethe	seethed	seethed, sodden
Sell	sold	sold
Send	sent	sent
Set, *be-*	set	set
Sit (to rest)	sat	sat
Shake	shook	shaken
Shall	should	———
Shape, *mis-*	shaped	shaped, shapen
Shave	shaved	shaved, shaven
Shear	sheared	shorn, sheared
Shed	shed	shed
Shine	shone, shined	shone, shined
Shoe	shod	shod
Shoot, *over-*	shot	shot
Show	showed	shown, showed
Shred	shred	shred
Shrink	shrunk, shrank	shrunk, shrunken
Shut	shut	shut
Sing	sang, sung	sung
Sink	sunk, sank	sunk
Slay	slew	slain
Sleep	slept	slept
Slide	slid	slidden, slid
Sling	slung	slung
Slink	slunk	slunk
Slit	slit	slit, slitted

Present Tense.	Past Tense.	Past Participle.
Smite	smote	smitten
Sow (to scatter)	sowed	sown, sowed
Speak, *be-*	spoke	spoken
Speed	sped	sped
Spell, *mis-*	spelled, spelt	spelled, spelt
Spend, *mis-*	spent	spent
Spill	spilt, spilled	spilt, spilled
Spin	spun	spun
Spit*	spit	spit
Split	split	split
Spread, *over-*, *be-*	spread	spread
Spring	sprang, sprung	sprung
Stand, *with-*, *under-*	stood	stood
Stave,	staved, stove	staved, stove
Stay,	staid, stayed	staid, stayed
Steal	stole	stolen
Stick	stuck	stuck
Sting	stung	stung
Stride, *be-*	strode, strid	stridden, strid
Strike	struck	struck, stricken
String	strung	strung
Strive	strove	striven
Strow *or* strew, *be-*	strowed *or* strewed	strown, strowed / strewn, strewed
Swear, *for-*	swore	sworn
Sweat	sweat, sweated	sweat, sweated
Sweep	swept	swept
Swell	swelled	swollen, swelled
Swim	swam	swum
Swing [*re-*, *over-*	swung	swung
Take, *mis-*, *under-*, *be-*	took	taken
Teach, *un-*, *mis-*	taught	taught
Tear	tore	torn
Tell, *fore-*	told	told
Think, *be-*	thought	thought
Thrive	throve, thrived	thriven, thrived
Throw, *over-*	threw	thrown
Thrust	thrust	thrust
Tread, *re-*	trod	trodden, trod

*Spit, to put on a spit, is regular.

Present Tense.	Past Tense.	Past Participle.
Wax	waxed	waxed, waxen
Wear	wore	worn
Weave, *un-*	wove	woven
Weep	wept	wept
Wet	wet, wetted	wet, wetted
Whet	whetted, whet	whetted, whet
Will	would	——
Win	won	won
Wind, *un-*	wound	wound
Work	worked, wrought	worked, wrought
Wot	wist	——
Wring	wrung	wrung
Write	wrote	written

REMARKS.—Verbs that have both a regular and an irregular form are said to be **redundant.**

Verbs that do not have all the principal parts,—*present tense, past tense, past participle,*—are said to be **defective.**

LESSON 254.

Miscellaneous Exercise.

1. Examples.

1. Although one were watching him closely, it would be impossible to detect the fraud.

2. If thou do these things, show thyself to the world.

3. Though he were encased in triple armor, he could not resist the stroke.

4. Though these three men, Noah, Daniel, and Job were in it, they could deliver but their own souls by their righteousness, saith the Lord God.—*Ezekiel* 14:14.

5. Had I the pinions of a dove,
    I'd fly away, and be at rest.

6. And thither the miser crept by stealth
    To feel of the gold that gave him health,
    And to gaze and gloat with his hungry eye
    On jewels that gleamed like a glow-worm's spark
    Or the eyes of a panther in the dark.

2. Seat Work.

Study the next lesson, and write the analysis of the first sentence.

LESSON 255.

Miscellaneous Exercise.—Continued.

1. Examples.

1. If thou art worn and hard beset
   With sorrows that thou wouldst forget,
   If thou wouldst read a lesson that will keep
   Thy heart from fainting and thy soul from sleep,
   Go to the woods and hills! No tears
   Dim the sweet look that Nature wears.
   —*Longfellow, p. 9.*

2. Our mother, while she turned her wheel
   Or run the new-knit stocking heel,
   Told how the Indian hordes came down
   At midnight on Cochecho town,
   And how her own great-uncle bore
   His cruel scalp-mark to fourscore.
   —*Whittier. p. 289.*

2. Seat Work.

Study the next lesson, and write the parsing of all the words in the second example.

LESSON 256.

Miscellaneous Exercise.—Continued.

1. Examples.

1. With beating heart to the task he went;
   His sinewy frame o'er the grave-stone bent;
   With bar of iron heaved amain,
   Till the toil-drops fell from his brows, like rain.
   It was by dint of passing strength,
   That he moved the massy stone at length.

I would you had been there, to see
How the light broke forth so gloriously,
Streamed upward to the chancel roof,
And through the galleries far aloof !
No earthly flame blazed ere so bright :
It shone like heaven's own blessed light,
   And, issuing from the tomb,
Showed the monk's cowl, and visage pale,
Danced on the dark-browed warrior's mail,
   And kissed his waving plume.
               —*Lay of the Last Minstrel.*

2. Few leaves of Fancy's spring remain;
   But what I have I give to thee.
             —*Bryant, p.* 112.

2. Seat Work.

Write the analysis of the first two *examples* of the next lesson, and parse the correlatives in the remaining examples.

LESSON 257.

Comparison Introduced by an Adjective.

1. Instruction.

1. *The pen is* **mightier than** *the sword.*
2. *They were* **more beautiful than** *other women.*
3. *He is* **worse than** *a thief.*

In the first sentence, the *pen* and the *sword* are compared in regard to the quality of might. *Mightier* denotes the quality, and by its form suggests a comparison of two objects in regard to that quality. It may be said to introduce the comparison, and the clause *"than the sword"* to complete it. That form which the adjective takes for the purpose of denoting comparison is called its **comparative form** or *comparative degree.* The comparative form of short words is usually made by the addition of *er,* while long words employ one of the adverbs *more* or *less* for the same purpose. Thus :—

Wonderful, *more* wonderful, *less* wonderful.

Some adjectives have very irregular ways of making their comparative form. For example :—

Good, *better.*   Bad, *worse.*

Adverbs sometimes take the comparative form; as,—

1. *He can write faster than I.*
2. *The Jordan flows more rapidly than the Hudson.*

In the *second sentence* at the head of this lesson, *more beautiful* means the same as *beautifuler;* so *more* is almost as much a part of the adjective as the termination *er*. The women represented by the pronoun *they* are compared with other women in regard to the quality of beauty. *Beautiful* denotes the quality, and *more*, like the termination *er*, suggests the comparison; the clause *"than other women"* completes it.

In the third sentence, the person denoted by *he* is compared with a thief in regard to the quality of badness. *Worse* denotes the quality, and by its form introduces the comparison which is completed by the clause *"than the thief."*

In the sentence, *The Jordan flows more rapidly than the Hudson*, the two streams are compared in regard to their manner of flowing. *Rapidly* denotes the manner, and *more* suggests that the flowing of the Jordan is to be compared with the flowing of some other stream.

2. Examples.

1. They were more frightened than we.
2. She can read better than I.
3. My health is better than it was when you were here.
4. It is better to be alone than in bad company.
5. You must bear greater troubles than these.
6. Beneath the shadow of their boughs the ground is not more still than they.—*Bryant, p.* 252.
7. Why should an American sailor be treated worse than a dog?
8. What is stronger than a lion? and what is sweeter than honey?

MODELS FOR ANALYSIS.

Ex.—Edwin is taller than George.

1. *Edwin* is the subject; *is taller* is the predicate; it' predicates a quality.

2. **Taller** denotes the predicated quality, and by its termination shows that two* things are to be compared with reference to this quality.

3. **Than George** is an elliptical clause, and completes the comparison introduced by *taller*.

4. **Than** introduces the clause, and indicates its use. *George* is the subject; *is tall*, understood, is the predicate.

*Ex.—The gambler drives a more beautiful horse than
his honest neighbor.*

1. *Gambler* is the subject, *drives* is the predicate, and *horse* is the object.

2. **Beautiful** denotes a quality of the horse, and **more,** like the termination *er*, shows that two things are to be compared with respect to this quality.

3. *Than his honest neighbor* completes the comparison introduced by *more*.

4. *Than* introduces the clause and indicates its use. *Neighbor* is the subject, and *drives*, understood, is the predicate.

Ex.—She dresses more expensively than she can afford.

1. *She* is the subject, *dresses* is the predicate, *expensively* tells how she dresses, and *more*, like the termination *er*, shows that two things are to be compared with respect to their expensiveness. Her actual mode of dressing is compared with the mode of dressing which she can afford.

---

*NOTE.—When more than two things are compared, the adjective or adverb takes what is called the *Superlative Form*. In short words, this form is usually made by adding *est* to the common form; but in long words, it is made by using *most* or *least* instead of the termination *est*.

MODELS FOR PARSING.

Ex.—Edwin is taller than George.

Taller is an adjective, qualifying, used with the copula to form the predicate. It is in the comparative form, and may be said to be correlative to *than*, for it awakens an expectation of a clause that will be introduced by *than*.

Than is a conjunction, subordinate; it is correlative to *taller*, and shows the relation of its clause to that word.

Ex.—The gambler drives a more beautiful horse, etc.

More beautiful is an adjective, qual., comparative form; added to the noun horse.

More is an adverb, added to beautiful to give it the comparative form. It is correlative to *than;* for it awakens an expectation of a clause introduced by that word.

Than is a conjunction, subordinate; it is correlative to *more*, and shows the relation of its clause to *more beautiful*.

Ex.—She dresses more expensively than she can afford.

More expensively is an adverb in the comparative form; added to the verb *dresses*.

More is an adverb, added to *expensively* to give it the comparative form. It is correlative to *than;* for it awakens an expectation of a clause introduced by that word.

Than is a conjunction, subordinate; it is correlative to *more*, and shows the relation of its clause to *more expensively*.

REMARKS.—If the ellipsis were supplied in the fourth sentence, it would read, "It is better to be alone than *it is* [*good*] *to be* in bad company." In this sentence, two conditions are compared,—that of being alone, and that of being in bad company. *To be alone* names one condition, and *to be in bad company* names the other; so each of these groups should be parsed as a *verbal noun*, the first in apposition with *it* expressed, and the second in apposition with *it* understood.

Note.—If after parsing these groups as a whole, it be thought worth while to take up the separate words, *to be* should be parsed as the infinitive of the copula, (a copula that still denotes the *existence* of the condition expressed by the words following it, but has lost its power to predicate that condition), and *alone* as an adjective, independent, or absolute. *In bad company* is a phrase in the same relation as *alone*, so the preposition *in* has no antecedent term of relation. The meaning is not for any *particular one* to be alone or in bad company, but for *any one*, and therefore forbids the application of these conditions to any particular person. It may be interesting to notice how these groups become verbal nouns. The thought brought out in sentence 4 might be expressed thus:—

When any one is alone, he is in a more favorable condition than when he is in bad company.

Now if we wish to name the thought predicated in each subordinate clause, we must convert each predicate into a noun, but in order to do this we must destroy its power of predication. This is done by changing the copula to the participial or the infinitive form. This gives us *being alone* or *to be alone* as a name for the thought expressed by the first predicate, and *being in bad company* or *to be in bad company*, for the second.

3. Seat Work.

Study the next lesson; write the analysis of sentences 9 and 10, and the parsing of the correlative words.

———•——

LESSON 258.

Clauses Introduced by As.

1. Instruction.

By studying the examples of the last lesson we see that *subordinate* conjunctions, as well as *coördinate* conjunctions, may have correlatives.

Clauses joined by subordinate correlatives are sometimes called **correlative clauses.** The subordinate correlative clause is an adverbial clause whose relation to some adjective or adverb is shown by correlative words.

The examples in the last lesson contain comparisons of inequality. In such comparisons the subordinate clause is always introduced by *than*, preceded by some correlative adjective or adverb in the comparative form. But we often wish to describe a thing by comparing it with something that has an equal amount of some quality. This is called a comparison of *equality*, and is illustrated by the examples of this lesson. It will be noticed that comparisons of equality employ the correlatives *as—as* or *so—as*.

2. Examples.

1. The peasant is as gay as he.
2. Man is not as wise as his Maker.
3. Fair is that land as evening skies.
4. Work as long as you can.
5. As far as the eye could reach, all was ruin and desolation.
6. Some think that she can sing as well as Jenny Lind.
7. Other men, as well as poets, may be lovers of the beautiful.
8. Our conquest there, after twenty years, is as crude as it was the first day.
9. Into Hiawatha's wigwam
    Came two other guests, as silent
    As the ghosts were, and as gloomy.
10. In many parts, the thirsty traveler discovers springs as bright and limpid as those of our New England hills.

MODEL FOR ANALYSIS.
Sentence 1.

1. *Peasant* is the subject; *is gay* is the predicate; it predicates quality.

2. *Gay* denotes the predicated quality, and **as** shows that two things are to be compared with respect to that quality.

3. **As he** completes the comparison introduced by the first *as*.

4. **As** introduces the clause, and indicates its use.

5. *He* is the subject, and *is gay*, understood, is the predicate.

MODELS FOR PARSING.

As *(the first one)* is a conjunctive adverb. As a conjunction, it is correlative to the second *as*, and as an adverb, it slightly modifies the adjective *gay*.

As *(the second one)* is a conjunction, subordinate; it is correlative to the first *as*, and shows the relation of its clause to *gay*.

REMARKS.—In sentence **7,** *as well as* is a coördinate conjunction; its office is like *and*, only it gives greater emphasis to the relation. It is said to denote emphatic correspondence. The same relation might be made more emphatic by the use of correlatives. Thus:—

Not only poets, but also other men, are lovers of the beautiful.

3. Seat Work.

Select correlative clauses joined by *as* and *than*.

LESSON 259.

Correlative Clauses with As and Than.

1. Examples.

1. My father is seven years older than my mother.
2. I have returned to refute a libel as false as it is malicious.
3. And the brown ground-bird in the glen,
   Still chirps as merrily as then.
   —*Bryant, p.* 51.
4. Be more anxious to acquire knowledge than to show it.
5.   The brook,
   Bordered with sparkling frost-work, was as gay
   As with its fringe of summer flowers.
   —*Bryant, p.* 30.
6. O ye wild winds! a mightier power than yours, in chains upon the shore of Europe lies.

7. Purple, and crimson, and scarlet, like the curtains of God's tabernacle, the rejoicing trees sank into the valley in showers of light, every separate leaf quivering with buoyant and burning life; each, as it turned to reflect or to transmit the sunbeam, first a torch and then an emerald.—*John Ruskin.*

2. Seat Work.

Write out the analysis of sentences 5 and 6 of the next lesson.

LESSON 260.

Correlative Clauses Denoting Consequence.

1. Examples.

1. The day was so stormy that it was not prudent to venture out.

2. He was so much injured that he could not walk.

3. The patient had gained so much strength that he was able to ride out.

4. John arrived as soon as I.

5. Then there escaped from her lips a cry of such terrible
  anguish
  That the dying heard it, and started up from their
   pillows.   *—Longfellow.*

6. Thus fares it still in our decay;
  And yet the wiser mind
  Mourns less for what Age takes away
  Than what it leaves behind.
     — Wordsworth.

MODEL FOR ANALYSIS.

Ex.—Virtue is so amiable that even the vicious admire it.

1. *Virtue* is the subject, and *is amiable* is the predicate; it predicates quality.

2. *Amiable* denotes the predicated quality, and

3. **So** indicates that a clause is to follow that will show the degree of the quality by telling what effect it produces.

4. **That the vicious admire it** tells the effect of the quality, and in that way shows how much of it the subject possesses.

5. **That** introduces the clause, and indicates its use.

6. *Vicious,* or the noun limited by it, is the subject of the clause, *admire* is the predicate, and *it* is the object.

7. *Even* gives emphasis to the assertion, and seems to suggest that it is true against what would be probable.

MODELS FOR PARSING.

So is a conjunctive abverb. As a conjunction, it is correlative to *that;* as an adverb, it slightly modifies the adjective *amiable.*

That is a conjunction, subordinate; it is correlative to *so*, and shows the relation of its clause to *amiable.*

2. Seat Work.

Write the analysis of sentence 6 of the next lesson, and the parsing of the correlatives in sentences 4 and 5.

———— • ————

LESSON 261.

Transposed Correlative Clauses.

1. Examples.

1. As the door turneth upon its hinges, so doth the slothful man upon his bed.

2. As a bird that wandereth from her nest, so is a man that wandereth from his place.

3. As is your influence, so is your destiny.

4. As the rose breathes sweetness from its own nature, so the heart of the benevolent man produces good works.
—*Dodsley.*

5. As round the reaper falls the grain,
So the dark host around him fell,
So sank the foes of Israel.
— *Whittier.*

6. One evening, after the sheep were folded, and we were all seated beneath the myrtle which shaded our cottage, my grandsire, an old man, was telling of Marathon and Leuctra; and how, in ancient times, a little band of Spartans, in a defile of the mountains, had withstood a whole army.—*Elijah Kellogg.*

MODEL FOR ANALYSIS.

Sentence 1.

1. *Man* is the subject, *doth turn* is the predicate, and *upon his bed* tells where he turns.

2. **So** indicates that the turning of the man is to be compared with a similar turning of something else.

3. **As the door turneth upon its hinges** completes the comparison introduced by *so*.

4. **As** introduces the clause and indicates its use.

5. Etc.

MODELS FOR PARSING.

As is a conjunction, subordinate; it is correlative to *so*, and shows the relation of its clause to *doth turn.*

So is a conjunctive adverb. It is correlative to *as*, and slightly modifies *doth turn.*

REMARKS.—In most of the examples of this lesson, the subordinate clause comes first, and the correlative conjunction at the head of it awakens an expectation of a principal clause containing a correlative word that will *introduce a comparison*. The correlative word in the principal clause introduces a comparison, and directs the mind backward to the subordinate clause which completes it.

The true relation of the subordinate clause in sentence **2**, may be seen by comparing the following equivalent expressions :—

1. A man that wandereth from his place is *like a bird that wandereth from her nest.*

2. A man that wandereth from his place is *as a bird that wandereth from her nest.*

3. *As a bird that wandereth from her nest, so* is a man that wandereth from his place.

These sentences all express the same thought. Each predicates a *condition* of the man that wanders from his place, and in each the condition is brought out *by comparison*. In the first, the comparison is completed by a *phrase*, and in the second and third, by a *clause*. This clause is substantive, for it is used with the copula to form the predicate.

In the second sentence, *as* introduces the substantive clause and indicates its use. It is a conjunction, subordinate; it shows that its clause will denote comparison, and that it is subordinate in rank.

In the third sentence, the clauses are transposed. *As,* in this sentence, is parsed just as it is in the model above. *So* is called a conjunctive adverb; it is correlative to *as,* and perhaps it slightly limits the verb.

2. Seat Work.

Study the next lesson; write the analysis of sentence 7, and the parsing of the conjunctive adverbs and subordinate conjunctions in sentences 1, 3, and 4.

LESSON 262.

Correlative Clauses.—Continued.

1. Instruction.

Sometimes the word *the* is used with an adverb in the comparative degree as a correlative for the purpose of showing corresponding increase or decrease. Thus :—

1. ***The more*** *we study,* ***the more*** *we thirst for knowledge.*
2. ***The fewer*** *friends we claim,* ***the fewer*** *ties are broken.*

In many instances, the increase and decrease are in inverse relation. Thus :—

The less *the passions are indulged,* ***the more easily*** *they are controlled.*

The, when used as above, is commonly parsed as an adverb, but it seems to have something of the nature of a conjunction; for the two *the's* are certainly correlative to each other, and indicate a relation between the clauses that would not necessarily exist if these words were omitted.

2. Examples.

1. As we do to others, so shall it be done to us.

2. The longer I use the book, the better I like it.

3. These English parks have trees as fine and as effective as any of ours.

4. O, teach him that the Christian man
     Is holier than the Jewish priest.
                 — *Whittier, p.* 70.

5. In the lone and long night-watches, sky above and wave below,
     Thou didst learn a higher wisdom than the babbling school-men know.   —*Ib., p.* 57.

6. We are so afraid of each other's doctrines, that we cannot cure each other's sins.

7. What he gives thee, see thou keep;
     Stay not thou for food or sleep:
     Be it scroll, or be it book,
     Into it, knight, thou must not look;
     If thou readest, thou art lorn!
     Better hadst thou ne'er been born.
                —*Scott.*

8. The gigantic genius of Shakspeare so far surpassed the learning and penetration of his time, that his productions were little read and less admired.

REMARKS.—In sentence **5,** the expression *sky above and wave below* consists of two absolute phrases joined coördinately by *and.* Each of the nouns *sky* and *wave* is independent with an adjective instead of a participle. Each expression comes from a clause having an adjective or adjective phrase in the predicate.

We have seen that clauses are abridged to absolute phrases by destroying their power of predication. This is done by changing the verb to a participle whenever the verb constitutes the entire predicate; but whenever the predicate consists of a copula and a noun, the copula is changed to a participle; as, *Paul being a Roman,* etc.

Whenever the predicate consists of a copula and an adjective, we may change the copula to a participle, or we may drop it entirely, as in the sentence which forms the subject of this remark.

In sentence **6**, *each* is used to show that the persons represented by *we* act reciprocally in being afraid of doctrines. *Each*, or the noun limited by it, is commonly regarded as being in apposition with *we*, and therefore in the nominative case; while *other's*, or the noun limited by it, is in the possessive case.

3. Seat Work.

Write the analysis of sentence 9, and the parsing of all the correlative words in the next lesson.

------•------

LESSON 263.

Correlative Clauses Denoting Purpose.

1. Instruction.

PUNCTUATION.—Correlative clauses are not usually separated by any mark of punctuation when the clause completing the comparison is introduced by *as* or *than*, or when the clauses are closely joined by *so that* or *such that*. But they should be separated by the comma whenever the second correlative word is followed by a comma, or when the correlative words stand at the head of their respective clauses.

Correlative clauses joined by other words than those mentioned above are generally separated by the comma.

2. Examples.

1. He visited the springs that he might improve his health.
2. Cæsar visited Britain, in order that he might conquer the inhabitants.
3. Live well that you may die well.
4. The foliage of the trees is as dense as ever, and as green.
5. Better is the storm above it, than the quiet of the grave.

6. The man traveled in order that he might regain his strength.

7. We can discover nothing so sublime as the spirit of self-sacrifice.

8. Shall your good State sink her honor that her gambling stocks may rise? .

9. As the tides of the sea arise in the month of September, flooding some silver stream till it spreads to a lake in the meadow, so death flooded life.

MODEL FOR ANALYSIS.

Sentence 2.

1. *Cæsar* is the subject.
2. *Visited* is the predicate.
3. *Britain* names the place visited by him.

4. **In order that he might conquer the inhabitants** tells why he visited Britain.

5. **In order** awakens an expectation of a clause that will tell why Cæsar visited Britain.

6. *That he might conquer the inhabitants* meets the expectation raised by *in order.*

7. *That* introduces the clause, etc.

MODELS FOR PARSING.

In order is a conjunctive adverb; it is correlative to *that,* and slightly modifies *visited.*

That is a conjunction, subordinate; it is correlative to *in order,* and shows the relation of its clause to *visited.*

3. Seat Work.

Study the next lesson, and select all kinds of correlative clauses.

LESSON 264.

Correlative Clauses.—Continued.

1. Examples.

1. They have given their lives, in order that the nation might live.

2. God sent his singers upon earth
   With songs of sadness and of mirth,
   That they might touch the hearts of men,
   And bring them back to heaven again.
   —*Longfellow, p.* 134.

3. O lady fair, I have yet a gem which a purer luster flings
   Than the diamond flash of the jeweled crown on the
      lofty brow of kings,—
   A wonderful pearl of exceeding price, whose virtue shall
      not decay,
   Whose light shall be as a spell to thee, and a blessing on
      thy way!   *Whittier, p.* 91.

4. The more the love of poetry is cultivated and refined, the more do men strive to make their outward lives rythmical and harmonious.

5. As I darkened the light, he cast his eyes toward the window, that he might catch the feeble rays of the moon.

6. The sun is so bright that it dazzles the eyes.

7.   The fingers of the rain
   In light staccatos on the window played,
   Mixed with the flame's contented hum, and made
   Low harmonies to suit the varied strain.
   —*Bayard Taylor.*

REMARK.—In sentence **3**, *as a spell*, is an elliptical substantive clause used with *shall be*, to form the predicate. It means "as a spell *would be.*"

2. Seat Work.

Study the next lesson, and select all kinds of correlative clauses.

LESSON 265.

Emotional Expressions.

1. Instruction.

Wonderful are the works of God!

This sentence not only predicates a quality of the works of God, but it also shows that emotion is awakened by the thought.

In spoken language the emotion is shown chiefly by the tone and modulations of the voice; but in written language the attendant emotion is shown by the arrangement of the words, and by the use of the exclamation point at the close of the sentence.

In the sentence given above, the word *wonderful* is put in a prominent position, because it denotes the quality that excites emotion. If the sentence were written thus: "The works of the Lord are wonderful," no emotion would be indicated.

Exclamatory sentences are generally introduced by some word which gives notice of the emotional character of the thought to be expressed. These words are *O, how, what*, etc.

2. Examples.

1. How grandly the huge waves mount toward the sky!
2. What fearful sounds come from the dark vault!
3. How his gray skirts toss in the whirling gale!
4. What a tale of terror their turbulency tells!
5. How pale is the face of that young sufferer!
6. How delicious, how real, are such remembrances!
7. With what a look of longing and sorrow she turned from us!
8. With what fearful eagerness the people watch for signs of rain!
9. With what a glory comes and goes the year!

10. How it tolls for the souls
     Of the sailors on the sea!
           —T. B. Aldrich.

11. How it clatters along the roofs, like the tramp of hoofs!

12. What soft, fleecy clouds floated in the clear, blue sky!

MODELS FOR ANALYSIS.

Ex.—How wonderfully the flowers are made!

1. This group of words is an exclamatory sentence; it predicates a thought, and shows that emotion is awakened by that thought.

2. *Flowers* is the subject.

3. *Are made* is the predicate.

4. *Wonderfully* shows *how* the flowers are made,— that they are so made as to excite wonder in those who behold them.

5. **How** shows that the *manner* in which they are made excites an *unusual degree* of wonder. It takes the most prominent place in the sentence in order to show what *modification* of the thought, excites the emotion.

Ex.—What blessings we enjoy!

1. This group of words is a sentence; it expresses a thought, and shows that emotion is excited by that thought.

2. *We* is the subject.

3. *Enjoy* is the predicate.

4. *Blessings* names the things that are enjoyed.

5. **What** seems to show that the blessings here meant are *peculiar*, and either *unusually great* or *remarkably abundant*. It takes the first place in the sentence to show that this *peculiarity* of the blessings is what excites the emotion.

MODELS FOR PARSING.

How is an adverb, added to *wonderfully* to show that the flowers are so made as to excite an *unusual degree* of wonder.

What is an adjective, added to *blessings* to show that the blessings are either *unusually great* or *very abundant*.

2. Seat Work.

Study the next lesson, and write the analysis of sentences 1 and 9.

LESSON 266.

Emotion Expressed by a Single Word.

1. Instruction.

1. *Alas! thy youth is dead!*
2. *Ah! how cold are their caresses!*
3. *Hark! I hear the tread of armed men!*

In the arrangement of the words in the first sentence there is nothing to indicate emotion.

Alas denotes an emotion of sadness, and the sentence that follows it shows what thought awakens the emotion.

The emotional character of the thought is still further shown to the eye by the exclamation point, and to the ear by the tones and modulations of the voice.

In sentence 2, the emotion is shown by the words *ah* and *how*. *Ah* is used expressly for that purpose. It is not really a part of the sentence, but stands alone, and is, to a great degree at least, independent. It denotes a sudden emotion of *grief* or *sadness*, and the sentence that follows it explains the cause. *How*, by its prominent position in the sentence, shows just what modification of the thought excites the emotion. It is the unusual degree of coldness. The quality itself is shown by *cold*, but the unusual or unexpected degree of the quality is indefinitely shown by *how*.

In the third sentence, *hark* is the predicate of a clause with *thou*, *you*, or *ye*, understood as its subject. It exhorts the person spoken to to act; but, at the same time, indicates an emotion of *fear* or *surprise*, without telling what awakens that emotion.

2. Examples.

1. Alas! the sweetness of Annette's manners was not the beaming of a lovely spirit.

2. Ugh! the old men all responded from their seats beneath the pine-trees.

3. Hark! distant voices ripple the silence deep.

4. Hurrah! there they come!

5. Bah! how disgusting are such actions!

6. Why! how you look!

7. Hush! came not faint whispers near?

8. There! my work is done.

9. See! a rocket cleaves the sky from the fort,—a shaft of light.

10. O, wash away these scarlet sins!

11. Well done! thy words are great and bold.

12. What! are these my guests?

REMARKS.—Sentences **7** and **12** are emotional and interrogative at the same time.

Sentences **1, 2, 3, 8, 9, 11,** are simply declarative, and followed by the period. The emotion is indicated by *alas, ugh, hark, there, see,* and *well done.*

Hark, hush, see, well done, are all elliptical clauses, but have been so much used as exclamations, that, when so employed, they seem to have nearly lost their original signification, and are commonly parsed as interjections.

3. Seat Work.

Write the parsing of all the exclamatory words in the next lesson.

LESSON 267.

Elliptical Expressions of Emotion.

1. Instruction.

Oh for a lodge in some vast wilderness!

The meaning of this sentence seems to be, "Oh how I long for a lodge in some vast wilderness!" The subject and predicate are both understood. *For a lodge, etc.*, modifies the predicate understood; it tells the tendency or direction of my longing. *Oh* denotes an emotion of intense earnestness, mingled, perhaps, with impatience. The cause of this emotion is not given.

PUNCTUATION.—Exclamatory expressions are usually followed by the exclamation point. Interjections are followed by this point when emphatic; but when they are not emphatic, yet require a pause after them, and are followed by an exclamatory clause, the comma is placed after the interjection, and the exclamation point at the end of the clause.

Whenever the interjection is so closely connected with what follows as to admit of no pause, the comma is omitted.

2. Examples.

1. Oh for faithful men in times of such fearful wickedness!
2. Alas! the weakness of human nature!
3. What! not up yet?
4. Farewell, a long farewell, to all my greatness!
5. What beautiful warm days we are having this month!
6. Bingo, why Bingo! hey, hey—here, here!
7. A Daniel come to judgment! yea, a Daniel.—
   O, wise young judge, how I do honor thee!
   —*Shakspeare.*
8. O God! I cannot bear this doubt
   That stifles breath.
9. Onward he rode, the pathway still
   Winding betwixt the lake and hill;
   Till, on the fragment of a rock,
   Struck from its base by lightning shock,
   He saw the hoary Sage:
   The silver moss and lichen twined,
   With fern and deer-hair checked and lined,
   A cushion fit for age;
   And o'er him shook the aspen-tree,
   A restless, rustling canopy.
   —*Scott, p. 385.*

3. Seat Work.

Study the next lesson, and write the parsing of the words in sentence 4.

LESSON 268.

Subject of the Last Lesson Continued.

1. Examples.

1. My heart is awed within me when I think
   Of the great miracle that still goes on,
   In silence, round me,—the perpetual work
   Of thy creation, finished, yet renewed
   Forever.   —*Bryant, p.* 80.

2. "Oho!" she muttered, "ye're brave to-day!"

3. "Fie, silly bird!" I answered, "tuck your head beneath your wing."

4. O men and brothers! what sights were there!
   White upturned faces, hands stretched in prayer!
                                   —*Whittier, p.* 811.

5. Up! up! my friend, and quit your books.

6. A pilgrim, when the summer day
   Had closed upon his weary way,
     A lodging begged beneath a castle's roof;
   But him the haughty warder spurned ;
   And from the gate the pilgrim turned,
   To seek such covert as the field
   Or heath-besprinkled copse might yield,
     Or lofty wood, shower-proof.
                                   —*Wordsworth, p.* 148.

2. Seat Work.

Study the next lesson, and write the analysis of examples 2, 5, and 7.

LESSON 269.

Quality Acquired or Discovered Through the Action of the Verb.

1. Instruction.

1. *The leaves* **turn brown** *in autumn.*
2. *The rose* **smells sweet.**

In the first sentence above, *brown* denotes a quality which the leaves acquire by the act of turning.

In the second sentence, *sweet* denotes a quality of the rose,—a quality discovered by the act of smelling.

In both instances, the quality is predicated. The verb predicates action, and does not represent it as being received by anything. . So far, it is like an intransitive verb; but in addition to doing this work, it shows that the quality denoted by the adjective that follows it, is predicated. In this respect it is like the copula. The adjective forms a part of the predicate as much as it does when used after the copula itself. Such a verb is called a **copulative verb.**

The *copula* is used with the adjective, simply to show that the quality is predicated; but the *copulative verb* used with the adjective to form the predicate does two things,— it predicates action, and at the same time shows that some other thought is predicated,—some *quality, action, state,* or *class,* denoted by a word that follows.

However different in other respects, all copulative verbs are alike in doing the work of a copula, in addition to predicating the thought which they themselves denote.

2. Examples.

1. At once his eye grew wild.
2. The eyes of the sleepers waxed deadly and chill.
3. Day by day her step grew weaker.
4. Ho, young Count of Greiers! this morning thou art ours.

5. She appears healthier than she is.
6. Methinks the night grows thin and gray.
7. The muscles become strong through exercise.
8. Level the landscape grew.
9. The world looks old and grim.

MODELS FOR ANALYSIS.

Ex.—The leaves turn brown in autumn.

1. *Leaves* is the subject.

2. **Turn brown** is the predicate; it predicates an action, and also a quality which the subject acquires through that action.

3. **Turn** denotes the action and predicates it.

4. **Brown** denotes the quality, and *turn*, like a copula, shows that the quality is predicated.

Ex.—The rose smells sweet.

1. *Rose* is the subject.

2. **Smells sweet** is the predicate; it predicates an action, and also a quality which is discovered through that action.

3. **Sweet** denotes the quality.

4. **Smells** denotes and predicates the action, and also shows that the quality is predicated.

MODELS FOR PARSING.

Turn is a verb, reg., copulative, indicative mode, present tense, 3d, plu., to agree with its subject *leaves*.

Brown is an adjective, qual.; used with the copulative verb *turn* to form the predicate.

3. Seat Work.

Study the next lesson; write the parsing of the copulative verbs, and the adjectives used with them to form the predicate.

LESSON 270.

Copulative Verbs Used to Predicate Accompanying State.

1. Instruction.

As may be seen by some of the examples in this lesson, the adjective following the copulative verb often denotes a condition or quality that *accompanies* the action or state expressed by the verb.

2. Examples.

1. Illuming the landscape with silver, fair rose the dewy moon and the myriad stars.—*Evangeline.*

2. But thicker and thicker a hot mist grew,
   Shot by the lightnings through and through,
   And muffled growls, like the growl of a beast,
   Ran along the sky from west to east.
   —*Whittier, p.* 298.

3. Their hearts beat but once, and forever lay still.
   —*Byron.*

4. And there the full broad river runs,
   And many a fount wells fresh and sweet.

5. The grass grows green where the frost has been,
   And waste and wayside are fringed with flowers.

6. Is this a time to be gloomy and sad,
   When our mother Nature laughs around;
   When even the deep blue heavens look glad,
   And gladness breathes from the blossoming ground?
   —*Bryant, p.* 105.

REMARK.—In analyzing sentence **1**, say, *Rose fair* is the predicate; it predicates action and an accompanying condition. *Fair* denotes the condition, and *rose*, like a copula, predicates that condition.

3. Seat Work.

Select examples like those in this lesson and in the preceding one.

LESSON 271.
Copulative Verbs Predicating Class.

1. Examples.

1. A region of repose it seems,
   A place of slumber and of dreams,
   Remote among the wooded hills.
   —*Longfellow.*

2. And Duncan pines a prisoner, fast within his father's towers.

3. Then from a neighboring thicket the mocking-bird, wildest of singers,
   Swinging aloft on a willow spray that hung o'er the water,
   Shook from his little throat such floods of delirious music
   That the whole air and the woods and the waves seemed silent to listen. —*Evangeline.*

4. Nor long may thy still waters lie
   An image of the glorious sky.
   —*Bryant,* p. 116.

5. Sometimes it seemed a prayer, and sometimes it sounded like swearing.

6. Dark and silent the water lies.

MODELS FOR ANALYSIS.

Ex.—She moved a goddess.

1. *She* is the subject.

2. **Moved a goddess** is the predicate; it predicates an action by which the subject manifests qualities that characterize a goddess.

3. **Goddess** names one of a class, and

4. **Moved** denotes the action by which the subject manifests qualities that belong to that class.

Ex.—She looked a queen.

1. *She* is the subject.

2. **Looked a queen** is the predicate; it predicates an action, and through that action qualities are manifested which characterize a queen.

3. **Queen** names one of a class, and

4. **Looked** denotes the action through which qualities are manifested that distinguish that class.

Ex.—He died an honest man.

1. *He* is the subject.

2. **Died an honest man** is the predicate; it predicates action of the subject, and also that at the time of that action he belonged to a class of men called *honest*.

3. **Man** names one of a class ; **honest** describes the kind of man here meant by assuming a quality of him ; and **died** predicates, not only the action denoted by itself, but also that at the time of that action the subject belonged to the class of men described in the words that follow.

Ex.—He turned beggar.

1. *He* is the subject.

2. **Turned beggar** is the predicate ; it predicates action, and also that through this action he became one of a class called *beggars*.

3. **Beggar** names one of the class.

4. **Turned** denotes the action through which he became a beggar.

MODEL FOR PARSING.

Ex.—She moved a goddess.

Goddess is a noun, com., 3d, sing., fem.; it is used with the copulative verb *moved* to form the predicate, and is therefore put in the nominative case.

2.   Seat Work.

Study the next lesson ; write the analysis of sentence 5, and the parsing of its verbs and predicate-adjectives.

LESSON 272.

Accompanying Action or State.

1. Examples.

1. The level sun, like ruddy ore,
   Lay sinking in the barren skies.—*Jean Ingelow.*
2. Here delicate snow-stars, out of the cloud
   Come floating downward in airy play.—*Bryant, p.* 225.
3. Beatitude seemed written in his face.
4. As o'er the verdant waste I guide my steed,
   Among the high rank grass that sweeps his sides
   The hollow beating of his footstep seems
   A sacrilegious sound.   —*Bryant,* 131.
5. The scene was more beautiful far to my eye
   Than if day in its pride had arrayed it:
   The land-breeze blew mild, and the azure-arched sky
   Looked pure as the spirit that made it.—*Thomas Moore.*
6.   The church of the village
   Gleaming stood in the morning's sheen.—*Longfellow, p.* 24.
7. The herd's white bones lie mixed with human mold.

MODELS FOR ANALYSIS.

Ex.—She sat weeping.

1. *She* is the subject.

2. **Sat weeping** is the predicate; it predicates posture with accompanying action.

3. **Weeping** denotes the action, but of itself has no power to predicate it.

4. **Sat** denotes posture and predicates it; it also acts the part of a copula in showing that the act of weeping is predicated.

Ex.—He went on his way rejoicing.

1. *He* is the subject.

2. **Went rejoicing** is the predicate; it predicates two associated actions.

3. **Went** denotes an action, and predicates it; it also acts the part of a copula in showing that the act of rejoicing is predicated.

4. **Rejoicing** denotes an accompanying action, but has in itself no power to predicate it.

Ex.—Fields lie deserted.

1. *Fields* is the subject.

2. **Lie deserted** is the predicate; it predicates two conditions.

3. **Lie** denotes a condition, and predicates it; it also acts the part of a copula in showing that the state denoted by the participle *deserted* is predicated.

4. **Deserted** denotes action received by the subject, and a consequent condition.

MODELS FOR PARSING.
Ex.—She sat weeping.

Sat is a verb, irreg., copulative, ind. mode, past tense. Verbs in this tense do not change their form for the person and number of their subject.

Weeping is a participle, present active; it denotes accompanying action, and is used with the copulative verb *sat* to form the predicate.

2.   Seat Work.

Study the next lesson; write the analysis of sentence 2, and the parsing of the verbs and participles in sentences 1 and 4.

LESSON 273.
Miscellaneous Exercise.
1.   Examples.

1. The rain-drops glistened on the trees around,
   Whose shadows on the tall grass were not stirred,
   Save when a shower of diamonds, to the ground
   Was shaken by the flight of startled bird.—*Bryant. p. 67.*

2. Colder and louder blew the wind,
   A gale from the northeast,
   The snow fell hissing on the brine,
   And the billows frothed like yeast.
   —Longfellow, p. 2

3. But courage, O my mariners!
   Ye shall not suffer wreck,
   While up to God the freedman's prayers
   Are rising from your deck.
   — Whittier, p. 315.

4. That withered trunk a tree or shepherd seems,
   Just as the light or fancy strikes the eye.

5. In fair wood like this, where the beeches are growing,
   Brave Robin Hood hunted in days of old;
   Down his broad shoulders his brown locks fell flowing,
   His cap was of green, with a tassel of gold.
   —Parker.

2. Seat Work.

Study the next lesson, and write the parsing of the words in example 2.

LESSON 274.

Miscellaneous Exercise.—Continued.

1. Examples.

1. As the weary traveler sees
   In desert or prairie vast,
   Blue lakes, overhung with trees,
   That a pleasant shadow cast;

   Fair towns with turrets high,
   And shining roofs of gold,
   That vanish as he draws nigh,
   Like mists together rolled,—

   So I wander and wander along,
   And forever before me gleams
   The shining city of song,
   In the beautiful land of dreams.

But when I would enter the gate
  Of that golden atmosphere,
It is gone, and I wander, and wait
  For the vision to reappear. —*Longfellow, p.* 228.

2. Suspended cliffs, with hideous sway,
    Seemed nodding o'er the cavern gray.

2. Seat Work.

Write the analysis of examples 1 to 4 of the next lesson, and the parsing of all the words in their predicates.

LESSON 275.

Double Object Consisting of a Noun or Pronoun with an Adjective.

1. Instruction.
1. *We thought* ***that the man was insane.***
2. *We thought* ***the man insane.***

In the first sentence above, the substantive clause "*that the man was insane*" is the object of the verb *thought*. In the second sentence, "*the man insane*" is the same clause in an abridged form; it means the same that it did in its complete form, and is used for the same purpose.

Now if we use a pronoun in place of the noun *man*, we shall see that *him* is required instead of *he* or *his*. The sentence would then read, "*We thought him insane.*" From this we learn that the subject of an abridged clause is put in the objective case whenever the clause is used to complete the meaning of a transitive verb. An abridged clause used in this way is sometimes called **a double object.**

2. Examples.
1. They thought me mad.
2. Do you believe me sincere?
3. That experience made us more cautious.

4. Some call him stingy.

5. I consider the boy honest.

6. What makes the sky so bright?

7. Spake full well, in language quaint and olden,
   One who dwelleth by the castled Rhine,
   When he called the flowers, so blue and golden,
   Stars, that in earth's firmament do shine.

Stars they are, wherein we read our history,
   As astrologers and seers of eld;
Yet not wrapped about with awful mystery,
   Like the burning stars which they beheld.

—*Longfellow, p.* 4.

MODEL FOR ANALYSIS.

Ex.—We thought him insane.

1. *We* is the subject.

2. **Thought him insane** is the predicate; it predicates an action and the conclusion reached by that action.

3. *Thought* denotes the action, and **him insane** tells what we thought,—the conclusion reached by thinking.

4. **Him insane** is an abridged clause, and means the same as *that he was insane.*

5. **Him** is the subject of the abridged clause, and

6. **Insane** denotes a condition of the person alluded to by *him.*

7. *Thought,* like a copula, shows that the condition denoted by *insane* is predicated.

MODELS FOR PARSING.

Thought is a verb, irregular, copulative, active voice, indicative mode, past tense. Verbs in this tense do not change their form for the person and number of their subject.

Him is a pronoun, personal, 3d, sing., mas.; it is subject of an abridged clause which is the object of the verb *thought,* and for this reason it is put in the objective case.

Insane is an adjective, qualifying, used with *him* to complete an abridged clause.

REMARKS.—In sentence **3,** *made us cautious* is the predicate; it predicates an action and its effect. *Made* denotes the action, and *us cautious*, the effect.

Us cautious is an abridged clause, and means the same as *that we should become cautious;* but the complete form is never used after the verb *make*. *Us* is the subject of the abridged clause, and *cautious* denotes a quality which the action of the verb causes us to acquire.

In sentence **7,** *call him stingy* is the predicate; it predicates an action, and a belief or accusation made known through that action. *Call* denotes the action, and *him stingy*, the belief or accusation.

Him stingy is an abridged clause, and means the same as *that he is stingy;* but the complete clause is never used after the verb *call*. *Him* is the subject of the abridged clause, and *stingy* denotes a quality of which the person is accused through the action of the *verb*. If we should substitute *say* for *call*, then the complete form of the substantive clause would be used; as, "Some say *that he is stingy*."

3. Seat Work.

Study the next lesson, and write the analysis of sentence 4.

LESSON 276.

Subject of the Last Lesson Continued.

1. Examples.

1. The fruit made the boy sick.
2. They made him joyful.
3. Yeast renders bread porous.
4. She hears the sea-birds screech,
   And the breakers on the beach
      Making moan, making moan:
   And the wind about the eaves
   Of the cottage sobs and grieves;

> And the willow-tree is blown
> To and fro, to and fro,
> Till it seems like some old crone
> Standing out there all alone
> With her woe,
> Wringing, as she stands,
> Her gaunt and palsied hands,
> While Mabel, timid Mabel,
> With face against the pane,
> Looks out across the night,
> And sees the Beacon Light
> A-trembling in the rain.
> —*T. B. Aldrich.*

5. Shorter and shorter the twilight clips the days.

2. Seat Work.

Study the next lesson, and write the parsing of the verbs, participles, and predicate adjectives, in examples 6, 7 and 8.

LESSON 277.

Abridged Clause, with To Be, As, As Being.

1. Instruction.

To be, as, or *as being,* may be used between the subject and adjective of the abridged clause, but this does not affect the construction. These words are mere connectives, used to make the relation between the adjective and the subject of the abridged clause more prominent.

2. Examples.

1. They regard themselves as wiser than other men.

2. We supposed them to be truthful.

3. We regarded him as being too indolent to hold his position long.

4. For winter maketh the light heart sad,
   And thou, thou makest the sad heart gay.
   —*Longfellow, p.* 19.

5. He sailed as midshipman.

6. He turned pale on hearing that his execution was to take place the next day.

7. The prisoner looked happy when he was told that his mother had come to see him.

8. The black-walnut logs in the chimney
Made ruddy the house with their light.

9. I think him dishonest.

REMARKS.—Some difference of opinion prevails in regard to the parsing of *as* when used as it is in sentence **5,** above. Since *as midshipman* tells in what capacity he sailed, some regard it as an adverbial phrase, and parse *as* as a preposition. But this sentence is very much like, *She moved a goddess,* or, *He died a hero;* so some parse *midshipman* as they do *goddess* and *hero* in the sentences just quoted, and *as* as a mere sign of apposition.

3. Seat Work.

Study the next lesson, and write the analysis of sentence 2.

LESSON 278.

Promiscuous Exercise in Copulative Verbs.

1. Examples.

1. But brighter than the afternoon
That followed the dark day of rain,
And brighter than the golden vane
That glistened in the rising moon,
Within, the ruddy firelight gleamed;
And every separate window-pane,
Backed by the outer darkness, showed
A mirror, where the flamelets gleamed
And flickered to and fro, and seemed
A bonfire lighted in the road.
—*Longfellow, p. 292.*

2. Yester morning I saw the lesser lake completely hidden by mist; but the moment the sun peeped over the hill, the mist broke in the middle, and in a few seconds stood divided, leaving a broad road all across the lake.—*Coleridge.*

3. We regard him as competent.

4. I believe him to be honest.

3. Seat Work.

Study the next lesson; write the analysis of the first and fifth examples, and the parsing of the words in the second and third.

LESSON 279.

Copulative Verbs in the Passive Voice.

1. Examples.

1. We were made more cautious by that experiment.

2. The boy is considered honest.

3. He is known to be guilty.

4. The government of Edward the Fourth, though it was called cruel and arbitrary, was humane and liberal, when compared with that of Louis the Eleventh, or that of Charles the Bold.—*Macaulay's Essays, Vol. 1, p. 62.*

5. The small hand that trembled
    When last in my own,
   Lies patient and folded,
    And colder than stone.
                    —*Elizabeth Whittier.*

6. On the morrow we will meet,
    With melancholy looks to tell our griefs,
    And make each other wretched.
                    —*Bryant, p. 112.*

7. Ha! how the murmur deepens!

MODEL FOR ANALYSIS.

Ex.—*It was thought advisable to give up the expedition.*

1. *It* is the subject.

2. **Was thought advisable** is the predicate; it

24

predicates an action received by the subject, and also a quality of the subject.

3. **Was thought** denotes the action, and **advisable** denotes a quality which the action of the verb attributes to the subject.

4. *To give up* names the action which is represented by *it*.

5. Etc.

MODELS FOR PARSING.

Was thought is a verb, irregular, copulative, passive voice, indicative mode, past tense, 3d sing., to agree with the subject *it*.

Advisable is an adjective, qualifying; used with the copulative verb *was thought* to form the predicate.

To give up is a verb, irregular, transitive, active voice, infinitive mode, present tense; it is here used to name an action, and thus becomes a verbal noun; it explains what is meant by *it*, and is therefore put in the same case.

2. Seat Work.

Study the next lesson, and write the analysis of sentences 4 and 5.

LESSON 280.

Double Object Consisting of Two Nouns.

1. Examples.

1. I think him a villain.

2. They elected him president.

3. 'Twould make the earth a cheerless place
   To see no more of these.

4. In the time of Homer, the Greeks had not begun to consider themselves as a distinct race. —*Macaulay's Essays, Vol. 1, p.* 172.

5.   Scarlet tufts
   Are glowing in the green, like flakes of fire;
   The wanderers of the prairie know them well,
   And call that brilliant flower the Painted Cup.
   —*Bryant, p.* 196.

6. On the evening of the next day, at sunset, the shattered ice, thus frozen, appeared of a deep blue, and in shape like an agitated sea.—*Coleridge.*

7. The Latin writers looked on Greece as the only fount of knowledge.

8. They called him John.

MODELS FOR ANALYSIS.

Ex.—Some thought him an impostor.

1. *People* or some other noun understood is the subject.

2. **Thought him an impostor** is the predicate; it predicates an action, and the conclusion reached by that action.

3. **Thought** denotes the action, and **him an impostor,** the conclusion.

4. **Him an impostor** is an abridged clause, meaning the same as *that he was an impostor.*

5. *Him* is the subject.

6. **Impostor** names one of a class to which the person belongs that is represented by *him.*

7. *Thought,* like a copula, shows that the fact of his belonging to that class is predicated.

Ex.—Affliction made him a better man.

1. *Affliction* is the subject.

2. **Made him a better man** is the predicate; it predicates action, and the effect of it.

3. *Made* denotes the action, and *him a better man,* the effect.

4. *Him a better man* is an abridged clause meaning the same as *that he should become a better man,* but the complete form is never used after the verb *make.*

5. *Him* is the subject.

6. *Man* names one of a class to which the person belongs that is represented by *him.*

7. *Made,* like a copula, shows that the fact of his belonging to that class is predicated.

MODEL FOR PARSING.

Man is a noun, com., 3d, sing., mas.; it is used to complete an abridged clause, and since it names one of a class to which the subject of the clause belongs, it is put in the same case.

REMARKS.—In sentence **2,** *elected him president* is the predicate; it predicates an action, and the effect produced upon the object that receives the action. *Elected* denotes the action. *Him* alludes to the person that receives the action. *President* names one of a class of which the person becomes a member through the act of being elected; or we may say that it names the office which he acquires through the action of the verb.

Him president is an abridged clause, but the complete form is not used after this verb.

In sentence **6,** *of a deep blue,* and *like an agitated sea,* are adjective phrases used with the copulative verb *appeared* to form the predicate.

In sentence **8,** *John* is the name which the person receives through the action of the verb.

2. Seat Work.

Study the next lesson; write the analysis of sentence **6,** and the parsing of the words used in predicate.

————►•-•——

LESSON 281.

Subject of the Last Lesson Continued.

1. Examples.

1. We knew the thief to be an Indian by his tracks.

2. A brook came stealing from the ground.

3. Some thought him an excellent speaker, but others regarded his style as too showy for sound reasoning.

4. Thou'lt find Him in the evil days
    An all-sufficient strength and guide.

5. Chains are round our country pressed,
   And cowards have betrayed her,
   And we must make her bleeding breast
   The grave of the invader.
   —*Bryant*, *p.* 108.

6. She stood one moment statue-still,
   And, musing, spake in undertone,
   "The living love may colder grow;
   The dead is safe with God alone."
   —*Elizabeth Whittier.*

7. Grief wastes my life, and makes it misery.

8. Our country calls, away! away!

REMARKS.—In sentence **4,** *strength* names a quality, but is used figuratively to denote a source of strength. This it may be made to do on account of the close relation existing between the quality and the source of it. *All-sufficient* assumes a quality of the source of strength here meant.

In sentence **7,** *misery* names a condition. His life is said to be misery, because so much misery attends it.

2. Seat Work.

Study the next lesson, and write the analysis of sentences 1, 2, and 3.

LESSON 282.

Copulative Verbs in the Passive Voice Followed by a Noun.

1. Examples.

1. The Swiss and Spaniards were, at that time, regarded as the best soldiers in Europe.

2. He was everywhere known as the king's favorite.

3. Sunderland, in spite of the very just antipathy of Anne, was made Secretary of State.—*Macaulay's Essays, Vol. 1, p.* 204.

4. She haunts the Atlantic north and south,
   But mostly the mid-sea,
   Where three great rocks rise bleak and bare
   Like furnace-chimneys in the air,
   And are called the Chimneys Three.
   —*Longfellow. p.* 280.

5. Full knee-deep lies the winter snow,
   And the winter winds are wearily sighing;
   Toll ye the church-bells sad and slow,
   And tread softly, and speak low,
   For the old year lies a-dying.
   —*Tennyson.*

MODELS FOR ANALYSIS.

Ex.—He was called a hero.

1. *He* is the subject.

2. *Was called a hero* is the predicate; it predicates an action received by the subject, and that by this action the subject is put in a class called heroes.

3. *Was called* denotes the action, and predicates it.

4. *Hero* names one of the class to which he is said to belong.

5. *Was called*, like a copula, shows that the fact of his being put in that class' is predicated.

Ex.—Jackson was elected president.

1. *Jackson* is the subject.

2. *Was elected president* is the predicate; it predicates action received by the subject, and that by this action the subject becomes one of the class called presidents.

3. *Was elected* denotes the action, and predicates it.

4. *President* names one of the class of which he became a member, and

5. *Was elected*, like a copula, shows that the fact of his becoming a member of that class is predicated.

MODEL FOR PARSING.

Ex.—He was called a hero.

Hero is a noun, com., 3d, sing., mas.; used with the copulative verb *was called* to form the predicate. It names one of a class to which the subject belongs, and is therefore put in the same case as the subject.

2. Seat Work.

Study the next lesson, and write the analysis of sentence 8.

———•———

LESSON 283.

Double Object Consisting of an Infinitive and its Subject.

1. Examples.

1. Who caused your stern heart to relent?
2. The doves besought the hawk to defend them.
3. Permit your mind to reflect gravely.
4. Fingal bade his sails to rise.
5. 'Tis working with the heart and soul
   That makes our duty pleasure.
   —Phebe Cary.
6. It's odd how hats expand their brims as youth begins to fade,
   As if when life had reached its noon, it wanted them for shade. *—Oliver Wendell Holmes.*
7. He demanded permission to leave the army.
8. I heard the trailing garments of the Night
   Sweep through her marble halls!
   I saw her sable skirts all fringed with light
   From the celestial walls!
   —Longfellow, p. 2.

MODEL FOR ANALYSIS.

Ex.—The colonel ordered the regiment to advance.

1. *Colonel* is the subject.

2. **Ordered the regiment to advance** is the predicate; it predicates action, and the contemplated effect of that action.

3. **Ordered** denotes the action, and

4. **The regiment to advance,** the anticipated result of that action.

5. *Regiment* is the subject of the abridged clause.

6. *To advance* is the infinitive of the predicate; it names the action which the regiment is ordered to perform.

MODEL FOR PARSING.

To advance is a verb, regular, intr., infinitive mode, present tense; it is here used to name an action and thus becomes a verbal noun; it completes an abridged clause which is object of the verb *ordered*, and is therefore put in the objective case.

2. Seat Work.

Select five examples of the copulative verb in the passive voice followed by a noun.

LESSON 284.

Review Exercise.

1. Examples.

1. It was a hundred years ago,
    When, by the woodland ways,
    The traveler saw the wild deer drink,
    Or crop the birchen sprays.

2. The conditions which had been imposed on him made him a mere vassal of France.

3. The griefs of life to thee have been like snows
    That light upon the fields in early spring,
    Making them greener.
    —*Bryant. p.* 232.

4. Ghost-like and pale he wandered,
    With a dreamy, haggard eye;
    He seemed not one of the living,
    And yet he could not die.
    —*Ibid. p.* 158.

5. He bids us to watch and be ready,
   Nor suffer our lights to grow dim;
   That when He may. come, he will find us
   All waiting and watching for him.

6. Time makes us eagle-eyed.
             —*Alice Cary.*

2. Seat Work.

Study the next lesson, and write the analysis of sentences 4 and 9, and the parsing of the words in sentences 7 and 8.

LESSON 285.

Copulative Verbs in the Passive Voice Followed by an Infinitive.

1. Examples.

1. We were told to sit still.
2. You are requested to sing.
3. The soldiers were commanded to fire.
4. The men of Israel were led to worship false gods.
5. They told him to come.
6. The Greeks were taught to use letters by Cadmus.
7. They were ordered to leave.
8. He bade me rejoice.
9. To number his virtues is to give the epitome of his life.
10. George was called to recite.

MODEL FOR ANALYSIS.

Ex.—The regiment was ordered to advance.

1. *Regiment* is the subject.

2. **Was ordered to advance** is the predicate; it predicates two actions of the subject. The first is received by the subject, and the second performed by it. The action performed is anticipated as the result of the action received.

MODEL FOR PARSING.

To advance is a verb, regular, intransitive, infinitive mode, present tense; here used as a verbal noun to name an action of the subject. It is taken with the copulative verb to form the predicate, and is therefore put in the nominative case.

2. Seat Work.

Write the analysis of sentence 1 of the next lesson, and the parsing of sentence 2.

LESSON 286.

Miscellaneous Review.

1. Examples.

1. Above low scarp and turf-grown wall
   They saw the fort-flag rise and fall;
   And, the first star to signal twilight's hour,
   The lamp-fire glimmer down from the tall light-house tower.
   —Tent on the Beach.

2. He was seen to fall.

3. In the genial breeze, the breath of God,
   The unseen springs come spouting up to light.

4. Just above yon sandy bar,
   As the day grows fainter and dimmer,
   Lonely and lovely, a single star
   Lights the air with a dusky glimmer.

5. During more than forty years, he was known to his country neighbors as a gentleman of cultivated mind, of high principles, and of polished address.—*Macaulay's Essays, Vol. 1, p. 58.*

6. Gliding by crag and copsewood green,
   A solitary form was seen
   To trace with stealthy pace the wold,
   Like fox that seeks the midnight fold,
   And pauses oft, and cowers dismayed,
   At every breath that stirs the shade.—*Scott, in Rokeby.*

2. Seat Work.

Select examples of all kinds of Copulative Verbs.

LESSON 287.

Miscellaneous Review.—Continued.

1. Examples.

1. And now there came both mist and snow,
    And it grew wondrous cold;
    And ice, mast-high, came floating by,
    As green as emerald.
        —*Samuel Taylor Coleridge.*

2. The silver fair-browed moon rose in the purple sky, and looked down, calm and silent, as God looks on the scene of misery and oppression,—looked calmly on the lone black man, as he sat with his arms folded, and his Bible on his knee.—*Harriet Beecher Stowe.*

3. The wagon rolled up a weedy gravel walk, under a noble avenue of China trees, whose graceful forms and ever-springing foliage seemed to be the only things there that neglect could not daunt or alter,—like noble spirits, so deeply rooted in goodness as to flourish and grow stronger amid discouragement and decay. —*Ibid.*

4. The English seem as silent as the Japanese, yet vainer than the inhabitants of Siam.—*Goldsmith.*

2. Seat Work.

Write the analysis of sentence 2 of the next lesson, and the parsing of all the words in its predicates.

LESSON 288.

Miscellaneous Review.—Continued.

1. Examples.

1. Peace to the just man's memory; let it grow
    Greener with years, and blossom through the flight
    Of ages; let the mimic canvas show
    His calm benevolent features; let the light
    Stream on his deeds of love, that shunned the sight

Of all but Heaven, and in the book of fame
 The glorious record of his virtues write,
And hold it up to men, and bid them claim
A palm like his, and catch from him the hallowed flame.
—Bryant, p. 11.

2. And the crescent moon, high over the green,
  From a sky of crimson shone
On that icy palace, whose towers were seen
  To sparkle as if with stars of their own;
While the water fell with a hollow sound,
 'Twixt the glistening pillars ranged around.
—Ibid, p. 170.

3. I saw the waning lights in the skies
  Blown out by the breath of morning;
And the morn grow pale as a maid who dies,
  When her loving wins but scorning.
—Phebe Cary.

Miscellaneous Examples.

1. The house had been large and handsome. It was built in a manner common at the South; a wide veranda of two stories running around every part of the house, into which every outer door opened, the lower tier being supported by brick pillars.

But the place looked desolate and uncomfortable; some windows stopped up with boards, some with shattered panes, and shutters hanging by a single hinge,—all telling of coarse neglect and discomfort.—*Mrs. Stowe.*

2.   He lay
Reposing from the noontide sultriness,
Couched among fallen columns, in the shade
Of ruined walls that had survived the names
Of those who reared them; by his sleeping side
Stood camels grazing, and some goodly steeds
Were fastened near a fountain; and a man,
Clad in a flowing garb, did watch the while,
While many of his tribe slumbered around.

And they were canopied by the blue sky,
So cloudless, clear, and purely beautiful,
That God alone was to be seen in heaven.
                                        —Byron.

3. If I could but arouse in other minds that ardent and ever-growing love of the works of God in the creation, which I feel in myself,—if I could but make it in others what it has been to me—

> The nurse,
> The guide, the guardian of my heart, and soul
> Of all my moral being,—

if I could open to any the mental eye which can never be again closed, but which finds more and more clearly revealed before it, beauty, wisdom, and peace,—in the splendors of the heavens, in the majesty of seas and mountains, in the freshness of winds, the ever-changing lights and shadows of fair landscapes, the solitude of heaths, the radiant face of bright lakes, and the solemn depths of woods,—then, indeed, would I rejoice.—*Wm. Howitt.*

4. Born and educated in camps, Montcalm had been carefully instructed, and was skilled in the language of Homer as well as in the art of war.—*Bancroft.*

5. The sisters were together,—together for the last time in the happy home of their childhood. The window before them was thrown open, and the shadows of evening were slowly passing from each familiar outline on which the gazers looked. They were both young and fair; and one, the elder, wore that pale wreath the maiden wears but once. The accustomed smile had forsaken her lip now, and the orange blossoms were scarcely whiter than the cheek they shaded. The sisters' hands were clasped in each other, and they sat silently watching the gradual brightening of the crescent moon, and the coming forth, one by one, of the stars. Not a cloud was floating in the quiet sky; the light wind hardly stirred the young leaves, and the air was fraught with the fragrance of early spring flowers.—*Jane Worthington.*

6. There are some hearts like wells, green-mossed and deep
        As ever Summer saw;
    And cool their water is,—yea, cool and sweet;—
        But you must come to draw;

They hoard not, yet they rest in calm content,
   And not unsought will give;
They can be quiet with their wealth unspent,
   So self-contained they live.

And there are some like springs, that bubbling burst
   To follow dusty ways,
And run with offered cup to quench his thirst
   Where the tired traveler stays;
That never ask the meadows if they want
   What is their joy to give;—
Unasked, their lives to other life they grant,
   So self-bestowed they live!

And ONE is like the ocean, deep and wide,
   Wherein all waters fall;
That girdles the broad earth, and draws the tide,
   Feeding and bearing all;
That broods the mists, that sends the clouds abroad,
   That takes, again to give;
Even the great and loving heart of God,
   Whereby all love doth live.
                       —Caroline Spencer.

7. What if there was a spring-time of blossoming but once in a hundred years! How would men look forward to it, and old men, who had beheld its wonders, tell the story to their children, how once all the homely trees became beautiful, and earth was covered with freshness and new growth! How would young men hope to become old, that they might see so glad a sight! And when beheld, the aged man would say, "Lord, now lettest thou thy servant depart in peace, for mine eyes have seen thy salvation."—*Theodore Parker.*

8. She filled the helm, and back she hied,
   And with surprise and joy espied
     A monk supporting Marmion's head;
   A pious man, whom duty brought
   To dubious verge of battle fought,
     To shrive the dying, bless the dead.
   Deep drank Lord Marmion of the wave.
                       —Walter Scott.

9. We sit around the fireside, and the angel feared and dreaded by us all comes in, and one is taken from our midst. Hands that have caressed us, locks that have fallen over us like a bath of beauty, are hidden beneath shroud-folds. We see the steep edges of the grave, and hear the heavy rumble of the clods; and, in the burst of passionate grief, it seems that we can never still the crying of our hearts. But the days rise and set, dimly at first; seasons come and go; and little by little the weight rises from the heart, and the shadows drift from before the eyes, till we feel again the spirit of gladness, and see again the old beauty of the world.—*Alice Cary.*

10. Dark as the forest leaves that strew the ground,
The Indian hunter here his shelter found;
Here cut his bow and shaped his arrows true,
Here built his wigwam and his bark canoe,
Speared the quick salmon leaping up the fall,
And slew the deer without the rifle-ball.
   —*John G. Brainard.*

11. On one side, the bank is almost on a level with the water, and there the quiet congregation of trees stood, with feet in the flood, and fringed with foliage down to its very surface. Vines here and there twine themselves about bushes or aspens or alder trees, and hang their clusters, though scanty and infrequent this season, so that I can reach them from my boat. I scarcely remember a scene of more complete and lovely seclusion than the passage of the river through this wood.—*Hawthorne.*

12. All day, as day is reckoned on the earth,
I've wandered in these dim and awful aisles,
Shut from the blue and breezy dome of heaven.
   .   .   .   .   And now
I'll sit me down upon yon broken rock,
To muse upon the strange and solemn things
Of this mysterious realm.
   —*Prentice.*

13.   .   .   .   .   Beautiful
Are all the thousand snow-white gems that lie
In these mysterious chambers, gleaming out
Amid the melancholy gloom; and wild
These rocky hills and cliffs and gulfs; but far
More beautiful and wild, the things that greet

The wanderer in our world of light,—the stars
Floating on high, like islands of the blest;
The autumn sunsets glowing like the gate
Of far-off Paradise; the gorgeous clouds
On which the glories of the earth and sky
Meet, and commingle; earth's unnumbered flowers.
All turning up their gentle eyes to heaven;
The birds, with bright wings glancing in the sun,
Filling the air with rainbow miniatures;
The green old forests surging in the gale;
The everlasting mountains, on whose peaks
The setting sun burns like an altar flame.
                                   —*Ibid.*

14. Up the long ascent it moved,—that shadow of our mortal sorrow and perishable earthly estate,—that shadow of the dead man's hearse,—along the way his feet have often trod, past the spring over whose brink he may have often bent with thirsting lip, past lovely green glades, mossy banks, and fairy forests of waving ferns, on which his eye had often dwelt with a vague and soft delight; and so passed out of our view. But its memory passed not out of our hearts that day.—*Sarah J. Lippincot.*

15. There needs no other proof that happiness is the most wholesome moral atmosphere, and that in which the immortality of man is destined ultimately to thrive, than the elevation of soul, the religious aspiration, which attends the first sober certainty of true love. There is much of this religious aspiration amidst all warmth of virtuous affection. There is a vivid love of God in the child that lays its cheek against the cheek of its mother, and clasps its arms about her neck. God is thanked—perhaps unconsciously—for the brightness of his earth, on summer evenings, when a brother and sister, who have long been parted, pour out their heart-stores to each other, and feel their course of thought brightening as it runs. When the aged parent hears of the honors his children have won, or looks round upon their innocent faces as the glory of his decline, his mind reverts to Him who in them prescribed the purpose of his life, and bestowed its grace.—*Harriet Martineau.*

16. "Twice have I sought Clan-Alpine's glen
      In peace; but when I come again,
      I come with banner, brand, and bow,
      As leader seeks his mortal foe.

For love-lorn swain, in lady's bower,
Ne'er panted for the appointed hour,
As I, until before me stand
This rebel Chieftain and his band!"

"Have, then, thy wish!"—he whistled shrill,
And he was answer'd from the hill;
Wild as the scream of the curlew,
From crag to crag the signal flew.
Instant, through copse and heath, arose
Bonnets and spears and bended bows;
On right, on left, above, below,
Sprung up at once the lurking foe;
From shingles gray their lances start,
The bracken bush sends forth the dart,
The rushes and the willow-wand
Are bristling into axe and brand,
And every tuft of broom gives life
To plaided warrior armed for strife.
That whistle garrison'd the glen
At once with full five hundred men,
As if the yawning hill to heaven
A subterranean host had given.

Watching their leader's beck and will,
All silent there they stood, and still.
Like the loose crags, whose threatening mass
Lay tottering o'er the hollow pass,
As if an infant's touch could urge
Their headlong passage down the verge,
With step and weapon forward flung,
Upon the mountain-side they hung.
The Mountaineer cast glance of pride
Along Benledi's living side,
Then fix'd his eye and sable brow
Full on Fitz-James—"How say'st thou now?
These are Clan-Alpine's warriors true;
And, Saxon,—I am Roderick Dhu!"
—*Scott.*

17. The village was buried in deep sleep, but the woods were filled with large parrots, which, being awakened, made a prodigious clamor. The Indians, however, thinking the Spaniards all destroyed, paid no attention to these noises. It was not until their houses were assailed, and wrapped in flames, that they took

alarm. They rushed forth, some with arms, some weaponless, but were received at their doors by the exasperated Spaniards, and either slain on the spot, or driven back into the fire. Women fled wildly forth with children in their arms, but at sight of the Spaniards glittering in steel, and of the horses, which they supposed ravenous monsters, ran back, shrieking with horror, into their burning habitations. Great was the carnage, for no quarter was shown to age or sex. Many perished by the fire, and many by the sword.—*Washington Irving.*

18. Amid all this, the center of the scene,
　　The white-haired matron, with monotonous tread,
　　Plied the swift wheel, and with her joyless mien
　　Sat like a fate, and watched the flying thread.

　　She had known Sorrow. He had walked with her,
　　Oft supped, and broke with her the ashen crust,
　　And in the dead leaves still she heard the stir
　　Of his thick mantle trailing in the dust.
　　　　　　　　　　　　　—Thomas Buchanan Read.

19. Thought is deeper than all speech;
　　Feeling, deeper than all thought;
　　Souls to souls can never teach
　　What unto themselves was taught.
　　　　　　　　　　　　　—Christopher Cranch.

20. It was a wild, forsaken road, now winding through dreary pine barrens, where the wind whispered mournfully, and now over log causeways, through long cypress swamps, the doleful trees rising out of the slimy, spongy ground, hung with long wreaths of funereal black moss; while ever and anon the loathsome form of the moccasin snake might be seen sliding among broken stumps and shattered branches that lay here and there, rotting in the water.—*Mrs. Stowe.*

21. Yesterday thy head was brown as are the flowing locks
　　　of love;
　　In the bright blue sky I watched thee towering, giant-
　　　like, above.
　　Now thy summit, white and hoary, glitters all with sil-
　　　ver snow,
　　Which the stormy night hath shaken from its robes upon
　　　thy brow;

And I know that youth and age are bound with such
mysterious meaning,
As the days are link'd together, one short dream but
intervening. —*Goethe.*

22. Shall I ask the brave soldier who fights by´my side
In the cause of mankind, if our creeds agree?
Shall I give up the friend I have valued and tried,
If he kneel not before the same altar with me?
—*Moore.*

23. O my ears are dinned and wearied with the clatter of
the school:
Life to them is geometric, and they act by line and
rule;—
If there be no other wisdom, better far to be a fool!
Better far the honest nature, in its narrow path content,
Taking with a child's acceptance, whatsoever may be sent,
Than the introverted vision, seeing Self pre-eminent.
—*Bayard Taylor*, p. 254.

24. You shall receive, my dear wife, my last words in these
my last lines; my love I send you, that you may keep it when
I am dead, and my counsel, that you may remember it when I
am no more. I would not with my will present you sorrows,
dear Bess; let them go to the grave with me, and be buried in
the dust. And seeing that it is not the will of God that I shall
see you any more, bear my destruction patiently, and with an
heart like yourself. . . . . To what friend to direct you I know not, for all mine have left me in the true time
of trial. Most sorry am I, that, being thus surprised by death,
I can leave you no better estate; God hath prevented all my
determinations,—that great God which worketh all in all; and if
you can live free from want, care for no more, for the rest is
but a vanity; love God, and begin betimes—in him you shall
find true, everlasting, and endless comfort; when you have
travailed and wearied yourself with all sorts of worldly cogitations,
you shall sit down by sorrow in the end. Teach your son also
to serve and fear God whilst he is young, that the fear of God
may grow up in him; then will God be an husband to you, and
a father to him,—an husband and a father that can never be
taken from you.—*Sir Walter Raleigh.*

25.   With quickened step
Brown night retires : young day pours in apace,
And opens all the lawny prospect wide.
The dripping rock, the mountain's misty top,
Swell on the sight, and brighten with the dawn.
Blue, through the dusk, the smoking currents shine ;
And from the bladed field the fearful hare
Limps awkward ; while along the forest glade
The wild deer trip, and often turning, gaze
At early passenger. Music awakes,
The native voice of undissembled joy,
And thick around, the woodland hymns arise.
Roused by the cock, the soon-clad shepherd leaves
His mossy cottage, where with peace he dwells;
And from the crowded fold, in order, drives
His flock, to taste the verdure of the morn.
                                        —*Thomson.*

26. It is imagined by many that whenever they aspire to
please, they are required to be merry, and to show the gladness
of their souls by flights of pleasantry and bursts of laughter.
But though these men may be for a time heard with applause
and admiration, they seldom delight us long. We enjoy them a
little, and then retire to easiness and good-humor, as the eye
gazes a while on eminences glittering with the sun, but soon turns
aching away to verdure and to flowers. Gayety is to good-humor
as animal perfumes to vegetable fragrance. The one overpowers
weak spirits, and the other recreates and revives them.—*Dr.
Samuel Johnson.*

27. Some feelings are to mortals given,
With less of earth in them than heaven;
And if there be a human tear
From passion's dross refined and clear,
A tear so limpid and so meek,
It would not stain an angel's cheek,
'Tis that which pious fathers shed
Upon a duteous daughter's head!
                        —*Scott. in Lady of the Lake.*

28. Knowledge and Wisdom, far from being one,
Have oftimes no connection. Knowledge dwells
In heads replete with thoughts of other men;
Wisdom in minds attentive to their own.

Knowledge, a rude unprofitable mass,
The mere materials with which Wisdom builds,
Till smoothed, and squared, and fitted to its place,
Does but encumber whom it seems t'enrich.
Knowledge is proud that he has learned so much;
Wisdom is humble that he knows no more.
—*Cowper.*

29. Poetry is commonly understood to have two objects in view; namely, advantage and pleasure, or rather a union of both. I wish those who have furnished us with this definition had rather proposed utility as its ultimate object, and pleasure as the means by which that end may be effectually accomplished. The philosopher and the poet, indeed, seem principally to differ in the means by which they pursue the same end. Each sustains the character of a preceptor, which the one is thought best to support if he teach with accuracy, with subtlety, and with perspicuity; the other with splendor, harmony, and elegance. The one makes his appeal to reason only, independent of the passions; the other addresses the reason in such a manner as even to engage the passions on his side. The one proceeds to virtue and truth by the nearest and most compendious ways; the other leads to the same point through certain deflections and deviations, by a winding but pleasanter path. It is the part of the former so to describe and explain these objects, that we must necessarily become acquainted with them; it is the part of the latter so to dress and adorn them, that of our own accord we must love and embrace them. . . . . Poetry addresses her precepts not to the reason alone; she calls the passions to her aid : she not only exhibits examples, but infixes them in the mind. She softens the wax with her peculiar ardor, and renders it more plastic to the artist's hand. Thus does Horace most truly and most justly apply this commendation to the poets :—

> What's fair, and false, and right, these bards describe,
> Better and plainer than the Stoic tribe.
> —*Lowth.*

30. In youth from rock to rock I went,
From hill to hill in discontent
Of pleasure high and turbulent,
Most pleased when most uneasy;

But now my own delights I make,—
My thirst at every rill can slake,
And gladly Nature's love partake
  Of thee, sweet Daisy!
            —Wordsworth, p. 137.

31. Yet, ah! why should they know their fate
Since sorrow never comes too late,
  And happiness too swiftly flies?
Thought would destroy their paradiso.
No more;—where ignorance is bliss,
  'Tis folly to be wise.
          —Gray.

32. A transition from an author's book to his conversation, is too often like an entrance into a large city, after a distant prospect. Remotely we see nothing but spires of temples and turrets of palaces, and imagine it the residence of splendor, grandeur, and magnificence; but when we have passed the gates, we find it perplexed with narrow passages, disgraced with despicable cottages, embarrassed with obstructions, and clouded with smoke.—*Dr. Samuel Johnson.*

33.   Drowsed by the soft,
Delicious greenness and repose, I crept
Into a balmy nest of yielding shrubs,
And floated off to slumber on a cloud
Of rapturous sensation.

                  When I woke,
So deep had been the oblivion of that sleep,
That Adam, when he woke in Paradise,
Was not more blank of knowledge; he had felt
As heedlessly, the silence and the shade;
As ignorantly had raised his eyes and seen—
As, for a moment, I—what then I saw
With terror, freezing limb and voice like death,
When the slow sense, supplying one lost link,
Ran with electric fleetness through the chain
And showed me what I was,—no miracle,
But lost and left alone amid the waste,
Fronting a deadly pard, that kept great eyes
Fixed steadily on mine. I could not move:

My heart beat slow and hard; I sat and gazed,
Without a wink, upon those jasper orbs,
Noting the while, with horrible detail,
Whereto my fascinated sight was bound,
Their tawny brilliance, and the spotted fell
That wrinkled round them, smoothly sloping back
And curving to the short and tufted ears.
I felt—and with a sort of fearful joy—
The beauty of the creature: 'twas a pard,
Not such as one of those they show you caged
In Paris,—lean and scurvy beasts enough!
No; but a desert pard, superb and proud,
That would have died behind the cruel bars.

I think the creature had not looked on man;
For, as my brain grew cooler, I could see
Small sign of fierceness in her eyes, but chief,
Surprise and wonder.   More and more entranced,
Her savage beauty warmed away the chill
Of death-like terror at my heart; I stared
With kindling admiration, and there came
A gradual softness o'er the flinty light
Within her eyes; a shadow crept around
Their yellow disks, and something like a dawn
Of recognition of superior will,
Of brute affection, sympathy enslaved
By higher nature, then informed her face.
Thrilling in every nerve, I stretched my hand,—
She silent, moveless,—touched her velvet head,
And with a warm, sweet shiver in my blood,
Stroked down the ruffled hairs.   She did not start;
But in a moment's lapse, drew up one paw
And moved a step,—another,—till her breath
Came hot upon my face.   She stopped: she rolled
A deep-voiced note of pleasure and of love,
And gathering up her spotted length, lay down
Her head upon my lap, and forward thrust
One heavy-moulded paw across my knees,
The glittering talons sheathing tenderly.
Thus we, in that oasis all alone,
Sat when the sun went down: the pard and I,

Caressing and caressed : and more of love
And more of confidence between us came,
I grateful for my safety, she alive
With the dumb pleasure of companionship,
Which touched with instincts of humanity
Her brutish nature. When I slept, at last,
My arm was on her neck.
         —*Bayard Taylor*, p. 236.

34. It was not without some awe and apprehension that I
approached the presence of my father. My infancy, to speak the
truth, had been neglected at home; the severity of his look and
language at our last parting still dwelt on my memory; nor could
I form any notion of his character or my probable reception.
They were both more agreeable than I could expect. The domestic discipline of our ancestors has been relaxed by the phi-
losophy and softness of the age; and if my father remembered
that he had trembled before a stern parent, it was only to adopt
with his own son an opposite mode of behavior. He received me
as a man and a friend; all constraint was banished at our first
interview, and we ever afterwards continued on the same terms
of easy and equal politeness. He applauded the success of my
education; every word and action were expressive of the most
cordial affection; and our lives would have passed without a
cloud, if his economy had been equal to his fortune, or if his
fortune had been equal to his desires.—*Gibbon.*

35. Hark! 'tis the twanging horn! o'er yonder bridge,
That with its wearisome but needful length
Bestrides the wintry flood; in which the moon
Sees her unwrinkled face reflected bright:—
He comes, the herald of a noisy world,
With spatter'd boots, strapp'd waist, and frozen locks.
News from all nations lumbering at his back.
True to his charge, the close-pack'd load behind,
Yet careless what he brings, his one concern
Is to conduct it to the destined inn;
And having dropp'd the expected bag, pass on.
         —*Cowper.*

36. Difficulty is a severe instructor, set over us by the su-
preme ordinance of a parental Guardian and Legislator, who
knows us better than we know ourselves, as he loves us better

too. He that wrestles with us, strengthens our nerves, and sharpens our skill. Our antagonist is our helper. This amicable conflict with difficulty obliges us to an intimate acquaintance with our object, and compels us to consider it in all its relations. It will not suffer us to be superficial.—*Burke.*

37. Then kneeling down to heaven's Eternal King,
    The saint, the father, and the husband prays:
Hope "springs exulting on triumphant wing,"
    That thus they all shall meet in future days;
There ever bask in uncreated rays,
    No more to sigh, or shed the bitter tear,
Together hymning their Creator's praise,
    In such society, yet still more dear,
While circling time moves round in an eternal sphere.
                      —*Robert Burns.*

38. I see before me the gladiator lie:
He leans upon his hand; his manly brow
Consents to death, but conquers agony,
And his drooped head sinks gradually low:
And through his side the last drops, ebbing slow
From the red gash, fall heavy, one by one,
Like the first of a thunder-shower; and now
The arena swims around him; he is gone,
Ere ceased the inhuman shout which hailed the wretch
    who won.

He heard it, but he heeded not; his eyes
Were with his heart, and that was far away:
He recked not of the life he lost, nor prize,
But where his rude hut by the Danube lay;
There were his young barbarians all at play,
There was their Dacian mother—he, their sire,
Butchered to make a Roman holiday.
All this rushed with his blood. Shall he expire,
And unavenged? Arise, ye Goths, and glut your ire!
                      —*Lord Byron.*

39. Those who are in the power of evil habits must conquer them as they can;—and conquered they must be, or neither wisdom nor happiness can be attained;—but those who are not yet subject to their influence, may, by timely caution, preserve their freedom; they may effectually resolve to escape the tyrant, whom they will very vainly resolve to conquer.—*Dr. Samuel Johnson.*

40. Morn on the mountain, like a summer bird,
Lifts up her purple wing, and in the vales
The gentle wind, a sweet and passionate wooer,
Kisses the blushing leaf, and stirs up life
Within the solemn woods of ash deep-crimsoned,
And silver beech, and maple yellow-leaved,
Where Autumn, like a faint old man, sits down
By the wayside a-weary. Through the trees
The golden robin moves. The purple finch,
That on wild cherry and red cedar feeds,
A winter bird, comes with its plaintive whistle,
And pecks by the witch-hazel, whilst aloud
From cottage roofs the warbling blue-bird sings,
And merrily, with oft-repeated stroke,
Sounds from the threshing-floor the busy flail.

O what a glory doth this world put on
For him who, with a fervent heart, goes forth
Under the bright and glorious sky, and looks
On duties well performed, and days well spent!
For him the wind, ay, and the yellow leaves,
Shall have a voice, and give him eloquent teachings.
He shall so hear the solemn hymn that Death
Has lifted up for all, that he shall go
To his long resting-place without a tear.
—Longfellow, p. 7.

41.   Some drill and bore
The solid earth, and from the strata there
Extract a register by which we learn
That he who made it and reveal'd its date
To Moses was mistaken in its age.
Some, more acute and more industrious still,
Contrive creation; travel nature up
To the sharp peak of her sublimest height,
And tell us whence the stars; why some are fixt,
And planetary some; what gave them first
Rotation, from what fountain flow'd their light.
Great contest follows, and much learned dust
Involves the combatants; each claiming truth,
And truth disclaiming both. And thus they spend
The little wick of life's poor shallow lamp
In playing tricks with nature, giving laws
To distant worlds, and trifling in their own.
—Cowper.

42. Ask yourselves what is the leading motive which actuates you while you are at work. I do not ask what your leading motive is for working—that is a different thing; you may have families to support—parents to help—brides to win; you may have all these, or other such sacred and pre-eminent motives, to press the morning's labor and prompt the twilight thought. But when you are fairly *at* the work, what is the motive which tells upon every touch of it? If it is the love of that which your work represents,—if, being a landscape painter, it is love of hills and trees that moves you,—if, being a figure painter, it is love of human beauty and human soul that moves you,—if, being a flower or animal painter, it is love, and wonder, and delight in petal and in limb that moves you, then the spirit is upon you, and the earth is yours, and the fullness thereof. But if, on the other hand, it is petty self-complacency in your own skill, trust in precepts and laws, hope for academical or popular approbation, or avarice of wealth—it is quite possible that by steady industry, or even by fortunate chance, you may win the applause, the position, the fortune, that you desire; but one touch of true art you will never lay on canvas or on stone as long as you live.— *John Ruskin.*

43. I've watched you now a full half-hour,
  Self-poised upon that yellow flower;
  And, little Butterfly! indeed
  I know not if you sleep or feed,—
  How motionless! not frozen seas
   More motionless! and then
  What joy awaits you when the breeze
  Hath found you out among the trees,
   And calls you forth again!

  This plot of orchard-ground is ours,
  My trees they are, my sister's flowers;
  Here rest your wings when they are weary;
  Here lodge as in a sanctuary!
  Come often to us, fear no wrong;
   Sit near us on the bough!
  We'll talk of sunshine and of song;
  And summer days, when we were young;
  Sweet childish days, that were as long
   As twenty days are now.
     —*Wordsworth, p. 94.*

44. There is a pleasure in the pathless woods,
There is a rapture on the lonely shore,
There is society, where none intrudes,
By the deep sea, and music in its roar;
I love not man the less, but nature more,
From these our interviews, in which I steal
From all I may be, or have been before,
To mingle with the universe, and feel
What I can ne'er express, yet cannot all conceal.
—*Lord Byron.*

45. O, a dainty plant is the ivy green,
   That creepeth o'er ruins old!
Of right choice food are his meals, I ween,
   In his cell so lone and cold.
The walls must be crumbled, the stones decayed,
   To pleasure his dainty whim;
And the mouldering dust that years have made
   Is a merry meal for him.
      Creeping where no life is seen,
      A rare old plant is the ivy green.

Fast he stealeth on, though he wears no wings
   And a staunch old heart has he!
How closely he twineth, how tight he clings
   To his friend, the huge oak-tree!
And slyly he traileth along the ground,
   And his leaves he gently waves,
And he joyously twines and hugs around
   The rich mould of dead men's graves.
      Creeping where no life is seen,
      A rare old plant is the ivy green.

Whole ages have fled, and their works decayed,
   And nations scattered been;
But the stout old ivy shall never fade
   From its hale and hearty green.
The brave old plant in its lonely days
   Shall fatten upon the past;
For the stateliest building man can raise
   Is the ivy's food at last.
      Creeping where no life is seen,
      A rare old plant is the ivy green.
      — *Charles Dickens.*

46. The melancholy days are come, the saddest of the year,
   Of wailing winds, and naked woods, and meadows brown
      and sear.
   Heaped in the hollows of the grove, the autumn leaves
      lie dead;
   They rustle to the eddying gust, and to the rabbit's tread.
   The robin and the wren are flown, and from the shrubs
      the jay,
   And from the wood-top calls the crow through all the
      gloomy day.

   Where are the flowers, the fair young flowers, that lately
      sprang and stood
   In brighter light and softer airs, a beauteous sisterhood?
   Alas! they all are in their graves; the gentle race of
      flowers
   Are lying in their lowly beds with the fair and good of ours.
   The rain is falling where they lie; but the cold Novem-
      ber rain
   Calls not from out the gloomy earth the lovely ones again.

   The wind-flower and the violet, they perished long ago,
   And the brier-rose and the orchis died amid the summer
      glow;
   But on the hill the golden-rod, and the aster in the wood,
   And the yellow sunflower by the brook in autumn beauty
      stood,
   Till fell the frost from the clear cold heaven, as falls the
      plague on men,
   And the brightness of their smile was gone from upland,
      glade, and glen.

   And now, when comes the calm mild day, as still such
      days will come,
   To call the squirrel and the bee from out their winter
      home;
   When the sound of dropping nuts is heard, though all
      the trees are still,
   And twinkle in the smoky light the waters of the rill,
   The south-wind searches for the flowers whose fragrance
      late he bore,
   And sighs to find them in the wood and by the stream
      no more.   —*Bryant.*

47. The Assyrian came down like the wolf on the fold,
And his cohorts were gleaming in purple and gold;
And the sheen of their spears was like stars on the sea,
When the blue wave rolls nightly on deep Galilee.

Like the leaves of the forest when summer is green,
That host with their banners at sunset were seen;
Like the leaves of the forest when autumn hath blown,
That host on the morrow lay withered and strown.

For the Angel of Death spread his wings on the blast,
And breathed in the face of the foe as he passed;
And the eyes of the sleepers waxed deadly and chill,
And their hearts but once heaved, and forever grew still!

And there lay the steed with his nostril all wide,
But through it there rolled not the breath of his pride;
And the foam of his gasping lay white on the turf,
And cold as the spray of the rock-beating surf.

And there lay the rider distorted and pale,
With the dew on his brow and the rust on his mail;
And the tents were all silent, the banners alone,
The lances unlifted, the trumpet unblown.

And the widows of Ashur are loud in their wail,
And the idols are broke in the temple of Baal;
And the might of the Gentile, unsmote by the sword,
Hath melted like snow in the glance of the Lord!

—Lord Byron.

48. Let me have men about me that are fat;
Sleek-headed men, and such as sleep o'nights:
Yond' Cassius has a lean and hungry look;
He thinks too much: such men are dangerous.

—Shakspeare.

49. The Being that is in the clouds and air,
That is in the green leaves among the groves,
Maintains a deep and reverential care
For the unoffending creatures whom he loves.

— Wordsworth, p. 186.

50. It was the pleasant harvest time,
    When cellar-bins are closely stowed,
    And garrets bend beneath their load.

    And the old swallow-haunted barns—
    Brown-gabled, long, and full of seams
    Through which the moted sunlight streams,

    And winds blow freshly in, to shake
    The red plumes of the roosted cocks,
    And the loose hay-mow's scented locks—

    Are filled with summer's ripened stores,
    Its odorous grass and barley sheaves,
    From their low scaffolds to their eaves.

    On Esek Harden's oaken floor,
    With many an autumn threshing worn,
    Lay the heaped ears of unhusked corn.

    And thither came young men and maids,
    Beneath a moon that, large and low,
    Lit that sweet eve of long ago.

    They took their places; some by chance,
    And others by a merry voice
    Or sweet smile guided to their choice.

    How pleasantly the rising moon,
    Between the shadow of the mows,
    Looked on them through the great elm-boughs!—

    On sturdy boyhood sun-embrowned,
    On girlhood with its solid curves
    Of healthful strength and painless nerves!
    *   *   *   *   *   *   *

    ,But still the sweetest voice was mute
    That river-valley ever heard
    From lip of maid or throat of bird;

    For Mabel Martin sat apart,
    And let the hay-mow's shadow fall
    Upon the loveliest face of all.

    She sat apart, as one forbid,
    Who knew that none would condescend
    To own the witch-wife's child a friend.
    —*Whittier. p.* 218.

51. Their light-arm'd archers far and near
    Surveyed the tangled ground,
Their center ranks, with pike and spear
    A twilight forest frown'd,
Their barbed horsemen, in the rear,
    The stern battalia crown'd.
No cymbal clash'd, no clarion rang,
    Still were the pipe and drum;
Save heavy tread, and armor's clang,
    The sullen march was dumb.
There breathed no wind their crests to shake,
    Or wave their flags abroad;
Scarce the frail aspen seem'd to quake,
    That shadow'd o'er their road.
Their vanward scouts no tidings bring,
    Can rouse no lurking foe,
Nor spy a trace of living thing,
    Save when they stirr'd the roe.
The host moves like a deep-sea wave,
Where rise no rocks its pride to brave,
    High-swelling, dark, and slow.
The lake is pass'd, and now they gain
A narrow and a broken plain,
Before the Trosach's rugged jaws;
And here the horse and spearmen pause
While, to explore the dangerous glen,
Dive through the pass the archer-men.

At once there rose so wild a yell
Within that dark and narrow dell,
As all the fiends, from heaven that fell,
Had peal'd the banner-cry of hell!
    Forth from the pass in tumult driven,
    Like chaff before the wind of heaven,
        The archery appear;
For life! for life! their plight they ply—
And shriek, and shout, and battle-cry,
And plaids and bonnets waving high,
And broadswords flashing to the sky,
    Are maddening in the rear.
Onward they drive, in dreadful race,
    Pursuers and pursued;

Before that tide of flight and chase,
How shall it keep its rooted place,
  The spearmen's twilight wood?—
"Down, down," cried Mar, "your lances down!
  Bear back both friend and foe!"—
Like reeds before the tempest's frown,
That serried grove of lances brown
  At once lay level'd low;
And closely shouldering side to side,
The bristling ranks the onset bide.
               —Scott, p. 233.

52. This is the forest primeval. The murmuring pines and
    the hemlocks,
Bearded with moss, and in garments green, indistinct in
    the twilight,
Stand like Druids of eld, with voices sad and prophetic,
Stand like harpers hoar, with beards that rest on their
    bosoms.
Loud from its rocky caverns, the deep-voiced neighboring
    ocean
Speaks, and in accents disconsolate answers the wail of
    the forest.

This is the forest primeval; but where are the hearts
    that beneath it
Leaped like the roe, when he hears in the woodland the
    voice of the huntsman?
Where is the thatch-roofed village, the home of Acadian
    farmers,—
Men whose lives glided on like rivers that water the
    woodlands,
Darkened by shadows of earth, but reflecting an image
    of heaven?
Waste are those pleasant farms, and the farmers forever
    departed!
Scattered like dust and leaves, when the mighty blasts
    of October
Seize them, and whirl them aloft, and sprinkle them far
    o'er the ocean.
Naught but tradition remains of the beautiful village of
    Grand-Pre'.   *—Longfellow, p.* 95.

53. The stars are forth, the moon above the tops
    Of the snow-shining mountains.—Beautiful!
    I linger yet with Nature, for the night
    Hath been to me a more familiar face
    Than that of man; and in her starry shade
    Of dim and solitary loveliness
    I learned the language of another world.
    I do remember me, that in my youth,
    When I was wandering,—upon such a night
    I stood within the Coliseum's wall,
    Midst the chief relics of almighty Rome.
    The trees which grow along the broken arches
    Waved dark in the blue midnight, and the stars
    Shone through the rents of ruin; from afar
    The watch dog bayed beyond the Tiber; and
    More near, from out the Cæsars' palace came
    The owl's long cry, and, interruptedly,
    Of distant sentinels the fitful song
    Begun and died upon the gentle wind.
    Some cypresses beyond the time-worn breach
    Appeared to skirt the horizon, yet they stood
    Within a bowshot,—where the Cæsars dwelt,
    And dwell the tuneless birds of night, amidst
    A grove which springs through leveled battlements,
    And .twines its roots with the imperial hearths.
    Ivy usurps the laurel's place of growth;—
    But the gladiators' bloody Circus stands,
    A noble wreck in ruinous perfection,
    While Cæsar's chambers and the Augustan halls
    Grovel on earth in indistinct decay.—
    And thou didst shine, thou rolling moon, upon
    All this, and cast a wide and tender light,
    Which softened down the hoar austerity
    Of rugged desolation, and filled up,
    As 't were anew, the gaps of centuries,
    Leaving that beautiful which still was so,
    And making that which was not, till the place
    Became religion, and the heart ran o'er
    With silent worship of the great of old!—
    The dead, but sceptered sovereigns, who still rule
    Our spirits from their urns.
                        —*Byron.*

SYSTEMATIC CLASSIFICATION OF THE PARTS OF SPEECH.

SUBSTANTIVES.

A **substantive** is,—

1. A noun; or a letter, sign, or figure, used to represent its own name.

2. A word, phrase, or clause, used in the office of a noun.

NOUNS.

Names, of every kind, are called **nouns**.

A **common noun** names any one of a class.

A **proper noun** distinguishes some particular individual of a class.

A **collective noun** names a collection of objects.

An **abstract noun** names a quality.

A **verbal noun** is a participle or an infinitive used to name action, being, or state.

PRONOUNS.

Pronouns take the place of nouns, by alluding to persons or things previously named, to the speaker, or to one or more persons spoken to.

A **personal pronoun** shows its person by its form.

A **relative pronoun** shows the relation of its clause to the word represented by the pronoun.

An **interrogative pronoun** is used in asking a question.

A substantive is said to be in the **first person**, when it represents the speaker; in the **second person**, when it represents the person spoken to; in the **third person**, when it represents a person or thing spoken of;—

In the **singular number**, when it means but one; and in the **plural number**, when it means more than one;—

In the **masculine gender**, when it denotes a male; in the **feminine gender**, when it denotes a female; and in the **neuter gender**, when it denotes an object that has no sex.

A **pronoun must agree** with its antecedent in person, number, and gender.

A **collective noun, as antecedent**, must be represented by a pronoun in the singular number, when the entire collection is taken together as a unit; but when reference is had to the individuals that make up the collection, the pronoun must be in the plural number.

When a pronoun represents **two or more antecedents** taken conjointly, it must agree with them in the plural number; but when its antecedents are taken separately, the pronoun must agree with the one next to it.

A noun or a pronoun should be put—

In the **nominative case,**—

When it is the subject of a sentence or clause.

When used in predicate with the copula.

When in apposition with any word in the nominative case.

When independent by address; by exclamation; with a participle or an adjective; or by pleonasm.

When used after a copulative verb as an attribute of the subject.

When used after the participle of the copula in a verbal noun.

In the **possessive case,**—

To denote ownership; kindred; authorship; origin; fitness; time, weight, measure; etc.

When in apposition with any word in the possessive case.

When subject of an abridged clause, and followed by the participle of the copula.

In the **objective case,**—

When it is object of a verb or a participle.

When object of a preposition.

When in apposition with any word in the objective case.

When it is subject of an infinitive in an abridged clause that is object of a preposition.

When it is attribute of an object after a copulative verb.

When it is used after a passive copulative verb whose indirect object is made its subject. (See note, p. 407.)

VERBS.

A true **verb** denotes action, being, or state, and predicates it.

A **regular verb** forms its past tense and past participle by adding *ed* to its present indicative; while an **irregular verb** forms its past tense and past participle in some other way. **Redundant verbs** have both a regular and an irregular form. **Defective verbs** lack some of the principal parts, and so cannot be used in all the tenses.

A **transitive verb** represents an action as being received by something. The **active voice** represents the subject as acting; the **passive voice** represents its subject as being acted upon.

An **intransitive verb** does not represent its action as being received by anything. It sometimes predicates existence or state.

The **copula** predicates the existence of some quality or state denoted by an adjective or noun that follows it.

A **copulative verb** predicates not only the act, being, or state denoted by itself, but it also does the work of a copula in predicating the action, quality, or state, denoted by some other word.

MODES AND TENSES.

Mode is the manner in which the verb predicates.

The **indicative mode** represents the act, being, or state as actually existing or occuring.

The **potential mode** predicates the power, necessity, duty, etc., of its subject to act, to exist, or to be in a certain state.

The **imperative mode** commands, exhorts, or entreats.

The **infinitive mode** (so called) has no power to predicate, and consequently has no person and number.

The **subjunctive mode** is used to express what is doubtful, contingent, or merely supposed.

The indicative mode has six tenses; the potential, four; the imperative, one; and the infinitive and subjunctive, each two.

The **simple-tenses,**—past, present, future,—are used to denote the time indicated by their respective names.

The **perfect tenses,** as their names denote, represent action as completed,—the present perfect, at the time of speaking; the past perfect, at some point of time in the past; and the future perfect, at some point of time in the future.

The **person and number** of a verb is the inflection [*change of form*] required by the person and number of its subject.

When the **subject of a verb** is a collective noun in the singular number, the verb must be in the plural number if the individuals composing the collection are regarded separately; but if the whole collection is taken as a unit, the verb must be in the singular number.

Whenever a verb has **two or more subjects** taken together, it must be in the plural number; but if the subjects are taken separately, the verb must agree with the one next to it.

PARTICIPLES.

Participles assume action, being, or state, but have no power to predicate. They are sometimes classed among verbs, because they are derived from verbs, and retain much of the nature of the verb. In their use, however, they are like adjectives, being employed to limit nouns and pronouns.

When a participle is used to name an act, being, or state, it is called a **participial noun.**

A **present participle** represents its action as present at the time denoted by the predicate of its clause.

A **past participle** represents its action as past at the time denoted by the predicate of its clause.

A **perfect participle** represents its action as completed at the time denoted by the predicate of its clause.

The present participle has two forms,—the active and the passive. The past participle sometimes has an active meaning and sometimes a passive, but its form is always the same as that of the present passive.

The perfect participle has three forms,—the **common,** the **progressive,** and the **passive.** Each of these forms *assumes* just what a perfect tense of that form would *predicate.*

The **infinitive** is like the participle in being derived from a verb without having the power of predication; but differs from it in its form and in some of its uses.

MODIFIERS.

Modifiers are words used to introduce some circumstance of quality, condition, time, place, manner, purpose, or cause, or in some other way to restrict or extend the application of words.

ADJECTIVES.

A **qualifying adjective** is added to a noun or a pronoun to assume quality or condition.

A **limiting adjective** is added to a noun or a pronoun to restrict its application in some other way than by denoting quality, condition, or kind.

The so-called **pronominal adjectives** are used to limit a noun understood, and are supposed to represent that noun.

Interrogative adjectives are used in asking questions.

ADVERBS.

An **adverb** is added to a verb, a participle, an adjective, or an adverb, to tell *when, where, how, why, how long, how far,* or *how much.*

A **relative adverb,** like a relative pronoun, shows the relation of its clause to the word which the clause limits.

A **conjunctive adverb** is one that has, to some degree, the nature of a conjunction.

Interrogative adverbs are used in asking questions.

A **modal adverb** modifies the manner of assertion, and not the action of the predicate.

Both adjectives and adverbs have a **comparative** and a **superlative form** for the purpose of denoting comparison.

RELATION WORDS.

PREPOSITIONS.

A **preposition** introduces a phrase, and shows the relation between the word which the phrase limits and the substantive which forms the essential element of the phrase.

The relative pronoun and the relative adverb are both relation words, but have already been defined.

The copula, also, is a relation word, showing the relation between the subject and whatever is predicated of it.

CONJUNCTIONS.

A **coördinate conjunction** is placed between coördinate elements to show that they are equal in rank, and if they are dependent, that they are alike related to the word which they limit.

A **subordinate conjunction** introduces a clause, shows it to be subordinate in rank, and generally indicates its use.

EMOTIONAL WORDS.

Interjections are words used expressly to denote emotion.

NOTES.

PECULIAR CONSTRUCTIONS.

1. Obj. case after copulative verb in passive voice.

> *That experience taught us a useful lesson.*
> *A useful lesson was taught us.*
> *We were taught a useful lesson.*

In the first sentence above, *lesson* is the direct object of the verb, and *us* the indirect, or object of the prep. *to* understood. In the second sentence, the direct object (*lesson*) is taken for the subject, and the verb is changed to the passive voice; but in the third sentence, the indirect object of sentence 1 (*us*) is made the subject of the verb in the passive voice; but the direct object (*lesson*), although it still receives the action, is no part of the subject—does not belong to it in any sense—and so remains in the objective case. The verb seems to be passive in regard to *we*, but active in regard to *lesson.*—(*See Greene's Analysis, p.* 99, *b.*)

2. Abridged clause with " being."

> *His nationality prevented his election.*
> *His being a Jew prevented his being elected.*
> *That he was a Jew prevented that he should be elected.*

By comparing these sentences it will be seen that *being a Jew* and *being elected* are abridged predicates used as nouns. *Being elected* is a passive participle used as a noun; it is the passive voice of the verb, with its power of predication destroyed. *Being a Jew* should be parsed together as a noun, and then *being* and *Jew* may be parsed separately. *Being* is the participle of the copula, and *Jew* is used with the participle of the copula in the predicate of an abridged clause, and is therefore put in the nominative case.

> *I was not aware that it was he.*
> *I was not aware of its being he.*

In the second sentence above, *being he* is a verbal noun, object of the preposition *of*, and limited by the possessive pronoun *its;* but *he* is in the nominative case.—*Greene's Anal., pp. 204, 205.*

3. Preposition used in predicate to give an intransitive verb a passive meaning.

> *His mates laughed at him.*
> *He was laughed at.*

In the first sentence above, the phrase *at him*, though called adverbial, does not modify the verb in regard to time, place, manner, cause, or purpose; it shows the *tendency* or *direction* of the action, and so much resembles an objective element that the object of its preposition is called the *indirect object* of the verb.

In the second sentence the indirect object is made the subject of the sentence, but the preposition is retained in the predicate to show that the person represented by the pronoun sustains the same relation to the action as in the preceding sentence. *Was laughed at* may as well be parsed together as an intransitive verb, with a meaning somewhat like that of a verb in the passive voice.

4. Group of words in possessive case.

If the group is complex, the possessive sign is added to the noun that comes nearest to the limited noun. Thus:—

> The *Earl of Chatham's* last speech.
> For my *servant David's* sake.
> For *David my servant's* sake.

If the group be a couplet or a series denoting *separate* possession, the possessive sign is added to each term; but when the couplet or series denotes *joint* possession, the possessive sign is added to the last term only. Thus:—

> *Colburn's, White's,* and *Olney's* arithmetic.
> *Allen* and *Greenough's* Latin Grammar.

5. Verb agreeing with its logical rather than its grammatical subject.

> *The horse and carriage (the conveyance) is waiting.*
> *Bread and milk is good food.*
> *The horse and the carriage are waiting.*
> *Bread and milk are both good articles of food.*

By noticing the sentences above, it will be seen that when two grammatical subjects are so closely united in sense that the mind takes them as one, the verb should be in the singular number. The subject may also be so emphatically distinguished as to require a verb in the singular number, as:—

> *The wife, as well as the husband, was convicted.*
> *The doctor, and the sexton too, was imprisoned.*
> *Thine is the kingdom, and the power, and the glory.*

6. For want of a pronoun in the third singular that can include both sexes, the masculine is often used; as,—

The teacher should maintain his authority by the mildest means possible.

7. Nominative absolute with a phrase.

They went out one by one.

Flake after flake
They sink in the dark and silent lake.

Day by day the sky is cloudless and blue.
They grew together side by side.
The sisters' hands were clasped in each other.

From an examination of the sentences above, it will be seen that the nominative absolute is often followed by a phrase instead of a participle or an adjective.

Sometimes this phrase is adverbial, and sometimes adjective; for sometimes it would limit the verb, and sometimes it would be used with the copula in predicate, if the phrase absolute were converted into a clause.

The last sentence means the same as though it read, The sisters' hands were clasped *each in other.* Such phrases are not usually set off.

8. Than whom.

"Which, when Beelzebub perceived, than whom,
Satan except, none higher sat," etc.
　　　　　　　　　　　　—*Paradise Lost, B.* 2, *l.* 300.

"The objective, *whom*, is here preferred to the nominative *who*, because the Latin ablative is commonly rendered by the former case, rather than by the latter; but this phrase is no more explicable according to the usual principles of English grammar, than the error of putting the objective case for a version of the ablative absolute. If the imitation is to be judged allowable, it is to us *a figure of syntax*—an obvious example of *Enallagé*, and of that form of Enallagé, which is commonly called *Antiptosis*, or the putting of one case for another."—*Brown's Grammar of English Grammars, p.* 675, *ob.* 18.

PUNCTUATION.

1. Punctuation of adverbial elements.

Nothing has been said in this book in regard to the punctuation of adverbial elements. In general, the pauses required in reading have very little to do with the punctuation; but to this the adverbial element seems to be an exception; for whenever it requires a pause before and after it to bring out the sense, it should be set off by the comma. This is most commonly the case when the adverb is parenthetical or inverted.

2. Quoted expressions.

Quoted expressions should be enclosed in double quotation marks; and a quotation that is included within another quotation should have single quotation marks. When the quotation is a complete clause, a comma should precede it; when it is long, emphatic, or formally introduced, it should be preceded by a colon. When the quotation is direct, the first word should begin with a capital letter.

This work does not claim to be complete on punctuation; a thorough work on punctuation would constitute a good sized volume in itself.

LETTER WRITING.

The model on the next page will give some useful hints to those who are not familiar with the most approved forms for beginning, closing, and directing an ordinary letter. The parts requiring particular attention are briefly noticed below:—

1. **The Heading.**—This tells where and when the letter was written; and if no other instructions are given, it is supposed to show how a reply is to be directed. It should be placed toward the right and near the top of the page, and may consist of one or more lines, according to its length and the width of the page. The proper punctuation is shown in the model.

2. **The Margin.**—Do not forget to leave a fair margin on the left-hand of each page. It should be from a half-inch to an inch in width, according to the size of the page, and of uniform width from top to bottom.

3. **The Address.**—This should be placed at the left of the page, next to the margin, and one or two lines below the heading. It usually consists of some term or honor, affection, or relationship, and is commonly punctuated as in the model. Some, however, prefer the colon after the last word, and others the comma without a dash.

4. **The Subscription.**—This consists of the name of the writer, called his signature, preceded by some expression of respect or personal regard. The different lines of the subscription should begin each farther to the right than the one above it, and the first word of each should have a capital initial. The punctuation may be learned from the model.

The full name and the residence of the person addressed should then be written at the left and a little below the signature.

5. **The Superscription.**—This consists of the name of the person to whom the letter is to be sent, written on the envelope, and followed by the name of the Post-office, county, and State, where the letter is to be delivered. The name, especially if quite long, should begin near the left end of the envelope, and not much above the middle. Below the person's name should be the name of his post-office, county, and State, each on a separate line, and each line beginning a little farther to the right than the one above it.

Great pains should be taken to make every word of the superscription so plain that it cannot be mistaken.

(430)

SPECIMEN LETTER.

Battle Creek, Michigan,
Friday, June 10, 1881.

My dear Father:—

Accept my most hearty thanks for your kind letter, and for the generous supply of means which it inclosed. I was in no need of money, for I still have quite a sum left from what you last sent me.

I prize your letter most of all for the good counsel it contains, and for its pledges of confidence in my sincerity. I trust your good words will not be lost upon me, etc.

I am, as ever,

Your affectionate son,

William C. Caswell.

Mr. Leonard F. Caswell,
Shingle Creek,
St. Law. Co., N. Y.

SUPERSCRIPTION.

STAMP.

Mr. Leonard F. Caswell,

Shingle Creek,

St. Lawrence Co.,

New York.

INDEX.

www.ingramcontent.com/pod-product-compliance
Lightning Source LLC
Chambersburg PA
CBHW030956110726
47900CB00004B/1297